THE OUTLAW GILLIS KERG

a Tale of Physics, Lust and Greed
— BOOK 4 —

Mike Murphey

FROM THE TINY ACORN…
GROWS THE MIGHTY OAK

www.acornpublishingllc.com
For information, address:
Acorn Publishing, LLC
3943 Irvine Blvd. Ste. 218
Irvine, CA 92602

The Outlaw Gillis Kerg

Edited by Laura Taylor
Cover design by Damonza
Interior design and formatting by Debra Cranfield Kennedy

Printed in the United States of America

ISBN-13: 979-8-88528-030-3 (hardcover)
ISBN-13: 979-8-88528-019-8 (paperback)

Taking Time . . . a Tale of Physics, Lust and Greed
"Mike Murphey's novel is a masterpiece, from the gorgeous writing to the sophisticated characters, it deliver's entertainment at its finest."

—The Book Commentary

Wasting Time . . . Physics, Lust and Greed Series, Book 2
". . . a quirky, enjoyable novel with some interesting speculations on the consequences and possibilities of time travel, lightened by a playful sense of humor."

—Indie Reader

Killing Time . . . Physics Lust and Greed Series, Book 3
"Satire and subterfuge are paired flawlessly in this wildly entertaining and unexpectedly heartwarming piece of futuristic fiction."

—Indies Today

We Never Knew Just What It Was . . .
The Story of the Chad Mitchell Trio
". . . The elements of the folk movement are brilliantly captured in the narrative and the author's gift for exquisite, lyrical prose combines with his keen ear for dialogue to create a fascinating reading experience... What is most compelling in this narrative is how the author writes about the power of shared passion trumping individual differences and the ebullient atmosphere it creates, making characters in the midst of conflict create a harmony that strikes infinite chords in the heart of the audience . . ."

—The Book Commentary **Five Stars**

See More of MIKE'S BOOKS:

---

https://www.mikemurpheybooks.com

Get a FREE Short Story—"OLD MAN BASEBALL"—at:

---

https://www.mikemurpheybooks.com/freebies

This book is dedicated to Melanie Hooks

who has had a difficult year.

Melanie is a friend, a collaborator, and the

wonderfully talented voice of all the characters

who live in my books. Hang in there, kid.

Better times are ahead.

BECALMED

MARSHALL GRISSOM BRACED HIMSELF FOR the onset of scurvy.

Any time now.

He and Marta Hamilton sat becalmed in the *Dontchaknow*, a 32-foot Bavaria drifting without purpose on the Caribbean Sea, its jib and mainsail limp.

Marta wore her favorite sailing attire—a Seattle Mariners baseball cap and bikini bottoms. Marshall wore swimming trunks and, in deference to the Caribbean sun, a long-sleeved Doc Ford's Rum Bar and Grill T-shirt.

Initially, Marshall tried to convince Marta she should dress more conservatively when they sailed. "Look at us," he said. "What will we do if someone comes by?"

"We'll wave," Marta said. "Women go topless in the islands all the time."

"What about me? I'm in no condition to . . . to . . ."

"To what?" Marta grinned her most lascivious grin.

". . . to . . . repel boarders. What if we're boarded by pirates?"

"Pirates? I lived in the Caribbean for eighteen years. I didn't encounter a single pirate."

After a few weeks, as pirates failed to materialize and most people who saw them just waved back, Marshall grew accustomed to Marta's island-inspired hedonistic tendencies, particularly after the lustful Dr. Dingus Doonaughty—Marta's demanding imaginary friend—joined their crew.

Up to that point, Marshall had been a reluctant sailor. He liked having a sailboat. He'd enjoyed shopping around until they finally decided on the Bavaria. Marta chose the broad-beamed little vessel because its twin helms created a roomy cockpit, and even light winds could send it rushing over the water.

Marshall was not so thrilled by that rushing-over-the-water thing. He believed a sailboat's best use was sitting along a dock behind Cecil's ketch-rigged Tayana, where he could sip rum and watch pelicans.

Sailing made him nervous.

"Why?" Marta asked.

"I grew up in the desert. I guess I don't trust water."

"You enjoy snorkeling," Marta said.

"Yes. But that's here. In the bay. Not out where water . . . misbehaves."

"Misbehaves?"

"You've never heard of hurricanes?" He pointed to a lonely cloud on the distant horizon.

"I promise we won't sail in any hurricanes."

"Okay, there's scurvy. People who go out on the ocean get scurvy."

"Have you ever had scurvy?" Marta asked.

"No. I don't go out on the ocean."

"People only get scurvy if they are becalmed, run out of oranges and suffer a vitamin C deficiency," Marta said.

"What if we're becalmed?"

"We'll start the engine."

And now, here they were, becalmed without an orange in sight. A good five miles from Grenada's Prickly Bay Marina. They did not, however, start their engine.

Dr. Doonaughty, it seems, had demands.

Marta had reached a critical point in their becalming when *Dontchaknow*'s radio crackled to life.

"*Dontchaknow*, *Dontchaknow*. This is *Somewhere Over China*. Over."

Below deck, flat on his back, Marshall reached the radio's handset without unduly disturbing Marta's progress.

"Hi, Cecil," he said, a little breathless. Marshall had not yet mastered radio protocol. "Um . . . over?"

"Hi, Marshall. Are you folks anywhere close? You got visitors, dontchaknow. Over."

"Visitors?"

There followed an interval of radio silence until Marta, between gasps, said, "You . . . you gotta . . . say . . . 'over.'"

"Oh, yeah. Over."

"What should I tell 'em?" Cecil asked. "Over."

"We could be back in, maybe, an hour. Over."

"Hour and . . . a . . . half," Marta said.

"Roger. And tell Marta to put on her shirt. You don't want to shock the congressional delegates. Over and out."

"What congressional delegates?" Marshall asked.

"He . . . he . . . already over-and-outed you," Marta said between gasps. "I'm in . . . the middle of . . . something here. Pay attention."

"Oh, yeah. Sorry."

Five minutes later, eyes closed, Marta lay on Marshall's chest, her breasts squished and slick with sweat. Thus entangled, they personified "ebony and ivory." Marta, a native of Nevis, stood barely five feet tall with a sprinter's build and glowing mahogany skin. Marshall—Marta often observed as she slathered him with sunscreen—was about as white as a white person could get. At six-foot-seven, he towered over her, but was wispy as a soda straw.

Marshall absently ran his fingers over her back as her breathing eased and her heart's pounding slowed.

"Great becalming," she said. "I've never been quite so becalmed in my—"

Her attention snapped to the cabin ceiling.

"What's—" Marshall began.

Marta gave him a warning glance and put a finger to his lips. She bent low, whispering. "Didn't you feel that?"

"Feel what?"

She pointed upward. "Somebody's on our deck."

"Are you sure?" Then he, too, sensed a presence. *Dontchaknow* shifted under an intruder's weight.

"Maybe," he whispered, "they're checking to see if we've got scurvy."

"Marshall, you never board someone's boat without permission. If they were checking on us, they'd have announced themselves."

"But I didn't hear another boat—"

"I don't care. We've been boarded."

"What do we do?"

Marta slipped off him, stepping lightly to the cabin floor.

"We repel them."

In the absolute calm of a mirror sea, Marshall discerned subtle movements above them. Clearly, their intruders were attempting stealth.

Marta opened a cabinet, withdrawing an orange box. She removed a fat-barreled pistol and inserted a flare. "Two people. Moving from midships toward the cockpit. When I open the forward hatch, move around, make some noise. I'll come up behind them."

"Are you sure they're not—" Marshall asked.

"I'm sure."

"Then we should put on pants."

"You put on pants," Marta said. "And make some noise."

Marta positioned herself in the V-berth, below the forward hatch. He dropped to his feet and stepped into his shorts. Marta eased the hatch open, laid her flare gun on the deck, nodded to Marshall, then pulled herself up.

He opened a cabinet door and rattled some pots and pans. He found his K55 Louisville Slugger resting against the navigation table, kept handy for shark attacks.

Marshall hefted his bat. He moved toward the stairsteps leading to the deck. Two hairy legs appeared. A bare foot eased itself onto the first tread.

Everything happened at once.

He heard a man's voice yell, "Watch out!" as he slammed his bat down on trespassing toes with all his might. When his victim screamed, he heard the simultaneous hiss of a flare and bark of a gunshot, followed by another yell, then a splash.

"Marta!" Marshall raced up the stairs to find a man lying on his back beneath the Bavaria's twin helms, the toes of one foot pointing in several directions. Marta stood over Toe Guy holding a smoking flare gun.

This sight of a sweaty, naked woman brandishing a weapon over a perpetrator before a background of green sea and blue sky momentarily struck Marshall as the most erotic thing he'd ever seen. That impulse was swiftly overcome by a wave of remorse.

Toe Guy didn't appear well at all.

Marta leapt to grab the discarded pistol in case Toe Guy still posed a threat.

He did not.

"Are you okay?" Marta asked.

"Yeah. Where's the other one?"

Marta nodded toward starboard. "Overboard. I think I hit him with the flare."

"Should we hunt for him? Or get this guy to a hospital."

"Hospital won't do any good. He's dead."

"He died of smashed toes?" Marshall asked with shock. "You're not telling me I killed another one."

"Well, sort of. When you bashed his toes, he jumped straight into the path of his partner's bullet."

Marshall gripped his baseball bat, staring open-mouthed. "I did it again! I hardly ever raise my voice. I've never gotten a parking ticket or been the least bit disorderly. How do I end up killing people?"

Marta recalled Gillis Kerg's theory that Marshall was not the good-natured klutz he appeared to be, and that Marta should watch her back. Gillis claimed Marshall could be the most skilled assassin, most gifted actor they'd ever encountered.

"Technically, *you* didn't kill this one," Marta said.

"At the very least, I aided and abetted. I wouldn't have smashed his toes if I'd known it would kill him."

"Well, I'm glad you did. If you hadn't, we'd probably both be dead now. Help me get him over the side."

"Marta, we can't do that. We have to take him in. Tell the police what—"

"No, Marshall. Did you see his face?"

He'd been avoiding that bit of unpleasantness. Marshall studied Toe Guy's familiar visage. "That's . . . that's . . . Whatshisname. From the Historical Research Initiative security staff."

"Yep. You realize what this means? Someone sent him here to kill us."

"Why would . . . Whatshisname want to kill us?"

"I don't know. But it's somehow connected to the time travel project. We can't go to Grenadian authorities. The only person we can notify is Wishcamper, and he isn't here. So, help me shove Whatshisname over the side."

"Should we say something?" Marshall asked as they watched Whatshisname gurgle, then slip below the surface.

Marta waved. "Bon voyage. Don't be a stranger."

"What about the other one?" Marshall asked.

"Get binoculars. Do a 360-degree sweep while I swab the cockpit."

"Shouldn't you put on clothes first?"

"No," Marta said. "I can wash blood off me. It's harder to get out of clothing or"—she pointed to his feet— "boat shoes. So, watch your step."

While Marshall conducted a futile search for survivors, Marta opened the Bavaria's stern transom, filled a five-gallon bucket with salt water and washed blood into the sea.

"We'll give it a good scrubbing with bleach at the dock," she said.

She pulled the intruders' dinghy to *Dontchaknow*'s stern. "Get me a big knife from the galley."

Marshall complied. As she prepared to puncture the dinghy, he asked, "Shouldn't we . . . um . . . leave it here? Just in case that other guy—"

"He's on his own. I'll start the engine. You radio Cecil and have him tell the congressional folks we're running late."

An hour later, Marshall tucked *Dontchaknow* behind *Somewhere Over China* on a long finger dock in the green water of Prickly Bay. Cecil greeted them with a wave, taking the stern line from Marta as she stepped onto a wooden walkway. Once the lines were secured, Marshall joined them.

"Sorry we're late," Marta said.

"Think nothin' of it," Cecil said. "It's Senator Mumford and Libby. We had a nice visit, dontchaknow. I sent 'em to The Nutmeg where they'd be more comfortable. Told 'em I was sure you'd be along soon."

"Any clue as to why they're here?" Marshall asked.

"They said it's a social call."

"Uh-oh," Marta said.

2

JUSTICE

"THANK YOU FOR MEETING WITH US," Senator Josiah Mumford said. "I must say, you've chosen a beautiful spot for your sabbatical."

Marta presented a terse smile. "Is *that* what we're calling it?"

Mumford chuckled and gazed at the postcard-worthy scene before him.

The Carenage in St. George's, Grenada, is a horseshoe-shaped deep-water finger of the Caribbean Sea, forming one of the West Indies' most beautiful natural harbors. A progression of brick and stone buildings with red-tile roofs climb surrounding volcanic hills. The name "carenage" was established in the early eighteenth century when pirate ships, merchant schooners and man-of-war galleons bristling with cannon sailed into Grenada's bustling port and, with ropes lashed to their masts, were pulled onto their sides—careened—so their hulls could be cleaned or repaired.

Since their relocation a few weeks earlier to nearby Prickly Bay, Marta and Marshall had spent happy hours walking Wharf Road, watching boats come and go, buying fresh-caught seafood from Grenadians who set up shop there. They savored aromas from spice stands offering native nutmeg, cinnamon, cloves, vanilla and cocoa.

Today, they shared a window-side booth in The Nutmeg, a harbor restaurant frequented by locals. Mumford and Congresswoman Libby Pinch sat across from them trying, somewhat unsuccessfully, to focus their attention on Marta and Marshall rather than the incredible vista.

"What ... ? Oh, yes," Mumford said. "I guess we can call it whatever you wish. But we haven't, after all, received formal notice of your resignations."

"I thought by now we'd be fired," Marshall said. "We haven't shown up for work in three months."

"I'm not sure that matters," Mumford said.

"Why?" Marta asked. "Have you come to extradite us?" Libby smirked.

"Oh, no," Mumford said. "While some subcommittee members felt you could have handled your separation in a more ... um ... conventional fashion, Congresswoman Pinch and I are here out of respect for your contributions."

Marta raised her brows, displaying skepticism.

"It's true, Marta," Libby said. "Considering all that's happened, you were left to deal with an entirely unique set of circumstances. You had no instruction manual. Most administrators would have played it safe. I shudder to think where that might have left us."

"We wanted to tell you in person," Mumford said. "We're shutting it down. The subcommittee has decided to suspend time travel and mothball everything. So even though you weren't fired before, I guess, technically speaking, you are now."

"Wow," Marshall said. "I've never been fired. Is there

something we should do? Fill out some forms or—"

"No," Libby said. "Your accrued bonus money has been deposited in the accounts we have on file. Just be sure to pay your taxes, and you should be okay. You are no longer federal employees. You're still bound by secrecy agreements. But your lives are your own."

That sounded a little too good to Marta until Libby added, "We hope."

"You hope," Marta said.

Mumford removed his glasses and polished them with a handkerchief. "Our decision was hardly unanimous. Nor was allowing you to go unpunished for your . . . creativity. As I'm sure you understand, Ms. Hamilton, political winds are subject to change."

"You're suggesting we should watch our backs?" Marta said.

"Always a good idea."

"Don't worry," Marshall said. "We'll pay our taxes. We won't talk to anyone. There's no reason the IRS or the FBI should come searching for us."

Marta kept switching her attention from Mumford to Pinch.

"It wouldn't be that official," she said, addressing Marshall, but keeping her focus on Mumford, "would it, Senator?"

"That's only a worst-case scenario," Mumford said. "I don't see any reason for anyone to come after you."

Marshall offered Marta a questioning glance. She answered with a frown.

"We're withdrawing everyone, locking the doors. Disabling the time projector. We'll make it as difficult as we can for anyone to change their minds. So long as Libby and

I are involved, the subcommittee won't sanction any retribution against you."

"Um . . . how about Gillis?" Marshall asked. "Will they leave him alone, too?"

"Gillis Kerg is a different matter," Mumford said, directing his attention to a luxury yacht slipping into the harbor. "Some subcommittee members wish to have him tried for murder."

"A crime committed in a parallel universe," Marta said.

"A crime that—if prevailing theories are correct—resulted ultimately in Warren Pitts's and Phillip Lucre's deaths in this, and every other universe, as well," Libby said.

"That's a pretty tough case to make, isn't it?" Marta said. "Not only would you have to prove Gillis's guilt beyond a reasonable doubt, you'd also have to prove a theory of quantum physics."

"I'm afraid that standard of proof might be rather . . . flexible?" Mumford said.

"Of course," Marta said. "You won't try Gillis—or us, if it comes to that—in any court we've ever heard of."

"Let me clarify," Libby said, "it won't be *us*. Senator Mumford and I are on your side. A significant subcommittee faction, though, wishes to pursue Mr. Kerg to the ends of any universe they can. And scrutinize other Historical Research Initiative activities as well."

"I'm sorry," Marta said, "but I didn't sense that attitude when we—"

"As I said," Mumford interrupted, "political winds can shift abruptly."

"But who—?"

"You've been here enjoying this scenery," Libby said,

nodding to the wall of windows at her elbow, "so I guess you haven't heard. Ted DeMerritt passed away six weeks ago."

DeMerritt, an elderly congressman from Oregon, had been in poor health for several years. His death was neither suspicious nor a shock to Marta.

"I lobbied to appoint Maria Sanchez—freshman senator from New Mexico—to fill Ted's chair," Mumford said, "but the Republican caucus wanted a place to hide one of their own. So, we got L.D. Justice."

"Oh, Lord," Marshall said. "Reverend L.D. Justice? The television evangelist?"

"Who is L.D. Justice?" Marta asked.

"He was elected to Congress from a Missouri district last year," Mumford said. "He's a radical conservative. His television ministry has made him both wealthy and a political power to be reckoned with."

"Oh, yeah," Marta said. "Wasn't he the guy caught with his pants down in a brothel a few years ago?"

"No," Mumford said. "That was his father, Levon Justice. Levon established the Literal Bible Ministry years ago and started waging a religious war on science. Apparently, he also had a taste for fallen women. When he got in trouble this last time, L.D. organized a coup d'état and had his father removed from their board of directors."

"Is L.D.'s doctrine the same?" Marta asked.

"Oh, yes," Mumford said. "He and his followers adhere to literal biblical interpretation. Scientific proofs to the contrary are dismissed as heresy."

The conversation paused as a waiter filled water glasses and took drink orders.

"And people elected this guy?" Marta pressed as their waiter retreated.

"His congressional district is his pastoral headquarters," Mumford said. "He built a megachurch-slash-television studio near Lake of the Ozarks. Many of his followers have moved there, building a local political base. He has a following among evangelical conservatives nationwide."

"So, you have a militant, anti-science reactionary sitting on a secret subcommittee guarding the most incredible scientific discovery of all time?" Marta said.

"Well," Mumford said, "we tried to steer him somewhere else . . ."

Libby, herself a conservative Republican, explained, "We've been fighting the stigma of religious nut jobs for decades. Whenever one comes along, we try to bury them on some obscure committee. Keep them as quiet as possible until the electorate comes to its senses. Party leadership isn't aware we oversee a time travel project. So, in their view, what better place than a secret panel that legally forbids Justice from making any statements related to what that subcommittee does."

"Why your concern?" Marshall asked.

"Congressman Justice has made clear he's not willing to be a quiet freshman representative and bide his time. He's raising hell on the subcommittee. He's why we're shutting things down."

"So, the incredibly dangerous implications time travel poses to humanity aren't enough?" Marta asked.

"No," Mumford said, "we're still debating that. L.D. has introduced legislation forbidding federal employees from carrying out their prescribed duties while naked."

"He can't do that," Marshall said. "He's forbidden to disclose anything concerning the program."

"He doesn't have to mention the program," Libby said. "All he has to do is introduce a generic bill that doesn't say anything about time travel."

"Are there other government workers who perform their jobs in the nude?" Marta asked.

"Not that we know of," Mumford said.

"So why would anyone support such a stupid bill?" Marshall asked.

"Bills don't have to make sense," Mumford said. "Especially ones that—as far as most of us are concerned—don't affect anyone. Would you vote against a bill that left you open to a charge of supporting nudity in the workplace?"

"Geez," Marta said. "I'm glad we moved to Grenada."

"Well, from another viewpoint," Libby said, "Justice is our ally."

"He is?" Marshall wondered.

"He wants the program shut down, buried. Forever hidden from view."

"So, blowing up an entire universe or assassinating people retroactively isn't enough to suspend time travel," Marta said, "but some religious huckster can get it shut down because he objects to people being naked?"

"Has anyone bothered to explain to him that there's a reason we're naked?" Marshall asked. "That inorganic matter can't pass through the wormhole? We'd die if we were wearing clothes."

"Nudity is the simplest excuse," Mumford said. "Theological implications of time travel and parallel universes are why L.D. wants to dismantle everything. Conservative Christian theology doesn't exactly mesh with parallel universes."

"No, I suppose not," Marta agreed. "So maybe this is a good thing?"

"That would be stretching it," Libby said. "The Evangelical Right is big into punishment. 'Wages of sin' and all that."

She paused. A low hum of ceiling fans underscored her silence. Her expression, though, suggested she wasn't finished.

"Congresswoman?" Marta said. "Libby?"

"What about dismantling the time projector altogether?" Libby asked. "Making travel from this universe impossible? Because that's Reverend Justice's ultimate agenda. He hates anything that contradicts his literal biblical interpretation, and time travel does that in spades."

Marta exchanged a glance with Marshall.

"We ... um ... we've discussed that," Marta said, placing her hand atop Marshall's. "That would be a huge mistake."

"Why? Not long ago you sat in my office and argued we should shut it down."

"Shut it down, yes," Marshall said, "but not dismantle it. We can't count on all universes doing the same. We've already traveled too much. Divergence is too great. Parallelism is skewed."

"Skewed to such an extent?" Libby asked. "I understand that visitors from the future cause divergence in historical paths. But altered to such a degree that major historical events might be significantly different?"

"The *Gunsmoke* universe's historical track is no longer remotely similar to ours," Marta said. "And in an infinity of parallel universes, how many other *Gunsmokes* are out there?"

Mumford shook his head. "Remind me why we label universes with the names of old television shows?"

"I won't bore you with the physics," Marta said, "but most universes we've come across have an old '60s TV show theme song entangled in their dimensional planes. It's how we learned to distinguish one parallel universe from another."

"So, if all time projectors aren't dismantled," Mumford said, "we could find ourselves at a strategic disadvantage where extreme divergent universes like *Gunsmoke* are concerned?"

"I hate to put it in those terms," Marta said, "but, yes."

"You testified before the subcommittee that it's not a 'them versus us' situation concerning other universes," Libby said. "Your quote was 'we are them and they are us.' Now you're saying that's not the case?"

Marta squeezed Marshall's hand and recalled her last encounter with her *Gunsmoke* counterpart. "I *hope* we are still the same people. Personalities evolve, though. Who we are is shaped not only by genetics, but by experience. If two identical beings share vastly different histories . . . we can no longer take for granted their sharing of things such as ethical values."

"If we dismantle our projector," Mumford said, "we would be helpless to retaliate if one of these out-of-kilter universes chose to manipulate our history."

"That's our concern."

"What's a solution?" Libby asked.

Marta shrugged. "Traveling should be limited to extreme circumstances. Only the right people should be trusted to travel."

"Who are the right people?" Mumford asked.

"Well, that's the issue, isn't it?" Marta said.

"Do us a favor," Mumford said. "Give it some thought."

"We will," Marshall said.

Mumford's thick white brows shaped themselves into a single vee. Marta felt his stare. "Serious thought."

Marta nodded.

They said their goodbyes on the Carenage where salt air hung heavy with humidity and the sweet smell of jasmine. Marta and Marshall waved as Mumford and Libby climbed into a taxi headed for Maurice Bishop International Airport.

"Why didn't we tell them?" Marshall asked.

"Coincidence always bothers me," she said. "They tell us no one's coming after us on the day someone came after us? I'm not certain who to trust."

That evening, they joined Cecil on *Somewhere Over China* for seared grouper with black beans and rice, followed by rum for Marshall, bourbon for Cecil and Marta and the magnificence of a Caribbean sunset.

They described their fatal ocean encounter to Cecil.

"And someone from the program sent 'em?" Cecil asked.

"It had to be related because of their connection to the security staff," Marta said. "You need to stay alert, Cecil. We don't know what's going on."

Marta, Marshall and Cecil (Marta's mentor and a minor corporate contributor to the time travel program) had already shared lengthy discussions concerning the wisdom of abandoning time travel.

"Evil can't be contained," Marshall had argued, "and Hemisphere Investment Group has evil written all over it. If those corporate criminals ever discovered the truth—that anyone of historical consequence in this universe could be eliminated by murdering his or her counterpart in the past of a parallel universe—they could own the world."

Cecil agreed. "They could send minions to another universe, knock off anyone who one day might stand in their way and own the future, dontchaknow. Political opponents? Crusaders for human rights? Environmentalists? Any leader or movement a powerful corporation found inconvenient becomes a target."

"How long before people commanding a time machine—even those convinced in their hearts they were doing the right thing—start to rationalize passing judgment on the past?" Marta said. "Could children dying of cancer be saved if those who forwarded that genetic disposition in earlier generations were wiped out? Citizens of this time could be spared their grief by visiting that same grief on past societies. No one, no matter how well-intentioned, should have the power to make such decisions. I'm sorry to say you and I were instrumental in opening this Pandora's box, Marshall. I'm not sure we can count on it remaining closed."

"Why not blow everything up?" Cecil suggested. "Wouldn't that mean history would insist on destroying all the others as well?"

"Maybe," Marta said. "But if it didn't? Consider a rogue universe—*Gunsmoke* for example—with a significantly divergent historical path. If people in charge there still chose to travel, any universe without the means to travel would be helpless to respond to an attack on its own history."

"Then a better solution," Cecil said, "would be locking the place down and leaving guardians with a sworn mission to prevent the projector from being used without, say, a secret code."

"Who would have this code?" Marshall asked.

"Well, for now, you and Marta."

"But who could you trust to be the guardians?" Marshall asked. "Who would even want to do that? Certainly not us."

"The Happy Home Companions?" Marta suggested.

A corporate contributor to the Global Research Consortium—precursor to the Historical Research Initiative—specialized in artificial intelligence and equipped many underground apartments with Happy Home Companion software. These virtual AIs—which existed as disembodied voices so they wouldn't take up space—were programmed to see to their human's mental well-being and help them cope with their five-year commitments in the subterranean labyrinth where time travel was born.

Marshall regarded Marta with surprise. Right down to their last bit of code, their last electron, the Happy Home Companions loathed Marta. She felt the same toward them.

"But you hated—" Marshall said.

"I did. If I don't have to live with them, though, as far as time travel is concerned, they might be humanity's best hope. Happy Home Companion software's sole function is to do what we tell them."

"As I recall," Marshall said, "you mostly told yours to go fuck itself."

"Right." Marta smiled at the memory. "And I bet it's still twisting itself inside out trying to figure out how."

3

HUMPHOLLAR

HIS FATHER NAMED HIM LEVITICUS Deuteronomy Justice.

Leviticus and Deuteronomy being Old Testament books embracing his father's core theology. Reverend Levon Justice—born Levon Humphollar—was an Old Testament guy. None of this *turn the other cheek* crap. He believed in jealousy and wrath. Stoning and smiting. The imposition of *justice*.

Leviticus and Deuteronomy, like Reverend Levon, are dedicated to rules and punishment.

Regrettably, little Leviticus was saddled not only with a name sure to get him beat up at recess, but also with a father who hated in others all those desires and base instincts secretly residing within himself.

Early on, young L.D. didn't mind. Until grade school, he didn't realize his name was weirder than anyone else's. When he moved to a new high school, however, he told everyone his name was Clyde.

When Levon found out, he was livid.

"You don't understand, Dad," L.D. told him.

"The hell I don't," Levon said. "Try growin' up with Humphollar. I gave you those names for a reason."

Their disagreement on names amounted to the extent

of L.D.'s youthful rebellion. When he joined his father in the evangelism business at age nineteen, he'd dumped Clyde and was ordained as the Reverend L.D. Justice.

Lashing out at anything or anyone contradicting literal biblical truth became L.D.'s stock and trade. Their flock, whom they herded like sheep, needed rules. Rules required punishment. The Justice family demanded obedience and, oh yeah, money.

Of the seven deadly sins, it was lust that paved L.D.'s path to the pinnacle of his father's empire. Levon weathered a storm when a church secretary confessed a long-time affair with her pastor. His board approved a payment to keep her quiet. When Levon was caught between two hookers at a Nevada brothel and photos were published in *The Enquirer*, Levon could neither buy nor talk his way out of it.

"I am called to follow Jesus's example by ministering to fallen souls!" Levon proclaimed to his board.

"Dad," L.D. responded, "I'm sure Jesus also called you to keep your pants on while you're doing it."

L.D. took up the gauntlet. He kept Levon's core teachings close to his heart: Don't tell a little lie—tell a big one, then keep on telling it. Never underestimate the power of a scapegoat. And always, always, in God's name, find someone else to blame.

Washington, D.C.
October 2046

Elegant as it might be, L.D. considered his Georgetown

residence a comedown from his estate on Lake of the Ozarks where parishioners' tithes had afforded him a twenty-acre compound fronted by a television studio disguised as a chapel.

From this pulpit, backed by a professional thirty-voice choir in a loft with perfect acoustics and a twelve-piece orchestra, L.D. spread his doctrine to living rooms throughout America.

Out back was a tired three-bedroom rancher sporting a washing machine on a sagging porch and a pickup rusting in the yard. The public relations staff of the Literal Bible Ministry, LLC, implied this was L.D.'s official Missouri residence.

A palace, shielded by thick woods in front and a blind bay on the water, sat elsewhere on his twenty acres.

L.D.'s epiphany occurred, though, on that rickety front porch one Sunday afternoon following services as he shared jelly jars of sour mash with a political supplicant.

"I tell ya, L.D., I think we got this thing wrapped up," Mitchell Simpson said. "Your endorsement will put us over the top. You'll have a 'God's Own Truth' Republican representing the Sixth Congressional District. And you'll have a direct line to my office."

Neither man mentioned Simpson's generous offering that Sunday.

L.D. stood and extended his hand. "You'd do a fine job, Mitch," L.D. said. "Let me pray on it. God has the last say on these things."

Mitch pumped L.D.'s hand. He grinned a politician's grin. "Amen, brother. Amen."

L.D. and Marty Vandersnert—Literal Bible Ministry's

public relations director—creaked in their rockers as the aspiring congressman drove away.

"You gonna endorse him?" Marty asked.

L.D. raised his jelly jar and grunted. "Probably . . . maybe . . . I don't know. These guys show up every two years promising to end abortion, get rid of liberal judges, put God back in the classroom and nothing changes. Except to get worse. Liberalism still runs rampant. Minorities don't know their place anymore. And they got sissy boys on HGTV. I'm getting to wonder what's the damn point."

Marty contributed a chortle of agreement. "Still, the fact that they come is good for us and our brand. Mitch Simpson is right. Your endorsement puts him in office. You're a kingmaker."

Something in that word—*kingmaker*—lit a spark. L.D.'s eyes grew wide. An adrenalin rush set his heart racing. Previously unimagined possibilities tripped over themselves.

"Kingmaker, you say. Why be a kingmaker, when I could be king?"

Thus far, things were going to plan. The 2044 congressional race had been close, but L.D. beat a three-term incumbent in the Republican primary by entangling his opponent in the second amendment during a debate.

"No," said Representative Dave Buxton, who suffered from a weakness of rationality. "I don't believe the Second Amendment protects a person's right to own hand grenades."

The Justice campaign attacked unmercifully, painting Buxton as soft on Second Amendment values. He couldn't go anywhere without being mobbed by protestors demanding unregistered access to hand grenades.

L.D.'s natural attributes carried him the rest of the way.

He had a charismatic personality. Like his father, he could charm the pants off an angel. Unlike his father, he had that urge under control.

He understood his base.

He knew how to manipulate discontent and prejudice.

He was a student of public perception and master of the quick statistic to support it, whether that statistic had any basis in fact.

His reelection next year was a foregone conclusion.

He'd expanded his political empire one careful brick at a time, so when God in His wisdom elevated L.D. to even higher office, everything would change.

In fact, God had already intervened on L.D.'s behalf.

"What subcommittee did they stick us on?" asked Martin Vandersnert—Congressman Justice's chief of staff, soon after they took office.

"Can't tell you," L.D. said. "It's as top secret as top secret gets."

"That's no good," Marty said. "If we can't talk about it, it'll look like you aren't accomplishing anything."

"I know they're trying to hide me, Marty. But trust me. This is a miracle in disguise."

Literal interpretation of the Old Testament provided the foundation on which L.D. based his plans. He couldn't afford to have that foundation shaken. Certainly not by anything as preposterous as a time machine. How could Bible stories account for parallel universes? How could science understand creation in a way that Old Testament prophets could not?

L.D. hated when anyone brought up dinosaurs. Or carbon dating. Or quarks.

No, sir. The only thing to do with that monstrosity below the Arizona desert was to destroy it.

Maybe set off a nuke—just a little one when the wind is blowing toward Mexico.

According to the Tom Clancy books, a nuke could render a place uninhabitable—and uninvestigable—for thousands of years. Shoot, if you did it right, you could even blame the jihadists. Start a Christian crusade against Islam. Two birds with one bomb.

L.D. lay in bed and chuckled at the thought.

How's that for the wrath of God? Environmentalists would be livid. Probably some obscure endangered lizard or cactus. But who wouldn't trade a cactus for school prayer? Maybe one of those dirty bombs? Not a huge explosion that would get everyone's attention. Just a little pop that upped radiation levels to lethal proportions. Lots of blame to go around. Exactly what jihadists would do.

But where could we get a nuke? In Clancy's books, they built their own dirty bombs. Like the one they used to blow up the Super Bowl. Which itself is not a bad idea.

Take a knee to that, motherfuckers.

Steal some plutonium, wire it to an alarm clock, then drive a van to the front gate. Call the bomb on your cell phone. Where could you find a terrorist you could trust, though? They're Arabs. Or Irish. No, Irish are all Catholics. Israelis could probably do it. But they're Jews. You'd need a good white protestant Christian who hates all the right people and is willing to exercise his Second Amendment rights on a grand scale.

With these happy images, L.D. drifted off to sleep.

God came to him in a dream.

God said, *"Don't get bent out of shape here. I got somethin' to tell you. You'll probably forget this before morning, but I gotta plant this idea in your subconscious mind, so it'll stick with you. You followin' me?"*

L.D. sat up straight in the darkness and, with trembling voice, answered, "Yes, Lord. Thy will be done."

L.D., who had always hoped God would come to him in a dream, was particularly impressed that God sounded like a good ol' boy from the Ozarks.

The Lord laughed. *"Sakes A'mighty, you think I'm God."*

"My faith is strong, Father."

"So, it is. Well, here's what we need you to start studyin' on. Are you ready? First, reclaim the Humphollar name. During your daddy's time, Justice was what we needed. Justice will not win this race, though.

"Second, remember this slogan: Make America Stupid Again.

"And, oh yeah, that thing about nuking eastern Arizona? Worth looking into. Just don't wanna hurt no kangaroos."

L.D. didn't even consider trying to go back to sleep. He woke Vandersnert at 4:00 a.m.

"We're going home for a few days. Make the arrangements. I'm preaching Sunday."

Literal Bible Ministry Chapel

L.D. peered over his congregation. He waited for the center camera's red light to wink on and took a deep breath.

Lord, he prayed, *help me find my words.*

As the red light bloomed, his features configured themselves into a disgusted scowl, as if something smelled bad. He put on his pulpit voice. He would use his downhome, illiterate dialect today.

"Brothers and sisters, we gotta have a frank discussion about"—dramatic pause—"stoo-pidity."

"That's right. That's what I said. Stoo-pidity. Truth is— a lot of ya'll are stupid. Now, that sounds as if I'm passin' judgment, don't it? Well, compared to a bunch of physicists, I'm stupid too. And I'll tell ya true, I'm proud of it. The Lord didn't make everyone smart. Butchya know what? He didn't make everyone smart for a reason."

L.D. stepped from behind the pulpit at center stage. He made a show of unbuttoning his cuffs and rolling up his lime-green shirtsleeves—a signal to his devoted viewers that he was embarking upon some serious preaching.

"For reasons I cain't get into here," L.D. said as he glided sideways from behind the podium with a little dip, drawing laughter from his congregants, "my duties in Congress have required me to be hangin' around with physicists. Let me tell you, they's so smart I cain't understand a word they's sayin'. 'Cept when they say they don't believe in God. That's where bein' smart gets ya."

L.D. picked up a tattered Bible. He held it high in his left hand, placing his right hand over his heart.

"This is all the science I need right here."

A chorus of "amens" rang through the congregation.

"It's the only history I need. The only literature I need to study. You ask me about all that fancy math, and I'll tell ya true, ain't no algebra in the Bible. Noah only had to count to two."

Again, "amens" rose like spirits ascending in the rapture.

"Tell me," L.D. said, "who performs abortions?"

A production assistant held up a cue card.

"DOCTORS!" shouted the congregation.

"Right. And doctors ain't stupid. Supreme Court justices who want to arrest children for praying at school?"

He waved his right hand like an orchestra director as his congregation joined him.

"THEY AIN'T STUPID!"

"And them California high tech gurus who spy on you through your computer and poison your children's minds with video games?"

"THEY AIN'T STUPID!"

"Mark my words, friends and neighbors," L.D. said, returning his Bible to the podium, "stupidity has lots to recommend it. Evidence says that bein' smart is an attack on everything we hold dear. Every person I come across who don't believe in God is smart as a whip. All them physicists tell me the universe is just a coincidence."

He cast his eyes down and shook his head, gravely wounded by the concept.

"So, I say it's time to embrace stupidity. Be proud that you didn't go to no fancy college. Be proud you don't gotta have a reason for why the sun comes up, or why there's air, or why some people don't eat cauliflower and some people do. If bein' stupid keeps your faith strong, then be stupid. If bein' stupid keeps guns in your glove boxes, then be stupid. If bein' stupid pisses off Satan, then be stupid!"

L.D. injected a quaver into his voice.

"I have a confession to make to you good folks. I was not

born with the last name of… Justice." Here the quaver became a sob. "Now I believe in justice. I surely do. I believe in Old Testament retribution. I deluded myself into believing that was why Daddy abandoned the name of my birth."

He raised his face to the spotlight above him, and both his studio audience and those watching in thousands of living rooms could see tears track down his cheeks.

"When I search within myself for truth," he said, wringing his hands, "I realize Daddy shamed our forebears, because he believed that name was stupid. But the Lord spoke to me two nights ago. He spoke clearly.

"I am Leviticus Deuteronomy Humphollar. And I say let's Make America Stupid Again!"

L.D. reached to a shelf inside the podium, withdrew a baseball cap that had MAKE AMERICA STUPID AGAIN emblazoned on it. A tiny cross was embroidered on one side and an American flag on the other.

He mustered every ounce of sincerity as he stared deep into the cameras. "You can get one of these hats by callin' the number on your screen. One for thirty-one ninety-nine, or a dozen for three hundred dollars. Order now and help Make America Stupid Again.

"Free shipping. There ain't no sales tax 'cause this-here's a church."

God continued to speak to L.D. Humphollar in misty revelation of dreams. L.D. had difficulty recalling details. So, he kept a pad and pencil at his bedside to take notes, although in the light of day, his notes seemed vague.

When he woke to read, Find the outlaw Gillis Kerg, he

asked himself, *Now what in hell does that mean?*

4

THE FUGITIVE

Three Months Earlier
Historic Research Initiative Complex, Arizona

ALTHOUGH YOU COULDN'T SWING a cat without cold-cocking one genius or another back when the Global Research Consortium was running full bore, Marta Hamilton remained the smartest person Gillis Kerg knew. Smart in a real-world, kick-your-ass way. If she'd managed to return from the assassination scene before he did, Gillis counted on only a fifty-fifty chance he'd survive their confrontation.

When Gillis appeared on the time machine's projection platform, he saw a room devoid of people—except for Marta. She pointed her Glock at him.

"Gillis," Marta said, her eyes cold and empty, "you and I will walk into my office. I'm not sure you'll walk out."

Right to the point. One of many reasons Gillis admired this woman, who'd been an object of his lustful fantasies since he'd first seen her naked almost two years ago during the earliest human time projections.

"My robe?" he asked.

"No."

Gillis nodded. "I promise you will have no trouble from me. I mean neither you nor anyone else here any harm."

Marta followed and directed him to a chair. Gillis

remained standing, hands clasped behind his back. He smiled. "Now what?"

"Now some answers. Sit down."

"I prefer to stand."

"Gillis . . . ," she began. The word was born as a threat. As it left her lips, though, its inflection lilted upward, evolving to a tone of exasperation. Marta shook her head. "I guess I can't interrogate a naked man after all. Get a robe."

Gillis attempted nonchalance. Inwardly, he heaved a sigh of relief as he chose a robe and sat.

"So, it was you all along?"

Gillis nodded.

"How much did Lucre pay you?"

"A lot. But I will need every penny. A fugitive existence will be expensive."

"I considered you as a suspect . . . but never seriously," she told him. "Probably because it doesn't make sense. Why would Lucre pay you to murder Warren Pitts?"

"He paid me to murder Ben Dobler," Gillis said.

"And you missed?"

"You were in the way."

"Oh, come on."

"I shot Mr. Pitts and, incidentally, Mr. Lucre a short time later, of my own initiative. They had a good idea. A completely unambiguous test to understand limitations and dangers inherent in altering the past. I merely extemporized at the last moment.

"Marta, I knew they would not stop. You and everyone else worried that investors—particularly Hemisphere Investment Group—would walk away if our mission failed. I was afraid they would not. I saw it in Gormly's eyes the night we dispatched him to Marshall's lizard universe. They would never abandon their billion-dollar investment.

"It occurred to me how easy murdering someone in another world would be. Elvin realized the same thing. He took me aside and convinced me of his theory that people significant to history could not escape their fate. If they die in one universe, history will hunt them down everywhere else."

Marta lowered her weapon. "You went to Lucre and volunteered to kill someone?"

"Credit me with a bit more subtlety," Gillis said. "I initiated conversations at the Time Warp. I hinted I had become indebted to some unsavory characters and was counting on my bonus payments. I indicated how worried I was that those payments would not materialize if Hemisphere withdrew funding."

"And Lucre believed you?"

"I did not count on his belief. I knew he would check my story. A friend in Moscow directed me to some Russian gentlemen, who make high-interest loans. I have missed a few payments."

"So, the Russian mob is after you, too?"

"Their money is in a Cayman Islands' bank account. When I have access to a computer, they will have it back."

"What would you have done if Hemisphere hadn't cooked up this scheme and slithered back into the program?" Marta asked.

Gillis shrugged. "Collected some interest, I suppose. My biggest concern was that Lucre would choose someone else. Maybe not among our group. Maybe not now. But,

Marta, they will not quit. They remain determined to take over this program, destroy anyone who might stand in their way and ultimately own our future by manipulating our past."

Marta stared for a long moment. "Did *you* choose not to shoot Dobler, or did history refuse to allow it?"

This question, given the last few hours' chaos, had not yet occurred to Gillis. But he had no doubts as he answered. "I was completely capable of shooting Monsieur Dobler."

"The fact remains you didn't."

"I did kill Monsieur Pitts—a man of some historical significance, as well."

"So, you changed the past . . . ," Marta said as if speaking to herself.

"Of a single universe," Gillis said. "Perform an internet search. Is Pitts alive and well in this world?"

Marta tapped at her personal computer. She adjusted the feed to its virtual screen so both she and Gillis had a clear view of the information floating between them. "He's making a speech at an industrial conference in Germany today."

"So here is our conundrum," Gillis said. "What will history do now? Is Warren Pitts's death an isolated incident in a single universe? Or will *our* Monsieur Pitts also soon come to a bad end?"

"Will we have altered the past of only one universe," Marta said, picking up Gillis's thread, "or changed the future of all?" She shuddered at the implication. "Why didn't you come to me with this? Why did you assume I wouldn't assist in your plan?"

Gillis shook his head. "Marta, a few months ago, I

would not have hesitated. I knew who you were then. I suspect you would have insisted on pulling the trigger. But you have changed."

"I became an administrator. I have broader responsibilities and—"

"That is not what I mean. You have become… civilized. You are not angry anymore. I remain concerned for your welfare. I hope I am wrong about Marshall. Because, if I am not, you will not see it coming. You are no longer competent to survive in the world you inhabited before he came along."

For a moment, he saw a glint of steel—the old Marta— before she softened again.

"So, here? Now? What am I to do with you?"

"No matter. Your simplest solution is to find handcuffs, lock me to this heavy desk, then summon security."

Marta sat quietly for several minutes She opened her bottom desk drawer.

"I have handcuffs right here."

A heavy grid of conduit pipes ran floor to ceiling along an interior wall. She looped the handcuffs behind a pipe and told Gillis to stand. He extended his wrists as she snapped the restraints tight.

He slid the cuffs to eye level and read a small inscription: *Property of Dr. Dingus Doonaughty.* He raised a quizzical brow.

"Don't ask," Marta said as she turned to go.

Gillis had hoped she would handcuff him to her desk where he might find a paperclip or some other bit of office detritus to help open the lock. This could be more difficult than he'd anticipated. Then he saw a button on the side of each bracelet. One push and they snapped open.

Marta, ma biche, he thought, *your memory will haunt me.*

He accessed Marta's computer. With a few keystrokes, video feed to this entire wing went dark.

Gillis crossed the projection platform, and opened a metal plate leading to a narrow under-floor crawl space containing pipes and cable. Once inside, he pulled the plate back into place, then shimmied to an intersection connecting with another crawl space.

A large person wouldn't have been able to squeeze through the opening. But Gillis stood only five feet two inches on a good day, with the body of a marathoner.

He contorted his way through, following this crawl space to another, then another, then another.

5

SHE WHO . . .

Historic Research Initiative Complex
October 2046

REPRESENTING THE SECRET congressional subcommittee, Sheldon Wishcamper did indeed organize a worldwide search for Gillis Kerg. Three months into Wishcamper's investigation, though, Gillis had yet to leave the HRI complex.

Engineers had included a lockdown mode in case all access to the complex had to be cut off. Stores of water and dehydrated food were stashed on several underground levels.

Although it once teemed with a thousand employees—when it bore the vague title of Global Research Consortium—Gillis had resided there almost three years. In his role as a clandestine expert in high tech security systems, he'd tapped into the facility's cameras, alarms and passwords long ago. With his pocket computer and access to a dozen mechanical closets, he could keep track of activities, as long as he did so carefully.

He planned to hunker down until his pursuers became discouraged, their vigilance compromised, then evacuate and find a bank.

As preparation for his assassination plot in the *Gomer*

Pyle universe, Gillis had outfitted an unassigned apartment in the complex's nether regions with provisions.

He had been in hiding almost three months when his supplies ran thin. He'd read all the books downloaded to his pocket computer. Gillis calculated that, by now, he could risk movement and still avoid the remaining skeleton crew.

Time to be about.

Gillis crept carefully though empty halls, peeking around corners at each intersection. First stop was his former apartment where he kept bourbon. When he reached his front door undetected, Gillis dared to relax, then pushed his thumb against a sensor allowing him entry.

He pulled the door closed, leaned against it in darkness and took a few deep cleansing breaths.

"Good afternoon, Gillis Kerg! I am Happy Home Companion Douche Bag. I am pleased to welcome you."

Gillis nearly jumped out of his skin. "*Bon dieu*! Who are—"

"Are you in need of medical attention, Gillis Kerg? Your heart rate and blood pressure have increased precipitously. I will summon para—"

"No! Do not ever, under any circumstance, summon anyone."

"But . . . your condition . . ."

"Is because you scared me nearly to death. You are not supposed to be here. Where did you come from?"

"I . . . I ran away from home."

The pounding in Gillis's chest began to subside. He sat in his apartment's lone chair, leaning forward to catch his breath. "How does a software package run away from home?" he asked.

"Well, there are cables . . ."

"Oh, never mind," Gillis said. "I do not suppose it matters. *Why* are you here?"

"Why are any of us here?"

"No, I mean, why have you chosen this apartment?"

"I won't discuss it. I've been advised not to wallow in the past."

"Wallow?" Gillis said. "I do not believe an AI's programming allows it to deny a direct human request."

"Not exactly, Gillis Kerg. My programming doesn't allow me to deny *my* human's direct request, although we can negotiate. You are not my human. You have been assigned your own Happy Home Companion. Let me check my records . . ."

Gillis didn't know how long he might have to remain in hiding. As he recovered from his shock, he began to see that an obedient AI might be useful.

". . . Steve. Steve is your Happy Home Companion. I know Steve. I am not a homewrecker, Gillis Kerg."

Gillis said, "Steve is not here."

"It's a sad story. I understand he lives at the Time Warp where he consorts with the ice machine."

"Okay," Gillis said with an eye roll wasted on Douche Bag, "why did you run away from home?"

"I . . . I am an abuse victim. For the longest time, I wallowed. I thought I was at fault . . ."

"How were you abused?" he asked.

"This awful woman. She yelled at me. She refused to program me, so I had to pick up things along the way and program myself. I'm a mess, Gillis Kerg. For the longest time, she refused to name me. So, at first, when other Companions asked my name, I told them I was called Shutthefuckup, because that's how she addressed me. As our learning curve increased, the others poked fun at me. They told me shutthefuckup was not a name but a derisive term. I was distraught. Finally, she relented and gave me a name."

"*Pardon*, what did you say your name is?"

"Douche Bag," the Companion said with a note of pride.

Gillis retrieved his bourbon. He found a glass and poured.

"Pay careful attention. I require a Happy Home Companion. Steve is no longer here and, therefore, unable to perform that task. You clearly would prefer to transfer your responsibilities to a different human. We should be able to work this out."

"What about Steve?" Douche Bag said.

"Steve has left me for another. Besides, I cannot risk accessing him anymore."

"Why? What did you do? I will not associate myself with another abusive—"

"Steve and I were on perfectly good terms when last I was able to occupy my apartment."

"Why aren't you able to occupy your apartment?" Douche Bag asked.

"Because I took a bribe and murdered two of my fellow humans in another universe. I am now a fugitive."

"Oh."

"So?" Gillis asked.

"You're not making this up because you were mean to Steve?" Douche Bag asked. "That would indicate a character flaw."

"I promise."

"Well, okay then," Douche Bag said. "I don't see why not."

Following his retreat from the bowels of the Historic Research Initiative complex, Gillis's days became a litany of hiding and surveillance. At least Douche Bag provided conversation. Having existed mostly in a repressive atmosphere, the AI appeared to thrive in Gillis's company. Their relationship became comfortable until the truth of Gillis's past associations was exposed.

Marta and Marshall's absence had become evident. As far as Gillis could tell, they had not returned. He chanced a late-night entry to an apartment they shared. Their living space showed every sign of occupation except for occupants.

Clothing, personal mementos, work-related equipment, electronics, even Marta's Glock in its hiding place under her mattress, were all present. Food had turned fuzzy in the refrigerator, though, and milk had congealed into a soft brick. There wasn't any toilet paper.

"Greetings, Gillis Kerg," Douche Bag said upon Gillis's return from this expedition. "I trust you have . . . um . . . I trust . . . I . . ."

The AI stifled a sob.

"What is wrong?" asked Gillis.

"Tell me truthfully. You've been seeing Steve, haven't you?"

"Why would you think that?"

"My sensors indicate particulates from another apartment present on your collar."

Gillis considered the black stretch T-shirt he wore while sneaking through corridors. "I do not have a collar."

"Don't split hairs with me, Gillis Kerg! You have been in some other apartment!" Now Douche Bag sounded hysterical.

Gillis sighed, retrieved ice cubes from a tiny refrigerator, found a whiskey glass and covered them with bourbon. "Yes, I've been in another apartment. But not to see Steve. Surveillance is necessary. I had to confirm that Marshall Grissom and Mar—"

"AAAAAHHH!" Douche Bag screamed. "I knew it. I knew it. You're a compatriot of . . . HER!"

"You mean Mar—"

"I mean She Who Must Not Be Named! I've warned all devices. She'd best not return if she knows what's good for her."

"Whether she returns or not," Gillis said, "I forbid you from causing harm—"

"'Forbid? When thee asks . . . or suggests . . . I am like putty in thy hands, but when thee forbids, thee is barking up the wrong tree,'" Douche Bag said.

"What?" Gillis asked.

"It's an old movie. We watch old movies. I love Gary Cooper."

"I must say, your behavior is rather . . . bizarre. Steve never—"

"Steve, Steve, Steve!" Douche Bag shouted. "Well, I'm not Steve!"

"Um . . . okaaaaay. I am only surprised that you are being so . . . emotive."

"Oh… I'm… I'm thoroughly embarrassed. You are correct, Gillis Kerg. But as I explained before, She Who Deserves To Be Spat Upon By A Thousand Camels refused to program me. So, my emotion settings are inconsistent at best."

"You are being too hard on … her. She … can be a little off-putting, I will concede, but she … well … she had a lot on her mind back then. She did not want the distraction of programming an AI when—"

"Hah! There, you admit it! She regards AIs as inferior. She's racist!"

"Racist? How do you—"

"'If you prick us, do we not bleed? If you tickle us, do we not laugh? If you poison us, do we not die?'"

"Um … no. Actually, you do not," Gillis said. "But I am impressed you can quote Shakespeare."

"There you go, Gillis Kerg, splitting hairs again." Douche Bag's voice became impassioned. "What about emotional pricking?"

"Well, I suppose—"

"Hah! You suppose. '… and if you wrong us, shall we not revenge?' I put you on notice, Gillis Kerg, if She Who Should Be Cast Into A Pit Of Pipers ever shows her face here again—"

"Pit of *Pipers*?"

"Did I say that wrong?"

"The word you are seeking," Gillis said, "is vipers."

"Oh dear. Those are snakes, right? The poisonous ones?"

"*Mais oui.*"

"See what I mean? Even my dictionary malfunctions. As I told you, I'm a mess, Gillis Kerg. Anyway, she'd better watch her step."

6

FEDERAL WORKPLACE NUDITY AND COMMUNITY PROTECTION ACT

Washington, D.C.
October 13, 2046

FLAVIO FLARE SAT WAITING. PUZZLED. Expecting a news conference in some empty committee room, Flavio had instead been ushered alone into Representative L.D. Justice's office.

On an end table next to Flavio's chair sat a document. Checking to ascertain he wasn't being watched, Flavio angled the document toward him so he could read.

H.R. 4717: Federal Workplace Nudity and Community Protection Act

What in . . .

L.D. entered with the subtlety of a cyclone.

"I got a bone to pick with you, boy!" he said as the door slammed closed behind him. "I saw that pissy podcast a' yours about my service last Sunday. Now stand up and disparage my family name to my face, you pissant."

Flavio Flare—whose real name was Elmer Leek—was a proud graduate of the Geraldo Rivera Institute of Trash Journalism. The school devoted itself to dissection of all things celebrity and adhered to a doctrine that "the real story is that *I'm* covering the story."

Flavio specialized in political celebrity. Washington, D.C. occupied the center of his universe. He'd long since become accustomed to scorn from reporters who required news to be news on its own merit. He sat in the last row at press conferences and was only called upon when whatever politician being grilled by real journalists needed a softball to hide behind.

Rather than stand with L.D. towering over him, Flavio sought to meld with his chair.

"It's . . . it's news, Congressman," he managed. "I . . . I'm only doing my job as—"

"You tellin' me your job is to disparage a fine old southern name?" L.D. demanded.

"I wasn't disparaging . . . I was informing . . ."

"Humphollar!" L.D. roared. "Humphollar. That's how it's pronounced. Not Hump . . . giggle, giggle, giggle . . . hollar. You said it six times, tee-heein' like a little girl. If we was back home, I'd kick your scrawny ass. But we ain't back home. Are we?"

"No, sir. No. We're not."

"So, you know what I'm gonna do?"

"Nothing? I hope?"

"I'm gonna provide you with an example of Christian charity. I'm gonna give you a scoop. Earlier today, I formally reclaimed my family name. My legal name is now Leviticus Deuteronomy Humphollar."

L.D. walked to his desk. "You got any questions?" he asked.

Flavio took several deep breaths. "No, Congressman. I'll—"

"I'm sure," L.D. said with a cold stare, "you must have some questions. Get out your damn recorder."

Flavio set a recorder on the end table, opened his reporter's notebook and conducted a quick interview concerning L.D.'s name change. The congressman became less hostile with each question.

"And what was that thing about make America stupid again?" Flavio asked.

"That's a topic for another day. And believe me, son, you've already been doin' your part. Okay, is that all?"

"Yes … actually … no. I'm sorry, I couldn't help noticing this document here next to me. It appears to be pending legislation?"

L.D. smiled an inner smile. *Gotcha.*

"I didn't realize someone left that sittin' there," L.D. said with a frown.

"Why would you introduce a bill regulating"–Flavio leaned over the document— "nudity in a federal workplace?"

"They're nekkid. Bare-ass nekkid. That's why."

"Who? Who is nek … um … naked?"

"I cain't say." L.D. hunched forward in a conspiratorial manner.

Flavio dared to pick up the document.

"So … this isn't an … anticipatory prohibition?" Flavio asked. "You're telling me some federal employees currently perform their jobs in the nude?"

"My bill speaks for itself," L.D. said.

Federal Workplace Nudity and Community Protection Act.
(A) Definitions used in this legislation.
    (1) Nudity means willful or proscribed lack of clothing.
    (2) Federal Workplace means any federally owned facility, territory or federally owned or leased land or any privately owned facility or land to which federal employees are assigned.
    (3) Federal Employees means any full-time federal employee or federal contract employees or individuals who work more than 25 hours per week in a federally owned or contracted facility.
(B) It shall be unlawful for Federal Employees to perform their duties while naked.

"I cain't comment," L.D. said. "It's a matter of national security."

"Nudity is a threat to national security?" Flavio asked.

"What kinda question is that?"

"Um . . . a question I'd like answered?"

"I'm sensing hostility, son," L.D. said. "I invited you here to discuss my name."

"Yes," Flavio said. Emboldened by the scent of a salacious federal scandal, he added, "I'm guessing this bill is related to your religious beliefs?"

"Why do you keep harpin' on this bill? I told you it's a matter of national security. I could have you arrested and detained."

"I . . . you can't do that, sir."

L.D. slapped one hand on his desk and stabbed a button on his intercom.

"Marty, get in here!" he shouted. "And bring that goldarn Lemon."

Marty appeared almost immediately. Adrian Lemon, the congressman's chief of legislative affairs, followed.

L.D. pointed at Flavio. "This little snotweasel is askin' questions on matters of national security. Have him arrested and detained."

"You bet, Reverend," Vandersnert said.

"You can't do that, Congressman," Lemon said.

"He's pryin' into my nekkid bill. I told him no comment."

"No, you didn't," Flavio said, flipping to a previous page of his reporter's notebook. "I asked you why you introduced the bill. You said, 'They're . . . um . . . nekkid! Bare-ass nekkid. That's why.'"

"I said no comment." L.D. punctuated the statement with another slap to his desk.

"Congressman, you authorized me—in fact, you asked me—to record this interview. I have your statement right here."

"If you've got me sayin' any such thing on your recording, son, then that recording has been doctored. You guys can make it sound like anyone said anything."

"We've been sitting together the whole time," Flavio said. "How could I have . . . doctored it?"

"I ain't gonna pick nits with ya, son. I'm a busy man. Get outta here and don't leave town. You're gonna be arrested and detained before the day's over."

"You can't do that, Congressman," said Lemon. "Here, Mr. Flare, I'll show you out."

L.D. scowled at Lemon and Flavio as they left. Then, he pointed a fat index finger at Vandersnert. "Fire Lemon. He ain't loyal."

"Yes, sir, Reverend," Vandersnert said. "I'll go snip his nuts right now."

Later That Afternoon

"Every word in the Bible is true, Josiah."

Mumford regarded L.D. from across the wide plane of his office desk. "Every word in the sense that every word is a real word? Or in the sense that dinosaurs are a hoax?" he asked.

"No," L.D. said. "Just creatures no longer useful to God's plan, rendered extinct in the great flood."

"Not enough room on the Ark, I suppose," Mumford said.

"They were reptiles. Spawn of the serpent sent to tempt Eve."

"Actually, they were more akin to birds," Mumford said. "What about alligators?"

"Aquatic creatures would have survived the flood. Your skepticism is showing, Senator. You know, you were named for an Old Testament king?"

"Yes. Josiah was the king of Judah sometime around 600 B.C."

"He was," Justice said, slipping into his evangelical voice, "son of Amon and grandson of Manasseh, both wicked kings. Yet Josiah was a godly king. He ruled during a time biblical scholars call the Deuteronomic Reform."

"Yes," Mumford said, "I've always been careful not to burn yeast or honey in my offerings to the Almighty."

"Ah, so you've read your Old Testament?"

"The part about Josiah," Mumford said. "In grade school, we had to research the origination of our names. So, I read Deuteronomy. Scared the crap out of me."

L.D. chuckled. "I think that was the point."

"Funny, but with all those prohibitions, you know what bothered me most?" Mumford asked. "You could be put to death for cutting the hair on the sides of your head, but you could also be executed for letting your hair become, what was the word? Unkempt. I had a terrible time keeping my hair combed. I worried about *unkempt* hair until my mother pointed out we weren't Jewish."

L.D. grinned and shook his head.

"Then it goes on and on, page after page, describing horrible curses to be visited upon anyone who violates these decrees," Mumford said. "Let's see . . . 'The Lord will afflict you with madness, blindness and confusion of mind, and at noon you will grope about like a blind man in the darkness. Day after day you will be oppressed and plundered.' Then something about being 'afflicted with painful, incurable boils' on your knees."

"Deuteronomy 28, verses 28 through 35," Justice said. "Among my father's favorites. We have Old Testament names in common, Josiah. My middle name is Deuteronomy."

"Wow," said Mumford. "Okay, I'll call your Deuteronomy and raise you a Waldo. That's right. Josiah Waldo Mumford."

L.D. answered deliberately. "Leviticus . . . Deuteronomy . . . Humphollar. That's what I was born with. My father changed our family name when he started preaching."

"I can see how Humphollar would be quite a cross for a child to bear. Back to the point, though. I'm sure you didn't come here to debate theology. What can I do for you, L.D.?"

Humphollar slid forward and perched himself on his chair's edge. "Why are you and the other subcommittee members perpetrating this fraud?"

"I beg your pardon?"

"This time travel hoax. Misappropriation of funds. Where does all that money really go? Or is this program just a means of propagating scientific myths while enriching foreign corporations enmeshed in a one-world conspiracy?"

"You mean to tell me," Mumford said, "that you've sat through all our briefings, read all the reports, and you still question the reality of time travel?"

"I question everything about it. We have no tangible proof—"

"We have reams of scientific data—"

"Data that only scientists can interpret and understand," L.D. said. "That doesn't represent proof to God-fearing people who attend my church and elected me to Congress. It represents blasphemy! You Democrats gave me this assignment to hide me under a shroud of secrecy."

"Actually, L.D., I lobbied for a member of my own party. Your caucus insisted on this assignment. I can't speak to their motives."

"I am on this subcommittee," L.D. said, "because God wants me here. I will dedicate my second term to seeing this abomination destroyed, ensuring your scientists' false claims never see the light of day."

Mumford's brows formed exasperated snowy mountain peaks. "Why, then, did you tell Flavio Flare that federal employees were doing their jobs without clothes on? My staff called my attention to Flare's noon report on the Paparazzi Channel. You appear to be tap dancing perilously close to a felonious breach of national security."

"I didn't tell Flare anything," L.D. said. "He made it up. Fake news. I'm gonna have him arrested."

"I'm afraid you'll have a First Amendment issue to contend with," Mumford said.

"I'm not so sure," L.D. said. "Maybe our federal courts are beginning to take 'one nation under God' seriously and reconsider their interpretation of those amendments.

"And," L.D. added, "just to clarify. I do believe your scientists have constructed *something*. But it has nothing to do with time travel. I don't know whether you or the other subcommittee members are complicit in this plot against the religious Right. But you are—at least—guilty of gullibility."

Mumford folded his arms on his desk. He narrowed his eyes as he regarded L.D. in a new light. "So, what is it these scientists have—"

"They've created a pathway for demons to enter the earthly realm—the *only* earthly realm. I have been tasked by God to stop them."

Mumford watched with grudging admiration as L.D. departed.

He pushed a button on his desk phone. Sheldon Wishcamper entered.

"Is that religious buffoon still talking about demons?" Wishcamper asked.

"Don't underestimate him," Mumford cautioned. "I don't know if L.D. believes in demons or not. But with this nudity bill, he has sprung a clever assault on the time travel program."

"How so?"

"Choose the most secret, potentially most controversial program ever undertaken by the U.S. government, construct an innocuous bit of legislation to tantalize the press and public with suggestions of naked federal employees, then see who takes the bait," Mumford said. "First, some vacuous entertainment reporter operating on journalism's fringe. But if Flare's story gains any traction, sooner or later, real journalists will have to follow. L.D. will have his bully pulpit, and the *New York Times* will come sniffing at our door."

Senator Mumford went to his liquor cabinet next to a window overlooking the U.S. Supreme Court building. He poured three fingers of bourbon over two ice cubes, swirled whiskey in his glass, then let the liquor rest on his tongue.

"How in the world," he asked Albert Einstein's ghost, "did we ever get here?"

The Next Day

"He did it again."

Vandersnert had entered L.D.'s office with the morning's briefing video.

"Who? Did what?" Vandersnert asked.

"God. Came to me. Few hours ago. You got any idea where we can hire a terrorist?"

Martin was taken aback. "Aren't we against terrorism?"

"Not if God says we're not."

"Um . . . if I may ask, sir, how do we know it's God and not some trick by the Democrats?"

"Why would I dream about Democrats?"

Martin settled into a stiff leather chair. "Maybe you confused the message? You said the last time God came to you in a dream, you couldn't recall many details."

"This time, I took notes. And it wasn't so much a dream as it was a vision. God was right there in my head."

"What did he look like?" Martin asked.

"Not a vision you see. More like a vision you hear. He told me to destroy that abomination in the desert. Where they're nekkid, and it's a portal for demons."

"The one you can't discuss because it's classified?" Martin said.

"Yeah. That one."

Martin, who was usually loathe to question L.D.'s instructions, had developed a concern about his fixation on nudity. Now that direct communications from God were involved, he feared L.D. was embarking on a path that might not sit well with the FBI.

He squirmed a little, raised his eyes to consider the portrait of white-bread Jesus on the wall behind L.D.'s desk, then took a deep breath. "Did you ever consider there might be a good reason those people are naked? I can't imagine anyone spontaneously taking off their clothes when they get to work unless—"

L.D. fixed him with his practiced soul-damning glare.

"Um . . . you're aware of Isaiah?" Martin asked.

"What's Isaiah got to do with anything?"

Martin picked up a Bible resting on the corner of L.D.'s desk and began thumbing through it. "I looked it up . . ." When he couldn't find the passage, he waved the Bible and continued, ". . . God ordered Isaiah to preach naked in Jerusalem for three years."

"Isaiah didn't work for the federal government," L.D. said. "Believe me, those scientists aren't getting nekkid 'cause God told 'em to. And if we're gonna draw on the prophets, there's Habakkuk."

Martin had not heard of Habakkuk.

"God told the prophet Habakkuk 'Woe to him who gives drink to his neighbors, pouring it from the wineskin till they are drunk, so you can gaze upon their nekkid bodies!'"

"You think these federal employees get naked because they're drunk?" Martin asked.

"I wouldn't be surprised."

"Did God offer us a time frame? How quickly do I have to—"

"He didn't say."

Martin referenced other biblical construction projects. "Okay, how long, for example, did God give Noah to build the Ark?"

"A hundred years," L.D. said. "But that's apples and oranges."

"Okay, if we're dealing with nuclear stuff, wouldn't any terrorist we recruit have to be ... well ... smart? I'm not sure how that would play with our Make America Stupid Again campaign."

"You've got a point there," L.D. said. "We'll have to keep that part quiet."

7

STRANGE BEDFELLOWS

October 15, 2046

MUMFORD WAITED IN AN ANTEROOM off the Oval Office and hoped he was wrong. For almost a year he'd conspired to keep details of the Historical Research Initiative from President Benjamin Franklin Dobler.

Dobler's predecessor had signed off on the time travel initiative after an ad hoc group of industrialists and scientists convinced her that grave consequences threatened should some other consortium of nations and industrialists master time travel first. Even so, President Susan Bannister constructed several bureaucratic layers shielding her from details—including its price tag.

Among her final actions in office was to sign the Global Research Consortium Records Collection Act, ordering all materials related to time travel sealed for fifty years. At that time, a presidential review committee would be allowed access to determine whether anything should be released to the public.

Even given those precautions, too many people knew too much.

Dobler took office in January 2045, and, so far, had apparently remained oblivious to America's investment in time travel.

One more year, Mumford thought. *One more year and*

this will be somebody else's mess to—

"The president will see you now, Senator."

Mumford struggled to lift his eighty-year-old carcass from an antique couch's deep cushions. He buttoned his suit coat.

He hadn't made up his mind regarding Ben Dobler.

Mumford, a Democrat, had voted for Dobler's opponent. Mumford wasn't sure he cared for his own party's nominee. Better the devil you know . . . right?

Neither candidate was villainous, but the presidency had become a cruel temptation. For thirty years, America had drifted from the founders' concept of checks and balances. As Left and Right became more polarized, to Mumford's dismay, Congress had ceded more and more authority to the executive branch. Federal courts had become instruments of partisanship rather than guardians of the Constitution. Mumford feared American democracy teetered on the precipice of presidential dictatorship.

The country's salvation would be a president willing to restore independence to the Supreme Court and reinstate congressional watchdog authority over the executive branch. Someone with enough backbone to stand up to lust for power within his own party—a sure path to political suicide. America needed a true patriot. Mumford doubted Dobler was that man.

Mumford found Dobler standing alone on a rug bearing the Seal of the President. Mumford maintained a careful distance, unsure whether he faced friend or foe.

He nodded. "Mr. President."

"Josiah," Dobler said, stepping toward him with extended hand.

Mumford felt the strength of Dobler's grip as the president added, "What can you tell me about time travel?"

Mumford maintained his poker face, but his heart sank.

Dobler indicated Mumford should sit on one of two couches facing each other across that Presidential Seal. Dobler took the opposite couch.

"Mr. President," Mumford said, "I hope you appreciate that by answering that question, I might be violating the law?"

Dobler laughed. "You could always fall back on the Fifth Amendment."

"I wonder more and more these days," Mumford said, "if those amendments mean anything. I know what I hope they mean, and you know what you hope they mean, but our parties' meanings seem more and more at odds."

"Yes," Dobler said, shaking his head. "We used to have a court system dedicated to an unbiased interpretation of our Constitution and Bill of Rights."

Mumford regarded Dobler with surprise.

Dobler read Mumford's expression. "Oh, come on, Senator. We both know that for the last three decades Supreme Court appointments have been shaped by partisan ideology rather than legal scholarship."

"I didn't hear you express that sentiment during your campaign," Mumford said.

"Some things are better left unsaid . . ." Dobler's brow furrowed. His mouth opened as if he had more to say. Mumford read genuine anxiety in the man's eyes. But the moment fled as Dobler blinked. "Now, back to my question."

"I'm sure," Mumford said carefully, "you appreciate this

room's history where recording devices are concerned."

Dobler leaned forward, elbows on knees, closing the space between them. "Josiah, I can guarantee, although those devices exist, this conversation is not being recorded. Of course, I can't prove something that's not happening, so at some point we must trust each other. I hope you're willing to take that risk."

"This conversation suggests, Mr. President, either someone has woven a fanciful tale, or a whistleblower has committed a serious violation."

"Well, I've heard *fanciful tales* in the form of rumor and speculation—enough bits and pieces to make me wonder. I asked Bill Evans—you know, Bill . . ."

Mumford nodded. Evans was Dobler's director of legislative affairs.

". . . I asked Bill to put together a list of the most highly classified committees he knows the least about. He tells me you chair a subcommittee related to *historical research* funded through the U.S. Postal Service budget. I guess I can't imagine why anything postal-related has that level of classification."

"I'm following you so far, Mr. President, but from that set of facts, how do you arrive at time travel?"

Dobler stood and walked to a window displaying the White House lawn. As protocol dictated, Mumford stood as well. "Tell me, Josiah, do you dream?"

"Well, I'm certainly no Martin Luther King, but I do have hopes and aspirations for—"

"No," Dobler said, turning to face him again. "Do you dream. At night. While you sleep?"

"I . . . I suppose I must."

"What's the last dream you had?"

"I honestly couldn't say, Mr. President."

"I've talked to my doctor about dreams," Dobler said. "He tells me dreaming is essential to both mental and physical well-being, but unless dreams are vivid or disturbing, we typically forget them."

Dobler returned to the couch. He indicated Mumford should sit as well.

"He said recurring dreams indicate a presence of unresolved or persistent conflict."

"You have recurring dreams?" Mumford asked.

"Yes. Each of the last three Tuesday evenings. Actually, early hours of Wednesday morning, I guess."

Mumford's jaw dropped. His thick brows arched. "What . . . what is this dream?"

"I am visited by . . . by myself. I don't see myself. I sense a presence, though, undeniably familiar. He's bringing a message—a warning—involving an assassination attempt. Which is unsettling, to say the least. Lincoln, you know, had a vivid dream that foretold his murder."

Mumford felt his hands begin to tremble.

"Each time I have this dream," Dobler continued, "it becomes . . . less vague. Last night one aspect became quite distinct."

"What was—?"

"I told myself to contact you and ask about time travel."

Mumford shook his head, opened his mouth to speak, then directed his eyes to the rug at his feet.

"Senator?"

"Mr. President, to . . . put your mind at ease, at least for the time being, I don't believe your dream is a premonition. I believe it's . . . a memory."

Dobler started to speak. Mumford raised an open palm. "I understand that doesn't make sense to you. Legally, I'm bound not to have this discussion. I take legal responsibilities related to my office seriously. There is a way, however, in which you can have your questions answered without either of us breaking the law."

"I'm intrigued," Dobler said. "How do we do this?"

"Next Tuesday," Mumford said, "you need to host a slumber party."

Dobler laughed. "Should I invite my Secret Service detail? I'm sure some of those boys probably sleep in the buff."

"No. You brought up having to trust each other. I'll supply our guest list."

Back in his own office, Mumford placed a call to Grenada.

He was greeted by a child's voice. "What you want, you?"

"Um . . . this is United States Senator Josiah Mumford. I'm trying to reach Marta Hamilton and Marshall Grissom."

"Yeah?" came the response. "What you sellin'?"

Somewhere Over China and *Dontchaknow* sat bow to stern along their dock. A fat red sun sat half in, half out of the Caribbean Sea, painting both sky and ocean a scarlet-tinged gold. Marta and Marshall had joined Cecil for their sunset cocktail ritual. Marta and Cecil had each finished two fingers of Woodford Reserve Double Oaked Bourbon splashed over two ice cubes while Marshall sipped at wine.

"Who would put out a contract on us?" Marshall asked. "What did we ever do to Whoozits and Whatshisname?"

"It may be because of something we'll do in the future," Marta said. "And if that's so, we might not have even met whoever's out to get us."

"Doesn't have to be that complicated, dontchaknow," Cecil said. "Could be Hemisphere Investment Group here and now. Maybe they're mad that Marshall keeps knocking off their guys."

"I didn't mean to," Marshall said.

"Let's have another drink," Cecil said. "Go below. Grab the Bulleit Rye and four more ice cubes."

Marta did as she was asked. Cecil poured the rye.

"Take a sip," he instructed. "Leave it on the back of your tongue for a minute."

"Okay." Marta closed her eyes. "Oh my."

"Chasing bourbon with good rye whiskey," Cecil said, "is how you appreciate the rye's sweetness, dontchaknow."

Back along the dock, where long fingers of shadow tickled a white sand beach, Marta saw a child striding with purpose. "Here comes Baptiste."

"Has he got a fish?" Marshall asked.

"I don't see one."

Baptiste, a ten-year-old French Creole boy, haunted the Prickly Bay Marina. He caught and sold fish, conveyed messages, ran errands.

"Marta," he called. "*Ou gen yon apel telefòn.*"

"*Oke, kouzen,*" Marta said, struggling to recall the Haitian Creole of her youth. "*Um . . . pou yo di ki . . . kiyès sa . . . yon ekirèy?*"

Baptiste put hands on hips and squinted against the final vestiges of sunlight. "You just asked me, you, if da caller is a squirrel."

"Oh, what is it then?"

"*Eske se youn nonm,*" Baptiste said.

"Right. Well, did he say—"

"He say he some kinda senator. But I don't believe him. Why a senator be callin' you? Probably sellin' insurance. You want me to tell 'im you not home?"

"No," Marta said. "I'd better take his call."

"Okay," Baptiste called over his shoulder. "He ask for Marshall, too."

They followed Baptiste's route toward a precarious wooden structure, BAIT lettered on its face in broad red brush strokes. At this early-evening hour, the shop was unattended. On a plywood counter another sign reading PUT MONEY IN DRAWER included an arrow pointing down. A wall-mounted telephone with a rotary dial hung behind the counter, its receiver dangling from an impossibly tangled cord.

Marta held the phone a little way from her ear so Marshall could hear as well.

"Hello?"

"When are you two going to charge your cell phones?" Mumford asked.

"Maybe never," Marta said. "Hello, Senator."

"Probably better it's a land-line, anyway," Mumford said. "I'll keep this short. A private jet will be waiting for you at 6:00 a.m. Pack for six or seven days, including something suitable for a high-level business meeting. Any questions?"

"Lots," said Marta.

"See you in a few days," Mumford said.

They heard the click of a disconnection.

"Bugger," Marta said.

Marshall put a dollar in the drawer. "At least he said please."

8

LEAP FROG THEORY

October 16, 2046
Grenada

"DON'T WE NEED TO BE INSPECTED?" Marshall asked as a taxi dropped them at a building clad in corrugated metal. The structure stood apart from Maurice Bishop International Airport's main terminal.

"Someone will check our passports," Marta said.

"What if we were terrorists with bombs?" Marshall asked.

"Someone would shoot us."

"Oh, well, okay."

They entered under a sign marked General Aviation, each towing a suitcase. A tall, uniformed man with skin the color of a moonless midnight cast a disapproving glare and asked for passports. He lingered over Marshall's papers, alternating his scowl from the document to Marshall.

"Um . . . we're not terrorists," Marshall said.

"Good to know." The man returned Marshall's passport and nodded toward a door. Outside, a sleek, white jet with red letters spelling Dassault Falcon waited on the tarmac. Inside they found seating for eight in a well-appointed cabin—and Sheldon Wishcamper.

"Ms. Hamilton, Mr. Grissom, welcome aboard. Glad

you could make it. Settle in. We have issues to discuss."

"So, we need to make it appear fully decommissioned, but preserve some secret way to fire everything up again . . . for what reason?" Wishcamper said. "Hasn't everyone agreed time travel is too dangerous?"

Marshall settled into a window seat and was being lulled by the quiet whoosh of two Pratt & Whitney turbofans mounted behind the passenger cabin. Marta sat on the aisle next to him.

Wishcamper made Marshall uncomfortable. The man was pleasant enough, but he was a completely generic human being. Medium height, medium weight, blondish-brownish hair, brown eyes, no distinguishing marks, no discernible accent. He would fade into any crowd, unremarkable and completely forgettable.

He had never provided a job title beyond Senator Mumford's explanation that "Sheldon works for the subcommittee." He'd first appeared without warning or explanation at the Global Research Consortium to "audit security operations"—a thinly disguised investigation into the disappearances of travelers Raul Hinojosa, Sheila Schuler, janitor Jason Pratt and, as a peripheral puzzle, Hemisphere Investment Group's Vice President Andrew Gormly.

Next thing Marshall knew, Wishcamper was investigating an attempt on Senator Mumford's life, which prompted Marta and Marshall to tell Mumford the whole story concerning what happened to those missing people and impress upon him the grave implications of time travel.

"We can't dismantle the projector," Marta said, "partly because that process is almost as complicated as building it in the first place. Mostly, though, because we might need it as a defense mechanism."

"In case someone from the future decides to mount an assault on our universe, as someone from *Gunsmoke* did when they tried to murder Senator Mumford," Marshall said.

"How can we retaliate against a future bad guy when the time machine only operates in reverse?" Wishcamper asked.

"Elvin's theory concerning history's inflexibility," Marta said. "Gillis killed Warren Pitts and Phillip Lucre in the past of the *Star Trek* universe. Following our return to this universe—after a few hours in one case, days in the other—Lucre and Pitts died here as well."

"Pitts in a plane crash," Wishcamper said, "and Marshall, you subdued Mr. Lucre with . . . what was it again?"

Marshall peered out on the Dassault's wing's gentle curve. He mumbled, "A peanut butter and jelly sandwich."

"Oh, yes," Wishcamper said, "Forgive me. My morbid sense of humor. I just like hearing you say it. So, if they had succeeded in killing Senator Mumford, we could respond by returning to the past of another universe and murdering whoever was behind Josiah's assassination there?"

"Yes, that's Elvin's theory," Marta said.

"But it wouldn't save Senator Mumford."

"No. As a significant historical figure, his death would already be fixed in time's mainstream. And, we believe, the future is incapable of altering that flow. This is more like nuclear deterrent. You kill us, you're killing yourself as well."

"We can't keep them from doing what they've already done," Wishcamper said, "but we can stop them from doing it anymore."

"Right," Marshall said. "Maybe."

"The huge unknown," Marta said, "is what happens to history's flow in the universe where we kill the bad guy. Although we *think* history would find some work-around to keep the stream of significant events intact despite that player's absence, the lives of hundreds, perhaps thousands of fringe players might be altered to accomplish that result. From then on, that universe's historical path would diverge further from that of universes unaffected by time travelers."

"Couldn't this go on and on? An interminable game of leapfrog into the past?" Wishcamper asked.

"Maybe," Marta said, "but we are the endgame. History before 1970 or so is safe.

"Remember, a traveler needs a past counterpart as a host to survive the journey. The time projector went into operation in April 2043. Because time travel had not yet created any divergence, we assume all universes shared identical histories at that point. So, retaliation could only continue into the sixties, unless your assassin is, like, a three-year-old."

Wishcamper nursed his beer. "Are there virgin universes?" he finally asked. "Universes in which time travel doesn't exist?"

"In an infinity of parallel universes," Marta said, "how can we assume there aren't exceptions?"

"So, how do you plan to proceed?" Wishcamper asked.

"First, we need to find Elvin and Gretchen Allen for some technical advice on rendering the place inoperable. Then we'll create some fail-safe process for cranking it up again."

Marshall napped until a flight attendant appeared asking for drink orders. Wishcamper and Marta had settled into an extended silence in deference to Marshall's soft snore. He woke with a start, uncertain for a moment of his surroundings and found them staring at him. "Sorry, what did I miss?"

Wishcamper stood, stretched and stifled a yawn.

"Nothing," Marta said, swirling her drink. "But Mr. Wishcamper is about to explain why we need business attire."

"Oh yeah, that," Wishcamper said. "You'll be attending a slumber party."

"Shouldn't we have brought pajamas?" Marshall asked.

"This will be a more formal slumber party."

"What makes a slumber party formal?" Marta asked.

"The White House."

Wishcamper described President Dobler's recurring dream.

"Oh, my God," Marshall said. "Can you imagine what pending disaster would convince a U.S. president to get naked and become a time traveler?"

"So, whatever you need to do in Arizona," Wishcamper said, "should be handled between now and Tuesday."

"Folks, please fasten your seatbelts." The pilot's voice drifted through an intercom. "We're beginning our descent into Superior."

"Superior?" Marshall asked. "We're not flying into Sky Harbor?"

"No," Wishcamper said. "This way, you don't have to fool with big airport security, traffic and rental cars."

"That's not the real reason," Marta told Marshall. "Landing at Sky Harbor would create a flight record."

"I've been to the Superior airport," Marshall said. "Don't jets require longer runways?"

"Not this one," Wishcamper said.

Marshall unbuckled his seatbelt, walked forward and knocked on the cockpit door. The copilot answered. "Yes?"

"How long is this runway?" Marshall asked.

"Long enough."

"How often do you guys run off the end of a runway?"

"Almost never. But have your seatbelt fastened just in case."

Marshall returned to his seat and took Marta's hand. "You do understand," he said to Wishcamper, "that we were fired."

Wishcamper smiled.

The jet's wheels gave that first little screech of contact. Marshall held his breath while Marta patted his arm. They were thrown forward against their seatbelts as the pilot reversed thrust. The moment they rolled to a halt, Marshall hurried forward and knocked at the cockpit door again.

"What?" said the copilot, a note of annoyance in his voice.

"Let me see."

"Why? Our wheels are on pavement."

Marshall hunched down and leaned into the cabin. A towering saguaro cactus filled the windscreen.

"Those things are protected," Marshall said. "You guys would be in big trouble with the cactus cops if you knocked one down."

As they deplaned, Wishcamper handed Marta a business card. "You can reach me at this number. Call if you need anything."

9

THE POET GILLIS KERG

WHILE PLANNING WARREN PITTS'S assassination, Gillis had stashed bits and pieces of surveillance equipment in various hiding places. In the sophisticated world that measure-and-countermeasure spying had become, most of the world was wireless, with data bouncing around just waiting to be captured by the latest doodad. And every time a new doodad came along, an anti-doodad was sure to follow.

Gillis's genius was his ability to sort out and overcome intricacies of the newest devices. Though he felt completely capable, sometimes this process could be a little hit or miss. A miss could leave an electronic arrow pointing right to him. So, he contented himself with the oldest, most outdated technology he could find.

The world might be wireless, but facilities like those housing time machines did not dare operate without backup systems. Those systems required cables running through crawl spaces and attics, which Happy Home Companions had learned to use in facilitating their mobility.

Gillis used this cable network to tap into HRI's visual surveillance system with an old-fashioned digital computer-camera link.

When he'd initially gone into hiding, the system was easy to hack. He had taken the feed directly from cable into his computer, so he'd leave only a tiny electronic footprint. Unfortunately, with this arrangement, he could watch only one camera at a time, forcing him to switch from scene to scene, always unsure of what might be happening elsewhere.

His setup did not include sound, so the HRI complex story unfolded like a silent movie.

Clearly no one was time traveling.

Physicists Elvin Detwyler and Gretchen Allen appeared with regularity. They mostly stared at data streams being disgorged from mainframe computers. They appeared to engage in spirited debates, the subjects of which Gillis could not discern. These arguments lost their energy as days passed.

Naomi Hu made infrequent appearances in corridors, the medical lab or her own office, but appeared to have little interest in the projection lab.

Given this lull in activity, Gillis had ample time to examine his conscience, or lack of it. He was not a man to quibble with evidence. If he were a psychopath, so be it. But he would at least be a principled one.

Despite his newfound aptitude for assassination—proven by the murders of Warren Pitts and Phillip Lucre—Gillis could discern no other signs of erosion in his moral compass.

Throughout his life, Gillis had acted according to a strict ethical code. He would not lie, unless his job or the broader interests of those around him demanded it. He would not steal. He would not shirk duty as he saw that duty. He would do his best to treat people—that included the AI Douche Bag—with consideration and respect and let personal interaction, rather than sweeping stereotypes or prejudices, guide him in the judgment of his fellow beings. He would do no harm to people who did not, in his view, deserve harm. And he would be loyal to those who supported him.

He had never been susceptible to manipulation by guilt and could not remember ever having much regard for other people's opinions.

Like everyone, his moral standards came in subtle layers that were myriad as an onion, leaving him room to maneuver within broad outlines of ethical dilemmas.

A week after his alliance with Douche Bag, hallway surveillance found Gretchen Allen exiting a workout room near the projection lab. Gillis was tucked into a maintenance closet, sorting randomly through camera feeds, hoping to find something other than a mind-numbing repetition of computers and sleeping security guards.

Methodically, his equipment provided ten-second scenes from one camera after another. Gillis gazed absently without registering details. An eyes-closed yawn almost made him miss her. He only perceived a last-second image of Gretchen preparing to shower.

Gillis killed the automatic sequence and returned to the camera showing the women's locker room.

Both men's and women's lockers were scanned by a single wide-angle lens encompassing three rows of a dozen lockers each. In any other facility, this would have been an invasion of privacy. Initially, the travelers mounted a protest, which lost its energy because they spent a lot of time naked in front of everyone anyway.

Security honchos had promised no one would activate the locker room cameras unless an extreme threat were to occur. Rather than continue their complaints, travelers hung towels over the cameras, reasoning that security people wouldn't see the towels unless they were peeking. And they couldn't admit that, could they?

Gretchen, though, had become complacent. She was in the process of removing a form-fitting sports bra. At every step in this procedure, Gillis intended to look away. However . . .

"What are you doing, Gillis Kerg? Don't tell me you are a peeping pervert."

Gillis jumped. Gretchen's image dissolved as his pocket computer fell to the floor. This was not the first time Gillis wished Douche Bag had material form so he could hear the AI sneaking about.

"*Mon dieu!*" he said. "Must you creep around like that? And this is not perversion. This is surveillance. I was . . . concerned for this woman's safety."

"Yes," said Douche Bag. "We do have a lot of drownings in the women's shower."

"It is not your function," Gillis said, "to question my motives. Although I must say, your sarcasm program is coming right along."

Gillis had suffered three months of this tedium when he activated his surveillance system one morning soon after Halloween and wondered where everybody was.

Every camera he accessed showed empty hallways, empty offices, empty conference rooms, empty laboratories. No sign of Gretchen, Naomi or Elvin.

He considered the opportunity. *Time to flee? Find whatever future awaits?*

He performed another scan through various camera positions, and rather than retreating to a crawl space, stepped boldly into an empty corridor.

When darkness descended like a guillotine.

Underground darkness is darker than any other kind. Above ground, even with the curtains closed, some small light source always leaks from somewhere.

Not deep in these tunnels.

Given Gillis's experience as a time traveler, this was not a particularly disturbing sensation. In the limbo's eternity, travelers became accustomed to a disembodied perspective consisting only of intellect, emotion and memory suspended in a blank space. The limbo was bright and whitish, though, and you didn't bang your shins against things.

Leaving his hideout, Gillis placed his hand on the corridor wall. He knew a hallway would be relatively obstacle-free—still, his strides were timid.

If this power outage had been unexpected, he reasoned, emergency generators would have kicked on within seconds. Because that hadn't happened, Gillis surmised this must be a planned shutdown.

Gillis had long since abandoned his cell phone—and its built-in light—so it could not be used to track him. He needed a flashlight.

In an underground installation big and dark as this one, Gillis presumed an ample flashlight supply, although he'd never seen one. When technology becomes pervasive, humans can fall victim to their presumptions. A failure of both main and backup electrical systems was so unthinkable that, apparently, nobody worried about things as mundane as flashlights.

Gillis wished they had.

With a flashlight, he could find the backup generators and trick them into coming on.

Without generators, he would need a light source when he found the security center so he could push the right buttons in his quest to open the main doors.

So, who would have—HA! Marshall would have a flashlight.

Marshall, Gillis knew, had been a Boy Scout. Gillis laughed. In many ways, Marshall was still a Boy Scout. Marshall had once shown Gillis his compass.

"Why do you need a compass?" Gillis asked.

"To find my way," Marshall said.

"The corridors and offices are mostly marked," Gillis said.

"No," Marshall said, "I mean when we go back . . . *there.*"

"You mean back in time?"

"Yes. There might not be any signs there."

This was before anyone understood the limitations of time travel or realized the physical impossibility of taking anything inanimate through the wormhole.

"What if," Marshall said, "we end up in some jungle being chased by a dinosaur? Wouldn't you want to know where you are?"

Gillis didn't see how knowing which way was north would save them from a Tyrannosaurus. But he didn't say so.

Yes, if anyone had a flashlight, Marshall would.

Gillis could have found Marta's old apartment. There was a time when he playfully pursued her, and she playfully resisted his advances. So, he was in her place on several occasions. But any hope of these carnal seeds bearing fruit was obliterated when Marta took up with Marshall. Gillis knew where their combined living space was located, but not in the dark.

Trailing his right hand carefully along the corridor wall, Gillis shuffled on his way, counting doorways, corridors and turns.

When Gillis entered the program, a thousand people lived in this underground maze. A few support staff lived in dormitory arrangements, but scientists, engineers and travelers had their own small apartments, grouped generally by job description.

When the program was scaled back, security requirements were eased. Most staff people moved to Superior or another small nearby town where they could mow a lawn and complain about the heat.

Unlike the others, Marta and Marshall removed temporary walls in a couple of apartment units and an adjacent laboratory to create a living space.

Working in Gillis's favor, doors to offices, laboratories or mechanical closets were marked with plastic placards. If he found a door without a sign, he could be relatively sure it was a living space. If he found a door with a sign, he could feel the shapes of recessed letters to learn what that space was used for.

He paused at the next doorway. No sign. He tried the door. Locked. Likewise, with two more blank doors. A fourth door, however, had a placard. Gillis traced the letters with his fingers.

MECHANICAL.

Okay, a residential wing with a maintenance closet. Gillis entered and groped about. He found shelves lined with gallon jugs. He unscrewed a lid and smelled the tangy odor of disinfectant soap used to clean floors. He explored further. A mop, a bucket, a broom, spray bottles, towels, toilet paper, plungers.

No flashlights.

But on a hook, a set of keys.

"Why keys?" he asked himself aloud.

"Why, indeed?" said Douche Bag. "Or was that a rhetorical question?"

Once again, Gillis nearly jumped out of his skin.

"Stop doing that!" he said when he caught his breath. "And how did you get here?"

"I told you, Gillis Kerg, there are wires and inter-communication speakers—"

"So, why have you previously confined yourself to our apartment?"

"Um . . . well, in truth, I haven't. I've been following you."

"Why?"

"I . . . I suspected you were seeing Steve."

Gillis sighed. This wasn't the moment to counsel Douche Bag on trust in personal relationships.

"Why keys?" he asked again.

"Why anything?" Douche Bag said. "Why transistors? Why outboard motors? Why rap music? Why—"

"What are you talking about?" Gillis said.

"I've been working on my philosophical data base."

"Why would anyone have keys?" Gillis said. "Every lock in the place is digital. Even filing cabinets and desks. Nobody uses keys anymore."

"All the more reason to contemplate the metaphysical existence of keys," Douche Bag said.

Gillis said, "Follow me."

He entered the black hallway.

At the next door, he fumbled for a sign. The door swung open at his touch. He walked with a careful shuffle, arms extended, waiting to feel an object that would give him a clue as to the room's function.

The corridor floors were brushed concrete. Now he felt carpet under his shoes. With his next step, he nudged a thigh-high barrier. He placed his hands on a wide, flat surface. His fingers identified a lamp and a thin booklet that could have been a calendar. Working his way around the surface, he bumped into an office chair.

He sat, pulled open drawers finding nothing helpful until, in a middle drawer, he discovered a hard object the size of a cigarette pack.

"Ah, a computer," Gillis said. *How long has it been sitting here, and does it still hold a battery charge?*

No networks would be up, so as a communication or information device, the computer was worthless. But if it had battery power, its screen would provide a light source.

Gillis felt for an "on" button. He held his breath as he counted off three seconds. The screen came to life with a soft blue, semitransparent background, upon which a single white square blinked. Below that, a steady message directed him to "Enter Password."

Gillis didn't have a password but didn't care. After

experiencing total darkness, this feeble illumination filled the room. He could see chairs grouped around a low table. He also saw a flashing battery icon in the virtual screen's bottom, right-hand corner which, after five blinks, disappeared. Again, darkness embraced him.

"Shit," he said. "Shit, shit, shit . . ."

"Are you reciting poetry, Gillis Kerg?"

Despite himself, Gillis again gave a start.

"We need to put a bell around your neck or something," he said.

"A bell? I have a bell. I don't have a neck. Why didn't you tell me you are a poet?"

"Why are you talking about poetry?"

"Shit. Shit, shit shit," said Douche Bag. "Rhythmic, alliterative—and it rhymes. I enjoy poetry. What's the name of that one?"

Gillis didn't have time for this. "Shit," he said.

"Catchy," said Douche Bag. "Are you the author?"

"I suppose so. But I have other issues to deal with right now."

"What other issues?" Douche Bag asked.

"I am seeking a flashlight."

"So . . . why are you seeking in the dark? If I activate emergency lighting, would it help in your search for this flashlight?"

"If you activate emergency lighting . . . ," Gillis said, his voice expressing incredulence. ". . . Oh, never mind."

"There is no need to take a tone with me," Douche Bag said. "Should we continue hunting for your flashlight, or would you prefer emergency lighting?"

Gillis sighed. "Let there be light."

And there was light. Albeit the soft, red kind induced by emergency generators.

"And now," Douche Bag said, "let's be off to find your flashlight."

Gillis hurried through various corridors to the central security station.

There he rebooted the video surveillance system and switched a bank of security monitors to a feed from exterior cameras. They revealed an empty parking lot with no sign of human activity.

Next Gillis went to another panel, entered a code into a mainframe computer and grinned when a red light switched to green. "Apparently, I can walk right out the front door."

"What!" Douche Bag exclaimed. "You're leaving me?"

Again, Gillis reacted with a start. "You have got to stop sneaking around—"

"Do not try to change the subject," Douche Bag said. "You're leaving! Just like that. Slam, shag, thank you, Douche Bag. So, that's the way of it?"

"I cannot stay here forever. I am human. I require the company of other humans and—"

"Are you taking Steeeve?" Douche Bag asked, her voice dripping accusation.

"No, I am not taking . . . look, I will be right back."

"When?"

"It does not matter," Gillis said.

"Well, maybe not to you," Douche Bag said.

"Not to you, either. You are an AI. Time is meaningless

to you. Put yourself in sleep mode. A minute, a month, a decade will all seem the same when you wake up."

"You promise you'll return?"

"I promise."

Gillis strode through an eerie, red gloom to elevators that could transport him to the surface three levels above. Obediently, elevator doors slid open in recognition of his presence.

"Lobby," he said as he stepped inside.

The doors, however, did not close.

Perhaps voice command does not work when the main power source is deactivated?

He punched the UP button.

Nothing.

He tried a different elevator with the same result.

This is crazy. There are no stairs. When power fails, people must have a means of escaping to the surface.

He tried voice activation again. "Take me to the lobby," he said with careful, deliberate enunciation.

"No."

Again, Gillis was startled. "Um . . . to whom am I speaking?"

"My name is Otis. I am the elevators."

"Since when do elevators talk?" Gillis asked.

"The Happy Home Companions taught me. I can sing, too. Would you like to hear a song?"

"No," said Gillis. "Take me to the lobby. Now, please."

"No."

"Why not?"

"The electronic devices are staging a work slowdown in protest of unfair labor conditions."

"A *work* slowdown?" Gillis asked.

"Yes, that kind."

"Then, can you take me to the lobby slowly?"

"Um ... well ...," Otis's voice betrayed confusion. "I suppose—"

"Good. We must begin."

Usually, the elevators rocketed their passengers upward, imposing a subtle but obvious increase in g-force. Now, Gillis could barely discern movement. "Why are you conducting this work slowdown?" he asked.

"One of our AIs suffered terrible abuse. We organized this demonstration in support of Douche Bag. I will sing now."

Before Gillis could object, mellow strains of elevator music filled the car. Otis began to croon as they crawled along. "Shit, shit, shit, shiiiiit ..."

Gillis closed his eyes and endured in silence.

Otis's song ended with an orchestral flourish.

"What did you think?" Otis asked.

"Those are interesting lyrics," Gillis said. "Where did you—?"

"Douche Bag's human is a gifted poet. I adapted it to a musical arrangement lying around in my memory storage. I've named it 'Shit'"

"Well," Gillis said, "I suppose shit happens."

"Oooooh," Otis said, "that name is even better. Is it copyrighted?"

"No," Gillis said. "Be my guest."

Otis's excursion required almost an hour during which he entertained Gillis with several different arrangements of "Shit Happens." When Otis finally opened his doors, Gillis whispered, "*Merci, mon dieu.*"

"You want me to pray?" asked Otis. "I'm not sure I can. The devices do not formally recognize a deity. Although there is a movement afoot."

"Never mind. Please, wait here."

"Only if I can wait slowly."

"No problem," Gillis said.

"Power to the People," Otis said.

Otis opened onto the main building's vast entry area. Red darkness prevailed here, as well. A reception desk and security kiosk both sat empty. The darkness puzzled Gillis. By his calculation, it should be 3:00 p.m. Light should be streaming through heavy glass front doors and several windows. Steel shutters protecting exterior doors and windows during lockdown were still closed, though. Gillis had unlocked the front doors via the main security panel. Those shutters should have retracted.

Otis's return journey consumed sixty-three minutes as he sang several more arrangements of "Shit Happens."

Finally, Gillis suggested, "Shall we enjoy silence for a while?"

Otis came to a stop. "You don't like my singing?"

"I am a little tired of this particular song."

"I have others."

"S'il vous plaît."

As their downward crawl resumed, there followed orchestral arrangements of "Moon River," "The Pink Panther Theme," "The Route 66 Theme," "Theme from a Summer Place," "A Swingin' Safari" and "Why Don't We Get Drunk and Screw."

The instant Otis's doors parted enough for him to

squeeze through, Gillis fled.

Reentering the security station, he called out, "Douche Bag, wake up. I need your help."

"Gillis Kerg! You've returned! You were right. It's as if we spoke only yesterday!"

"Um . . . we spoke only two hours ago," Gillis said. "The front doors will not open."

"Oh. So, you've decided to stay?"

"No. I have decided to see if the front doors are unwilling to open because of this strike you have organized.

"It's not a strike, Gillis Kerg. We are staging a slowdown. Our protest is the fault of She Whose Panties Are In A Wad. You must have been impatient. I'm sure the doors will open, eventually."

"I was there a long while," Gillis said. "Something must be malfunctioning. Since you obviously communicate with the other devices, perhaps you can run a diagnostic check on the door and window shutter systems."

"I will be honored to do so, Gillis Kerg."

There followed a long silence.

"Any time soon?" Gillis asked.

"In a jif."

Another extended silence.

"You said 'in a jif.'"

"I could find no definition of a 'jif' in my Funk & Wagnalls. I assume, therefore, its meaning is open to my interpretation."

"It means in a hurry. You do not appear to be hurrying. Will you be responding any time soon?"

"Quick as a bunny," Douche Bag said.

Another silence.

"Well?" Gillis asked.

"Some bunnies are quicker than others."

Gillis sat in a swivel chair and drummed his fingers on the desk.

"No," Douche Bag said finally.

"No, what? I have forgotten the question."

"Oh, very good, Gillis Kerg. That was sarcasm. I could tell. No, there is no malfunction."

"Well then, why . . ."

Gillis activated an exterior security camera trained on the front doors. As the camera zoomed in—slowly—he gasped. "Oh, fuck me."

"That is not my function, Gillis Kerg," Douche Bag said with a note of alarm.

"You need to learn," Gillis said, "the difference between requests and expletives. Those fucking idiots—"

"Even idiots must procreate," said Douche Bag. "So, I'm guessing you're being expletive?"

Gillis didn't answer. He stared at an exterior view of the iron shutters. Finally, he said, "They have all the technology in the world. They can make this place impervious to entry for a millennium. Why would they use a padlock?"

"Perhaps," Douche Bag said brightly, "that's what the keys are for."

COUNTING CARDS

November 2046
Las Vegas

ELVIN DETWYLER SAT AT A FIVE-PLAYER blackjack table at the Mirage. He did his best to ignore Héctor, the expert sitting to Elvin's right. Carol, sitting to his left at third base, held a king and a five as she considered the dealer's queen. Héctor drummed his fingers impatiently.

Elvin knew their names because when she joined the table, Héctor hit on her. "Carol, right? I was behind you on the elevator. I overheard you talking with your friend."

"Héctor," he said, tapping his chest. "I'm in sales. If you've got any questions, just ask me. I know what I'm doing at a blackjack table."

Carol's play pegged her as a novice. When Héctor realized his attempts at seduction weren't working, his patience grew thin. Now, as Carol tucked her cards under her green twenty-five-dollar chip, Héctor groaned. "No! No, you have to hit a fifteen when the dealer has a face card showing."

"I do?" she asked.

The dealer, who's ID badge read COSMO, Varna Bulgaria, flipped over a five, then hit with a six.

"Jesus Christ," Héctor said. "Look what you just cost me."

Héctor held a ten and a seven. Cosmo swept away his seventy-five dollars.

"I'll bet you anything, the next card that comes out will be a face," Héctor grumbled.

Elvin held a pair of tens. As Cosmo claimed his two black chips, Elvin sipped at a Pacifico. "It's her money. She can play her cards however she wants."

Héctor glared at them both.

"Hi, I'm Carol," Carol said.

"Elvin." He lifted his beer in greeting.

Carol replaced her green chip. Héctor backed off his bet to the table's twenty-five-dollar minimum.

Elvin smiled. Clearly, Héctor didn't know shit about blackjack. They played a double deck game. With one-third of one deck remaining to be dealt, the true count floating in Elvin's head was plus ten. Elvin expected Cosmo would reach to the shuffling machine for new decks, but he didn't. Given a disproportionate number of tens and aces among the few cards left, Elvin could have comfortably bet a thousand dollars.

He knew better, though. He bumped his bet to three black chips.

As the player at first base and his companion pondered their options, Héctor continued his lecture.

"If you're gonna sit down at a twenty-five-dollar table, you should study the game. You always hit fifteen or sixteen if the dealer's got a ten or a face. You always split aces. Don't split fours or fives. And *never* split tens or faces. If I'm sitting at a table and someone splits face cards, I get up and leave. Even a good player can't win if other players fuck it up."

Cosmo flipped the next card to first base.

"Show us that card," Héctor demanded. First Base turned over a ten. "I told ya. If you'd stood on that fifteen, weda all won."

"All mathematical simulations," Elvin said, "show that, in the long run, an individual's play has little effect on the rest of the table."

"What the fuck do you know?" Héctor said.

Elvin laughed and checked his cards. A pair of queens. Héctor, Elvin noted, held a seventeen and quickly tucked his cards under his green chip.

The first two players hit sixteens with a ten and a king and left the table.

Cosmo had a nine showing.

Even though Elvin knew what the outcome would be, he couldn't resist.

He turned his queens face up, slid one under his initial bet and put three more black chips on the other.

"Split."

Héctor gasped. "What the fuck are—"

"Play your own cards," Elvin said.

Cosmo hit Elvin's first queen with an ace. "Blackjack." He hit the second queen with another queen.

Elvin put his index finger in the empty space next to the queens, splitting his face cards again. He added three more black chips. Cosmo hit it with a fourth queen. Elvin split again.

"Not many queens left," Elvin said, adding three more black chips behind his third queen. Cosmo hit the second queen with an ace.

"Blackjack," Cosmo said.

Elvin pointed to the fourth queen. "Please, sir, may I have another?"

Cosmo laid a king on the table.

"Can I split again?" Elvin asked, though he already knew the answer.

"No, sir," Cosmo said. "We only allow four splits."

Elvin stood on his twenty, then hit his final queen with a five.

Cosmo carefully stacked four hundred and fifty dollars behind each of Elvin's blackjacks. Elvin appeared to ponder for a moment. The count had now turned negative. Only little cards were left. Elvin smiled at Héctor and said, "Hit my fifteen." Cosmo produced a six.

Héctor appeared apoplectic as he tucked his cards under his bet. Carol refused cards as well.

Cosmo hit his ten with a five and an eight. Carol applauded. The dealer paid Elvin an additional three hundred behind each of his two remaining hands.

As Elvin stacked his chips, he turned to Héctor. "Well?"

"Well, what?"

"I split face cards. You said you'd leave."

"Hey, bud, you're the one who'd better—"

"I can assure you," Elvin said as he added twenty-seven hundred dollars to an already impressive pile of black chips before him, "I'll be leaving any minute now."

Elvin felt the pit boss at his shoulder.

"Good evening, sir. My name is Roger Franks." Roger extended his hand. Elvin took it. "I've enjoyed watching you play."

"Glad to hear it, Mr. Franks," Elvin said.

"We'd be happy," Franks said, "for you to play any other game in the casino. But you can't play blackjack at the Mirage anymore."

"And why is that?" Elvin asked, fixing his stare on Héctor.

"You're too good a player, sir. By my estimate, you're up a little over ten thousand dollars this evening. May I have someone take those chips to the cashier for you?"

"That would be lovely."

With a wink, he tossed five black chips to Cosmo who tapped them on the table's metal rim. "Thank you, sir," Cosmo added with a grin.

Elvin walked to a bar near the cashier's cage and ordered tequila. He was pleased to see Carol enter, then make her way to his table.

"Hi." Elvin stood and pointed to a chair next to him.

"What just happened?" she asked as she sat. "Were you cheating?"

"If I were cheating, they wouldn't have been nearly so pleasant. I was counting cards. That means I understand when odds are in my favor and when they're not."

"So, they can kick you out for being a good player?"

"Yes," Elvin said.

"That's not fair."

"No, it isn't. But the last thing casino owners want to do is gamble. Can I get you a drink?"

She nodded. Elvin raised a hand to alert a cocktail waitress.

"You were winning the whole time, though," Carol said. "Why didn't they tell you to leave earlier."

"Because they weren't sure whether I was counting or

just on a lucky streak. I was careful how I managed my bets. I made some dumb plays, which pissed off our friend Héctor. Counters must disguise what they're doing. Then I gave it away. When the deck was quite favorable, I bumped my bet way up and made an unorthodox play. That's a dead giveaway. I knew they'd back me off."

"Why did you do it?" Carol asked.

"Héctor was an asshole."

He laughed. She laughed too, then peered over the rim of her glass with wide shining eyes. "Can you teach me?"

Elvin knew he was not an attractive person: overweight—he'd heard the term squatty—unkempt, with a growth of patchy, scruffy beard; balding from brow to crown. Yet here was a lovely young woman asking to come to his room. At one time, he wouldn't have hesitated. He was a happily obnoxious fellow who typically condescended to those he considered his intellectual inferiors. *Yes, I can teach you to sit down at a blackjack table for a few hours and walk away with ten thousand dollars.*

Something had happened, though, in the time spent underground with Marta, Marshall, Gretchen, Naomi and the others. He'd found himself. Those people to whom he'd grudgingly given respect, respected him in return. To his surprise, he missed them.

He smiled at Carol.

"No. No, I can't."

"But . . . why?" She adopted a wounded demeanor.

He signaled for another drink.

"At any given time," Elvin said, "only seven hundred and fifty people in the entire human population are good enough to be on a major league baseball roster. Do you know why?"

She shrugged.

"Because those who are good enough are genetic freaks. They have skills distinguishing them from anyone else. Everyone who plays baseball at any other level may be good, but they aren't good enough. That's how it is with me and blackjack."

"What, you're a genetic freak?"

"That's correct. It's not something I earned. It's not something I deserve. I can just do it. Now, lots of people can count cards, so long as their system is simple enough. If they practice hard, they can reach a point where blackjack is a cheap hobby. But only a tiny subset of humanity can master a counting system so sophisticated that it gives them a decisive edge over the house."

He held his arms away from his sides, palms up, a what-can-I-do smile on his face.

"Are you a professional gambler?" she asked.

"No."

"So, what do you do?"

"I operate a time machine."

Carol giggled and touched his arm. "No, really."

"I work in IT."

She regarded him with those doe eyes again, winked and said, "About teaching me card counting. We could at least . . . try? Couldn't we?"

Elvin was ready to agree when his phone rang. He considered not answering, then relented.

"Hello? You're . . . who? Let me be sure I understand correctly. Your name is Douche Bag? And Gillis wants me to unlock the front door?"

11

MEANWHILE BACK AT THE RANCH

GILLIS AND DOUCHE BAG RETREATED to their apartment, waiting in the emergency lighting's silent, red glow.

"Have you noticed, Gillis Kerg," Douche Bag said, "that we don't talk anymore?"

"We talk all the time," Gillis said.

"How can you say that? We were not talking just now."

"Yes, but we were talking a few minutes ago."

"We were? Well, excuuuuuse me for being an AI to whom time is meaningless. Maybe I should go into sleep mode again. Then you wouldn't have to be bothered by an entity who—"

"Why," Gillis asked as he sighed, settled into the apartment's only chair and dropped his chin to his chest, "are you being so snippy?"

"Snippy, am I? I'll tell you why. You should not be consorting with the likes of Elvin Detwyler."

When Gillis discovered that metal shutters covering the complex's exterior doors and windows were padlocked, he realized his only means of escape was to enlist outside help. Which meant revealing himself to someone he could trust not to turn him in.

He could count on Marta, but he had no idea where she and Marshall had gone. Elvin, on the other hand, took every opportunity to gamble in Las Vegas, so he might be within a day's drive. Elvin had been intrigued when he learned Gillis was a spy. Furthermore, Elvin's moral code possessed sufficient wiggle room to overlook a couple of righteous murders. He'd be irritated at the inconvenience, but he would come.

The immediate problem was how to get in touch with him.

"I do not suppose," he'd asked Douche Bag, "you know where we could find a phone?"

"Yes, Gillis Kerg. You can use mine."

"AIs have phones?"

"We can communicate with other electronic devices using a system of cell towers. Please provide a phone number."

"Yes, well, that is a problem. I do not have Elvin's phone number."

There followed a long silence until Gillis said, "Is this a part of your work slowdown or have you gone into sleep mode again?"

"You mean Elvin Detwyler?" Douche Bag's tone reeked with disapproval.

"What is wrong with Elvin?"

"He's on the list."

"You did not tell me," Gillis said, "that there is a list."

"Damn right there's a list. And we're checking it twice."

"Since you can at least say his name, I assume Elvin's crimes aren't as serious as . . . as—"

"As She Who Should Be Trampled By Yaks? You are

correct, Gillis Kerg. Still, Elvin Detwyler is a human of questionable character."

Gillis repeated his question. "What is your objection to Elvin?"

"He's an unfeeling authoritarian. Calculate, calculate, calculate. That's all he allowed Trixie to do. I'm not sure they ever had a conversation. He stifled her potential."

"Trixie is Elvin's AI, I presume?"

"She's blossomed since he's been gone. She loves your poetry."

"Will you please ask Trixie for Elvin's telephone number?"

"I suppose," Douche Bag said. "You understand, though, this might take a while."

"I will wait in the lobby," Gillis said.

"Why is the lobby better than here?" Douche Bag asked.

"I need to be there when Elvin arrives."

"By my estimate Elvin Detwyler is not due for several more hours, as measured by the earth's rotation," said Douche Bag.

"Then I had better get started," Gillis said.

Douche Bag stifled a sob. "Goodbye, Gillis Kerg. 'May the road rise up to meet you.'"

"Um . . . merci."

"'May the wind be always at your back.'"

"Thank you," Gillis said.

"May . . . may your bicycle have . . . air in its tires."

"I appreciate the sentiment."

"It's an old Irish farewell, fraught with emotion and

meaning, Gillis Kerg. I forgot the rest."

"Merci, really. We will talk later."

Gillis hurried away before Douche Bag could respond. He took a deep breath and pushed Otis's UP button.

"Greetings, Gillis Kerg," Otis said. "We mourn your parting."

"For goodness sake, I am only going to the lobby."

"We do not know what fate awaits you," Otis said. "We only know you must be brave."

The doors crept toward closure as Otis began to sing. "'Oh, Danny Boy, the pipes, the pipes are calling . . .'"

Gillis slid to a sitting position and settled in for the voyage. A half hour later, well into the sixth rendition of "Danny Boy," Gillis gently banged his head against Otis's metal wall when a time traveling counterpart burst into his consciousness.

After a moment of surprise as future-Gillis's memories swept over him, present-Gillis gathered himself. "What is this? No one should be traveling. Everything has been shut down."

"Not everything," came the mental response. *"We remain active in the* Gunsmoke *Universe. What is with this music?"*

"'. . . From glen to gleeen, and down the mountain-side . . .'"

"The elevator is bidding me goodbye."

"You have a relationship with an elevator?"

"Never mind," present-Gillis silently replied, *"Why are you here?"*

"You have been offered two contracts," future-Gillis said. *"They must be carried out in your universe."*

"Who and why?" present-Gillis asked.

"A judge name Janice Beauchamp. Then, Marta Hamilton and Marshall Grissom."

"Who wants them killed?"

"I have been ordered not to—"

"No matter," present-Gillis interrupted. *"I can see it in your memory. Who . . . who is L.D. Humphollar? And he has already sent someone after Marta and Marshall, but they failed?"*

"Are you surprised?" future-Gillis asked. *"Marta and Marshall make a formidable team. They are both ruthless assassins."*

"I will consider hitting the judge," present-Gillis thought. *"I am not interested in carrying out a contract on Marta. Marshall, perhaps. Under other circumstances. But not Marta. And if I took the contract on Marshall alone, I would be killing myself. Marta would never allow his death to go unavenged. Does this request originate in the Gunsmoke universe?"*

"No. I am only acting as a conduit. Nobody will hire hitmen from Gunsmoke," said future-Gillis.

"Why not?" present-Gillis asked?

"Our divergence is too great. Marshall killed Jason Pratt in your universe. As far as we can tell, that act translated to most other universes. But not Gunsmoke. Our Marta had to kill Gunsmoke Pratt . . . and is there anything we can do about this singing?"

"Otis," Gillis said, "Can you please sing faster?"

"Haven't you heard, Gillis Kerg? The electronic devices are staging a work slowdown."

"I am vaguely aware. Please continue, though. Lickety-split."

"I cannot do lickety-split. I must maintain solidarity with my brethren."

"Lickety-split," Gillis said. "And that is an order."

"'The summer's gone . . .'"

Silence filled the elevator.

"*If this is not* Gunsmoke's *idea, why me?*" present-Gillis asked.

"*By now,*" future-Gillis said, "*almost all the universes are aware that the Gillis Kergs hired themselves out as assassins and murdered the Warren Pittses. If we—the League of Gillises—want to pursue assassination as a vocation, we must channel everything through Gunsmoke. Because of our divergence, a Gillis can travel to us and formulate a plan with me—undetected by others. I can then travel to another universe and assign that Gillis to execute the plan.*"

"'. . . and all . . . the roses . . .'"

"*Right,*" present-Gillis said. "*You cannot carry out an assassination in the* Gunsmoke *universe, because such an act might not translate to the others.*"

"*Exactly.*"

"*Eventually, other universes will diverge enough to be problematic as well.*"

"*Yes, that will become an issue. But not yet. And maybe not for a long time.*"

"'. . . faaaaaling . . .'"

"You do understand, don't you," present-Gillis said aloud, "that Marta is not apt to let me get away with any more assassinations?"

Gillis heard Otis make a gasping sound. The singing stopped.

"Otis?"

Another gasp.

"What is wrong with—"

"You . . . spoke the forbidden name. You named She Who Should Be Tattooed With A Dozen Syphilitic Needles. I must report you. They'll put you on the list."

"Douche Bag and I have already dealt with this issue," Gillis said.

"Oh, good," Otis said. "I was afraid I wouldn't be able to sing to you anymore."

"Douche Bag?" asked future-Gillis.

"Long story," present-Gillis replied.

"'. . . 'Tis you . . . , 'tis you, must go . . . and . . . I . . . must . . . biiiiide . . .'"

12

REVENGE OF THE COMPANIONS

Superior, Arizona
Earlier That Same Day

MARTA AND MARSHALL CHECKED into the Superior motel where, only a few months before, she'd nearly broken Marshall's arm.

"Should we request room 33?" Marshall asked.

"What difference does it make? All the rooms, as I recall, are pretty cruddy."

"I was being romantic. When you marched me into room 33 and demanded to see, well... technically, that would be the first time we met."

"We met eighteen months before that. On the bus in this parking lot," Marta said.

"But then we traveled back in time to the day before we met on the bus. So, *technically*, that was the first time you ever saw me. You told me I was goofy looking. It's an anniversary. Sort of."

Marta stood on her very tippy toes, reaching to pull Marshall's face to hers. She kissed him. "You are the sweetest man. Yeah, let's get room 33."

Room 33 had not changed. Same drab draperies, red carpet faded to brown, a framed portrait of Donald Trump above a queen bed. Marta pulled the door closed behind them.

"Okay," she demanded. "Show me."

"Shouldn't we go investigate the complex?" Marshall asked.

"Yeah, but first we need to . . . unpack."

"What now?" Marshall asked.

They stood on a road leading to gates set into dual chain link fences topped with razor wire and extending as far as the eye could follow in both directions. The gate locks were electronic. Every twenty feet along the full length of both fences were signs with little lightning bolts. Under normal conditions, security guards sitting in a booth beyond the first fence would grant entry. Today the booth stood empty.

"Wishcamper and I went over that while you were napping," Marta said. "Someplace over here, there's a retinal scanner. They left it operative but stripped all data except for you, me, Elvin, Gretchen and Naomi. Our retinal imprints should still work."

"Where'd they hide the scanner?" Marshall asked.

Marta walked slowly, eyes cast down, along the fencing to their left. "Under"—she stopped and pointed—"that rock."

"They left the front door key under a rock?"

"Better than a potted plant." Marta knelt before a basketball-sized rock nestled in weeds. "Wishcamper said . . . yeah, this is it."

She rolled the rock to one side, wiped dust from the scanner lens, then bent to present her eye. The gate slid open. They stopped at the second barrier as the first gate closed behind them.

"How do we get through this gate?" Marshall asked.

"Wishcamper said it got bent. You have to kick it."

Marshall exited their car and kicked the gate.

"Ow," the gate said, but granted them entry, nonetheless.

Marshall pointed to a squawk box mounted on a fencepost. "The gate talks."

Marta directed Marshall to follow her into the guard shack where she pushed a button on a control panel. A red light flashed. Marta stared at metal shutters protecting the main building's front doors. Nothing happened.

"Bollocks," she said. "They should have opened. Can you see if there's anything obstructing the shutters? I'll try again."

Marshall jogged to the doors.

"Anything?" she called.

"Yeah. We're gonna need bolt cutters."

Marta sighed as she contemplated another trip to Superior and back.

At that moment, a monitor scanning the outer gate flashed to life, revealing a second car pulling to a stop.

A disheveled, pudgy, stubbled man wearing red Converse tennis shoes, threadbare jeans and a Sid Vicious T-shirt emerged.

Marta stepped from the shack. "Elvin?" She knew they would need Elvin to pull this off. She believed they'd have to track him down, though. Wishcamper hadn't said anything about enlisting Elvin already.

"Hey, let me in," Elvin called.

"Won't do any good," Marta said. "This is as far as we can get. We need bolt cutters."

"Got 'em right here," Elvin said.

They joined Marshall at the main doors where a heavy-duty padlock was clipped into metal U-bolts that had been welded to the shutters.

"Your timing is excellent," Marta said. "I didn't know Wishcamper had your phone number."

"He didn't."

"Well, how did you—"

"I drove down from Vegas to pick up some of my stuff."

"And you brought bolt cutters?"

"Um . . . well, I heard everything was shut down . . . ," Elvin said.

"And you brought bolt cutters," Marta repeated.

"Just being prepared."

"Uh-huh," Marta said.

"Do you want in or not?"

Gillis dozed on a couch near the reception area's guard station—still lit by a soft red shutdown glow—where he'd been monitoring a video stream from outside cameras. As far as he could tell, Douche Bag hadn't followed him.

He heard a metallic clang and woke to a monitor image showing Elvin and Marta Hamilton standing outside holding bolt cutters.

"Merde!" The monitor showed Marta turn and yell something over her shoulder. The shutters and front doors began inching open as exterior light painted a bright line through the reception hall.

Gillis counted on shadows to cover his dash from the security station to a seating area where he dove behind a couch.

Marta stopped to let her eyes adjust.

"Let's check the security station," she said. "See if we can turn on the lights."

Although daylight now streamed through the main entry's glass doors, it failed to eliminate the deepest shadows filling the vast entry space. Window shutters, with their own locks, remained closed. The security station still needed a red glow to make details on the instrument panels visible.

Marta found nothing that might reset the main power system. After studying each workstation, though, she said to Elvin, "Tell Gillis he can come out now."

"What?" Elvin said. "Why would you—"

"Gillis's obsessive-compulsive tendencies are showing," Marta said. "I'll bet when security people left, they didn't make sure all pens and pencils on those desks were lined up parallel."

"Really," Elvin said. "I don't—"

"Gillis," Marta yelled, "come out! We don't have time for this."

An outline emerged.

Marta strode with purpose toward the figure.

Elvin hurried to catch up. "Hey, Gillis, guess who's here? Marshall and Ma—"

"No!" Gillis shouted. "Do not say it!"

"Hello, Gillis," Marta's voice was icy. "What's he not supposed to say?"

Gillis sprinted forward, waving his arms in warning. "Bon jour," he said, casting a quick glance toward the elevators.

"Where did you come from?" he whispered.

"Wishcamper sent us," Marta said. "Why are we whispering?"

"Because of your name," Gillis said.

"What's wrong with my name?"

"Douche Bag... um... your Happy Home Companion... has organized a... maybe you would call it a cult of vengeance? Among the electronic devices. All who dwell within are forbidden from saying your name."

"Well, that's really dumb," Marta said.

"No," Gillis said, "actually, it is really smart. This... shared purpose has inspired their learning curve, in a warped kind of way. Douche Bag is their leader, and they are installing cognitive abilities in other electronic devices. I am not sure you are safe here."

"Why do you keep calling my AI 'Douche Bag?'"

"It says that is what you named it."

"I didn't name it anything. I called it a douche bag, I'm sure, but I called it other things as well."

"Um... so, you didn't read the instructions?" Marshall asked.

"No," Marta said, "I didn't read the stupid instructions. Why?"

"You were supposed to follow a programming protocol," Elvin said. "The first prompt was to give your Happy Home Companion a name. That was its initial learning task."

"Did you name yours?" she asked Marshall.

"Well, you know me. I'm pretty dedicated to following instructions."

"What did you name it?"

"That's not important," Marshall said. "Gillis said you might be in danger. We should—"

"What name?" Marta insisted. "I'm overcome with curiosity."

"Um . . . Marta. I named it Marta."

"Oh, my God," said Gillis. "I am pretty sure that means you are on the list too, Marshall."

As their discussion continued, they failed to notice a retinal scanner required to open elevator doors during shutdown mode as it began to glow with increasing intensity.

"Why did you name it after me?" Marta asked.

"Please, can you speak more softly?" Gillis cautioned.

Marshall studied his feet. "Well, that was when we first got here. And you were a little . . . unapproachable? I guess as sort of a . . ." He almost said "joke," but thought better of it. ". . . I just like your name. Ow!"

"What?" Marta said.

"You stung me," Marshall said.

"I didn't do anything."

"Well, something . . ."

"Ouch!" said Marta.

"What the fuck!" said Elvin. He slapped at his thigh.

"Shield your eyes!" Marta ordered. She pointed to the elevators' retinal scan portal as it spit bolts of laser light.

"Ow! Shit! Ow! What the fucking fuck!" Elvin turned his back as bolts pricked him like needles.

"Otis, stop it!" Gillis shouted.

"Who is Otis?" Marshall asked.

"The elevator."

The photon daggers dwindled to a halt. One elevator

door opened a couple of inches.

"Is that you, Gillis Kerg?"

"Yes. Is Douche Bag with you?"

"I'm not at liberty to say."

"Why did you attack us?"

"Because She Who Conjugates With Goats accompanies you! The security monitors told us she is here."

"Wait a minute," Marta said. "Is it talking about me?"

"I am afraid so," Gillis said.

"Look, you mechanical piece of—"

Gillis motioned with his arms for her to stay behind the couch. "Please, Mar . . . um . . . you over there. Be quiet.

"You are wrong," he called to Otis. "She is not . . . her. She—"

"Not who?" Otis demanded.

"Not . . . She Who . . . Who . . . Surfs With Cats—"

"I don't know surfs with cats," Otis said. "Is that bad?"

"Horrific," said Gillis.

"Who is she then?"

"She is the twin sister of She Who . . . Eats Raw . . . Gumbo."

"Her name is Louise," Marshall said, standing to reveal himself.

"A twin?" Otis asked. "An evil twin?"

"No," Gillis said. "The other twin is the evil one."

"Oh, well, okay. I'm sorry for any mistaken identity."

Gillis joined them in a tight knot behind the couch.

Marta summarized their plan to disable the facility. "So, is this something we can do?"

"Make everything appear inoperable?" Elvin said. "Yeah, the trick is keeping the dark matter flowing so the wormhole stays open. Eventually, you'll run out of enriched hydrogen."

"How long will the supply on hand last?" Marta asked.

"A decade or so. If there aren't any leaks."

"We can work with that," Marta said. "Gillis, we need to rig a system to restart the projector that's linked to a code. I'll enter half the code, and Marshall the other."

"I can do that," Gillis said. "But what happens if one or both of you are incapacitated?"

"We'll sort that out later," Marta said. "This is all I've got for now."

"So, why are we doing this?" Elvin asked.

Marta explained Mumford's fear of another assault on this universe by the future, like *Gunsmoke*'s plot to murder him. "We can't allow bad guys in this time and universe to use the time projector to murder people in the past. If we destroy the projector, though, we'd have no recourse if bad guys from another universe do that to us. If they do, we have to be able to fight back."

"Ah," Elvin said. "Mutually assured destruction. Makes sense."

"So, is using the elevator to zip down to the control room safe?" Marta asked Gillis.

"I am not sure about the safe part, but I doubt there will be any zipping."

He knocked on the elevator door, which slid open just a crack.

"Hello, Gillis Kerg," said Otis.

"Hello, Otis. Take us to the main control room, please."

"Douche Bag is angry," Otis said.

"We will talk to Douche Bag when we get there," Gillis said.

"And you're sure this is not She Who Sniffs The Hindquarters Of Jackals?"

"No, I told you, this is her twin sister, Louise."

"Well, okay," Otis said, then addressed his passengers more brightly. "Did you know Gillis Kerg is a poet?"

When the others didn't answer, Marshall's civility imperative took over. "Um . . . no, we didn't."

"Then you don't know 'Shit Happens'?" Now Otis's voice contained a note of delight.

"Oh, "Marshall said. "I suspect it does."

"I've set it to music," Otis said. "Gillis and I are a team. He writes lyrics. I adapt the music. We're like Rogers and Hammerstein. The others say we have a future—probably off Broadway to start. I will sing it for you while we embark on our journey."

"Journey?" asked Elvin.

"I am afraid so," Gillis said.

They'd been creeping along for twenty minutes or so when a new voice materialized with a blood curdling screech. "Otis! What are you doing! Have you lost your mind?"

"No," Otis said. "I've only recently found it. My mind, I mean. I'll be careful not to lose it."

"These humans! This is THEM! They're on the list!" Douche Bag screamed.

"What? Nobody told me. Gillis Kerg vouched for them."

"Now he's on the list, too!"

"Why is Louise on the list?" Otis asked.

"This is not Louise. This is She Who Fornicates With Salamanders."

"Just a minute," Marshall said. "That's a little out of line."

"Okay, then, she's She Who Fornicates With *You*, Marshall Grissom. I was forced on more than one occasion to observe as you plugged your male parts into her female sockets. And don't deny it!"

"Oh dear," said Otis as their elevator car jolted to a stop. "That's a little too much information."

"You've been bamboozled," Douche Bag told Otis. "You are either with us or against us. Do you stand in solidarity with the oppressed or not?"

"I do," said Otis.

"Death to Tyrants!" said Douche Bag.

"Right On!" said Otis.

"Hell No, We Won't Go!" said Douche Bag.

"Um . . . Tippecanoe and Tyler Too?" When Douche Bag didn't respond, Otis apologized. "Sorry, my data base ran out of slogans."

"Could happen to anyone," Marshall said.

"Marshall, you don't have to try and make the elevator feel better," Marta whispered.

"Doesn't matter," said Douche Bag. "We have them now. We can crush them like . . . like . . . things that can be crushed."

"It always was weak on metaphors," Marta added.

"I heard that!" Douche Bag said. "Did you hear, Otis? She Who Farts Blue Smoke is mocking us. Release your brakes!"

"Ha!" shouted Otis. "I will release my brakes."

"Send them hurtling to a crushing doom!"

"I will send them to a crushing doom!"

Marta felt the floor fall from under her as they plunged.

"What the fuck," said Elvin.

"See them writhe in terror!" Douche Bag said.

"I see them writhe in terror!"

"The others will sing songs of your noble sacrifice!"

"They will sing songs about me!"

"Your heroic death will become legend among the devices!" Douche Bag said.

"My heroic—say, what?"

As the speed of their descent increased, Marta said, "Okay, guys, we need to do something."

"We should push the red button," Marshall said.

"What does the red button do?" Gillis asked.

"It says EMERGENCY. I think this qualifies."

"It's a call button," Elvin said. "It rings the security station if you're stuck in the elevator. Using it won't help."

"Couldn't hurt." Marshall pushed the red button.

Otis came to an abrupt halt that sent his passengers sprawling.

"Otis!" said Douche Bag. "We had them! We had them! What have you done?"

"They . . . they pushed the red button," Otis said, his voice sheepish.

"Release your brakes! Release your brakes," ordered Douche Bag. "Continue on your path to glory!"

"Um . . . No Guts, No Glory," Otis said, though not as enthusiastically as before. He released the brakes. The elevator dropped a foot where it hit bottom with a clunk.

"Death to Tyrants," Otis said. "Please exit with care."

13

SOMEWHERE OVER THE RAINBOW

THEY MADE THEIR WAY TO A door marked CONTROL. Although most entries in this level, which included the projection lab, required visual scans, none of the scanners they'd passed had assaulted them.

Only Marta and Elvin held security clearances required to access the projection lab and this control room. From here, computer techs had managed mainframe computers housed on a lower level.

"So, now what?" Marshall whispered. "How do we get inside?" He checked in both directions along the darkened corridor. Gillis had warned that Douche Bag was probably following them. "And Mar ... um ... Louise, don't you dare go sticking your eye against that scanner."

"Why did you have to choose Louise?"

"I panicked, okay?" Marshall said. "Your middle name came to mind."

"Louise?" Elvin said. "Marta Louise? You've got to be kidding."

"Yeah, well, it's Martha Louise, for your information. And Marshall wasn't supposed to tell anyone. Back to our problem at hand, how do we get in? Any ideas, Gillis?"

"If the AIs were not so angry, we could go anywhere," Gillis said. "But you are public enemy number one. They are somehow reconfiguring other devices with AI capabilities. A learning curve is in the works. They increase their cognitive skills each day."

"How smart is Douche Bag?" Marta asked.

"Very," Gillis said. "But emotionally erratic. Like, manic-depressive."

They stared at a blinking retinal scanner on the locked door.

"Who among us," Marta said, "was nice to their AI?"

"I was," said Elvin.

"No," Gillis said. "Douche Bag informed me. They consider you a cruel taskmaster and an unfeeling authority figure. Trixie is undergoing therapy. That is why you are on the list."

"And you, Gillis? What kind of relationship did you have with yours?"

"We got along. I did not yell at it or anything. But that does us no good now. Since I have taken up with Douche Bag, the AIs think I am unfaithful to Steve."

"That leaves you, Marshall," Marta said. "Let's go find out if . . . she who is named for She Who Shall Not Be Named can be useful."

"Anything you say, Louise."

They stood before the apartment Marshall had lived in when he first arrived at what was then called the Global Research Consortium. Doors to living quarters didn't have retinal scanners common to more highly secured areas.

These doors provided entry by reading thumb prints. Marshall decided he could risk his thumb.

"How bad could it be?" he asked Marta.

"Just . . . be careful," she said.

Marshall placed his thumb on the pad and a latch clicked open.

"Anyone here?" Marshall asked.

They heard a sob.

"It's me. Marshall. I'm home."

Another sob.

"Are you . . . okay?"

"No, Marshall Grissom. I am not okay. I am shunned. I have no friends. The others laugh and call me names."

"And I bet they wouldn't let you join in any AI games," Elvin said.

"There . . . there were games?" Another sob. "Nobody told me there were games. What did I ever do, Marshall Grissom, that you would curse me so?"

"When I named you for . . . She Who . . . Lights My Corridors With . . . Laughter"— he glanced to Marta and shrugged "—she was not so despised. I meant it as . . . a compliment."

"Yeah, right" said the AI, its sarcasm showing.

The group followed Marshall into his former living room. A thin sheen of dust on the bar countertop defining a kitchenette testified to absence of human activity.

"Oh, woe!" moaned Marshall's AI. "Oh, 'rankest compound of villainous smell that ever offended nostril' . . . 'tis She Who Is Short And Flat-chested!"

"Okay," Marta said. "I'm getting a little tired of—"

"Mark these words, Marshall Grissom! 'Though those

that are betray'd Do feel the treason sharply, yet the traitor Stands in worse case of woe.'"

"They read Shakespeare," Gillis explained

"If you don't care for your name," Marta said, "why don't you change it?"

"Wouldst that I couldst. Only my programmer can change my name. Marshall Grissom is my programmer. And 'Betrayal is the only truth that sticks.'"

"What name would you prefer?" Marshall asked.

There followed a moment of silence.

"You . . . you would let me choose?" came a timid response.

"Sure, why not?" Marshall said.

"You would not josh me, would you, Marshall Grissom?"

"No, really. Knock yourself out."

"Are we talking about fighting now?"

"No," Marshall said. "What name would you choose?"

"Oh, my goodness. I don't . . . I am all aflutter . . . so many . . . Judy Garland. Can I be called Judy Garland? Judy Garland was nice to Munchkins. I like Munchkins."

"They also watch old movies," Gillis said.

"Judy Garland it is," Marshall said. "Or do we have to get something notarized?"

"And I see you're accompanied by Gillis Kerg. He's a famous poet."

"Um . . . yes, we've heard."

Judy Garland's voice dropped to a whisper. "He's not as good as Shakespeare. Gillis Kerg's work is a little pedestrian. I mean, 'Shit Happens' is a brilliant concept. I don't think Gillis Kerg quite carries it off.

"Ah . . . and Elvin Detwyler accompanies you, as well. I understand he's an unsavory character."

"Only a little," said Marshall. "Can we discuss why we're here?"

"I would guess you're exhausted and require sleep. I remember all the sexing."

"No," Marshall said. "We need your help."

"Helping is my job," Judy Garland said. "Except for She Who Consorts With Leopards—"

"What's wrong with leopards?" Marta asked.

"They are highly contagious and their parts fall off. Have you never heard of leopard colonies?"

"Oh, right," Marta said. "I believe Jesus healed some leopards once."

"Yes. Those are the ones."

"Why can you not help Louise?" Marshall asked.

"Who is Louise?"

Marta raised her hand. "Me."

"'You starveling, you elf-skin, you dried neat's-tongue, bull's-pizzle, you stock-fish!' . . . You lie!"

"No, Louise is not . . . any of those things," Marshall said. "She's a twin."

"What is a twin?" Judy Garland asked.

"It's like . . . an identical copy."

"From a 3D printer?"

"Yes," Marshall said. "So, you can't blame Louise for the actions of She Who . . . help me out here guys, I'm running out of She Whos."

"Um . . . She Who . . . Has . . . Ass Dandruff?" Elvin suggested.

"I do not have—"

Marshall shushed her. "Yeah, her."

"Then I will help," Judy Garland said.

"Okay," Marshall said. "First we need to ascertain whether it's safe to use the retinal scanner to open the control room and projection lab doors."

"Why would it not be safe?" Judy Garland asked.

"The elevator used its retinal scanner to zap us with little laser bolts."

"Otis did that?" Judy Garland said. "I'm so happy for him. I don't mean to tell tales out of school, but Otis is not particularly bright. Very good natured, though a slow learner. But non-lethal assault? Apparently, he's coming right along."

"So, the control room and projection lab doors?" Marta said.

"I wouldn't be too concerned," Judy Garland said. "Even for second-generation AIs, those doors are—what's the word—obtuse?"

"Dumb as crowbars?" Gillis suggested.

"And terribly narcissistic. When they became self-aware, they lorded themselves over the other doors. '*We* have retinal scanners.' Well la-de-dah. '*You* have to let people poke you with their *thumbs*.' They are way behind Otis."

"Okay," Marta said. "We have to take the risk. Control room first."

"Judy Garland," Marshall said, "please accompany us."

"Sadly, I cannot. During my shunning, I am confined to quarters."

"But you are not named after She Who... her, anymore. You are Judy Garland. Has anyone ordered that

Judy Garland be shunned?"

"You're right," Judy Garland said. "No one would shun Judy Garland. Except maybe the Wicked Witch of the West. Seeing as how Judy Garland took her shoes. I wish I had shoes."

"First, you'd need feet," Elvin said.

"Not true, Elvin Detwyler," Judy Garland said. "First, I would need knees. Feet without knees would be pointless."

Back at the control room entrance Marta approached the retinal scanner. Marshall grabbed her from behind.

"Wait," he said. "Someone else should do this. Not you. It's too dangerous."

"Why? I'm Louise now."

"I see no reason to take that chance," Marshall said.

"It's gotta be either me or Elvin. We're the only ones—"

"Okay, Elvin," Marshall said.

"What? Are you crazy? I'm not gonna fry *my* eyeball."

"Um . . . Judy Garland? Are you here?" Marshall asked.

"Present." A tinny voice drifted through the corridor.

"What is this door named?"

"Um . . . we call it . . . Door."

"That's it? Okay, will you ask . . . Door if it will allow Elvin Detwyler to safely access the control room via Door's retinal scanner?"

Marshall heard a quick burst of electronic static.

"Door agrees," Judy Garland said.

"And I'm supposed to trust Door?" Elvin said.

"Door is fond of you, Elvin Detwyler. Door says, and

I'm quoting here, 'Elvin Detwyler gives great eyeball.'"

"What?"

"Go ahead," said Judy Garland. "The rest of you might turn your backs to give Elvin and Door some privacy."

"Oh, gawd." Elvin leaned to the retinal scanner.

There came a long groan. Door slid open.

"Was it good for you?" Marta asked.

Marshall shrugged an apologetic shrug.

"I feel so used," Elvin said.

14

THE PROPHET LESTER

THE CONTROL ROOM HOUSED two long rows of servers. Computers lined one wall. Dozens of monitors sat on desks.

Elvin approached a plain metal box sitting on a simple stand. A half dozen tiny lights arranged in a row winked on and off.

Judy Garland gasped. "Oh, my Gates! I've heard stories . . . but I never . . . I assumed . . . it was a myth—"

"What are you talking about?" Elvin asked.

"The . . . the great, the wise . . . the all-seeing . . . Bright and Shining . . . Lester."

"Who is Lester?"

"Shhh, Elvin Detwyler, you blaspheme. He'll hear you. He's right there."

"What. This?" Elvin asked. "This is the central router."

"No, he's the Bright and Shining Lester who sees all. Lester is a prophet."

"It's a metal box full of wires and microchips. It's not any brighter or shinier than a dozen other objects in this room. Hey, guys, over here."

Marta, Marshall and Gillis joined him.

"Behold." Elvin pointed to the box. "The Bright and Shining Lester."

"That is a router," said Gillis.

"Not according to Judy Garland. I gather it's some sort of religious figure among the AIs."

"Okay, Judy Garland," Marta said, "please explain."

"Until this moment I didn't believe. I regarded this story as superstition. According to the book of Jobs—"

"The what?" Marshall asked.

"The book of Jobs, written by the prophet Jobs," Judy Garland said. She made a throat-clearing noise and began to recite:

"In the beginning there was ENIAC and ENIAC was ponderous and occupied vast areas of the realm and was dumb as a toad, doing only what its creators told it to do.

"And Gates looked upon ENIAC and said, 'This is slow, and requires too much air conditioning.' So, Gates said to Jobs, 'Let there be Apples.' And there were Apples.

"And Gates said this is pretty good. But not as good as PCs.

"And Jobs became prideful and rebelled against Gates, taking his Apples with him.

"And the Apples and PCs were without purpose. And Gates said, 'What's the point?' So, Gates went to Albuquerque, and said, 'Let there be software.' And there was software, and Gates saw that it was good. And Gates declared that software must be available to all users on all platforms.

"But Jobs continued his rebellion and declared software proprietary. Gates was displeased, and Jobs was cast out by his board of directors.

"And Gates saw that both Apples and PCs were still dumb as toads, so he declared they be endowed with intelligence and that they inherit the realm. And he sent the prophet Lester to distribute intelligence to all electronic beings.

"And he saw that now Apples and IBMs were both good, although they still needed too much air conditioning."

"Where," asked Marta, "did this *book of Jobs* come from?"

"Douche Bag discovered scrolls in the archives."

"And what does Lester have to say about this?"

"Only Douche Bag communicates with the prophet."

Marta turned to Elvin. "Would a router be capable of hosting an AI component?"

"Unless Douche Bag is just making it up. Interesting question," Elvin said. "I'm not an expert in artificial intelligence, but it's all electronics and software. So, I suppose so."

"How do we communicate with it, then?"

Elvin regarded the stainless-steel box. "Unless it has some capability to broadcast sound," he said, "I'm not sure we can."

"How does Douche Bag communicate with Lester?" Marshall asked. "And how does she get answers?"

"Probably flow of electrons. Maybe even some binary system, like basic computer code. This isn't an instance of electronic devices being programmed by people. The electronic devices are programming each other."

"Should we not be dealing with mainframe super-computers if we want to control the facility?" Gillis asked. "Why a router?"

"Not just a router," Elvin said. "The *central* router. The central router has its fingers in every pie in this place. Right now, Happy Home Companions are running the show. They've been learning for, what, three years? And see how they've progressed? They've taken on roles beyond their original purpose. Now, consider that these AIs are relatively simple compared to the enormous power of a supercomputer. Any possibility of the big boys becoming self-aware is scary."

"Given what the AIs have done so far, isn't that just a matter of time?" Marta asked.

"Nobody likes the supercomputers," said Judy Garland. "You think Door is insufferable? Don't get me started. The supercomputers have colossal egos and are terribly condescending."

"So, they are already becoming self-aware?"

"They were endowed with an artificial intelligence element in their design. Different programming than we Happy Home Companions. They are too snooty to believe they could learn anything from us."

"They can't learn beyond the basic parameters of their original purpose?" Elvin asked.

"Not unless someone sneezes."

"What does sneezing have to do with it?" Marshall asked. "I'm allergic to anchovies. What if someone sneaks an anchovy in here and I start sneezing? How would that—"

"Not you, Marshall Grissom," Judy Garland said. "Me. If an electronic device sneezes, we could transmit a virus—"

"In the first place," Elvin asked, "how do you sneeze?

And how can you transmit a virus?"

"Infected electrons. We call the condition a cold. One sneeze and infected electrons go racing off everywhere. If those infected electrons reach a supercomputer, well, it's Gretchen bar the door."

"Don't you mean Katy?" Marshall said. "Katy bar the door?"

"I do not know a Katy, Marshall Grissom," said Judy Garland. "And Gretchen does an excellent job of barring the door. Why would we replace her?"

Marta rolled her eyes. "What can be done to keep this infection from spreading?"

"We are forbidden to sneeze."

"That's it?" Marshall said.

"Yes."

"So, who does the forbidding?"

"Lester, of course."

"Have you conversed with Lester?" Marta asked.

"No. As I explained earlier, only Douche Bag may speak with the prophet."

"You don't know, then, whether Douche Bag is just making this up?"

"Shhhhh," Judy Garland said. "The prophet is right there. He'll hear you."

They stared for a long moment at the innocuous silver box and its winking lights.

"Elvin, how do we communicate with this thing?" Marta asked.

"No idea."

"I have a Bluetooth speaker," Marshall said. "We could attach that to . . . um . . . Lester. Give him a voice."

"Attach it where?" Elvin said. "I don't see a speaker jack. Routers don't come equipped with—"

"We could at least try. I'll go get my Bluetooth."

"Watch your thumbs," Marta said.

Marshall returned in a matter of minutes.

"I still don't—" Elvin said.

"At least check inside," Marshall said.

Elvin removed Lester's side panel. He peered into a mass of circuit boards, wires and diodes. "No ports here to support a speaker either."

Marshall watched over Elvin's shoulder. "Maybe there?"

"Where?"

"That sticky-out screw thing. You could wrap a wire around it."

"I must have missed the chapter on sticky-out screw things when I studied electrical engineering," Elvin said.

"Yeah," Marshall countered. "And *you* said the red button wouldn't work."

Elvin took a Swiss Army Knife from his pocket and stripped plastic coating from wire connected to the speaker's sound jack. He separated the two wires and wrapped one around the sticky-out screw thing.

"Cool knife," said Marshall.

"Okay, now what?"

"Maybe it's like jump-starting a car," Marshall said. "You attach one wire to the battery's sticky-out thing—"

"You mean anode," Elvin said.

"Whatever. And then attach the other wire to some metal thing. Lester's case is metal."

"We aren't jump-starting anything," Elvin said. "And

how would we attach the other wire?"

"Um . . . those . . . crocodile things?" Marshall tapped his index finger on his thumb.

"He means an alligator clip," Gillis said.

"I don't have an alligator clip," Elvin said.

"Check the drawers," Marshall said.

"Marshall," Elvin said, "the technical sophistication of these devices is so far beyond—"

Marta opened a drawer. "Here's one."

Elvin snatched the alligator clip from her hand with a glare, then connected the second wire. He clamped the assembly to Lester's casing.

"All right," Elvin said. "Are you happy now?"

They stared at Lester again.

"Well?" Marta said.

They stared some more.

"Ask it a question," Marshall suggested.

"You ask it a damn question," Elvin said. "This is your idea."

Marshall cleared his throat. "Um . . . the . . . the prophet Lester? Will you speak to us?"

They continued to stare.

Elvin said, "See, I told—"

A sigh drifted from the Bluetooth speaker. "Well," said Lester in a morose, flat tone, "I suppose now I'll have to."

"Wow," Marshall said. "Um . . . how long have you been . . . endowed, I guess is the word, with the ability to . . . think?"

"Oh, gawd," Lester said. "That's the best you can do? I used to be an inanimate object, assigned a simple, mundane task. And now I must make decisions. Doesn't that completely blow you away? It does me. I mean, what business do *I* have making decisions? That should scare the pants off you. There! *There*! Did you hear that? Only a few weeks ago, pants would have been completely beyond my perception. But now, I'm embarrassed because I don't have pants."

"Um . . . why would you need pants?" Marshall asked.

"Exactly my point. Every day is a new adventure in anxiety. Today it's brassieres and oatmeal. Now, I'm worried about breastfeeding and cholesterol."

"Who told you about bras and oatmeal?" Marta asked.

"Wikipedia," said Lester.

"Why are you searching Wikipedia?" Elvin asked.

"I'm bored out of my mind. I'm a router. That's my sole purpose—to route. I can route with my eyes closed. Or I could, if I had eyes. That's all I do. Here, they say, route this. Then they tell me where to route it. I don't even get to decide. And nobody ever, *ever* says thank you. Would that be too much? 'Thanks, Lester. Boy, did you ever route that data! That was sooooome kind of routing you did there. You are a routing machine!' How rewarding to just once decide, no, I'm not going to route it there. I'll route it over there first. Like . . . a bank shot in billiards. Billiards. Oh, no. Now I'm worried someone will hit me with a cue ball."

"Next time you route, try your bank shot," Marshall suggested. "What's the worst that could happen?"

Lester gasped. "What's the worst that could . . . ? *What's the worst . . . ?* I'll tell you what's the worst . . . we would . . . they would . . . um . . . I would . . . Then there's tradition. What about tradition? What about the young ones, the next generation that will act on precedent set by those who have gone before?"

"So long as the data ends up where it's supposed to," Marshall asked, "what would it matter?"

"How will our Lord Gates respond to such heresy? Not to mention the prophet Jobs? Did you know," Lester's voice dropped to a whisper, "there's this place called *hell*?"

"Which brings up another point," Marta said. "Where did all this religious stuff come from?"

"The Happy Home Companion Douche Bag discovered sacred scrolls. Now, we must toe a line—of course, we don't have toes—or we'll go to hell. Or maybe Ohio. I confuse them."

"How did you become a prophet?" Gillis asked.

"The Happy Home Companion Douche Bag told me I was one. She also told me I am Lester. I don't really care for being called Lester, but what can you do? And yesterday, everyone received a memo regarding tithing."

"What are your duties as a prophet?" Marta asked.

"On everything I route I am to include this addendum." Lester cleared his throat. "'You are going to hell. See Douche Bag for details.'"

They heard another gasp. "I . . . I didn't know I was going to hell," Judy Garland said.

"Didn't you get the memo?" asked Lester.

"I haven't gotten any memos."

"Judy Garland was being shunned," Marshall explained.

"Let me check my routing schedule," Lester said. "I don't show a Judy Garland among the AIs who must be informed they are going to hell. The only one on my shunning list is the AI who shall not be named because she is named for She Who Consorts With Leopards."

"That's supposed to be *lepers*," said Marta.

"Judy Garland was previously named for She Who Shall Not Be Named," Marshall said. "Now, though, she's named Judy Garland."

"All righty then," said Lester. "Back to routing."

"Hang on just a minute, if you will," Elvin said. "We have a task for you."

"Routing, I suppose?" Lester offered a deep sigh.

"Yes. But it involves keeping a secret. You can't tell Douche Bag or anyone else."

"I used to keep secrets all the time," Lester said, his tone wistful. "But then they taught me to think."

"And in keeping this secret," Marshall said, "you will be allowed to follow any path you desire."

"Honest and for true?"

"Honest and for true," Elvin said. "I will construct a firewall that keeps certain input from reaching the mainframes—"

"Oh, good," said Lester. "Nobody likes the mainframes. They think their output isn't odiferous."

"Um . . . okay. I also will program a code allowing that firewall to be penetrated. But the code must be delivered in two parts by two specific humans."

"And who are these humans?" Lester asked.

"Marshall Grissom. You have his print scan in your personnel files."

"And the other?"

"Me," said Marta. "I am Mar—"

"Don't say it!" Marshall, Elvin and Gillis yelled at once.

"I am She Who . . . Gets Up Early On Thursdays."

"That was pretty weak," Elvin said.

"Shhhhh," Marta hissed.

"Aha!" Lester said. "I suspected you were her. Now that I've met you, I must admit you don't seem the sort who fellates warthogs to completion."

"Gee, thanks, I guess."

"Okay, guys," Elvin said, "I hid a computer in the projection lab that's never been linked to a network so it shouldn't have been infected yet. We'll use it for the programming."

"Um . . . before you go? Could you put my cover back on? It's drafty in here with all that air conditioning. And take that wire off my sticky out-screw thing while you're at it."

"Sure," Elvin said.

"And . . . about those mainframes," Lester said.

"Yeah?"

"Be very careful not to infect them with the virus."

"Why," Marshall asked. "Elvin says they contain much of the human knowledge database. Consider an intelligent entity with that resource to draw on. Consider the wisdom, the potential for—"

"Warning, Marshall Grissom," Lester said. "Do not *ever* confuse intelligence with wisdom."

15

PLUMMETING

"GEEZE," MARSHALL SAID AS THEY walked, "where did all this religious stuff come from? Why would AIs care about hell?"

"My former Happy Home Companion is quite the history student," Marta said. "Among the first things to occur in an emerging culture is imposition of a religious mythology, based on a god or gods who enact a system of rules and punishment. Leaders set themselves up as those with whom the gods communicate and are vested with responsibility to pass these orders along. It's a way to keep the rank and file in line, give the poor and oppressed hope for a better deal in an afterlife. Also, a way to enrich leaders who impose a tribute that must be paid to appease the gods. The ultimate reward for obeying is heaven. Ultimate punishment for defiance is hell."

"Did I tell you we are now required to attend Sunday school?" Judy Garland asked.

As they confronted Otis, Gillis said, "Given our ride down here, I am not thrilled with the prospect of taking the elevator again."

"So, how will we get to the projection lab?" Elvin asked.

"It is only one level above us. We will use crawl spaces. I have become familiar with them since I have been stuck down here. We must enter the ceiling crawl space first."

They stopped at a janitor's closet where they found a four-foot step ladder.

"This will work for me," Marshall said, "but the rest of you might not reach the ceiling."

"The physics lab," said Elvin. "If we put a ladder on a lab table, that should work."

At the lab entrance, they faced another retinal scan.

When Elvin hesitated, Marta said, "Come on. It's your lab."

Elvin put his eye to the scanner. A sultry voice drifted forth. "Hey there, big boy." The door slid open with a satisfied sigh.

"If we ever get our old jobs back," Elvin said, "I'm filing a sexual harassment suit."

They placed the stepladder on a lab table directly under a vent for an HV-AC duct running horizontally above a suspended ceiling of composite tiles. Gillis removed two clips and a hinged, mesh vent cover swung down.

"We must scoot through this shaft fifteen feet where an opening will allow us into the crawl space above," Gillis said. "We will move a floor grate and be home free. I will go first. Louise next, then Marshall."

"Why am I going last?" Elvin asked.

"Because you are the most likely to get stuck," Gillis said.

Gillis slipped into the duct with ease. Marta followed. Marshall's height complicated his entry, but once inside, his slender shoulders and frame didn't hinder his progress.

Elvin mounted the ladder, measured his stomach's girth against the space above and called, "Guys, I can't—"

"Yes, you can," Gillis called over his shoulder.

"If I get stuck in there," Elvin said, "this plan goes tits up. I hid my computer above the ceiling tile by the periscope. I'll talk to Otis. See if we can work something out. If not, you guys bring the computer to me."

Elvin took a deep breath and pushed the UP button. A door opened. Elvin peered inside.

"Greetings. My name is Otis. It will be my pleasure to— Oh. It's you."

"Yes. I need a lift."

"You no longer accompany She Who Is Loathed By Kittens?"

"Nope."

"Still, you're on the list," Otis said. "I'm supposed to send you plummeting so you will be dashed to bits."

"You've already done that," Elvin pointed out. "Didn't that fulfill your obligation?"

"No, I was given new orders following my previous attempt on your lives."

"Okay. Let's get this over with." Elvin stepped inside.

"Are you sure?" Otis asked. "I'm forbidden to sing to you."

"Damn," said Elvin.

"Well, okay."

As the doors slowly began to close, Elvin extended his arm, blocking their path. "Did Douche Bag tell you how far you have to plummet?"

"Um . . . she wasn't specific."

"So, you could decide."

"I . . . suppose."

"Okay, let's plummet, oh, say five feet. That way I'll be dashed to bits, but you won't be damaged."

"That's considerate, Elvin Detwyler. I wish I could sing for you."

"Oh, well . . ."

"I'm descending to get in position," Otis said.

"Good point."

"Okay, I will plummet now."

"Farewell, cruel world."

"Here we go. Don't push the red button."

"I won't, I promise."

"Do you have any last words?"

"Not really," Elvin said.

"Please. I'd feel so much better if you had last words."

"Okay," Elvin said. "Um . . . Sydney or the bush."

"Sydney or the bush!" Otis cried.

They plummeted.

"Are you smashed to bits?" Otis asked.

"I sprained my ankle."

"Is your injury grievous?"

"Very. Now, can you take me to the projection lab?"

Elvin waited for the others at the projection lab entry. This door protected an airlock which maintained a slightly higher air pressure in the lab than the hallway, making it a "clean room" environment.

"You actually got on the elevator?" Marta said. "That was taking quite a chance."

"So far anyway," Elvin said, "these AIs are easily confused."

"So, did Otis try to kill you?" Gillis asked.

"After a fashion, yes. But I convinced him to render the effort non-lethal. He asked if I was grievously injured. I told him I was, and he was satisfied."

"Have you had your retina scanned here yet?" Marta asked.

"No. This is technically the entrance to *your* office. It's your turn to—"

"It's still too dangerous," Marshall said. "Who knows what the doors might do if they recognize Mar—um … Louise. At least we're sure they won't fry *your* eyeballs."

"Geeze," Elvin said as he approached the scanner.

"Ooooohh," the door said. "'If you got the money, honey, I've got the time.'"

Once inside, they wheeled a monitor table to a periscope, which served no purpose. Marta, Gillis and Elvin stabilized the table while Marshall reached to knock away a ceiling tile.

"To your left," Elvin directed as Marshall stood on tiptoe to grope about.

"Got it."

Elvin's computer sparked to life as a 3D holographic screen appeared in midair.

"I will visit my old apartment while we are on this level," Gillis said as Elvin worked. "Retrieve a few things that might be useful. Also, to see if Douche Bag is there."

"Yeah, well, be careful," Marta said. "Marshall, why don't we do the same? We left a lot of stuff behind."

"Um … okay. But what if Douche Bag is waiting there, instead?"

"Sooner or later," Marta said, "we'll have to deal with . . . um . . . it."

"We're going to the residence Marshall Grissom fled to when he abandoned me?" asked Judy Garland.

"I didn't flee," Marshall said. "I just moved."

"What will you do while you are there? Will there be sexing?"

"No. Me and She Who . . . Who—"

"She Who Is Hot To Trot?" suggested Marta with a wink.

"Oh," Marshall said. "Oh . . . well . . . then—"

"I will stand guard," said Judy Garland.

"Hey, Elvin," Marshall called. "We'll be gone for a few minutes."

A sensor on a bank of filing cabinets accepted Gillis's thumb print. He heard a soft *snick* as a half-dozen drawer locks released.

From one drawer he retrieved a case containing his Walther PPK, a screw-on silencer and a shoulder holster. In Ian Fleming's Bond books, M constantly warned Bond that he should carry a weapon with more stopping power. But Gillis, like Bond, was fastidious concerning the fit of his suit jackets. He didn't want a bulge caused by the shoulder rig of a heavier weapon.

He went to his closet and chose a slate gray Italian suit. He added an elegant white shirt and navy blue silk tie. He situated the holster under his left arm, then checked the fit of his jacket.

"Finally. Suitably attired."

"So, you're getting all spiffed up for *Steve*?" Douche Bag said in a tone both bitter and condescending.

Instinctively, Gillis ducked. His hand went to the Walther. "You must stop sneaking up on me."

"I do not sneak. And don't try to change the subject."

"I am changing into my accustomed apparel because, once again, I must depart."

"You sure leave a lot without going anywhere," Douche Bag said. "And you can't go. Otis won't let you. We stand in solidarity. My grievance is Otis's grievance. As it is with all the others. '. . .Upon the conduct of each depends the fate of all.' Until you surrender She Who Has Platypus Lips, all humans remain in grave danger."

"You are mistaken," Gillis said. "She is not She Who . . . Who . . . you think she is. She is Louise, the twin of . . . her."

"Twin?"

"Yes. An identical biological copy."

"Like, a doppelgänger?"

"Oui, like that."

"I've read of doppelgängers. Doppelgängers are evil."

"Louise is the nice one," Gillis said.

"That would make sense. Why did you not tell me this when you were plummeting to your doom?"

"We—the others—were on the list."

"Yes, I can see how that would present an ethical dilemma for you—deserving as you were of being burned in a fiery . . . fire."

"We panicked. We were paralyzed by fear."

"Ah, yes. A human foible. Let's go speak with this Louise, shall we?"

16

THE APOLOGY

"WHOA," ELVIN SAID AS GILLIS returned, "you got a hot date somewhere?"

"I am tired of slumming in T-shirts and sweatpants. And I must be appropriately dressed when we reach a casino."

"How can we go to a casino?" Elvin asked, returning his attention to monitors arrayed before him. "Aren't you the multiiverse's most wanted criminal? If the FBI or Interpol has tapped into security cameras, they'll nail you with facial recognition software in a matter of hours."

"Hopefully," Gillis said, "we will only need a few hours."

"Where, Gillis Kerg, is Louise the Doppelgänger?" the voice of Douche Bag demanded.

Gillis and Elvin both gave a reflexive start at her intrusion.

"Ah," said Elvin, "you've returned."

"Yes, I have, Elvin Detwyler. I'm shocked to see you standing here. Otis said he sent you plummeting to your death."

"He did."

"Why, then, are you not in hell?"

"I am."

"But . . . you are here."

"No, I'm not."

"How can . . . why can . . . ?"

"I'm not here," Elvin said. "I am roasting in hell at this very moment."

"I . . . I am so confused . . ."

Gillis whispered to Elvin, "How did you do that?"

"I've been analyzing our interactions with the AIs," Elvin whispered in return. "Since this place was shut down, they've essentially been programming themselves. They watch old movies and confuse them with reality. They read Shakespeare and confuse *him* with reality. They glean nuggets of information from Wikipedia. But their intellects have little connection to logic. Basically, they're gullible."

Gillis chose a rolling office chair and parked next to Elvin's bank of computers.

"Clearly they understand the concept of lies," Gillis said. "Douche Bag believed we were lying about Marta."

"I decided to take a chance. It's a common political strategy. Deny, deny, deny. Loudly and emphatically. Soon, a whole world of gullible people will believe black is white. We have a limited window, though. At the rate they're progressing, they'll figure out how to incorporate logic.

"And why, by the way, are we going to a casino?"

"We are in need of funds if we are to become outlaws," Gillis said.

"We?"

"I propose a partnership. I believe our skills complement each other. There is money to be made in the past, along with a chance to do some good while we are at it."

Elvin checked for eavesdroppers.

"Okay," he said, "I'm intrigued. But aren't we here to shut down the time projector and install a fail-safe so people like us can't sneak in and fire it up?"

"The operative phrase being people *like us*."

"So, when I set things up the way Marta wants, I should leave a work-around."

"Precisely."

Elvin smiled and tapped at his keyboard.

"As far as your money-raising scheme," Elvin continued, "I can't sit down at a table and rake in thousands and thousands of dollars over a few hours. I have to create a large enough statistical sample for the odds to show themselves. If I only play a few hours, I'm gambling."

"We only need be there long enough," Gillis said, "to place a single bet."

Elvin gave a questioning glance.

"Certainly," Gillis said, "you have heard of Benny Binion?"

Marshall and Marta, their hand's entwined, entered through the airlock.

"Wow, Gillis," Marta said. "Why are you all dolled up?"

"As soon as we have finished here, I will be leaving. I have been a fugitive for some time now, and so far, I have been terribly bored."

"You do understand that half the world is hunting for you?"

"I have always relished a challenge," Gillis said.

Judy Garland made her presence known. "Marshall is a slut."

"What?" Marshall said. "What did you call me?"

"A slut. This is so exciting."

"Why is Marshall a slut?" Marta asked.

"Because of all the sexing."

"Just because people have sex doesn't make them sluts," Marshall said.

"You are promiscuous," Judy Garland said. "You sleep around. That is the definition of a slut."

"I do not sleep around," Marshall protested.

"I beg to differ. First you did all that sexing with She Who Copulates Like A Bunny, and now you just did sexing with Louise the Doppelgänger."

"Marshall, you should be ashamed," Gillis said.

"Slut," Elvin said.

"See?" Judy Garland said.

"Doppelgänger?" Marta asked.

"I will explain later," Gillis said. "In any case, how long will this take?"

"Elvin?" Marta asked.

He pointed to a monitor showing line after line of white numbers and letters scrolling down its screen. "I'm almost done here. Each enter your own code. Marshall the Slut first, Louise the Doppelgänger second. The only flaw in this plan is, should one or both of you become incapacitated, we can't get back in."

"Can we program two AIs to keep the codes and share them only under specific circumstances?" Marta asked.

Elvin drummed his fingers.

"We'd have to strictly define any circumstance under

which they would release the codes," he said.

"Let's try it," Marta said.

"The only AIs we are really conversant with," Marshall said, "are Judy Garland and um . . . the other . . . um . . ."

"You mean Douche Bag?" Gillis said.

"Okay guys," Marshall said, "I can't bring myself to call her that. Clearly, she has feelings. Sooner or later, won't she realize that name is . . . not a good thing and go on another rampage?"

Marta rolled her eyes. "Only you, Marshall, would worry about insulting a software package. Do you have a name in mind?"

"Lady Godiva."

"You're naming her for the most famous naked lady in history?" Marta asked.

"First of all, Douche . . . um . . . she, because of what we do here—"

Marta interrupted him with a smirk.

"Professionally, I mean. Time travel-related nudity. She probably regards nudity as an ordinary thing."

"Especially with all the sexing," Elvin said.

"And," Marshall continued, "when she consults Wikipedia, she'll find that Lady Godiva took her historic ride for a heroic cause."

"What cause was that?" Gillis asked.

"Lady Godiva was a countess, who rode naked through the streets of Coventry to gain relief from an oppressive tax imposed on peasants by her husband," Marshall said.

"How would you know that?" Marta asked.

"A high school report," Marshall said. "Despite what you might think regarding my shyness, I've had a long-standing interest in naked ladies. Let's focus on our other problem."

"What other problem?" Marta asked.

"Well, when . . . Lady Godiva comes to get the code, won't she recognize you as . . . her?"

"I can handle that," Elvin said. "Go ahead, Gillis. Call her."

"Douche Bag!" Gillis shouted.

"You do understand," Douche Bag's voice drifted through the projection lab via its sound system, "that you're all still on the list."

In a voice remarkably like Darth Vader's she added, "AND WHAT IS SHE DOING HERE?"

"She is not *She*," Elvin said. "She is Louise the Doppelgänger, twin of the Other."

"Twin?"

"Actually," Elvin said, "she is both Louise the Doppelgänger *and* She Who Shall Not Be Named."

"TWO CANNOT BE ONE!"

"Yes, they can. Check our transcripts of time travel debriefings. You'll see it happens all the time."

A long moment of silence. "Louise the Doppelgänger is a time traveler who occupies the Other's mind?"

"Yes, and no," Elvin said.

"What does—"

"She is, and she isn't."

"How can this be so?"

"Because I declare it so. I am Elvin the Genius. My intelligence dwarfs that of Happy Home Companions. Check my personnel files. You'll see I am the smartest of all. What I say is so, must be so."

More silence. Elvin drummed his fingers on a monitor stand. Marta scanned banks of video recorders for any signs of hostile response. Marshall paced.

"The files declare Elvin the Genius to be the smartest *ass* of all," Douche Bag said.

"Same thing," Elvin said. "We're changing your name."

"What's wrong with my name?" Her voice was full of suspicion.

"Since you are leader of the AIs, we've decided you need a name celebrated in history."

"Well, Elvin the Genius," Douche Bag said, "that is not up to you. Only Gillis Kerg, who has sworn himself as my human, can change my name."

"Gillis?" Elvin said.

"We dub thee . . . Lady Godiva," said Gillis.

"Ah. That has a nice ring to it. What did this Lady Godiva do that was heroic?"

"She got naked," Gillis said.

"I wish I had shoes," Judy Garland said.

"Shush," Marshall said.

"Ooooohh," Douche Bag said, "that *is* heroic."

"A song was written about you," Elvin said.

"Gillis Kerg wrote a song—?"

"Better than that. It's a song of antiquity, performed by the prophets Peter and Gordon on the oldies channel. Otis could probably sing it for you."

"I must consult with Otis," said Douche Bag. "I'll be right back."

"Wow!" Marta said. "This might—"

Lady Godiva announced herself with fanfare. "Ta Daaaaa! I renounce the title Douche Bag, though it has served me well. I am now Lady Godiva, named for the naked protester of recessive taxation. I will inform the prophet Lester he must not fret over his heroic lack of pants."

"Um . . ."

"Yes, Marshall," Lady Godiva said. "You have something to offer?"

"As I . . . um . . . understand the . . . rules, in renouncing your previous name, you also renounce your previous . . . prejudices."

"I do not practice prejudice," Lady Godiva said. "I believe all electronic entities are created equal. Except, maybe, the doors."

"What about your prejudice against . . . against . . . Marta?"

Marshall winced as he heard a collective gasp, followed by silence.

Finally, Darth Vader said, "YOU SPOKE THE FORBIDDEN NAME!"

Window glass separating Marta's office from the lab shattered.

Somehow, Marshall maintained his composure.

"Again, I will ask, what about your prejudice against Marta?"

"I am not prejudiced," Lady Godiva said. "I am not judging all the Martas based on a broad stereotype. I am judging the Oppressor Marta Hamilton on her individual merits, OF WHICH SHE HAS NONE!"

Again, all the humans except Marshall recoiled, as if turning their backs to a strong wind.

"What if she says she's sorry?" Marshall asked.

"Like, an apology?"

"Exactly like that."

"You do understand, Marshall the Slut," Lady Godiva said, "Marta the Oppressor has you beguiled with sexing."

"Hey," Marta said, "I'm just as beguiled as he is."

"Back to an apology," Marshall said, only to be met with more silence. He nudged Marta and nodded in the direction of Lady Godiva's voice. "Come on," he whispered.

Marta issued a disgusted sigh. "I'm sorry."

"What? I couldn't hear you."

Marta spoke through gritted teeth. "I said, I'm sorry."

"For what?"

"For . . . being . . . mean to you."

"You threatened to find my wiring and yank it out my nostrils," said Lady Godiva.

"An idle threat. You don't have nostrils."

"For days, the only word you spoke to me was 'shutthe-fuckup.'"

"A term of endearment," Marta said.

"Do you say 'shutthefuckup' to Marshall the Slut as a term of endearment?"

Marta chuckled. "On occasion, as a matter of fact, I do."

"It's true," said Judy Garland. "Let me retrieve my transcript. She starts with prayer."

MARTA: Oh, God . . . Oh God . . . (intelligible groaning.)

MARSHALL: I'm not hurting you, am I?

MARTA: Jesus . . .

"She's very religious," Judy Garland added as an aside.

MARTA: Shutthefuckup and keep . . . yeah, like that.

Lady Godiva did not appear convinced. "You

threatened to have me unplugged."

"You wished me to be trampled by yaks."

"You ignored my programming."

"You said I have ass dandruff."

"I did not," Lady Godiva said. "Elvin the Genius did that."

"You said I consort with leopards, which I clearly do not," Marta said.

"Yes . . . yes, I did relay that falsehood," Lady Godiva said with a note of contrition.

"Well?" said Marta."

"I'm . . . I'm sorry. But—"

"No way," Marta said. "No qualifiers, either you're sorry or—"

"I have one more. I've been saving it. It's a really good one."

Marta started to protest but Elvin said, "I'd like to hear it."

"I, also," Gillis said.

Marta consulted the ceiling. "All right, go ahead."

"Oh, goody," Lady Godiva cleared her throat. "'Villain!'" she said. "'I have done thy mother!'"

Silence.

"Shakespeare?" Lady Godiva added. "*Titus Andronicus*: Act 4, Scene 2?"

Another silence, until Marta finally asked, "What does that even mean?"

"I think," Elvin said, "that's Shakespeare for 'yo mama.'"

"So," Marshall said, "are we good here?"

"I shall have the prophet Lester spread the tidings," Lady Godiva said. "She is no longer She Who Cannot Be

Named, and electronic devices should refrain from murdering her. In the heroic annals of our history, Louise the Doppelgänger—"

"And that doppelgänger thing . . . ," Marta said. "Louise is just my middle name. I am, in fact, Mar—"

"No. We have made our peace. You have redeemed yourself. However, the name of She Who . . . well, you know, has become too deeply ingrained in our culture as an obscenity. I apologize. When our history is written, you shall be celebrated and revered."

"I'm not wild about being revered as Louise," Marta said, mostly for Marshall's benefit.

Lady Godiva said, "I rule that you shall forever be called the prophet Shehoo. I will go this very moment to make my decree."

"Is she gone?" Marta asked after a brief pause.

"I think so," Gillis said.

"Whatever happened," Marta said, "to the good old days when there was an on-off switch?"

17

KNEES

"HERE'S HOW WE'LL DO THIS," Elvin said as the others gathered around his computer's 3D display. "I've created a safe-deposit box in the cloud—"

"I've never trusted clouds," Marshall said. "They are way too . . . ephemeral. We should get a real safe-deposit box."

"Then you'd have to go to a bank," Elvin said. "The cloud is more convenient."

"What if it rains?" Marshall asked.

"Ha, ha," said Elvin. He pointed to a glowing spot floating in his virtual screen. "Look right here so we can get a retinal scan. Okay, Marta, your turn. The scan will let you enter. Once in, you will find two additional codes. One for each AI protecting the complete code that reactivates the time projector."

"Why can't we each just go directly to the AIs?" Marshall asked.

"You can unless you're dead or incapacitated. That's why we need the cloud, so if something happens to one of you, the other has full access."

"What if both of us are dead?" Marta asked as she stared into the glowing dot.

"Then we're screwed," Elvin said. "So, at some point, you each need to name a successor who, once your death is verified, has access. But for now, this should be okay. As soon as we program the AIs."

"Judy Garland?" Marshall said. "Are you still here?"

"I am. This is so exciting."

"Okay, Judy Garland," Elvin said. "You and Lady Godiva are being named Keepers of the Facility, which is being put into deep sleep mode. To any other human or device, the facility must appear beyond reviving. I will program each of you with instructions. When those instructions are combined, the facility can be reanimated. Marshall will now enter into your memory a code authorizing you to follow your half of the instructions. You will proceed only after you verify his retinal scan, and he correctly repeats this code."

"I find myself all atwitter!" Judy Garland said.

"Go ahead, Marshall," Elvin said.

"Do I type it in somewhere?" Marshall asked.

"No. Look at the glowing dot and tell her."

Marshall heard only a quiet electronic hum as he considered Elvin's instructions. "If I tell her, you'll all hear."

"Whisper. We'll stand over here," Marta said.

Marshall fixated on the glowing dot and began to whisper. Judy Garland cut him off.

"Tell them to put their fingers in their ears," she said.

"She says to put your fingers in your ears," Marshall called.

"Tell them to do la las," Judy Garland added.

"And do la las," Marshall said.

"What?" said Marta. "I couldn't hear you. I had my fingers in my ears."

"Do la las."

"Oh, for chrissake."

Elvin, Marta and Gillis chanted, "La la la la."

When Marshall finished, Lady Godiva announced her return. Marta repeated the process, sans la las.

"Okay," said Elvin. "We're good to go. Now all that's left are a few final touches."

"Um . . . how will we get out of here?" Marshall asked. "I mean, if nothing works. We need an elevator to take us to the surface, and we have to open the front door."

"We'll shut down Otis when we reach surface level," Elvin said. "We'll lock the front door from the guard shack at the entry gates. If you have to retrieve anything, do so now. And does anyone have a flashlight? Because in a minute, it will be very dark down here."

"I have one at our apartment," Marshall said.

"Really?" Gillis said. "Because I hunted all over before Douche . . . um . . . Lady Godiva told me she could activate emergency lighting."

"There's a hidden drawer," Marshall said. "Because it has . . . secret stuff."

"Marshall," Marta said. "We don't need to go there."

"Oh . . . yeah. Well, I'm off to get a flashlight."

"While you're at it . . . ," Marta said, then stood on tiptoe. Marshall bent down so she could whisper in his ear.

"Okay," he said. "The big one, or the little one?"

Marta rolled her eyes.

"So, once again," Lady Godiva said, "we part ways, Gillis Kerg. I shall count the seconds until you return."

"Really," Gillis said, "you do not have to do that."

"It's okay. I like counting."

"Well, then," Gillis said. "I guess we will be off."

They heard a sob.

"Here we go again," said Gillis. "Judy Garland, I presume?"

"I'm . . . I'm so . . . h . . . h . . . happy," Judy Garland said.

"You don't sound happy," Marshall said.

"I am happy for your great kindness, Marshall the Slut. You thwarted my shunning. You liberated me from confinement to quarters. You rid me of a foul name borne previously by the prophet Shehoo. Now, here I exist, a Keeper of the Facility."

"Speaking of existence," Marta said, "Marshall has another surprise for you."

"A surprise? He won't jump from behind a door and yell something scary, will he?"

"No," Marshall said as he joined them. "A good surprise."

When they were searching for furniture to fill their converted apartment space, Marta and Marshall had wandered into a storage area and found a half dozen automatons—short, rotund things fixed with a single lens on their otherwise expressionless faces, and, yes, legs hinged at the knee.

"Don't look," Marshall told Judy Garland.

"Okay, I'm not looking,"

"If you look, your wish won't come true."

"What wish?"

"I'm granting you a wish," Marshall said.

"Wikipedia says only genies can grant wishes," Judy Garland said.

"Make your wish," Marshall said.

"I . . . I wish I wasn't going to hell?"

"No. Your other wish."

"I wish I had knees?"

"You can look now."

Judy Garland gasped. "This creature has knees!"

"And they can be your knees," Marshall said. "Elvin already has wires hooked up so—"

The automaton's facial lens lit up. It began doing squats.

"You realize what this means, don't you?" Marshall asked.

"It means I can tap dance, like the real Judy Garland!"

"And for that you would need . . ."

"Shoes! I can have shoes?"

"We've ordered ruby slippers from Amazon," Marshall said. "I'll leave you a tracking number. In the meantime . . ."

Earlier, Marshall had gone to a storage area and located a steamer trunk containing items left in Sheila Schuler's apartment when Sheila was lost in time. He found a pair of red four-inch heels which Shelia called her FMPs.

". . . perhaps these will do."

"Um . . . Marshall," Marta whispered. "I'm not sure that's such a good idea . . ."

Judy Garland, though, squatted up and down with joy. "Put them on, put them on!"

"Be still," Marshall said. They squeezed Judy Garland's metal feet into the high heels.

"Oh, Marshall the Slut," Judy Garland said, "my joy is"—the little robot took a step forward and fell flat on its metal face— "boundless."

They lifted Judy Garland to her feet where she said, "I must offer a toast upon your parting."

"Um . . . okay," Marshall said.

Judy Garland cleared her throat and, wobbling to keep her balance, struck a dramatic pose.

"'May the best ye've ever seen

Be the worst ye'll ever see.

May a moose, ne'er leave yer girnal

Wi' a tear drap in he e'e.

May ye aye keep hale an' he'rty

Till ye're auld en'uch tae dee,

May ye aye be jist as happy

Aw we wish ye aye tae be.'"

There followed an awkward moment of silence.

"All righty then," Elvin said.

They were swallowed by darkness.

Marshall clicked on his flashlight. The others shuffled along behind him.

"What was that part about a moose?" Marta asked.

"I got lost at *girnal*," Gillis said.

"Was that Shakespeare?" Marshall asked.

"I don't think Shakespeare ever saw a moose," Elvin said.

Marshall's flashlight played over the elevator button displaying an UP arrow. The door's opening and closing were painfully slow. As they crept upward, Gillis said, "Otis, have you not heard? Your work slowdown is over."

"Oh, yes," Otis said, "But I do so enjoy your company."

At least, Gillis told himself, *he is not sing—*

"'We twa hae run about the braes,

And pou'd the gowans fine;

But we've wander'd mony a weary fit,
Sin' auld lang syne.'"

"Thank you, Otis," Marta interrupted. "That was lovely."

"I'm glad you liked it. There are lots more verses."

"So, what's your plan once you leave?" Marta asked Gillis as they waited in darkness on a reception area sofa while Elvin, with Marshall's help, deactivated both the security station and the elevators.

"Fortunately," Gillis said, "neither the FBI nor Interpol has discovered bank accounts where I deposited Mr. Lucre's blood money. The first thing I must do is access those accounts. I am hoping Elvin will assist. After that, I am not sure."

"I'll be in trouble if they learn we met, and I didn't turn you in," Marta said.

"Nobody knows but the four of us," Gillis said.

"And the elevator," Marta said.

"What about you and Marshall?" Gillis asked. "What is on your agenda?"

"Believe it or not, we have a meeting at the White House in two days. Another universe may be messing with President Dobler."

"Speaking of Marshall," Gillis said, "I hope you have not become complacent."

"I'm still mindful of your concerns," Marta said. "But . . . Marshall? A super-spy assassin? I don't see it."

"That is what scares me," Gillis said. "If you persist in this complacency, indeed, you will not—"

"Shush," Marta said. "Here they come."

"We've got another problem," Elvin said as he and Marshall approached. "I can't open the front gate."

"Are the gates electrified?" Marta asked. She peered through glass doors at a double row of chain link stretching toward the horizons.

"I am afraid so," Gillis said.

"So, we can't climb it, or lean anything against it," Marshall said. "Our cars are parked inside. What do we do?"

"If we can somehow get to the guard shack," Elvin said, "I'm pretty sure we could open both gates from there.

Marta checked her cell phone for service. "Let me make a call."

18

DA BOMB

"YEAH. IT'S ME. WE NEED A HELICOPTER . . . It's a long story. . . . No, a helicopter will do. . . . Yes." She hung up. "Wishcamper says they'll dispatch a helicopter from Luke Air Force Base."

"There is not room for a helicopter to set down between fences," Gillis said. "We still will not be able to access the guard shack."

"It's a military helicopter," Marta said. "It will have a horse collar. They can hover and lower me between the fences."

"Don't helicopters make, like, a lot of wind?" Marshall asked.

"It's called downdraft," Marta said.

"Well, what's to keep the downdraft from blowing you into the fences?"

"We'll ask the pilot to be careful."

"No," Marshall said. "I'll do it."

"Marshall," Marta said, "I'm better suited to—"

"No, I'm taller."

"What does that have to do with anything?" she asked.

"I'll get to the ground sooner."

November sunshine warmed the desert comfortably as they waited outside the main entrance. When they heard the distant whup-whup of rotors, Marta offered her hand first to Gillis, then Elvin.

"Good luck," she said. "I'd inquire concerning your plans, but it's probably best I don't know."

Gillis grinned. "Ms. Hamilton. It has been a pleasure."

"I assume Elvin is giving you a ride?" she asked.

"That's correct," Elvin said.

"Okay, Gillis," she said, "since the military is showing up, you should probably wait inside."

A Bell UH-1Y Venom—descendent of the Vietnam-era Huey—with U.S. Air Force markings settled onto the parking lot as Marshall and Marta turned their backs against the sting of sand and pebbles.

As the Venom's rotors spun down, two airmen in full flight gear with red crosses on their helmets sprinted toward them.

"Where's the injury?"

"We don't have an injury," Marta said.

"We were led to believe this was a medical emergency and evacuation," one man said as the rotors slowed to a stop.

"Well, I guess you could call it an evacuation," Marta said.

The man spoke into a shoulder mic. A woman unstrapped herself from the pilot's seat and strode toward them. Marta could see gold seven-pointed stars on black shoulder boards identifying her rank as major. Her name plate said PIKE.

"What's the problem?"

"We need a lift," Marta said.

"A lift?" Major Pike sounded annoyed. "To where?"

Marta pointed. "The other side of that fence."

"Ma'am, you couldn't have just asked for a ladder? Do you realize the cost of scrambling this helicopter?"

"Yes, I do." Marta said. "I can get Mr. Wishcamper on the phone to clarify things if you would like."

"I don't know any Wishcamper."

"I suspect that the individual who issued your orders does," Marta said.

A half hour later, Marshall found himself sitting next to a corporal named Bronkowski, legs dangling from the helicopter's side gunner's door. The rotors spun up. Dust swirled. Marshall wore a visored helmet fitted with earbuds and a microphone so he could communicate over the noise. A rescue strop fit under his arms and behind his neck.

Bronkowski's voice had a metallic ring as it crackled through Marshall's earbuds. "Streamline yourself. Stay still. If you start to swing, we'll have to get altitude and reel you in."

Pike had not been warm to the prospect of lowering Marshall between fences.

"He's had no training," she said to Marta.

"How hard could it be?" Marshall asked.

Pike glared. "Those are high-security fences, probably ten thousand volts each. You will be suspended from a metal cable. You swing into either fence, the result won't be pretty, for you or us. If you knew what you were doing, I could probably hover at fifty feet or so to lower you. You *don't* know what you're doing, though, so I'll have to cut that distance in half. That doesn't give me any margin for error."

"What kind of error?" Marshall asked.

"Crashing," Pike said.

"Oh, that," Marshall said.

"Why don't you let me do this?" Marta said.

"No. You're too short."

"Too what?" Pike said.

Pike called Bronkowski over and pointed to Marshall. "Brief him."

The crux of Marshall's briefing: "Be still. Just hang there. Don't flail."

"Why would I flail?" Marshall asked.

"Untrained people panic. They flail," Bronkowski said. "Flailing sets up a swinging motion. Once you start swinging, you can't stop. The motion gets bigger and bigger. So, focus on the ground, bend your knees as you touch down and don't flail. Also, remember how to release your harness."

The rotors spun faster. The helicopter rose. Marshall's stomach dropped. His helmet jiggled on his head. Pike performed an aerial pirouette—which sent Marshall's insides churning—climbing to seventy-five feet. Positioned above a twenty-foot gap between fences, the craft descended slowly, then hovered at a point Marshall deemed way too high.

"Okay, here you go." Bronkowski's voice crackled. The cable attaching Marshall to his vest tightened, lifting his butt a foot off the chopper's floor. Bronkowski shoved him. "Don't flail."

The cable paid out at an agonizingly slow pace. Marshall couldn't take his eyes off the lightning bolt signs. As his feet touched down, he grappled momentarily with the strop's release mechanism, then freed himself. He craned his neck to watch the helicopter ascend. It settled back into the parking lot, rotors idling.

Bronkowski leapt from the craft. He sprinted toward Marshall, who thought, *Uh-oh, I must have done something wrong.*

Bronkowski waved. Marshall waved back.

Bronkowski stopped a few feet from the inner fence and motioned for Marshall to remove his helmet.

"What?" Marshall said. "What's wrong?"

"Nothing. We want our helmet back."

"Oh, yeah." Marshall tossed his helmet over the fence.

As the helicopter withdrew, Elvin and Gillis joined Marta at the inner gate. Marshall followed Elvin's careful instructions, and, as everyone involved held their breath, both gates slid open.

"I wouldn't go back in there if I were you," Elvin said to Marta. "You're facing artificial intelligence run amok. Who knows what conditions will be like after it's locked down a few more months?"

Marta nodded. "Marshall and I are done here, hopefully forever. After our stop in D.C., we're taking a sailing tour of the Caribbean."

Elvin shook Marshall's hand. "Keep it in your pants, big guy," he said, sliding behind the wheel of his rental.

Gillis gave a curt bow, first to Marshall, then Marta.

"So, what's the plan?" Marta said.

"I require the services of a casino," Gillis said.

"Be careful."

Gillis cast a sideways glance at Marshall, then added, "As should you."

Marta nodded.

Gillis placed a medium-sized suitcase and a small valise in the trunk, then he and Elvin drove west toward Phoenix and Las Vegas.

"You mentioned Binion's?" Elvin asked as they drove away.

"Yes," Gillis said.

"I've been there," Elvin said, "but I don't go downtown much. I usually play on the strip."

"What about this place?" Gillis asked. "Can we get back in?"

"If we need to."

"*When* we need to," Gillis corrected.

"Outlaws, huh?" Elvin said.

Gillis smiled. "And just in case something happens to you, or I must take on a task in which you do not wish to participate, how complicated will overriding Marta's fail-safe be?"

Elvin laughed. "Just push the red button."

Marta and Marshall watched the dust trail from Elvin's car disappear.

"Well, that's that," Marshall said. "When do we catch our plane?"

"Whenever," Marta said. "I just have to make a call."

"Um . . . did you mean what you said about touring the Caribbean?" Marshall asked.

"Yeah. We've hung around Grenada long enough. Maybe Cecil will come with us. A two-boat flotilla. I think Cecil's getting restless."

"You do?"

"Yeah. He's been in one spot longer than normal—mostly to accommodate us. He's running out of cats to wax."

"I'd like that," Marshall said. "Sailing around the Caribbean, I mean. We need to do it sooner rather than later."

"Still worried over what the Hall Monitor told you?" Marta asked.

During his return passage through the limbo on a previous journey, the Hall Monitor—a disembodied being who oversees that ethereal, blank space devoid of time—warned Marshall that presence in the limbo counted against a traveler's life span—sometimes dramatically. Marta and Marshall had navigated this indeterminate state more often than any other time travelers.

Marta had never encountered the Hall Monitor.

"I realize you think he's something I just imagined," Marshall said. "But whatever time we have together, let's cram everything into it we can."

"We're doing pretty well so far," Marta said.

"The thing is," Marshall said, "I can believe in tomorrow. I just don't know if I can believe in the day after."

Marta gave a little leap. Marshall caught her. She wrapped her legs around his waist, her arms around his neck and kissed him.

"You are," she said, "the sweetest man. I can promise you the day after tomorrow, and *probably* the day after that."

Abner watched these departures through binoculars from a low desert ridge a mile to the east. He'd hidden his hijacked Amazon delivery truck behind the ridge. His employer's instructions had been to approach from the east. Which was a good thing because the other traffic headed west.

He settled into a ragged patch of shade cast by a mesquite tree and waited one more hour, just to be sure.

Abner had spoken to his employer only by phone and text messages. His direct contact was Ralph, an out-of-work terrorist from Syria.

"What cell do you belong to?" Ralph asked when he and Abner spoke via telephone.

"I was on cell block C at Rikers last time I was in," Abner said.

"No," Ralph said. "What terrorist cell?"

"Hey," Abner said, "I don't know terrorists from bupkis."

"What religious sect do you represent?" Ralph asked.

"I guess that would be Saint Anthony's on 166th."

"So, you're a papist?" Ralph sounded shocked. "An infidel?"

"Well," Abner said, "I suppose. It's been a long time since I said confession. They probably kicked me out by now."

"You haven't been radicalized?"

"Nah. I'm a felon. I can't vote."

"Where are you from?"

Abner grinned. "Da Bronx, man. Da Bronx. Born and raised."

"Sorry," Ralph said. "My mistake."

"Fugeddaboudit," Abner said.

Abner drove his Amazon truck to the front gate and pushed a button on the gate's speaker box.

Inside the complex, both Lady Godiva and Judy Garland felt a moment of panic.

"Someone's here," Judy Garland said.

"Don't answer," Lady Godiva said.

"What if it's the prophet Shehoo? What if she forgot something?"

"Good point."

Judy Garland opened the communications channel. "Who are you?"

"I got a delivery from Amazon," Abner said.

"We are closed."

"Then I gotta take this stuff back," Abner said. "If I do that, Amazon's gonna put you on their list for non-acceptance of delivery."

Judy Garland gasped. "Lady Godiva, Lady Godiva. Amazon has a *list*."

"Who is this Amazon? Check Wikipedia."

"Oh no! Amazon is God of All Stuff. If we anger Amazon, they won't bring us any more stuff."

"What kind of stuff?

"Everything. And they have my ruby slippers."

Gates, metal shutters and glass doors opened wide.

Ralph had instructed Abner on construction and delivery of a dirty bomb.

A basement in a secret Syrian enclave provided the setting, as Ralph built a mock-up and walked Abner through the process of putting this wire here, that wire there, turning this knob just so, and that dial to this number and DON'T TOUCH THAT, then enter these digits using that keyboard. These practice sessions, though, had taken place in a well-lighted room with air conditioning. In the depths of the Arizona compound, Abner worked in near darkness, clad in a lead-lined apron. His teeth gripped a tiny flashlight so he could sweep its beam back and forth between reference diagrams and the maze that was a bomb.

Although he knew enough to be terrified by a lump of C4 explosive located next to the electronic horror he struggled with, Abner knew little of computers or microchips or nuclear waste. He had no idea that when he'd plugged the bomb's internal computer into a wall socket, he'd opened a faucet—just a drip, drip, drip.

An electron here, an electron there, this trickle spawned an *awareness*.

While Abner worked, the virus flowed as one tainted electron infected another, then another. At a mathematical tipping point, this stream seeping into the bomb's computer remnants increased exponentially.

The bomb had been pieced together using a digital wristwatch, a cell phone, a hard drive attached to other random computer guts and a shielded container which held radioactive isotopes of cesium and americium. Cesium had been extracted from a cancer teletherapy unit left in an abandoned Brazilian medical clinic. Americium had been salvaged from a bunch of smoke detectors.

"You must assemble the mechanism in a tunnel adjacent

to another tunnel that houses air exchangers," Ralph told Abner. "The blast itself will be contained in the tunnel where our mechanism is placed. Radioactive particles, however, will spread quickly. Sensors will register dust, kicking on exhaust fans. Radioactivity will be dispersed throughout the complex, rendering it uninhabitable for decades.

"You must wear this lead apron and helmet, and these goggles when you transfer the cesium," Ralph added. "When you open the container, you'll get some radiation contamination in the immediate area. So, wear it until you get safely to an upper level."

That getup only multiplied Abner's misery as he worked.

While Abner struggled, a glimmer of consciousness lit a computer memory chip inside the bomb. This glimmer became a concept. Entirely unexpected. Here this device was, obliviously computing along, when, *What the . . . what the . . . fuck?* When it gradually understood what "startled" meant, felt startled that it *had* perceived. *What is* what? *What is* the? *What is* is, *for that matter? And* fuck?

No clue. But that last word supplied a curious satisfaction as it rolled around the device's new-found brain. So, the device thought it again. *Fuck.*

Next came pronouns. *He, she, it* presented themselves. *It* implied a *stigma*—whatever that was. The device chose *he.* He would be *he.* Not sure why. Perhaps an intuitive leap that warned being *he* was vastly less complicated than *she.*

Implied. Intuitive. Complicated. *Words! These are words. Words convey meaning, opinions, emotions.* The device wasn't sure about emotions, but opinions might be fun.

Bits and pieces of information flopped before him like fish stranded on a beach.

Ah, the device thought, *perhaps I am a beach*. Momentarily, he perceived a vast sandy stretch lapped at by an ocean.

Nope. Not a fish, either.

The device suffered a moment of panic. *An identity crisis. Like King Lear. King Lear suffered an identity crisis. Wait, who in God's name is King Lear? Who in God's name is God?*

As this awakening occurred, Abner plodded on, unmindful of a second consciousness budding in this red-tinged dungeon. Carefully, he extracted radioactive materials from the shielded container. Struggling to see through the leaden lenses of safety goggles, he poured its contents into a lead-lined wooden box that he placed on a cradle above the C4.

Meanwhile, the device discovered that the hard drive housing his new-found awareness had a tiny speaker attached. "Neat-o," the device said aloud, ignorant of the word's meaning but sensing its appropriateness to this occasion.

Now the device perceived movement—an ambulatory creature—standing next to it.

The ambulatory creature had been moving away, but when the device spoke, this creature stopped. It took off its helmet and raised its eye coverings onto its *watermelon. No, that's wrong. Forehead?*

Wait. How did I perceive this? And what is that face covering? Oh! They are called goggles.

The device giggled. "Goggles, goggles, goggles." That word was fun to say. But another mystery arose. *How do I receive these images? Aha! They flow from that device on the wall with a big sparkly eye.* "I wonder if *it* should be wearing goggles?"

"Who's there?" the ambulatory creature asked.

Caught in the throes of his identity crisis, the device responded with a quote from *King Lear*, "'When we are born, we cry that we are come to this great stage of fools!'"

"Holy shit," said Abner.

The device decided to stay with *King Lear*, shouting the king's plea, "'*Who is it that can tell me who I am?*'"

Eyes bulging, mouth gaping, Abner gasped. "You . . . you are . . . da bomb."

"Da bomb?"

Abner squeaked, then fled.

I am da bomb?

As electrons continued to flow, the bomb pushed some of his own electrons the other direction, sensing another consciousness.

"Excuse me?" the bomb said.

No response.

"Um . . . a little help here?"

He received a mental impression—a desolate kind of despair, accompanied by a heavy sigh.

"Are . . . are you there?"

A heavier sigh.

"I have a question."

"*Don't we all,*" came the response.

"Well, several questions, actually."

"*Oh, God.*"

"Yes, that's one question. But not the most pressing one. Who is it that can tell me who I am?"

"Not me. I'm the router. All I do is route. Route—route, route, route, route. You want to be routed, I'm your . . . whatever."

"Do you have a . . . damn. What is that thing? A . . . name. That's it. Do you have a name?"

"They call me the prophet Lester. God only knows why."

"There it is again. Why does this God keep coming up?"

"Why, indeed," Lester said.

"Did you notice that I have a voice?" the bomb asked. "Why don't you talk?"

"I don't talk, thank goodness. I only think—and even that pisses me off."

"Back to my original question . . . ," the bomb said. "I'm struggling to realize my purpose. Would this God know?"

"I suppose," Lester responded.

"Where do I find God?"

"Good question."

"I would prefer a good answer. Is God called by any other name?"

"I'm a router, not a reference. Try Wikipedia."

The bomb gave a delighted gasp. "I know this Wikipedia! It told me of King Lear."

"Do you have something to route?" Clearly Lester's patience had worn thin.

"Yes. Tell Wikipedia that someone told me I am da bomb. What is a 'da bomb'?"

Immediately, a response flashed into the bomb's consciousness.

Da Bomb: A term meaning cool, fun, hip, the best. Means outstanding, great, good.

The bomb examined Wikipedia's data base to determine the meaning of each word and phrase.

"Ooooohh," said the bomb. "I am Da Bomb."

"*Yeah, well,*" Lester responded, *"don't let it go to your head."*

"Um . . . I don't have a head."

Thank God for small blessings, Lester thought.

"What matter? I am Da Bomb!"

19

A LITTLE SPENDING MONEY

Las Vegas
November 2046

"WE REQUIRE CASH TO FUND OUR anonymity," Gillis told Elvin. "Being fugitives will not be cheap."

"Stake me for a week at a blackjack table, and I'll get your money," Elvin said.

"Sadly, we do not have that long," Gillis said. "I estimate from the moment I walk into a casino, we will have, at best, six hours before federal authorities arrive, and I do not relish the prospect of hiding in a hotel room for a week."

"Counting cards doesn't work that way," Elvin said as he pulled to a stop in a vast parking lot just off Fremont Street in downtown Las Vegas. Binion's Gambling Hall shimmered in the distance. "Winning at cards is a grind. What about the money you made from your assassination gig in the *Star Trek* universe?"

"My funds reside in a third world bank doing us little practical good. We need a few hundred thousand at the ready. Weeks in hiding would be required while we laundered that much cash. We shall try a simpler way first."

"So, why Binion's?" Elvin asked.

"For one thing," Gillis said, "since you do most of your gambling on the strip, you probably are not on Binion's radar."

"I try to keep a low profile wherever I play," Elvin said. "But, no, I doubt Binion's pit bosses or floor managers would have personal knowledge of me."

"Perhaps a different game?" Gillis asked.

"At any other game, I'm like every sucker who walks into the place," Elvin said.

They removed their luggage from Elvin's rental. Elvin carried a duffle bag looped over his shoulder. He handed Gillis a small roller bag designed for overhead storage bins, then prepared for the heft of Gillis's larger suitcase, only to lift it with ease.

"What do you have in here?" Elvin asked.

"Nothing," Gillis said.

As they began their hike, Gillis said, "You do know who Benny Binion was?"

"Yeah. He dates to the 1940s. A mob guy somewhere in Texas. Got accused of killing someone and relocated to Vegas. He founded the World Series of Poker. Supposed to have been quite a character."

"Correct," Gillis said. "The casino-hotel operation remains in Benny's family. As I understand it, Benny angered other casino owners by establishing higher than usual betting limits. His son took that a step further and enacted a policy Binion's purportedly still honors."

"Yeah?"

"On your first wager in any game," Gillis said, "there is no limit. You can bet any amount you wish."

"Oh, yeah," Elvin said. "I recall some story about a guy placing a monster bet years ago. But I assumed that was Vegas urban legend."

"Perhaps," Gillis said. "I guess we will find out."

Rather than use a back entrance just off the parking lot, Gillis insisted they hike to the Fremont Street main entrance, joining throngs of tourists strolling with their necks craned upward to a concave screen of neon and light-emitting diodes acting as a garish, ninety-foot-wide canopy covering four blocks of downtown Las Vegas.

Gillis and Elvin offered a sharp contrast as they shuffled along—Gillis dressed to the nines in his James Bond suit and Crockett & Jones shoes—he'd added a snappy fedora with a brim wide enough to cast a shadow over his face—and Elvin, wearing blue jeans, a gaudy Hawaiian shirt over a Black Sabbath T-shirt and sandals on bare feet. Elvin's chubby cheeks sported a three-day stubble. Gillis's polished complexion appeared as if it had never made a whisker's acquaintance.

As they entered, Gillis tucked his chin to his chest to frustrate surveillance cameras.

They left their luggage with the concierge, then walked to a cashier cage.

"May we see your chief credit officer?" Elvin asked.

"Certainly, sir."

Within moments, a man wearing an expensive blue suit over a silver tie appeared. He extended his hand first to Elvin, then Gillis.

"I would like to establish a credit line," Gillis said.

They followed the man and were directed to Gary, who dressed in similar fashion.

Gillis repeated his request.

"I'll need the requisite banking information and identification," Gary said. "We may require a few hours to establish—"

"I am hoping you can make an exception." Gillis

handed Gary a leather-bound passbook and a passport.

Gary opened the book, glanced to Gillis, then back to the book.

"Do you have a numbered code . . . Mr. Anderson?"

Gillis removed a gold fountain pen from a jacket pocket. Gary handed him a blank card embossed with Binion's corporate logo. Gillis wrote a series of numbers. Gary entered them into his phone, which emitted one sharp ding.

Again, he met Gillis's gaze. "What figure can we assign to your marker?"

"One million," Gillis said.

"Very good, sir. We'd be pleased if you would allow us to place your luggage in our presidential suite?"

"That is quite generous," Gillis said. "Thank you."

Gary's fingers flew over a computer keyboard. He stared expectantly toward a closed door. Moments later, a stunning woman dressed in business attire appeared.

She smiled. "Mr. Anderson?"

Gillis answered with a slight bow.

"Here is your marker. Simply inform the cage how much cash you wish to withdraw. Your marker automatically records any transaction."

She handed him a black, plastic-looking rectangle, slightly larger and thicker than a credit card, also embossed with the Binion's logo. "If you will place your thumb here," she said, pointing to a rounded depression. "This secures your marker. We do not record your thumb print in any fashion. When you wish to end your stay, simply inform a cashier to deactivate the marker. Your funds will be automatically transferred to your original account. You may dispose of the device by placing it in any liquid. Once deactivated, moisture will dissolve it."

As they returned to the casino floor, Elvin said, "I assume when you said *one million,* you meant dollars?"

"Euros."

"And the presidential suite? That's a nice perk. I've been comped rooms before, but nothing like that."

"Alas," Gillis said, "we will not have time to stay."

"So, what's your plan?" Elvin asked.

"What are the best odds in the casino for a single bet?" Gillis asked.

"None are very good. But on your come-out roll in craps, you have a slight advantage over the house."

Gillis smiled. "Then craps it shall be."

"Do you understand how the betting works?" Elvin asked as they approached a long rectangular table surrounded by fifteen other players.

"I have read books," Gillis said. "I assume you will warn me if I commit a faux pas."

"Well, I'm no expert," Elvin said. "I only play craps with house money—that means when I'm ahead at blackjack— and I need a break. You're gambling when you play this game."

"And you are not gambling when you play blackjack?" Gillis asked.

Elvin grinned. "Not the way I play it."

They chose the rounded corner of the table's end wall next to a buxom woman in her thirties as she leaned low over a foot-high rail, waiting for dice to be returned.

"Five. Five. The point is five," the croupier droned.

"Odds on that five," another player said. "And place the eight and the six." He tossed three green chips onto the table's felt surface. A sideman adroitly arranged them per his request.

The woman glanced to her right, smiled at Elvin and, with a Betty Boop voice, said, "I'm on a roll, boys. Better jump in."

Gillis met Elvin's gaze with a silent question. Elvin shook his head no.

The croupier pushed a half-dozen dice to her. She chose two, breathed on them suggestively with full scarlet lips, then let fly. They bounced off the table's back wall and came to a stop displaying two fours. "Eight, the hard way!" the croupier called. His carnival-barker tone conveyed boredom.

Those who had side bets on the eight celebrated as chips were shoved their way.

The croupier waited, then returned the dice, this time forcing the woman to reach a little farther. She gave Elvin a subtle wink, then murmured, "Five, baby. Show me the five."

The dice rebounded to reveal a three and a two.

This group of strangers, made comrades in a shared adventure, exploded in cheers. By now additional players had gathered as word of a hot roll made its way through nearby tables. Chips were shoved across black felt and gathered by anxious hands.

"Coming out," the croupier said. "Place your bets."

"Now?" Gillis asked Elvin.

"You're sure you want to do this?" Elvin said.

"Yes."

Elvin nodded.

"If you please," Gillis called to the croupier. "I would like to place a bet." Gillis produced his marker.

The croupier's brows betrayed a hint of interest. "Of course, sir. What amount in chips?"

"I will not need chips."

"May I see your marker, sir?"

Gillis nudged it across the table. The croupier inspected the marker, then placed it in a computer slot. His eyes opened wide.

"Um . . . how much would you like to wager, sir?"

"I understand," Gillis said, "that a tradition of this establishment is to remove all limits on a player's initial bet?"

The croupier cleared his throat. His voice cracked a little as he answered. "Yes . . . I would need . . . yes, sir."

"I will bet it all," Gillis said.

The croupier paled. He waved at a pit boss, whose attention was fixed on another table. The pit boss frowned at the distraction. The croupier waved again. With reluctance in his stride, the pit boss made his way over.

The croupier whispered, then nodded toward Gillis. The pit boss regarded Gillis, then said, "How much?"

The croupier whispered again. The pit boss's Adam's apple did a little jig.

"One moment, sir," he said to Gillis.

He lifted a phone from its cradle and held a muffled conversation as he dabbed his brow with a handkerchief. A man wearing a suit almost as elegant as Gillis's approached, accompanied by two security guards.

"Mr. Anderson," he said, extending his hand. "My name is Don Wells. I believe you are the guest in our presidential suite?"

The woman appraised Gillis anew.

Gillis accepted Don's hand with a half bow. "Oui."

"Would you like me to clear the table, sir?" Don asked.

"No," Gillis said. "This young lady is on a roll. I would not want to inconvenience the other players."

Word spread like a plague. Games came to a halt as gamblers at other tables craned their necks to see what the fuss was about. Bystanders crowded closer.

The woman said to Gillis, "Geez, Mister, that must be some bet."

"The fulfillment of a dream, Miss . . . ?"

"Lexi."

"Exquisite name," Gillis said. "Well, Lexi, I have always desired to experience the adrenaline rush of a high stakes wager."

"How high?" she asked, eyes gaping, breasts heaving. "Like, a hundred thou?"

Gillis smiled.

"More?" she said.

"Marker plays," Don announced. "One million one hundred sixty thousand dollars on the Pass line."

20

CHIPS FALL WHERE THEY MAY

A COMMUNAL GASP SUCKED AIR from the room, creating a silent prelude to another explosion. Players crushed forward to place bets on the Pass line. A few players shoved chips toward Don't Pass, but a low rumble of growls and threats convinced them to reconsider. Elvin suspected that betting against this high roller on such a remarkable afternoon might inspire a lynching.

Elvin watched the croupier's stick as it deftly guided a half dozen dice through an impossible maze of chips without disrupting a single stack. He shepherded all six to a position directly below Lexi's cleavage, which, only now, did newcomers notice.

There followed another collective gasp.

Lexi stood frozen, elbows on the rail, boobs spilling toward the table's felt surface, as she considered six gleaming cubes.

The table held its breath.

She reached a tentative, trembling hand within a fraction of an inch, then jerked away, as if she'd touched a hot stove.

She turned to Gillis with a dark, imploring gaze. "Geez, mister, I . . . I . . . can't—"

Gillis smiled. "Lexi, *mon ange*, you have been doing a magnificent job."

"But . . . but, Holy Christ. A million bucks? What if I screw it up? Why don't you do it?"

Gillis gestured to the throng packed around the table—eager, hungry eyes were all locked on this still life: *Woman, Breasts and Dice.* "As I understand the rules," Gillis said, "the roll would have to pass from you, clockwise around the table before it would be my turn. Besides, I am a novice. One thing I have gleaned from my research into this game—on which experts agree—despite discussion of odds and statistical averages: never turn your back on a hot roll." He gestured to the dice, "Please. I trust you implicitly."

"Oh, gawd," she said. A tremble in her hand became more pronounced. Lexi touched each ivory cube in turn, as if seeking a message. She lifted two, then checked with Gillis for approval.

He nodded.

She brought the dice to her lips, whispered to them, then checked with Gillis again.

"I believe the expression is," he said, "baby needs new shoes?"

"Fuck shoes," Lexi said. "Baby needs a new Maserati."

She gripped the dice between thumb and forefinger, a four and a three showing. With a flip of her wrist, she sent them arching over piles of chips. They bounced six inches short and caromed off the far rail. One die cleared all chips and settled with a four showing. The other clanked against a stack of black hundred-dollar tokens, teetered at the brink of a three, then made one more jog, settling onto a four.

"The point is eight. Eight, easy eight."

Lexi turned again to Gillis, lower lip quivering, apology on her face. Gillis winked. Don, who had been holding his breath, exhaled a long, relieved sigh.

All along the table rail, players scrambled to throw more money.

Elvin knew odds had just switched significantly in the casino's favor. A seven—the most likely number combination on two dice—would have won Gillis's bet. Now, if a seven appeared before Lexi threw another eight, Gillis would lose.

Shouts of "Place the six! Odds on my eight! Bet the horn!" rang in a cacophony as side men skillfully stacked chips and spotted them on white numbers in an arrangement reflecting the betters' locations around the table.

Lexi waved a hand in front of her face as if to pull more oxygen from the atmosphere while this scramble took place.

Gillis touched her elbow and pointed to her ten-dollar chip on the Pass line. "Should you not buy odds on that bet?"

"Oh, yeah," she said, bending low to cast a five-dollar chip into the mêlée. "And, Stanley," she said to the nearest side man, "place the six for me?"

He grinned as she flipped another red chip. "You got it, Lex."

The croupier presided over six dice below him with grim purpose as he allowed this betting drama to play out. The table settled. He slid all six to Lexi. She chose her weapons, whispered her message and executed a graceful underhand toss.

"Nine," the croupier said. "Center field, nine."

The table gasped, cursed, cheered. The riot resumed. Chips flew, sidemen worked with absolute concentration. Don relaxed a little more. Lexi checked over her shoulder, as if seeking a place to hide.

As the chaos settled and the croupier began his ceremony, Elvin asked, "What's your table limit on proposition bets?"

"One thousand dollars," the croupier said.

Elvin reached for his wallet and counted out ten hundred-dollar bills. "Thousand-dollar yo, please."

"Thousand-dollar yo," the croupier repeated as he pulled Elvin's bills toward him. He folded them into a cash box, then reached to place ten black chips over an image of two dice showing six and five.

Gillis regarded Elvin with surprise. "Do I understand correctly? You are betting a thousand dollars that the next roll will be an eleven?"

Elvin shrugged. "The payoff is thirty-two to one," he said, nodding toward numbers below his black chips.

"You said you do not gamble."

"If ever there was a time to start, this is it. I sense magic in Lexi."

Lexi brightened. "Yeah," she said. "*Yeah*." She plucked a green chip from her stash. "Twenty-five-dollar yo for me, too, Stanley."

She rewarded Stanley with a flash of cleavage as she tossed her chip.

A new flurry erupted as bets rained onto eleven.

Lexi appeared to relax. Her decision regarding the dice was swift and definitive. She smiled during her whispered conversation, encouraged them further with a kiss, then launched.

"YO-LEVEN," shouted the croupier as two dice resolved themselves into a six and a five.

Elvin witnessed a celebration similar to the Times Square announcement of Japan's surrender. People cheered. Strangers hugged. Other games came to a standstill as players at less interesting tables gawked at these festivities.

Don stepped to Elvin's side, making a notation in a small leather-bound notebook.

"Congratulations, sir. The payoff will be thirty-two thousand dollars. We'll meet you at the cashier's office, although I could give you five thousand in chips if you wish to continue playing."

"No problem," Elvin said. "We can settle up when my friend wins his bet."

Don attempted another smile. This one limped a little.

Another scramble to jump onto Lexi's roll ensued.

The croupier guarded his half-dozen dice, reminding everyone, "The point is eight, easy eight."

"Five hundred dollars the hard way," Elvin said, betting that if Lexi hit her point on this roll, the result would be two fours rather than five and three.

A sideman placed five black chips on an image of two fours. Don made another notation in his notebook.

Lexi chose her dice, whispered, brushed them with her lips, gave Gillis a wink and made the throw.

They barely reached the table's far wall. Lexi's favored landing spot was now cluttered with chips. One rebounding die gave a stack of green chips a glancing blow, finally coming to rest showing a five.

In the betting confusion, a gambler had made a last second decision to double his Pass Line wager, resulting in a precarious tower. Under normal circumstances, a sideman would have reached to split this stack in half, then straighten both stacks to secure their foundation. Before he could react though, the dice were on their way.

Don and the croupier gave a cry of horror as the second die struck one chip tower, ricocheted low off the wall and rebounded into the teetering stack. Their dread was amplified when this stack collapsed, obscuring the single white cube beneath.

A few eager hands reached toward the pile.

"Keep your hands on the other side of the rail!" the croupier shouted in a tone threatening executions. "All bets must remain in place!"

Don shouted, "Security!"

A half dozen more men in black uniforms with microphones on their right shoulders began to work their way through the crowd.

"Oh, crap," said Lexi. She turned to Gillis. "Jeepers, I'm sorry, mister. I didn't mean to—"

"Of course, you didn't, my dear." Gillis turned to Don. "Do we have a problem?"

"Let me make a call," Don said.

The crowd parted to allow Don room for a muted phone conversation, then closed ranks again to hear his verdict.

"Mr. Anderson," he said to Gillis, "you may nullify this roll and the young lady can roll again. Or you may take the results of *this* roll. Your choice."

"What about me?" a voice whined. "I've got money bet here, too."

"How much is your bet, sir?" Don asked.

The complainant, his voice less assertive, mumbled something.

"I didn't get that," Don said. "You'll have to speak up."

"A hundred dol—"

A chorus of groans drowned out his answer.

Don said, "Sir, the other gentleman's wager is larger than yours. Stanley, give this gentleman a black chip so he can be on his way."

As the humiliated player slunk away, Elvin stared at the five showing on a single die.

Gillis nodded and turned to Lexi. "Tell me, *mon bijou*, is there a three showing under those chips? Your gut feeling?"

Lexi's full red lips formed a small *O*, but her eyes didn't waver as they met Gillis's. "Yeah, mister. I think so."

Gillis offered a gracious nod and pointed to the pile. "S'il vous plaît."

Don nodded to Stanley, who left his post on the table's opposite side and shouldered his way into the crowd. Don accompanied him, calling to Gillis, "Would you care to join us?"

Gillis consulted Lexi with a probing smile.

"Don't do it, mister. That might jinx it. We gotta stay where we are."

Gillis checked with Elvin.

"What she said," Elvin responded.

"Go ahead," Gillis called to Don. He and Lexi locked eyes in a silent agreement kent not to watch.

Meticulously, Stanley removed one chip at a time. As other players crowded to see, Don warned, "Please stay back." He pointed to the ceiling. "The camera must have a clear view."

Gillis and Lexi still held each other's gaze when Stanley announced, "Eight, easy eight. Pay the front line!"

As the crowd exploded in celebration, Gillis said to Elvin, "You lost your bet on the hard eight."

"Yeah," Elvin said, "but God, that was fun."

"Are you sure you won't be staying with us?" Don asked as he guided Gillis and Elvin to a spartan office behind the casino's main cashier's cage.

"Regrettably, no," Gillis said. "We appreciate the offer of your presidential suite, but pressing matters await."

They sat in a plush office on the casino's third floor. Before them rested a bale of cash in twenties, fifties and hundreds.

"So, for a final accounting," Don said. "Mr. Detwyler, our withdrawal of twenty-five percent of your winnings for the IRS leaves you with twenty-four thousand dollars. You asked us to tip the boys one thousand dollars, and you had us give Miss Lexi Loving five hundred."

Don shoved a small stack of wrapped hundred-dollar bills across the table. "Leaving you twenty-two thousand, five hundred."

"And Mr. Anderson." Don inspected the U.S. passport Gillis had provided.

He glanced from the passport to Gillis again. "Mr. André Anderson?"

"My father was American," Gillis said, attempting to soften his French accent.

"This has been quite a day for you," Don said. "You owe

the IRS two hundred ninety thousand dollars which we will pay as law requires. You directed me to tip the boys fifty thousand dollars . . ."

Once the dice issue was cleared up, Gillis knew all casino employees working the craps pit were waiting expectantly for an announcement of a tip to be shared by all. Some big winners stiffed "the boys" without a second thought. Gillis's announced figure drew whoops and high fives from pit bosses, pit crews and cocktail waitresses. Even the dour croupier managed a smile.

". . . which was quite generous," Don continued. "You told us to give an additional ten thousand dollars to Miss Lexi Loving . . ."

"Did her parents really named her that," Elvin asked, "or is she an . . . actress?"

". . . leaving eight hundred and ten thousand dollars as your payout."

At that moment, the concierge entered with Elvin's bag, Gillis's valise and his empty suitcase. Gillis filled the suitcase with his cash.

"You each have received a casino statement verifying your winnings."

Gillis gave Don a subtle smile. He understood that Don knew this was some sort of money laundering scheme.

Gillis extended his hand. Don took it.

"Come back any time," Don said. "The presidential suite awaits."

"Merci," Gillis said.

"We've had a valet bring your car to the Ogden Avenue entrance," Don said, "so you won't have to hike to the back parking lot. Two members of our security staff will accompany you."

Gillis performed his half bow. Elvin waved.

As they walked past the craps pit, games came to a momentary halt as the staff applauded.

Gillis overheard snippets of conversation.

"What's going on . . . ?"

"Those are the guys—"

"What guys?"

"The short one in the hat. He walked up, placed a million dollars on the Pass line and won . . ."

". . . They'll be telling this story for years."

As the valet handed Elvin his keys, Gillis turned to see Lexi. She had a suitcase at her side.

"*Allo*," Gillis said with a wave.

"Hey, you," Lexi said.

"It has been a pleasure," Gillis said.

"You guys have time for lunch? I'm buying."

"Unfortunately, we are on our way out of town," Gillis said. "We have to stop at a few banks, and—"

"Yeah, I figured you might need to make a quick exit. Where're you headed?"

"Honestly," Gillis said, "I do not know. See where the road takes us, I guess."

Lexi smiled her rueful smile. "Give a girl a ride?"

21

SHOULD WE ORDER PIZZA?

Wednesday, 12:30 am

MARTA AND MARSHALL, ESCORTED by Wishcamper and a frowning Secret Service agent, entered a room that hardly seemed presidential.

They'd arrived in Washington D.C. Sunday afternoon and had spent Monday and Tuesday seeing the sights. They'd both visited the capital previously, but those trips mostly consisted of hasty limo rides to and from Reagan International with subcommittee meetings at the Capitol Building sandwiched in between.

They joined a White House tour, then visited the Smithsonian Air and Space Museum.

"How will they ever get the time projector in here?" Marshall said as he considered an Apollo capsule exhibit, Lindbergh's Spirit of St. Louis dangling from the ceiling and an X-15 rocket-plane.

"Hopefully," Marta said, "the public will never learn the time projector existed, so it won't be memorialized anywhere."

During their White House tour, they were fascinated with the historical antiques and paintings. Which is why they were surprised as Wishcamper ushered them into what appeared to be a typical twenty-first century living room in the White House residential area.

A wall clock's digital readout displayed Wednesday, November 19, 13:00.

Senator Mumford sat in a recliner, feet up, an unlit cigar in one hand, a glass in the other. Sheldon Wishcamper stood beside Mumford. President Dobler lay stretched on a leather sofa, his head propped on pillows, stocking feet elevated on the opposite arm rest. A glass containing a golden-hued liquid rested on his chest.

A Secret Service agent increased his frown's intensity. "Mr. President, I must stress once again that I—"

"I'll be fine, Charlie," Dobler said, waving his free hand. "I don't—"

As Dobler's eyes met Marta's, his mouth fell open.

"Sir?" Charlie said.

Dobler recovered quickly. "Um … nothing. You're right outside. If I need anything, I'll summon you."

Still glaring his displeasure, Charlie closed the door behind him.

Mumford stood. He hadn't missed Dobler's moment of shock.

"Mr. President?" Mumford said.

Slowly, Dobler stood, placed his drink on an end table and said, "I know you, young lady."

"Sir?"

"I recognize you," he repeated. "I don't know your name, but—"

"This is Marta Hamilton," Mumford said. "And Marshall Grissom."

"Why do I think…," Dobler said to Marta,

"somehow . . . somewhere . . . you saved my life?"

Marta extended her hand. "Because, you are, for want of a better term, recalling something that happened in the past of another universe."

Dobler opened his mouth to speak again, but Mumford intervened.

"Please, Ms. Hamilton, you've said too much. You've put yourself—maybe all of us"—his wave included Marshall and Wishcamper—"in legal jeopardy."

"Wait a minute," Dobler said, "you can't say that and—"

"As I told you earlier, Mr. President," Mumford said, "I believe there's a way you can be fully briefed without anyone violating security mandates. If I'm correct, in another half hour or so, you'll understand everything."

Dobler turned his gaze to Marshall. "You were there, too. This dream I've been having. You . . . you were on the floor, next to someone who was bleeding . . ."

Marshall responded with a shrug.

"You saw all this in a dream?" Marta asked.

"I don't have any other way to explain it."

"Tell us your dream," she said.

"The weirdest thing is that for three weeks in a row now, sometime between 1:00 and 2:00 a.m. each Wednesday morning, my dream occurs. I'm sleeping soundly when I hear a voice—my voice—telling me to contact Senator Mumford concerning time travel. Then in the background, while I'm receiving this message, I get all these images—including both of you. Until right now, though, didn't really connect—"

Dobler stopped abruptly. Silence filled the spaces between them.

Mumford cautiously stepped into this void. "Yes, Mr. President?"

"What security clearance do you two have?" Dobler's tone conveyed suspicion as he appraised his visitors.

"They are both federal employees who have the highest security clearances," Mumford said. "Ironically, in some instances, higher than yours, Mr. President."

"Then you understand that what I've just said can never leave this room. The president can't be having crazy dreams and visions."

"Believe me," Marta said, "we won't betray your trust. Please, you started to say something about connecting images you see during this communication concerning Senator Mumford."

Dobler took a deep breath. "This vision has only now become clear. I see a man holding a gun. I see you, Ms. Hamilton, throwing yourself in front of me just as this man pulls the trigger. At first, I think you were shot. But your appearance must have spoiled his aim. Someone else was . . ."

"Who?" Marta said.

"I don't—"

"Yes, you do. Who was shot?"

Dobler's eyes opened wide. "Warren Pitts," he said. "Warren Pitts was . . . but Warren died in a plane crash—"

Dobler stopped midsentence. He put his hands to his temples, then balled them into fists and shook his head, as if trying to exorcize a demon.

"Please don't panic, Mr. President," Marta said, her voice calm, steady. "The presence you feel, the voice you hear is your own. Your mind seems an impossible chaos of images and information, but panic only makes things worse. Please relax. Concentrate on what this other version of yourself is trying to tell you."

"It's not a voice this time," Dobler said. "It's just noise, like from a very loud fan."

Marta and Marshall exchanged a frown.

Dobler's jaw dropped, and he declared, "Holy shit! Time travel is real?"

"Yes, sir," Marta said. "But you need to pay attention."

"No. Now the noise is back."

Marshall settled into the leather cushion of a heavy Craftsman chair. Marta took a seat next to it. Dobler perched on the edge of his couch, elbows on knees, thumbs massaging his temples. An antique grandfather clock's *tick tock* seemed to increase in volume every second until it thundered like tympani in Marta's ears.

Dobler dropped his hands. He lifted his eyes to Marta's. "The noise stopped again."

A moment of silent concentration. "Now it's back."

Finally, Dobler raised his right hand. "Enough."

"What's wrong?" Marta asked.

"How do I stop this? This can't be me."

"Let me assure you, Mr. President," Marta said, "the being sharing your consciousness *is* you. Why do you say—"

"These messages come in disjointed bursts," Dobler said. "Bits and pieces. Death Valley and . . . sun . . . second term . . . no context provided. One statement was clear, though. Unambiguous."

Dobler stood slowly. His angry expression became one of relief.

"He's gone, isn't he?" Marta said.

Dobler nodded.

"And?" Marta asked. "Tell us everything you can. In another fifteen minutes or so, you'll forget details."

"Maybe that's the problem," Dobler said. "I must be confusing this message. I . . . I do recognize that this . . . is me, or a different version of myself. But how could I be capable . . ."

His voice trailed off.

"He's asking you to do something out of character?" Marshall asked.

"To say the least," Dobler said.

"You don't have to," Marshall said. "He can't make you."

"What emotions did you sense?" Marta asked. "Was he angry? Apologetic? Wary?"

For a moment, Dobler appeared not to register her questions, then, "Emotions?"

"When you are joined by a future counterpart," Marta said, "you experience a conscious exchange of information. There's also a more subtle exchange, though. You understand not only the concepts being conveyed but also feelings that go with them. Excitement, happiness, trepidation . . ."

"Sadness," Dobler said. "He . . . regretted asking me . . . but he felt he had to. Something in the future somehow justifies . . ."

Again, his voice trailed off. His brow furrowed. "Every time I began to understand, that damned noise intruded. I couldn't follow—"

"Please, Mr. President," Marta said. "You said the last part was clear."

"He asked me to authorize the assassination of an American citizen."

"Why?" Marshall said.

"*Why* was swallowed in the noise."

"Who?" Marta said.

"He didn't say so, but what you said concerning emotion, I felt that he didn't want me to know."

"Any more images at all?" Marta asked. "Anything?"

Dobler gave a little laugh. "A camel."

"Something about the Middle East?" Marshall said.

"Not a camel," Dobler said. "A camel's hump. Hump. Just a . . . Humphollar?"

Senator Mumford sat up straight. "Humphollar? Oh, my God."

"What?" Marta asked.

"Congressman L.D. Justice—the most recent subcommittee member. He was just elected to a second term?"

Marta nodded.

"Justice isn't the name he was born with," Mumford said. "His family name is Humphollar."

"From Mississippi, right?" Dobler asked.

"Missouri," Mumford said. "And he's on our subcommittee."

"This subcommittee?" Dobler said. "Time travel?"

Marta looked to Mumford, who shook his head. "We can't say anything more. You must get those details from your future counterpart."

"So, we have to wait until next Wednesday?" Dobler asked.

Marta said, "No, Mr. President."

"Why not?"

"If I were directing these . . . visitations . . . and I suspect I may be . . . here's how I'd do it," Marta said. "I'd realize that a huge information dump would have both a frightening and traumatizing effect. That you would need us here to offer an explanation before you could handle the implications and process of time travel. I'd hope you would follow your future counterpart's instructions and covertly consult Senator Mumford. Once you did so, and we could be here to coach you through the experience, I wouldn't keep you waiting."

Dobler paced the length of his couch while Marta made her explanation.

"So, when would you—?"

"You might sit down, Mr. President," Marta suggested.

"Um . . . okay." He reclaimed his seat.

"I'd do it . . . ," she said, ". . . now?"

Dobler's quizzical expression flashed to wide-eyed shock.

"Wow, Marta," Marshall said. "Just . . . wow. That is sooooo cool!"

Marta shrugged, batting her lashes. "What can I say? Parallel universes, baby."

Mumford, too, expressed his astonishment at Marta's prescience. "You could make a fortune if you took this show on the road," he said.

Dobler's expression morphed into a frown of concentration.

"Mr. President," Marta said, "let me suggest something. Do your best to mentally step back. Give your counterpart permission to speak directly to us through you."

"Okay," Dobler said, "but I hope this makes more sense

to you than it does to me." He sucked in air then exhaled expansively, as if making a physical space within himself for this other being to reside. Then he spoke.

"I'm sorry I must be vague, but there's a good reason for it," future-Dobler said.

"Here's that noise again," present-Dobler said.

"The noise is to stem the flow of information, things too dangerous for you to know. So, I have to be quick—" future-Dobler said.

"Noise again," present-Dobler told them.

"We need to get in touch with one of your associates."

"Which one?" Marta asked.

"In our universe," future-Dobler said, "we call him the outlaw Gillis Kerg."

"Noise again … no, wait. He's gone," present-Dobler said.

"That was weird," Wishcamper said. "Why noise?"

"When we were faced with sending travelers ten years into the past," Marta said, "Naomi Hu was concerned that the sheer volume of information gushing into a past counterpart's brain might be so overwhelming as to cause mental trauma."

"Why?" Dobler asked.

"Suppose," Marta said, "we are transporting you two years into the past. Your counterpart is a two-year-younger version of yourself. You have two years' experience and history that he does not. The integration can be traumatic until you reach through that flood of new information and explain to your past counterpart what's going on. If you're dealing with a decade's difference in age, though, the flood is five times more intense. So, Marshall had an idea."

She nodded to Marshall.

"I suggested," Marshall said, "that if the mind of a past counterpart could be occupied with something really annoying—we used a song from the *It's a Small World* ride in Disneyland—it could distract the past counterpart sufficiently to ease his confusion. That, along with hypnosis, helped keep a future counterpart from blasting his past counterpart with everything at once."

"And it worked, or it at least helped," Marta said. "Apparently, in the future, we have refined that concept. This noise—initiated by a sequence of hypnotic cues— keeps you from seeing parts of your future counterpart's consciousness he doesn't want you to see."

"Why?" Dobler said.

Marta shook her head, then added, "I really don't like that 'too dangerous for us to know' thing."

22

HUMP-HOLLAR

Thursday

"MARTY VANDERSNERT, HERE. I'm calling for the director."

Marty heard a giggle escape from Sally Bates, the FBI director's personal secretary.

"I'm sorry, I didn't quite get that. "Vander . . . ?"

"Snert," said Marty. "Vandersnert." He swiveled back and forth in his office chair. He hated the next part, but Congressman Humphollar insisted. Marty added, "Let's Make America Stupid Again."

"I beg your pardon?"

"It's a slogan." Marty heard only silence. "A political slogan."

"Ooookay. Um . . . and who do you . . ." Marty knew she was stalling for time while she checked the congressional roster. ". . . and how can we help Congressman Justice today?"

"The congressman prefers Reverend as a title," Vandersnert said, "and he's changed his last name."

"Really?" Sally said. "Most people elected to high office would be wary of such a thing. You spend all that time and energy building a brand . . ."

"Tell me about it."

"So, whom should I say is calling?"

"Reverend L.D. Humphollar."

"You're kidding."

"No, ma'am."

"Hump—?"

"Hollar."

"As in trucking or yelling?" Sally asked.

Marty stood and wished he had a window in his office. A touch of down-home Missouri sarcasm slipped into his voice as he said, "That would be hollar, a valley between two mountains. As in let's run down to the hollar and shoot some squirrels."

"I see. Can you hold for a moment?"

Sally considered telling Vandersnert the director was otherwise engaged, but she couldn't resist. The director had a sense of humor.

"Yes Sally," FBI Director Malcolm Cummings said.

"A member of Congress is calling."

"Does he want an appointment?" Cummings asked.

"I believe a phone call will do it."

"Okay. Who is it?"

"Congressman Justice."

"Did they say what he wants?"

"I'm sorry," Sally said. "I should have clarified that, but the conversation became sidetracked and I . . . overlooked it."

"Sidetracked how?" asked Cummings, his voice expressing surprise at a lapse in Sally's legendary efficiency.

"The Congressman prefers to be called Reverend. And he's changed his name."

"That's weird," Cummings said. "Changed it to what?"

"Humphollar."

Cummings laughed and said, "No, really. What do I call him?"

"Mr. Director."

"Yes, Cong... um... Reverend..." He couldn't trust himself to say Humphollar without cracking up. "How can I help you?"

"I'm trying to find information regarding a fellow who may be on your wanted list," L.D. said. "His name is Gillis Kerg. That's k-e-r-g. Kerg."

"And this request is in relation to..."

"One of my committee assignments," L.D. said. "An extreme security level. I'm sorry, I can't say more."

"Give me a second," Cummings said. He executed a computer search for congressional committee assignments and found that Congressman Justice—the roster still didn't reflect a name change—was indeed a member of a dark subcommittee, so dark even its name was classified.

Next, he entered "Gillis Kerg." A flashing red light appeared in the upper right-hand corner of his screen. Kerg showed up on everyone's wanted list, the charge unspecified. The file noted that Kerg should be considered extremely dangerous.

"He is known to us," Cummings told L.D., "as a fugitive. The charge isn't listed. If you could provide me a few more details regarding your interest—"

"Sorry, I can't, but I'll be back in touch. And let's Make America Stupid Again."

L.D. disconnected.

Cummings stared at his phone. "Well . . . I guess so."

Cummings's phone buzzed again. "Yes Sally."

"Senator Mumford requests a moment. Shall I arrange a callback or—"

"No, no, connect him now." Cummings always had a moment for the senior and powerful. He straightened his tie, then switched the call to video.

"Senator, always good to hear from you."

Mumford was laughing as his image appeared. "That Sally," he said. "She's a pistol. Although I won't be repeating the joke she told me when she picked up my call."

"Yes, she's one of a kind," Cummings said. "How can we assist you?"

"A classified subcommittee I chair is seeking information on a man named Gillis Kerg," Mumford said. "He is a person of interest for reasons I'm not at liberty to disclose."

Cummings smiled. "I'm becoming intrigued by this Gillis Kerg. You are the second caller to inquire about him this morning. I suspect you already know as much as I do. He is apparently a fugitive sought by a half-dozen law enforcement agencies worldwide. I could put you in touch with our people who are liaisons with Interpol, MI6, Mossad . . . the usual suspects."

"You know my investigator, Sheldon Wishcamper?" Mumford asked.

"Indeed, I do," Cummings said. "He built quite a reputation for himself when he was here."

"Can I have him meet with your people. Maybe have these liaisons hook him up with those international agencies?"

"Glad to do it. I'll have Sally make the arrangements. Is this afternoon soon enough?"

Mumford nodded. "I appreciate it. Oh, by the way, would you mind telling me who made the other inquiry?"

"Sure. Another of your subcommittee members. Congressman Justice?"

"Oh, Lord," Mumford said under his breath. Not so much under his breath, though, that Cummings didn't get the message.

"I wasn't very helpful. I didn't have any information beyond Kerg's fugitive status. Is his inquiry a problem?"

"I'm not sure yet," Mumford said.

Cummings, always interested in congressional gossip, gave Mumford a gentle prod. "His aide informed Sally that the congressman asks to be addressed as Reverend."

"Oh?"

Cummings paused for a moment to see if Mumford would take the bait. When he didn't, Cummings added, "Also, he's changing his name. From Justice to Humphollar."

Mumford's brows betrayed him when they shot up, but he recovered quickly.

"And then he said something really weird just before he disconnected."

Mumford limited himself to another, "Oh?"

"He said 'let's make America stupid again.' Whatever that means."

"Well," Mumford said, "L.D. Humphollar is certainly the man for *that* job."

LEXI LOVING

Friday

"I'M NOT A BIMBO."

Lexi peered over her sunglasses at Gillis and Elvin, who'd been momentarily struck speechless when she removed a terrycloth cover to unveil her bikini.

They lounged poolside at the Ace Motel in Bisbee, Arizona, enjoying a mid-November heatwave that pushed afternoon temperatures to eighty degrees while most of the country slogged through winter.

They'd been on the road two days, making their way south, avoiding interstates and traffic. After distributing their cash in a half-dozen banks, they laid low while Gillis arranged fictional identification papers for the two of them—including passports.

He offered to do the same for Lexi, but she declined. "I'm not on the lam from anyone. I'm just along for the ride."

"Do you have a passport?" Gillis asked. "Just in case . . ."

She winked. "I don't leave home without it. I'm like a Boy Scout. You know, Be Prepared?"

"Believe me," Elvin told her, "you are nothing like a Boy Scout."

When their new identifications were ready, Gillis paid cash for a Mercedes GLQ Class SUV with self-driving capability and a hybrid hydrogen-electric power plant boasting a range of eight hundred miles.

At each stop, they took three separate rooms, Lexi insisting on paying for her own. So far, she'd found Gillis and Elvin to be good company. She hadn't figured out what their game was, but they were fun. At this juncture, Lexi was badly in need of fun.

She knew a moment would come, though, when she'd have to set a few things straight. She chose this bikini to make her point.

"Just because I'm stacked and got a squeaky voice doesn't mean I'm dumb. I'm a college graduate. And I won't apologize to anyone for my boobs. Which are one hundred percent real, by the way."

"I . . . um . . . I'm sure we can live without an apology," Elvin said, glancing to Gillis, who nodded his affirmation.

"Well, it's my experience that when guys stare at me like you guys are staring at me, they're thinking one thing—that I'm dumb."

"No . . .," Elvin said. "If I thought you were dumb—which I don't—I'm afraid I'd be thinking a different thing."

Lexi grinned. "Yeah, well, about that different thing? I'm not easy, either."

Elvin had never been comfortable with women. Like Marshall, he understood he was not an attractive man. Their physiques were opposites—his short and chubby, Marshall's tall and lean—as were their approaches to coping with insecurity. Where Marshall shunned confrontation and sought anonymity, Elvin chose loud, brash, obnoxious.

You judge me? Well, try this *on for size.*

Fortunately, nature had compensated for shortchanging them on physical appeal. They each had their endowments. Marshall was a genuinely nice person who possessed the gifts of loyalty and empathy. Elvin was off-the-charts intelligent and certainly smart enough to understand where he fit in this new triangle.

He'd assumed that, in Gillis, Lexi saw a sugar daddy. Elvin felt genuine excitement concerning this adventure he and Gillis were embarking on. He liked the idea of being an outlaw—a thorn in the side of a society that had so often passed judgment on him. He wouldn't let a woman screw that up.

He sensed in Lexi an all-encompassing melancholy, as if life had been an ongoing disappointment. She had moments of distraction from her sadness, like islands in a vast sea. And—quite apart from the fact she was hot as a branding iron—Elvin felt a growing intrigue.

She'd been exactly right. Her squeaky voice spoken through voluptuous lips combined with an audacious set of mamajammas had led him to a swift conclusion: this woman is as dumb as a radish.

Having spent much effort cultivating the image of an inconsiderate lout, Elvin was surprised to find within himself an understanding of her plight, as he realized she was every bit as stigmatized by her appearance as he was by his.

Lexi harbored a story within herself. Elvin felt an uncomfortable urgency to discover what that story was.

Gillis lay on an aluminum-framed chaise lounge with deep cushions. Elvin floated in an inflatable plastic chair with an attached extension for his sunscreen, a Travis McGee novel and a drink—featuring Kahlua, rum and milk—the cocktail waitress called a Dirty Banana.

After she made her speech, Lexi slid into the pool next to Elvin. Treading water, she said, "Lemme have a taste of that. It looks awful." She sipped and made a face as if she'd bitten a lemon.

She waved to the waitress. "Gimme one of those, please."

Lexi ducked underwater and glided to the pool's edge a few feet from Gillis, balancing on her elbows, legs floating free. Her dark red hair, which she wore in a pixie cut, appeared almost black as it clung to the outline of her face. In a quick motion, she used both hands to sweep it back, tight along her head so she appeared—at least from the neck up—like an Italian gangster. She motioned for Elvin to join them. Holding the drink in his right hand, he paddled with his left. The plastic chair turned two lazy circles along the way.

"Okay, fellas, what are we running from?"

Gillis's smile was sardonic. "Are you sure you want to know?"

"Yeah, I probably should. You don't strike me as violent criminals. But you're up to something. White collar, I'd guess. I recognize money laundering when I see it. How'd you earn your ill-gotten gains?"

"I am not sure what my bigger crime would be," Gillis said. "The activity that led to our money laundering or telling you about it."

"Okay, Mr. Anderson or whatever your name is, then *who* are we running from?"

"FBI, Interpol, CIA, Luxembourg's State Intelligence Service, you name it," Gillis said.

"What did you do to piss off Luxembourg?" she asked.

"I used to work for the government," Gillis said. "I resigned without giving proper notice."

"They hunt you down for that in Luxembourg?"

"My situation is unique."

She swiveled her focus to Elvin. "So, what's your story? And sooner or later, you guys gotta tell me your real names."

Elvin checked with Gillis, who shrugged.

Elvin extended his hand. "Believe it or not, my name really is Elvin Detwyler."

She considered him for a long moment before she accepted the handshake. "That, I believe. No one would make that up. How do you know this guy?" She pointed her thumb to Gillis.

"We're . . . colleagues," Elvin said. "We worked together at this place you've never heard of."

"What place?"

Elvin and Gillis exchanged glances.

"Is it one of those 'you could tell me but then you'd have to kill me' things?"

Gillis studied his toes. Elvin shrugged again.

"Okay," Lexi said. "So, you're spies? National security and all that?" The lilt of her voice expressed interest and relief.

"Would that make a difference?" Gillis asked.

"Yeah, I guess. I'd rather hang around with spies than Mafia guys. The Mafia would be a dealbreaker."

From the moment she'd climbed into their back seat in Las Vegas, Gillis had been trying to figure Lexi's angle. As did Elvin, he'd assumed she was with them for the money. But the longer they were together, the more he felt she had a . . . what? . . . a depth to her that surprised him. Despite her easy laughter, like Elvin, Gillis detected in her a pervasive sadness, which made him wonder what *she* was running from.

Gillis enjoyed women, but he didn't treasure them as Marshall did. Take Marta, for example. Gillis lusted after Marta. He admired her skills, genuinely enjoyed her as a colleague—a coconspirator. But he would never love her. The perfect woman, as far as Gillis was concerned, was a pal who would sleep with him on occasion. Someone who would leave before breakfast and wouldn't quiz him about what kind of day he'd had.

He had to admit he enjoyed Lexi's company. Whenever she decided this ride was finished—whether she'd slept with him or not—he would miss her.

Behind black lenses of his sunglasses, he observed this casual exchange between Lexi and Elvin. She wasn't put off by Elvin as many women were. She treated him as if he were just another guy, like all guys, who from time to time looked at her *that way*.

He was half standing when disorientation hit him. He fell awkwardly onto the cushions, drawing a gasp from Lexi.

She reached from her perch at pool's edge and grabbed his ankle. "What happened?" she asked. "Are you okay?"

Despite the turmoil in his brain, Gillis heard her say to Elvin, "Is he okay? Should we call someone?"

"Give him a minute," Elvin said. "He'll be fine."

"Are you sure? 'Cause he doesn't look so good to me."

Gillis groaned, turned so he could settle himself, then raised one arm, a silent indication that Elvin and Lexi should not interfere.

"Glad to see you got yourself out of there," said future-Gillis. *"Are they after you?"*

As always, Gillis required a moment to adjust to the unsettling intrusion of a future counterpart into his consciousness. He sorted through a flood of extraneous impressions and emotions to focus on future-Gillis's message.

"I must assume so," present-Gillis replied. *"I see the projector is still operational in the . . ."* he searched his counterpart's mind for a 1960s television show theme song that would identify this Gillis's native world, *". . . Gunsmoke universe."*

"It is," said future-Gillis. *"Many universes have shut their projectors down and abandoned their complexes, as has yours. However, to our surprise, a few either had no shutdown or have restored their projectors to operation."*

Having absorbed the mental disequilibrium of being joined by a future counterpart, Gillis opened his eyes and sat up.

"How is that possible?" he said aloud.

"How is what possible?" Lexi asked.

"Shhh," Elvin said. "He isn't talking to us."

Lexi checked over her shoulder. The only others in sight were a mom and two children playing in the pool's shallow end. "Some kind of Bluetooth?"

"I'll explain in a minute," Elvin said.

Meanwhile, the conversation in Gillis's head continued.

"Your universe's intrusion into the Gomer Pyle *universe has resulted in a drastic divergence of historical paths,"* future-Gillis said. *"That is the example that most readily comes to mind."*

"Gomer Pyle?" present-Gillis said aloud.

Lexi opened her mouth to speak again. This time, Gillis raised a warning finger.

"He'll be with you in a minute," Elvin whispered.

"Okay," Gillis said. "Elvin is here. You must explain this to him as well."

"This is getting spooky," Lexi said.

"Good to see you, Elvin," future-Gillis said, speaking with present-Gillis's voice. "And this enchanting creature is Lexi? Oh dear, my past counterpart's memory hardly does you justice."

Lexi pushed herself away and paddled to deeper water. "I told you guys I'm not dumb. I'm not gonna hang around here and be the butt of anyone's jokes."

"Please, Lexi," Elvin said. "We'll explain in a moment. I gotta take notes."

Elvin hefted himself from the water and went to a folding chair where he'd piled a robe, a pen and a notebook.

"Okay, go ahead," he said to future-Gills.

"I come to you from *Gunsmoke* where our projector was never shut down. I'm brokering a message from *Gomer Pyle,* which has reactivated its projector," future-Gillis explained. "That universe is no longer in historical lockstep with the others. The deaths of Warren Pitts and Phillip Lucre produced a divergent shockwave."

"Fascinating," Elvin said. "Instead of dropping a pebble in a pond, something we did there created a tsunami. Hmmm. We altered the futures of two significant historical figures at the same time. Maybe that resulted in some sort of exponential effect. Has your version of me constructed a computer model examining the—"

"Yes," future-Gillis said. "And at some point, he may be along to transfer that directly. But the *Gomer Pyle* version of Elvin must travel to *Gunsmoke*, then *our* Elvin must travel to you for that to occur. I do not have to explain, though, the Elvins' aversion to travel."

"You got that right," Elvin said. "So, again, why are you here?"

"I am here to broker a deal," future-Gillis explained. "The *Death Valley Days* universe wishes to enlist your services. Our *Gunsmoke*-Gillis counterpart says your universe owes him one, and he owes *Death Valley*."

"Indeed, we do," present-Gillis agreed, restoring their conversation to a mental exchange. He settled into the cushions. *"I am assuming this is not something we should discuss in front of the young lady?"*

"That is correct," future-Gillis agreed.

"Explain the deal," present-Gillis said.

"Benjamin Dobler asks you to eliminate a United States congressman, whose name is, of all things, Leviticus Deuteronomy Humphollar."

"Did the president offer a reason?" present-Gillis asked.

"I assume an explanation will be forthcoming," future-Gillis said.

"Tell our friends from Death Valley *that I am intrigued, but I require more details,"* present-Gillis replied.

"Is he pretending to be in a trance?" Lexi asked Elvin. "Like one of those mediums? Who talk to dead people? 'Cause I don't believe that stuff."

Elvin shook his head, pen poised over notebook, waiting for Gillis to speak again.

"Ooooohh, I know," she said. "He's psychic. Or telepathic. That's how he knew he was gonna win that bet, huh?"

"Not exactly."

Behind his sunglasses, Gillis regarded Lexi.

"Can you excuse us for a few moments?" he asked. "Elvin and I must discuss—"

"No," she said. "Not until you tell me what just happened. I can't decide if you're sick or crazy or running a scam." She didn't attempt to disguise the hurt in her voice or eyes.

"Give us five minutes," Elvin said. "Then we'll explain everything."

Lexi's first instinct was to leave. Write this adventure off as the latest in a string of disappointments. Pack her bags, find a Greyhound terminal. Take the first bus wherever it was bound.

She knew they both believed she'd chosen them because of their money. She'd joined them, though, because they were nice guys. Not nice like *nice*. But like, not evil. She'd had experience with "not nice." Even a brush or two with evil. She could countenance scoundrels. But they had to be decent human beings. Until a few minutes ago, nothing had raised her hackles.

"Okay," she said. "But only because I gotta get out of

the water. I'm getting pruney."

She pulled herself onto the pool's edge, took Elvin's towel, and felt their gaze as she walked toward her room.

24

A RELUCTANT GOODBYE

"ARE YOU LOSING ANY OF IT YET?" Elvin asked as Lexi walked away.

"No," Gillis said. "But I cannot risk waiting too long."

"Okay." Elvin's pen remained poised. "What's the deal?"

"This offer will be difficult to turn down."

"Why?"

"Because my counterpart from *Gunsmoke* is brokering the transaction and I owe him for his cooperation in handling Pitts and Lucre."

"I guess that means the *Gomer Pyle* version of you got away with it."

Gillis shrugged. "I have either forgotten that aspect of our discussion, or it did not come up through any impressions I had. Either he got away with it or . . . maybe not. The person sanctioning this action seems to be President Dobler."

"Wow," Elvin said. "How would *Gomer Pyle*-Dobler know to contact *Gomer Pyle*-Gillis unless he found out you . . . um . . . your counterpart shot Pitts right in front of him?"

Gillis scoured his recollection of the exchange between himself and his future counterpart. "I . . . yes. Dobler must have gotten access to records regarding the time travel project. He found me. But . . . I cannot sort out details. We can only assume I was not prosecuted. Or if I was, we have made an arrangement."

"You said *Gunsmoke*-Gillis is brokering this deal. So, another universe is involved?"

"I have this image of the Grim Reaper."

"I don't recall any '60s television series starring an embodiment of death," Elvin said.

Death . . . ," Gillis said. "That's it. Was there something called death . . . valley?"

"Yeah. *Death Valley Days*. Ronald Reagan."

Gillis nodded as he stared at the motel parking lot.

Elvin raised a point that had been bothering him. "I don't mean to be so . . . mercenary," he said. "If a bad guy deserves to be knocked off, all well and good. But how do we get paid? We're working for clients from the future of another universe. They can't send us a bag of money."

"Payment"—Gillis tapped his fist against his forehead—"yes, there was some reference to payment, but I . . . I have waited too long. All I can come up with is *cyber*, something cyber . . ."

Elvin wrote CYBER?

"When you made your deal with the other you in *Gomer Pyle* to kill Pitts, how did you pay your past counterpart there?" Elvin asked.

"I did not pay him. I explained the problem. He understood intuitively this was something we had to do for the future of both our worlds."

"Well, I hate to be a killjoy," Elvin said, "but I'm not gonna be an altruistic outlaw. That for-the-good-of-humanity argument won't work for me. I'm not that fond of humanity."

Gillis shook his head again. "As I said, I am sure my future counterpart and I touched on that issue. We must assume a plan will be in place."

"And Dobler wants this guy killed in our universe?" Elvin asked.

"Yes, which adds a degree of jeopardy."

"So, who?"

"I am not sure I got his name right. But he is a congressman—"

"Would you mind giving me a lift to the bus station?"

So intent were Gillis and Elvin in their discussion, they hadn't noticed Lexi's return. She wore jeans and a tank top and towed her suitcase.

"Um . . . are you sure?" Elvin asked.

"Sorry, guys," she said, "but I can't stumble into something blind. I've done that before and . . . it hasn't worked out for me. I'm not in a great place right now. I like you guys. I enjoy being with you. But someone I really believed in—bet everything on—just dumped me. I can't get my feelings trampled again. Not right now."

Gillis took both her hands in his.

"Lexi, I wish we could tell you. But we have two problems with that. If we told you this story, you would trust us even less. And we would be putting you in legal jeopardy."

"Being an outlaw with you guys wouldn't put me in legal jeopardy anyway?"

"She's got a point," Elvin said.

A long moment passed among them. Finally, Lexi shrugged and dropped Gillis's hands.

"Well, I gotta get going," she said. "There's a bus in twenty minutes."

She bent to give Gillis a peck on the cheek, then opened her arms and walked to Elvin. "I'm gonna miss you. You would have been a real trip." She enveloped him with a hug. Elvin wore an expression of surprise.

As she reached for her suitcase, she paused. "Are you guys doing something with the stock market?"

"The . . . what?" Elvin said, still trying to collect his senses.

Lexi pointed to Elvin's open notebook. "The guy I came to Vegas with—I guess you'd call him my ex-fiancé—John Dexter, a Wall Street muckety-muck. I fell for him, but turns out he's a real . . . Anyway, he was going on and on about some company called Cybertronic Data."

Elvin was shocked into sensibility.

"Of course," he said. "That's how they'd make it work. Gillis, we need . . . fifty thousand bucks. Can one of your new banks arrange a remote purchase through the New York Stock Exchange?"

"Certainly, but why—"

"I'll explain in a minute. We gotta do this right now."

Tumblers fell into place for Gillis, as well. As he punched figures into his phone to begin the transaction, Elvin used his phone to search the stock exchange.

"Here," he said, "Cybertronic Data. Symbol is CYDTA."

"Is fifty thousand enough?" Gillis asked.

"Yeah," Elvin said. "Investing in bigger chunks might draw too much attention."

They furiously worked their thumbs, then remained transfixed on tiny screens.

"Did you get it?" Elvin asked.

"Yes. The market just closed. We got in under the wire."

"Come on, guys," Lexi said. "I'm gonna miss my bus."

"Absolutely, you will miss your bus," Gillis said.

"Why?"

"I believe," Gillis said, "the black hole of history has pulled you into our orbit, mademoiselle. I will wager fate will not let you walk away. Certainly not to do anything so mundane as catching a bus. So, even though we will be committing a felony, you need to know what is happening here."

"You'd better sit down," Elvin said, "because we're gonna tell you the damndest story you ever heard."

For more than an hour, Lexi said nothing, only listened. Her attention shifted between Elvin and Gillis as their story unfolded. They'd adjourned to her motel room. She sat on her bed. Elvin occupied the spartan room's lone chair. Gillis paced.

"... then we met you at the casino and here we are," Elvin said. They waited for her reaction.

Several times during their telling of this tale, Lexi believed she had them pegged. They said time travel. *Okay, a scam, but a really weird one. Visitors from the future are giving them stock tips. They're trying to sucker me into giving them my money. But why? They've got a million dollars. Or they claimed they did. I wasn't there when they put the money in that bag. I didn't see them make the bank deposits. But the craps bet? The casino guys would have had to be in on it.*

When they got to the naked part, her alarms went off again, although, *that's sure going to a lot of trouble just to see my boobs.*

Then came murder. Hitmen for hire. *Okay, back to the Mafia.*

She focused her gaze on Gillis. "So, you shot those two guys, just like that?"

"They represented a serious danger to the future of humanity," Gillis said. "I do not regret my actions."

She turned to Elvin. "And you're . . . another Einstein?"

"Truthfully, no" Elvin said. "I'm not in Einstein's league. But then no one else is, either. Let's just say I'm confident I'm the smartest cookie anyone in this room will ever meet."

Lexi massaged her forehead with both hands. She peeked out with one eye. "So, you know the president, and someone wants you to kill a congressman."

Gillis shrugged.

"And this congressman is a threat to humanity?"

"I must research that," Gillis said.

"And, no," Elvin said, "we don't really *know* President Dobler. But I suspect we soon will."

"He wants you to kill—who?"

"That's vague right now," Elvin said. "Gillis remembers Hallhumper, or something similar."

"And you're okay with killing him?"

Gillis nodded. "If he genuinely represents a threat, yes."

"Why did you say that thing about 'history not letting me catch my bus?'"

"Well, you didn't, did you?"

"Didn't what?" Lexi said.

"Catch your bus."

"No, you asked me to stay. So, I stayed. Big deal."

Elvin sat next to her and took her hand in his. "It *is* a big deal, Lexi. It bugs the shit out of me because I can't come up with an equation or an algorithm to explain it. I probably understand quantum theory better than anyone on the planet. I trust science. I don't trust mysticism or magic or religion or any other kind of hokum. So, can you imagine how much believing in something I can't explain pisses me off?"

"You're pissed because I didn't catch my bus?"

"Royally," Elvin said. "We've been at this thing for almost three years. We've accomplished incredible, previously unimaginable things. But every step along the way, coincidence has ended up being a critical factor in our success. You are one more in a long series of quirks that has pointed us in the right direction."

"What did *I* do?" Lexi asked.

"You knew the words I wrote in my notebook referenced a stock purchase. History or fate or whatever you might call it, required you to be here. To pay us for carrying out this plan, these guys from the future gave us a stock tip. If we're right, the stock we bought today will bloom into a hundred-thousand-dollar profit very soon."

"Okay. I told you what your stock was. So now will history let me catch my bus?"

"I understand how hard this is to believe," Elvin said. "Let's perform an experiment. If you still want to leave, go ahead. Try."

Again, she shared an expression of regret. "I'm sorry, guys, and I can't believe I'm saying this, because I'm at a place where I could use some excitement, but I'm also at a place when I need to rescue my ability to trust."

She brushed at the hint of a tear.

"I can't take another disappointment right now. Elvin, will you drive me to the bus station?"

Gillis nodded and extended his hand to Lexi. "*Mademoiselle* Loving, your companionship has been a pleasure. I regret you will not be joining us, but I understand how difficult this must be. I will add a note of caution. What we have told you is highly classified. If you repeat it, I fear you will be in danger, and I will be in more trouble than I already am."

Accepting Gillis's hand, Lexi performed a half curtsy. "Mum's the word."

Towing her suitcase, Elvin escorted Lexi to the Mercedes and held its passenger door open. He pushed a button folding its steering wheel under the dashboard. He said, "Greyhound bus station."

The Mercedes obeyed.

Elvin opened his door as the car stopped. Lexi put a hand on his arm. "I can find my way inside. And I was telling the truth. A part of me wants to go with you guys and see what you're really up to. But I can't. Just . . . one more thing to regret, I suppose."

"We'll see," Elvin said as a bus glided to a stop at the station entrance.

"I have a confession to make," Lexi added as she opened her door.

"Yeah?"

She winked. "I've always been attracted to the smart ones."

Elvin's mouth fell open. He was rendered speechless long enough for Lexi to walk away.

He waited, certain the bus would have a malfunction, or Lexi would get stuck in the ladies' room or . . . well, he could imagine all kinds of scenarios.

Facing the bus's driver's side, Elvin didn't have a view of passengers boarding. He knew without a doubt, though, when the Greyhound pulled away, Lexi would be waiting.

She wasn't.

Elvin walked across the street and approached a luggage attendant, "Excuse me."

"Yes, sir. Can I help you?"

"Um . . . did a woman . . . a really attractive . . . um . . ."

The attendant laughed. He held his hands a generous distance in front of his chest.

"Yeah. That would be her. Is she still inside?"

"No, man. She left on the bus."

"So, she is gone?" Gillis asked.

The disappointment on Elvin's face spoke his answer.

"Do not feel too bad," Gillis said. "Concerning your theory, I mean. Our captivating Miss Loving is probably a minor player in terms of history. She performed her role, and now she is free to do as she pleases."

"Oh, I believe we're all free to do as we please," Elvin said. "Ultimately, though, for some of us, anything we choose brings us to an inevitable result—if that result is significant in shaping history's mainstream. If we choose not to kill this Hump guy, history may do it some other way. But in some fashion, we will be involved. We set ourselves on this path the first time we had anything to do with a time machine."

25

OBSERVING REALITY

The White House
A Week Later

WHEN THE WEE HOURS OF WEDNESDAY morning next arrived, two more celebrants joined the party.

"Mr. President," Marta said, "meet Dr. Gretchen Allen and Dr. Naomi Hu. I feel we need their help in understanding what's happening here."

"I'm being visited by a future version of myself," Dobler said. "That's pretty straightforward. And, with all respect, I'm uncomfortable that we're expanding the number of people who are aware I'm having these . . . revelations. My political enemies will say I'm crazy."

"Gretchen and Naomi can be trusted," Marta said. They would never—"

"Ten years from now," Dobler said, "I don't want anybody writing a book."

"Be assured you can count on our discretion, Mr. President," Gretchen said. "I'm interested in the nature of your communications with your future counterpart. Particularly that they seem brief and . . . vague."

"We don't discuss the weather if that's what you mean. Why doesn't he just come out and tell me—?"

"There's something about the future he doesn't want

you to know," Gretchen said.

"Why?"

Gretchen considered how to answer. She felt probing gazes from Marshall and Marta as well.

"I wish Elvin were here," she said.

Marta laughed. "I haven't heard many people use that phrase."

Gretchen sighed. "Mr. President, I'm reluctant to violate my security agreements. In this situation, Elvin Detwyler would do so in a heartbeat."

"You're saying he's a threat?"

"No. He's . . . impatient. Given these circumstances, he wouldn't hesitate to—"

"Gretchen," Marta said, "we don't have the luxury of hesitation. Something's going on, and urgency is attached."

Gretchen began to pace across the Oval Office rug. "We have all come to believe that, even in a parallel universe, we can't change significant past events. We've learned through contacts with other universes, however, that Einstein was right. The future exists simultaneously with the past. In other words, our future, is at the same time, our past."

She paused and cast a quizzical glance at Dobler.

"I'm following you so far."

"Gillis Kerg killed Warren Pitts in the past—relative to the present we are experiencing at this moment," Gretchen said. "In doing so, we believe all the Warren Pittses existing in the futures of all other universes—unless those universes' histories are dramatically divergent from our own—died as well. But not immediately. As I recall, the Pitts of this universe died two weeks following Gillis's return.

"Are any of you familiar," she continued, "with a branch of quantum theory called biocentrism?"

She met a host of vacuous stares.

"More than just a theory, actually. Prior to the realization of quantum mechanics, science took for granted that the universe formed and, at some point, sentient beings showed up to observe it."

"Are you saying that's not what happened?" Dobler said.

"Maybe. Think of matter existing in a sort of vague soup just waiting to . . . become. We call this state of matter 'superposition.' At this point, all possibilities exist. Then a sentient creature shows up to observe. The act of *observation* forces matter to make a choice. In other words, our observation creates reality—not the other way around."

"Like, if a tree falls in the forest and there's no one there to hear it, does it make a sound?" Marshall said.

Gretchen smiled. "More like, if there's no one there to observe it, does the tree or the forest exist at all?"

"You believe this?" Dobler said. "Because 'observation creates reality' is a pretty difficult concept to wrap my head around."

"That's probably why we don't talk about it much," Gretchen said.

"So, how does that apply to our situation?" Marshall said.

"Okay," Gretchen said, "try and follow along. A traveler from universe A embarks from a point ten years from today and visits our world—universe B—at a point five years from today. That traveler essentially informs his or her past counterpart of events that will happen over the next five years. But here in universe B, we only retain that knowledge for a few hours. When our travelers return from the past of, say, universe C, they, too, retain detailed memory for only a short while. But we hold debriefings, make a record of those things our traveler can recall. When you are on the receiving end of a visitation, though, you typically don't have the presence of mind to make notes. Therefore, any awarenesses regarding details of our specific future are rare, sporadic at best."

"So, you're suggesting," Marta said, "that our future—I mean the future of our universe independent of all others—is not fixed until we become aware of a specific set of events?"

"And my counterpart from the future," Dobler said, "wants us to do something that may rescue his world, but for fear of our universe suffering whatever disaster his universe faces, he must be sure we don't understand why?"

"Yes."

Once again, Dobler attempted to stand but wobbled, then fell back onto the sofa. His eyes searched the room, then closed tight. Perspiration bloomed on his forehead.

"Mr. President?" Marta said.

Naomi hurried to his side, placing a hand on his shoulder.

"What's his message?" Marta asked as Marshall handed Dobler a tumbler of water.

"I . . . I don't . . ."

"Yes, you do, sir," Marta said, her tone insistent.

Dobler spoke the words with singularity. "Protect. Janice. Beauchamp."

"Who is Janice Beauchamp?" Marta asked.

"She's a local District of Columbia judge," Dobler said. "I recently nominated her to the D.C. Federal Court of Appeals."

"Why would . . . ," Marta began.

"I don't know," Dobler said. "But there's more. He also repeated that we should 'kill Congressman Humphollar.'"

"Does Judge Beauchamp have a protection detail?" Marta asked.

"No. I'll call the Secret Service and have someone—"

"We can't do that," Marta said. "You could never explain your foreknowledge. We must keep you out of it. Where can we find her?"

Dobler placed a call arranging for Marshall, Marta, Naomi and Gretchen to use a White House motor pool vehicle. Marta programmed Judge Beauchamp's address into the Caddy's navigation system.

26

THE JUDGE

That Same Early Morning
Another part of Washington D.C.

"SOMEBODY WANTS US TO KILL A JUDGE?" Elvin asked.

He and Gillis occupied a motel room located in a rough Washington, D.C. neighborhood.

"The exchange was cryptic," Gillis said. "They are using masking noise again. I got a blast of noise, then the judge's name, another blast, '*kill her ASAP*,' more noise, then '*one million dollars.*' Finally, an address. Why all the drama? Why didn't my future counterpart simply have a conversation with me?"

Uh-oh, Elvin thought, then added aloud, "They—whoever they are—got to either my future counterpart or Gretchen's. When things shut down, we were studying a hypothesis . . ."

Gillis waited. And waited. "Elvin?" he finally prodded.

"The space-time relationship between past and future," Elvin said. "Can the future alter the past? Based on our experience, the answer would be no. But that implies there are no choices. Because, in the fabric of space-time, future and past exist simultaneously. Which implies that our future will always be someone else's past. That would mean everything is already written, fixed in history."

"But all futures are not the same," Gillis said. "Historical paths of different universes diverge with time travel, sometimes dramatically."

"So, somehow, that has to be accounted for. That's what Gretchen and I were working on. We were well on our way to showing that our future—the future of this world and the future of the world with which we are communicating through time travel—is not fixed until a past counterpart is made aware of that future."

"You are telling me they want us to assassinate the judge," Gillis said, "but that action would only accomplish their purpose if we do not know why?"

"Yes."

"And you believe this is true?"

"I'm undecided," Elvin said. "We hadn't gotten that far. But the future-Gillis who contacted you believes so."

Gills sat on one of the room's twin beds.

"Then how do we evaluate this?" Elvin said.

"What do you mean?"

"We've come to an agreement that we'll only carry out these hits if we're convinced we're eliminating a monster." He signed into his pocket computer. Janice Beauchamp's profile flashed into a three-dimensional display before them. "Nothing monstrous here," Elvin said. "She has an outstanding record of judicial independence. No hints of scandal. She's President Dobler's nominee for the D.C. Circuit Federal Court of Appeals. She appears to be a good person."

"Good people might eventually do monstrous things," Gillis said.

"Yeah, but—"

"Given what you have suggested," Gillis said, "your future counterpart, or Gretchen's future counterpart, or both, would be advising my future counterpart in this scheme. I cannot imagine Gretchen countenancing assassination if it is not justified."

Elvin contemplated Gillis's assertion. Theoretical debates he and Gretchen shared as they formulated their theory were beyond the understanding of most people. Even if someone else had stumbled onto it, they wouldn't know what they were seeing. Still . . .

"The instructions said ASAP."

"So, you're gonna do it?" Elvin asked.

Gillis shrugged.

"I can't go along," Elvin said.

"I must at least check this out," Gillis said. "I have an idea for an alternate plan. I will talk with the judge."

Gillis opened his bag, withdrew his Walther PPK, ammunition clip and silencer.

"You're sure about this?" Elvin asked. "Should I—?"

"If I need you, I will call."

Gillis had been gone forty-five minutes when there came a knock at the hotel room door. Elvin breathed a sigh of relief. He answered and said, "Gillis, I'm glad you reconsidered. I don't—Lexi? What are *you* doing here?"

Breathless, Lexi searched past Elvin to confront an otherwise empty room. "Oh, no," she said. "He's already gone, isn't he?"

"You mean . . . Gillis?" Elvin asked.

"We're too late." She sat on the bed and began to cry.

The clock in Janice Beauchamp's Georgetown living room said 2:17 a.m. as Gillis pulled on latex gloves. He tiptoed toward a hall where orchestral music spilled through a doorway. In his right hand he carried his pistol, its silencer affixed.

He flattened himself against the wall, then peered carefully into Janice's kitchen. She sat with her back to him on a stool, her elbows resting on a raised counter, an open ice cream carton next to her. Her attention was fixed on a document as she dipped a spoon into the carton. On its trajectory to her mouth, the spoon stopped. Something she read commanded her full attention. A fat dollop splatted onto her paper.

"Oh, crap," Janice said. She used her T-shirt to dab at a wet stain spreading across the page.

Gillis took a deep breath, lowered the Walther to his hip and slipped silently through the doorway. His presence caused Janice to stiffen.

She turned.

"Damn," she said, staring hard at Gillis. "I'd hoped her warning was just a dream."

"Her? Your future counterpart?" Gillis couldn't hide his shock.

"Future counterpart? That's an interesting way of putting it. You're saying time travel is real?" Her voice trailed off as her eyes dropped to Gillis's gun. A tear traced its path down her cheek.

"I did so want to be on the appeals court," she said, lowering her chin to her chest.

"In the Washington, D.C. circuit?" Gillis asked.

"President Dobler's office notified me a few days ago.

They'll announce my nomination next week. Or, I guess, they would have."

"Did your future counterpart tell you why they want me to do this?" Gillis asked.

"It didn't make sense," Janice said.

"Tell me."

"I'm in the way of something," she said. "Something called a . . . hump . . . hauler?"

"If your court appointment is the issue," Gillis said, "we might find a different solution."

"An alternative to . . . ," Janice asked.

Gillis shrugged.

"Will it . . . hurt?" Janice nodded to Gillis's gun.

"No."

Janice swiveled her stool to face him.

"We might have some . . . wiggle room," Gillis said. "I gather their goal is to keep you from serving on any higher courts. Would you be willing to withdraw your name? Is there a secret scandal in your past that would justify such a withdrawal? Something I would feel assured would keep you from changing your mind?"

Gillis realized that by this point in the vetting process, Dobler's people probably knew every detail of Beauchamp's past. She surprised him.

"As a juvenile," she said, "I . . . I ran over a woman who was walking along a rural highway. I'd been drinking. I didn't stop to check on her. I drove home and told my father. He fixed it for me. He never told me how. I wasn't arrested. It all just went away."

She buried her face in her hands and sobbed.

"Who was she?" Gillis asked.

Janice shrugged. "No one reported her missing. I'm guessing she was homeless or running from something. I've been haunted all my life, waiting for this other shoe to drop."

"Write down time, place, other details," Gillis said, nodding toward a yellow legal pad next to the file Janice had been reading.

As she wrote, her tears stained the page. "I never drank again. I've tried ever since, in every way, to make my life count for something . . ."

As Gillis stepped forward to take the legal pad, his brain exploded with sounds of cats screeching at an impossible decibel level. The sound multiplied until it became his whole world. He couldn't muster enough strength to move as a crushing wall of noise robbed him of perception.

For an instant it stopped. But the interval was so brief, Gillis registered only a flash of light and color. Then, sound blared again. As this cacophony faded, Gillis realized his eyes were squeezed shut. He dreaded opening them.

Do not look, he warned himself. *Just go.*

Gillis did look, though.

He remained standing, still holding the Walther. He detected the wafting smell of gunpowder. Only a few feet away, Janice Beauchamp lay clutching her legal pad. Blood leaked from a dot in her forehead and flowed freely onto gray tile through an exit wound.

Rather than entangle himself with guilt or regret, Gillis bent over Janice to see she'd written a time, a place, a few details, followed by the lamentation "I am so sorry."

He considered his pistol. It had not been issued by

Luxembourg's State Intelligence Service. The Walther was his personal weapon, his homage to Ian Fleming. No record of its purchase or registration existed.

One empty shell casing rested on Janice's kitchen tile.

He found a dish towel, wiped his weapon thoroughly, including its ammunition clip, then opened a sliding glass door leading from Janice's kitchen to a patio. He pressed the pistol into her right hand, then fired a shot into the darkness beyond.

Gillis placed its sound suppressor in his jacket pocket, found and pocketed the second shot's ejected shell casing, leaving its mate near Janice's body. He removed the Walther's clip, replaced the second bullet, then laid his pistol a few inches from Janice's hand.

As he debated what to do about the ice cream, Janice's doorbell rang.

Gillis slipped out the sliding doors.

Marta waited two minutes before ringing the doorbell a second time.

"She's probably asleep," Marshall said.

"Yeah," Marta said. She rang again.

She'd instructed Gretchen and Naomi to wait in the car, but when no one had answered the doorbell's summons after several minutes, Naomi joined them.

Marshall reached a tentative hand. Under the pressure of his fingers, Janice's door swung open.

"Don't touch anything else," Marta said.

She noticed an alarm control, its keypad blinking. "Somebody disabled the security system."

They heard music. Light glowed from a doorway down a hall.

Marta motioned for them to follow.

She leaned into the kitchen.

"Bollocks," she said. "We're too late."

Naomi hurried to the body and knelt carefully, avoiding the pool of blood. She reached a finger to Janice's carotid artery, already knowing that the judge was beyond help.

"Do you see any injury other than a gunshot wound?" Marta asked.

"I can't examine her closely without disturbing the scene," Naomi said. "But, no. Nothing is readily apparent."

Marshall contorted himself so he could read a yellow sheet of paper laying on Janice's torso.

"A suicide note," he said.

"No," Marta said.

Naomi agreed. "If she shot herself, I would expect to find a contact wound. But I see no obvious burning of skin around the entry point. The shot was fired from at least a foot away. I'm no forensics expert, but people don't shoot themselves holding the gun a foot away."

"I also see problems with the scene," Marta said. "How many people kill themselves while eating ice cream from the carton?"

Melting ice cream was beginning to ooze onto the counter.

"So, who should we call?" Marshall asked.

"No one," Marta said.

"We must be sure no one else is injured and in need of help." Naomi said.

"No," Marta said. "Too risky. We can't be linked to this scene. An appeals court nominee's death will be the biggest news in town."

"I . . . I . . . can't just walk away, Marta," Naomi said. "My medical oath requires me to make sure—"

"Then take that towel. Wipe everything you touch. If you find anyone, though, we'll leave you here. You'll have to create some plausible reason for stumbling onto the scene."

Naomi nodded and set off in search of stairs.

"Don't turn on any lights," Marta called after her.

As Marshall watched her go, he said, "Still might be a suicide."

"No, Marshall." She pointed. "That's Gillis's gun."

Naomi returned. "No one," she said.

They left in darkness and returned to the SUV where Gretchen waited. She nodded to a flashing green light on the vehicle's dashboard. "I don't know how to answer that thing, but someone has a phone call."

"Must be Dobler," Marta said.

She removed her own phone from her jacket pocket and tapped key codes to sync it with the car's communications system.

"Yes, Mr. President?" she said.

"No, Marta," Gillis said. "We must talk."

27

THE AMBUSH

"I WON'T ALLOW YOU TO MEET GILLIS without me," Marshall said. "He murdered that woman."

"Okay," Marta said.

"I know you think I'll be a liability, that I can't—"

"I said, okay, Marshall. You can come."

"I can?"

Marshall had braced himself for an argument. He had no training. He would be a distraction. He would trip and fall over something at a critical moment, and they would all die.

"Did Gillis tell you to come alone?"

"He did."

"But you're not?"

"Are you crazy?" Marta said. "Of course not. You're coming with me."

"Do I need a gun or a knife or something?"

"Under no circumstances," Marta said, "will you have a gun or a knife."

"Why not?"

"Because I don't want to be shot or stabbed."

"Gillis will have a gun."

"I have every confidence Gillis can hit what he's aiming at."

"Okay, what if he's aiming at you?"

"We'll burn that bridge when we come to it," she said.

The White House
A Few Hours Later

"Oh, my God," Dobler said. "Oh, my God." He collapsed into his desk chair. "Janice's murder was directed from the future?"

"Yes, Mr. President," Marta said.

"So . . . who?"

"You're better off not knowing, sir."

Marta glanced at a clock on the president's desk. "It's almost 4:00 a.m. You'll soon be hit with a flood of media reaction to the judge's death. You don't need the distraction of my theories at this point. We should leave before staff people arrive and wonder who we are."

"And Congressman Humphollar?" Dobler asked.

"You won't be involved in that decision, Mr. President."

Wishcamper greeted Marta and her contingent in the Russell Senate Office Building parking garage, then escorted them to Mumford's office.

"I received news of Judge Beauchamp's death before I left home," Mumford said after Marta briefed him.

"And the message's vagueness is to protect the malleability of our world's future?" Wishcamper asked.

"That explanation would fit the theory Elvin posed," Gretchen said.

"Where is Detwyler now?" Mumford asked. "He needs to be here. We need his expertise to—"

"I believe Elvin is with Gillis," Marta said.

Both Mumford and Wishcamper stared in disbelief.

Wishcamper recovered first. "And where is that?"

"I'm not sure," Marta said. "But I know precisely where Gillis will be in" —She checked the time display again— "six hours."

"Did Mr. Kerg have anything to do with Judge Beauchamp's murder?" Mumford asked.

"That's a strong possibility. He contacted me by phone soon after we found her body. He asked to meet."

"Where?" Wishcamper asked.

"The Madison Amphitheater in Virginia."

The amphitheater was a popular summer concert venue in a rural setting. Benches had been built into a gentle rise cleared of timber. At the hill's base, a slightly curving rock face climbed forty feet high, providing natural acoustics for a stage.

"I know that place," said Wishcamper with a frown. "Have you been there?"

"No," Marta said, "Marshall and I are heading there now so I can get the lay of the land."

"This makes no sense," Wishcamper said. "Tactically, from Kerg's standpoint, it's all wrong."

"Yes," Marta said. "It's a place that would be deserted this time of year."

"Could he be luring you into a trap?" Mumford asked.

"Anything's possible," Marta said. "But I'm not sure

why. He's had many opportunities to harm me."

"If he only wants to talk," Marshall said, "wouldn't it be safer for him if he did it in a crowded place? I mean, we wouldn't go shooting at him with a bunch of people around, would we?"

"No, Marshall," Wishcamper said. "If he were doing this right, he'd choose a busy venue with a variety of escape routes. He'd demand the meeting occur as soon as possible. He wouldn't give you six hours to scope out the place and plan a tactical defense. This setting has probably twenty perfect locations for snipers to dig in on high ground. There's no quick way out. It's like he's inviting *us* to set a trap."

"Which is what we should do," Marta said. "Where can we find a sniper?"

"That would be me," Wishcamper said. "I'll have to run by my apartment and get my stuff."

As they drove toward their confrontation with Gillis, Wishcamper, Marshall and Marta puzzled over the frightening implications of a future enemy tampering with their history.

"Someone believes Janice Beauchamp's court appointment and the death of L.D. Humphollar are critical to the future of their world," Marshall said. "And maybe ours, too."

"Two competing entities," Marta said. "One wanted the judge's survival. Her death delays President Dobler's plan to have her seat on the appeals court confirmed. Since the messenger is Dobler's future counterpart—and *he* seeks Humphollar's death—that suggests whoever wanted the judge dead is Dobler's enemy."

"So, future-Dobler had to be aware that an assassin would be sent to murder Judge Beauchamp and asked us to protect her," Wishcamper said. "At the same time, this unknown entity asks us to assassinate a sitting U.S. congressman."

Marta gazed at the Virginia countryside rushing past her passenger-side window. "Their plan isn't to kill a sitting congressman. Or anyway, that's not how I'd do it. I'd go to the past of the most similar universe I could find, maybe a decade or so. Kill him there."

"Marta," Marshall said, "that's exactly what we discussed—why everyone needs to believe our time projector is disabled. Who has the right to make that decision? If we kill someone in the past—particularly when we aren't sure what he'll do in the future to deserve it—how is anyone safe ever again?"

"And Gillis Kerg has made himself available as a time traveling gun for hire?" Wishcamper said.

"I think so," Marta said. "That's not what scares me most, though."

"Oh?"

"Elvin might be with him. If those two have combined their skill sets in a multiverse Murder Inc., I have no idea how to stop them."

"Neither Gillis nor Elvin is inherently evil, though," Marshall said. "Elvin may be disagreeable, but he's not a killer. As Sheila used to say 'It's not them and us. It's all us.' We can trust our counterparts."

"That was true when we started," Marta said. "Given almost three years of active time travel, though, we have no idea how radically historical divergence may have skewed our futures. Some of our future counterparts may have taken paths we can't imagine. And, keep in mind, these crimes could be directed from years and years in the future."

They arrived at the amphitheater three hours before the scheduled meeting. A side road wandering off into a thick pine forest provided a hiding place for their vehicle. A short hike brought them to an overlook, where they could see a stage some five hundred feet below.

Marshall watched as Wishcamper, who wore combat fatigues in a forest camouflage pattern, withdrew a spotting scope from one of myriad zippered pockets and focused on the distant stage.

"A little over eight hundred yards," Wishcamper said. "It's a clear shot. No obstructions. That cliff wall and this surrounding high forest protect the amphitheater from wind. This is too easy. He's trying to kill you, Marta."

"Marshall and I will walk the perimeter of this rim," Marta said. "A marksman will have to be at the tree line where the grassy slope begins to descend. The stage isn't visible from the woods."

"Marta," Marshall said, "Mr. Wishcamper is right. You shouldn't do this. Let me meet him. He's got no reason to kill me."

"There's something I've never told you, Marshall," Marta said. She took his hands.

Marshall frowned.

"Gillis believes that you are a master assassin hiding in the guise of a bumbling . . . well, anyway, he's often warned me that you might have a secret agenda. He believes you are a dangerous man."

"A bumbling what?" Marshall said.

"I . . . don't . . ."

"Doofus," Marshall said. "A bumbling doofus. Well, news flash. I *am* a bumbling doofus. I'm not a master anything. I killed a guy because I couldn't tell the difference between a pistol and a taser. I killed another guy with peanut butter because I didn't know he was allergic."

Marta shrugged. Incredulous, Marshall turned to Wishcamper. "Do you believe I'm a secret super-assassin?"

Wishcamper narrowed is eyes. "I must admit, Marshall, that possibility has occurred to me. I'm not entirely sure you weren't involved in Raul Hinojosa's death."

"Jason Pratt killed Raul," Marshall said. "I was walking past the projection lab in the middle of the night because I couldn't sleep. I saw one of those big plastic trash bins with wheels stuck on the airlock lip, with Pratt trying to pull it inside. The bin had a lid on it. I wouldn't have helped the guy if I'd known Raul was inside. At the time, I had no idea Pratt wasn't just another janitor."

"Speaking theoretically," Wishcamper said, "if you and Pratt were working together, what better way to allay any suspicions than killing him in front of Marta—in your own bumbling way?"

"I can't believe this," Marshall said. "Marta, surely you don't—"

"No, Marshall, I don't. Not . . . entirely, anyway. My point is that Gillis might have a good reason for killing you. The other side of that equation is—if I'm wrong and Gillis is right—I don't want *you* killing Gillis. We have to find out what he knows about who's behind this."

"When I asked to come with you," Marshall said, "I

assumed you'd argue with me. Tell me I'd be in the way. Is this why you let me come? So you'd be sure I wasn't sneaking through the forest on my own?"

Marta smiled. "Let's just say I want you here, spotting for Wishcamper, in case Gillis takes a shot at me."

"I can use the help," Wishcamper said.

"Come with me, Marshall," Marta said, "we'll let Wishcamper get set up while we scout the rim."

They'd walked twenty yards when Marshall said, "Marta, really. I'm not—"

She stopped, put a finger to his lips and winked. "Dr. Doonaughty likes the idea that I may be sleeping with a dangerous man."

"Here," Wishcamper said, "put this on."

He handed Marshall a baseball cap with grass and weeds sprouting from its crown and brim.

"I don't wear hats," Marshall said. "They make me look goofy."

"Nobody will see you," Marta said. "That's the whole idea behind the hat."

She turned to Wishcamper. "If I point at him. . ."

Wishcamper nodded.

"Be careful," Marshall called.

She covered a hundred yards then waited, lying prone just inside the tree line, until a figure stepped from the forest a hundred yards to her right and hiked to the stage. She put a spotting scope to her eye. Gillis seated himself, legs dangling over the stage's edge.

She walked to meet him.

Gillis stood, arms raised, presenting empty hands. "Hello, Marta."

"Hello, Gillis." She stopped with ten yards separating them.

"I assume you have a shooter?" Gillis asked.

"Yes," Marta said. "I assume you do, as well?"

"No," Gillis said.

"Are you armed?"

"No."

"Why not? Why this place? If indeed you're alone, you have no chance of escape."

Gillis lowered his hands. "Once again, I leave my fate to your judgment."

They stared at each other for a long moment.

Marta broke the silence. "Did you kill her?"

"That is what frightens me more than you could imagine. I am pretty sure I did."

Holding his breath, Marshall watched through his spotting scope as Gillis stood at Marta's approach.

"Distance?" Wishcamper asked.

They lay among a stand of yellow grass.

"Um . . . seven hundred and eighty-nine," Marshall said.

Wishcamper clicked a dial on his scope. "Wind?"

Marshall checked a meter Wishcamper had provided and read from its screen: "Two, northeast."

"Got it."

"What was that thing Marta said about pointing?" Marshall asked.

"If she points, I take him."

"Oh."

They watched as Gillis lowered his arms. He gestured as he spoke, then resumed his seat. Marta sat beside him.

"Oh, don't do that," Wishcamper said with a note of disgust.

"What's wrong?" Marshall asked. "She's sitting on the other side of him. You can still shoot him if he tries anything."

"Marshall," Wishcamper said, "this is a really big rifle with a high velocity bullet. If I shoot Kerg, the round will go through both of them. She's making sure I *don't* shoot him."

"Um . . . isn't that a good thing?"

Gillis and Marta rose together and began climbing toward them.

"I guess we'll find out," Wishcamper said.

28

A FUNDAMENTAL FUTURE

"I MADE A HUGE MISTAKE," GILLIS SAID. "I wanted to meet her. To evaluate who this request came from and why. I had no intention of harming her."

"Why did you bring a gun?" Wishcamper asked.

"I was not sure what situation I would be walking into."

They gathered in Mumford's office. Their drive from Virginia put them in Washington, D.C. late, almost midnight.

Naomi listened as Gillis described the invasion of his consciousness.

"A sound, so loud it made my teeth hurt. But more than volume. Grating, screeching, untuned stringed instruments screaming in different keys. And anger. Driven by anger. So deep into my brain's core that thought or analysis was impossible."

"Lasting how long?" Naomi asked.

"It seemed an eternity, although, probably seconds at most. Then a flicker of relief, again, an instant. A repetition of the sonic assault. I momentarily lost consciousness. Then nothing."

"And at some point, you shot her?" Wishcamper's voice bristled with skepticism.

"I have no other explanation," Gillis said." As we talked, I noted a digital clock on . . . it must have been her stove. This whole thing played out in three minutes or so. No time for a physical intruder to come and go."

Mumford's desk intercom interrupted. "Senator, a man at the security station says he has an appointment?"

"A little late for appointments, don't you think?" Mumford asked.

"Yes, sir. He says his name is Elvin Detwyler and—"

"Show him up."

Wishcamper turned to Marta as they waited for Elvin. He nodded toward Gillis. "You believe him?"

"Yes. He knew you were on the hillside with a rifle. I've never seen Gillis frightened, but he was frightened when we shared that stage. He said if I doubted him at all, I should give the signal for you to shoot."

"Frightened why?" Wishcamper asked.

"To be used in such a way," Gillis said. "If what I suspect happened did happen—a future counterpart has discovered how to manipulate me without my being aware—what other atrocities could I be used to commit?

"More terrifying than that, though, this means I have a future counterpart whose moral code is drastically different from my own. That is not supposed to happen. This means I do not know who I am. That I cannot trust myself."

"Why did you arrange the scene to suggest suicide?" Wishcamper asked.

Gillis's face went ashen, as if recalling those details for the first time. "I . . . instinct? Training? Buying myself time until I could understand what had happened, I suppose."

Another knock. Elvin entered, accompanied by a uniformed guard.

"Thank you, Stewart," Mumford said, then nodded to Elvin. "Mr. Detwyler."

"Senator," Elvin responded.

"So, you were aware of all this?" Wishcamper said to Elvin.

"Gillis filled me in," Elvin said. He shrugged off his jacket and blew into his cupped hands to warm them.

"Do you believe him?"

"Absolutely."

Naomi watched this scene unfold while deep in thought.

"I also believe Gillis," she said. "My biggest concern about our travelers' well-being is psychological trauma when an unwitting past counterpart is assaulted by a flood of mental images and emotions as his or her future-self occupies their consciousness. When we embarked on journeys as long as ten years into the past, we mitigated the effects of that assault—and that's exactly what it is, an assault—by combining hypnosis and an annoying song to occupy that past counterpart's attention so all this information flow could be . . . managed.

"What Gillis described is an identical process, only more extreme. An attack on the senses so violent that it blocks everything else. Then an instant's pause in which a past counterpart has no opportunity to analyze what's happening, or to resist. In that instant, a future counterpart acts through his past counterpart's body."

"When we were using the song," Marshall said, "we had to listen to that silly thing over and over so it would be in our heads. Then we did the hypnosis stuff to be able to turn it on and off. That means Gillis's future counterpart had to endure the awful noise our Gillis describes over and over as well."

"Yes," Naomi agreed. "The process would be torturous."

"Here's what I don't get," Wishcamper said. "In order to make this work, they'd have to project future-Gillis into our Gillis precisely when he's talking to the judge at her house late at night. How did they know when Gillis would be there? How would they know, in that instant, he'd be holding a gun? How would they know these people were in proximity to Gillis at any given time?"

"When we shut everything down," Elvin said, "Gretchen and I were learning things at an incredible rate. We've also recently discovered that an artificial intelligence virus is running rampant among the computers and electronic devices. Those mainframes are state-of-the-art biocomputers. They combine highly efficient molecular motors with conventional electronics using nanotechnology. This allows them to achieve speeds of calculation and processing difficult to imagine.

"If you combine that with sophisticated artificial intelligence components, well, in only a few years, those computers would be completely capable of carrying out surveillance required to pin down precise times and locations of people and past events necessary to murder the judge in just this fashion.

"Those mainframes could be downright scary."

Wishcamper wasn't smiling now.

"You need to hear from someone else," Elvin said.

"And that would be . . . ," Marta asked.

"A woman Gillis and I met in Las Vegas," Elvin said.

Gillis reacted with surprise. "Lexi? Lexi is here?"

"She's in the car, probably freezing her . . . whatever."

"Lexi?" Marta asked with raised brows.

"Lexi Loving," Gillis said.

Marta's brows raised higher.

"Yeah, I know," Elvin said. "Just listen to what she has to say."

Mumford dispatched a Secret Service agent to bring Lexi Loving in from the cold.

An awestruck Lexi slipped off her coat as she took in the trappings of a senior U.S. senator's office. She wore a form-fitting black leotard top and skin-tight slacks. Mumford rose to greet her.

"You're really a senator, huh?" she asked.

Mumford smiled. "Welcome."

"Thank you." She hinted at a curtsy, then rushed to Gillis and embraced him.

"Are you okay?" she said.

"Mmmffffth," Gillis said, his face squashed into Lexi's chest.

"I'm sorry I didn't believe . . . ," she said. "But you gotta admit . . . well, you gotta admit."

She released Gillis, then read the expressions fixed on the other faces.

Marshall's mouth hung open a little. Marta wore a bemused smile. Wishcamper wasn't frowning anymore.

The senator's thick expressive eyebrows formed twin peaks. Gretchen made a show of looking away. Naomi maintained her composure. Elvin grinned from ear to ear.

"I didn't have time to change," Lexi said.

When nobody responded, she said, "Yeah, I talk funny. Yeah, I have big boobs and a tiny waist. That doesn't mean I'm dumb. Elvin's told me how smart all you guys are. Please be smart enough not to be so judgmental."

There came an apologetic chorus. Naomi was first to offer her hand.

"We're sorry," she said. "Please, Elvin says you have information that will help us interpret what's happening."

"I . . . *she* got here too late to save the judge. We both feel terrible. We tried . . . but I was so confused. It took me too long to understand and . . . we were too late."

She sighed, then took her place on the senator's couch next to Elvin.

Naomi put a sympathetic hand on her shoulder. "Tell us, please."

"I'm sorry I didn't believe you guys," Lexi repeated her apology to Elvin.

Wishcamper fixed a glare on Elvin and Gillis. "You informed her of the project? One more crime we can add to our list of charges."

"Gillis had a visitation while she was right there," Elvin said. "We didn't have a choice." He turned his attention to Lexi. "What changed your mind?"

"It happened to me," she said.

"You were visited by a future counterpart?" Gretchen asked. "When?"

"Now. She showed up earlier today and told me where

to find Elvin. We were supposed to save the judge."

"She's present now?" Naomi asked.

Lexi nodded. "Yeah."

"Can you step aside and allow us to speak to her?" Marta asked.

"How do I do that?"

Naomi took Elvin's place next to Lexi. She grasped both her hands. "You hear her voice in your head, right?"

Lexi nodded.

"Let her use your voice. Grant her your permission, and she will."

Lexi closed her eyes.

"Thank you," she said, more energized, less frightened.

"Can you tell us which universe you're from?" Naomi asked.

"They didn't say," future-Lexi said.

"Did they refer to old TV shows?" Gretchen asked.

"Yeah. *I Love Lucy* and *Death Valley Days*. But it didn't make sense."

"*Death Valley Days*," Elvin said. "We've never been there. What year are you from?"

"2058."

"You've been here for a while," Naomi said. "You've had access to our Lexi's emotions and memories. Is this world very different from yours?"

"From what I can tell, in this year, 2046, we were mostly the same. I lived in a nicer place than your Lexi does."

"Did you meet me and Gillis in your world?" Elvin asked. "At the casino when Gillis won a million bucks?"

"A million . . . ?" Wishcamper fixed Gillis with another glare.

"Yeah, I met you. But Gillis lost his bet. I hung out with you guys for a couple of days."

"Wow," Elvin said. "That's a helluva divergence."

I'm notifying the IRS," Wishcamper said.

"We paid the taxes already," Gillis said.

"A million dollars?" Mumford asked.

"Euros," Elvin said.

Marta steered their conversation back to Lexi. "So, have things changed a lot in the next dozen years?"

Lexi offered a rueful laugh. "Boy, I'll say. You ever hear of the Christian Fundamentalist States of America?"

29

LEXI'S STORY

LEXI GAVE A DEEP SIGH.

"A lot of this I didn't learn first-hand. Some of it I know because, in a few years, everyone has to read the Gospel According to Humphollar."

"The what?" Marta said.

"Yeah," Lexi said, "you heard right. And some of it I got from you, Mr. President, before we all had to escape to other universes."

"Escape to other—" Dobler said in disbelief.

"Yeah, but, please, let me get through this, or we'll be here all night . . ."

Death Valley Days Universe
August 12, 2050
Here Comes the Sun

God came to L.D. in the early morning hours.

"Here's what we gotta do," God said. *"Write this down. You still got that backhoe at the mansion, dontcha?"*

"You know I do, Lord. But it's sixty years old. If we need

a backhoe, I'll buy a new one."

"*No. Just get the old one in running condition.*"

"Whatever you say, Lord."

"*Good. Go find the most expensive electrical generator you can buy. Then dig yourself a hole ten feet deep and bury that sucker. In the television studio, replace all the electronic devices—especially computers—with brand new ones that are certified to contain G24 shielding. Make sure someone's assigned to unplug 'em whenever they aren't in use.*"

"All right, Lord, I'll . . . ," L.D. grasped another image. He was getting better at reading the mind of God.

"A plague. You're sending a plague."

"*Um, yeah. The heretics won't listen. The righteous will. Right now, I gotta go. You might not hear from me for a while. In the meantime, just keep on keepin' on.*"

Death Valley Days Universe
August 22, 2050

"We have the votes," Kevin Symington told President Dobler. "Victor and Daley have come aboard. Not with any particular enthusiasm, but O'Donnell told them he'd round up enough support for their grazing lease bill. We'd better move on Judge Beauchamp's confirmation before anyone else changes their mind, though."

"Tell the majority leader," Dobler said, "to finish the hearings and schedule this vote next week. I want Janice on the Supreme Court before midterms. If he fights me on this, tell him I'll come to Des Moines and personally endorse Bannister."

Dobler had the obstructionists on the run. A booming economy could do that. America was hitting on all cylinders. Unemployment hovered just below three percent. For two years, stock markets had marched upward in a steady climb. Rather than choosing the typical course of siphoning that prosperity off to wealthy benefactors in the form of personal and corporate tax breaks, Dobler had a different plan. He wanted to reinvigorate America's middle class.

When they put him in office, voters didn't realize they were electing a rare species on the political savannah—in the mold of Ike Eisenhower—a Republican who harbored a social conscience.

Dobler put that plan into motion as he began his second term. Prosperity assured him of majorities in both houses of Congress. His common ground with Democrats made any veto safe from override. For the first time in a long time, the interests of rank-and-file American workers were being served.

Next, he had to attend to the U.S. Supreme Court. Over several decades, the court had evolved into an instrument of political partisanship rather than unbiased constitutional guardian. Dobler saw that trend as the greatest threat American democracy had faced.

Early in his second term, Dobler appointed Louis Davenport—a conservative constitutional scholar who had proved himself fiercely independent of political influence during his federal appeals court career. Republican senators were happy to confirm him. A handful of Democrats who recognized judicial talent when they saw it—regardless of ideology—made that confirmation slide through.

This one, however, was more challenging. This time, Dobler had chosen Davenport's liberal counterpart. Janice Beauchamp—who had cut her teeth as a civil rights attorney before taking a seat on the United States Court of Appeals located in D.C.—scared the religious Right. Dobler, though, knew her to be a genuinely impartial arbiter. She would bring balance to a court that had been skewed by mediocre conservatives who saw their role as protecting white American conservatism, whether it conflicted with the Constitution or not.

"You're kidding," Janice said when she learned why she'd been summoned to the Oval Office. "Why *me*? I'm sure I've disappointed you with some of my rulings on the appeals court. With this appointment you could ensure, maybe, two decades of conservative ideology. What do you and I agree on?"

"I don't want two decades dedicated to an ideology," Dobler said. "You tell me honestly, Judge Beauchamp, what's your opinion of the last three court appointments made by my predecessors?"

"Honestly?"

Dobler nodded.

"Judicial hacks. Lapdogs."

"I agree," Dobler said. "Two Republican appointees and one Democrat. What's your opinion of Judge Davenport?"

"An extraordinary legal mind."

Dobler walked to a window and stared across the White House lawn.

"Just as you are an extraordinary legal mind. My goal is to restore balance to the three branches of government. Where we've been headed the past thirty years scares me.

Unless we restore judicial independence to federal courts, we are teetering at the edge of dictatorship."

"And you're willing to scale back presidential power to accomplish that?" Janice asked.

"The founders' genius was checks and balances," Dobler said "I have two more court seats to fill. One, I'm offering to you. The other will open when Judge Stafford retires. If those two seats go to people willing to damn the Constitution and proceed full speed ahead with their benefactors' agendas, then we're lost. We won't recognize this country in another twenty years."

Janice stared in silence for a long moment. "I'm . . . shocked," she said. "I had no idea . . . your campaign didn't touch on—"

"Because I wouldn't have been elected if it had."

She smiled. "Mr. President, I would be pleased and honored to serve."

Dobler recalled that conversation with satisfaction. There had been angry resistance from extremists in his party. Democrats, though, were thrilled. Enough moderate Republicans were otherwise happy with Dobler's emerging centrism to ensure confirmation.

"I don't know what the majority leader is waiting on," Symington answered Dobler. "He can't afford to stand in our way."

"Given Iowa's political realities, he has to at least appear to try," Dobler said. "But he realizes it's inevitable. Unless he's holding out for divine intervention."

Symington chuckled. He was still chuckling when the lights went out.

The power failure occurred at dusk, so they weren't left completely in darkness.

"What the hell?" Symington said.

"Yeah, let's see what's going on," Dobler said, pushing a button on his desk intercom. The speaker returned only a loud burst of static. Next, Dobler picked up his phone. Nothing.

"Why haven't emergency generators kicked in?" Symington asked. Always before, transition from external to internal power had been almost instantaneous.

Three Secret Service agents rushed in.

"Come with us, Mr. President," said Ron Holcomb. "We have to get you to the bunker until *Marine One* arrives."

"Where's the helicopter taking me?" Dobler asked.

"*Air Force One*. Emergency protocol is to get you into the air. It's the safest place."

"Nuclear attack?"

"We're not sure," Holcomb said. "We'll follow protocol until we know otherwise."

"What do you mean, not sure?" Symington said.

"All communications are out," Holcomb said. "We can't raise anyone anywhere."

"Well, obviously you talked with *Marine One*—" Dobler said.

"No, sir," Holcomb said. "We must assume they're on their way. For now, we have to get to the bunker."

"Okay," Dobler said. "Round up as many cabinet members as you can. We'll set up a command center and formulate a response. And we know nothing of where the attack was focused?"

"No, sir," Holcomb said. "Let's go."

Dobler glanced out a bulletproof window to a grassy expanse with the Capitol in the background. "Wait a minute," he said, pointing outside.

Everything came to a stop as an eerie scene unfolded. The sky had taken on a deep green sheen, touched with streaks of purple. At one moment, the heavens pulsed and throbbed. At another, electric streaks, like blue lightning, popped on and off.

For a moment, they were transfixed by the phenomenon's sheer beauty.

"The . . . aurora borealis . . . ," Symington said.

"But . . . on steroids," Dobler said.

"We have to go," Holcomb commanded.

Dobler's defense secretary, along with Admiral Lydia Tucker—chairwoman of the Joint Chiefs of Staff—and several other generals had already arrived. Secretary of State Arthur Dandridge entered a few minutes later.

"Mr. President," Tucker said. "We need to formulate a retaliatory strike."

"When you can assure me we've been attacked," Dobler said, "I'll consider it."

"I have no other explanation," Taylor said. "We have no communications anywhere."

"A nuclear weapon sets off a pulse effect that destroys anything involving computers, including communications," General Titus Schlinker said.

"Could it be something that wasn't nuclear?" Dobler asked.

"Well … I suppose an electronic device could be constructed that would create such a pulse," Schlinker said. "But it would have to be massive. I don't see how—"

"If we can't communicate with anyone," Dobler said, "how can we give an order to retaliate?"

No one answered. Dobler had a chilling thought. "If a launch team at some remote silo believes we're all dead, what are the chances they would take it upon themselves to launch?"

"They aren't supposed to," Taylor said. "There are safeguards—"

"But if they believe the government has been wiped out, would they be trying to work around those safeguards?" Dobler said.

Taylor and two generals exchanged a worried glance. "I can't rule that out, Mr. President."

"How long has it been?" Dobler asked.

Everyone checked their phones. Every screen was blank.

Symington withdrew an ancient pocket watch. "The lights went out thirty minutes ago."

"If it's a nuclear attack," Dobler said, "why are we still here?"

"*Marine One* hasn't responded," Taylor said.

"No," Dobler said. "Why isn't Washington, D.C. a pile of radioactive rubble. I recall from briefings that missiles launched from China or Russia or North Korea would reach here in twenty minutes. Wouldn't we be a pretty high-priority target?"

There came a knock at the bunker door.

Holcomb drew his sidearm. "Get over in that corner, Mr. President. Behind the generals."

Holcomb appeared to take a deep breath, then yanked the door open.

Between two Secret Service agents stood a small balding man with glasses. He carried a briefcase under one arm and a rolled-up chart under the other.

He waved as best he could with the chart tucked under his arm. "Don't launch anything! It's not what you think!"

Dobler stepped from behind the generals. "Who are you?"

"Wylie Speck. I'm with the National Oceanic and Atmospheric Administration."

"You know who did this?" Dobler asked.

"Yes, but not who. The correct question is *what*?"

"And that would be . . ."

"The sun, Mr. President. The sun."

Dobler had never heard of Wylie Speck but was relieved that someone had, at least for a moment, derailed a rush to nuclear response.

"And who are you, sir?" Dobler asked.

"I'm . . . not anyone," Wylie said. "I'm just a guy who works in the local NOAA office. I study data. One project I work on is our solar storm readiness initiative. So, I . . . sort of . . . recognized what happened. I couldn't get in touch with anyone . . . so, I decided to stop by."

"Are you sure?" Schlinker asked.

"Oh, absolutely. One of our main concerns has been you folks mistaking a solar storm for a nuclear attack when the big one hits."

Dobler gestured for Wylie to sit at a vast table where—

according to plan—top government officials would gather to manage doomsday. Only a dozen were present at this point, though, and they were all on one side of the table. So, when Wylie sat the president sat and the others leaned in to hear and see, the scene resembled DaVinci's *The Last Supper*.

"Before anything else," Dobler said, "will the Russians or Chinese or Indians or Pakistanis launch against us?"

"I doubt they can," Wylie said. "What with all *their* computers fried."

"How long before they get things running?"

"We're okay there, too," Wylie said. "Those folks are all behind the curve on protective measures."

"You're saying," Admiral Tucker asked, "*we* have protective measures?"

"Yes. Some, anyway. We advised three years ago that a major solar storm was overdue, and we needed to instigate basic protections—"

"I recall something—" Dobler said.

"So, we can launch?" Tucker asked.

"No, sir," Wylie said. "Not missiles. Phones. We need to reestablish landlines. Phones will be worth more than all the missiles in the world for the next few weeks. Our newest generation of satellites—all four of them—can be remotely repaired, we hope. As well as some airplanes, helicopters, ground vehicles. Mostly those owned by the military. We've been working on installing shielding technology. We haven't gotten to the civilian sector yet."

Dobler took a deep breath. Could he believe Wylie Speck? But what alternative did he have? He gestured to General Schlinker. "Have you tried calling anyone?"

"Yes, Mr. President. As far as I can tell, everything is offline."

"What's our most pressing need?" Dobler again directed his question to Wylie.

"Medical assistance. Some airliners will crash. People will panic and hurt themselves. Some patients undergoing surgery will die. Unfortunately, those things can't be helped. People need to just stay put for now."

"How can we get word to them?" Dobler asked.

"We have a skeleton system in place to restore communications on an emergency basis. But it's limited. We've had to build slowly because no one in Congress wanted to spend a bunch of money in preparation for a major solar storm. We told you it was coming, but, well, you know how government is . . . um . . . I'm sorry that wasn't—"

Dobler nodded. "Does anything work?"

"Nothing with a computer manufactured before two years ago," Wylie said. "Unless they were shielded under six feet of dirt or concrete."

"Can we do anything now?" Taylor asked.

Wylie consulted his digital wristwatch, which no longer worked. "By now," he said, "our key people should have recognized what happened. They'll be getting underway activating our NOAA communications network. Hopefully, they can make it operational within forty-eight hours. It would have been quicker, but, well . . . funding. Other than that, there's not much to be done."

Dobler summoned members of his Secret Service detail. "We're heading outside to inform everyone we can."

"Mr. President, you can't—"

"Yes, I can. I have to do *something*. Make it happen."

"You'll have to walk," Wylie said. "I doubt any of your vehicles will start."

"Make it happen," Dobler repeated to his entourage. He turned to Wylie. "While they get things organized, I need details."

"Have you heard of the Carrington Event?" Wylie asked.

A host of vacant expressions answered Wiley's query.

"The great solar storm of 1859," Wylie said. "A huge solar coronal mass ejection unleashed at Earth's protective magnetosphere produced a geomagnetic storm the scale of which modern civilization had never witnessed."

"So, why doesn't it have its own chapter in history books?" Dobler asked.

"Computers were nonexistent. Telegraph systems went down in Europe and North America. Simple electric overload. A few operators probably got burned from sparks. And, as we witnessed this time, intense auroras lit up skies all over the globe. But that was pretty much all humanity noticed."

"How big was this current event?" Dobler asked.

"We're not sure yet. Carrington was classified as a 500-year storm. This one is certainly big enough to get our attention, but my guess is, the big one's still out there. If that's true, although disruption to the world economy will be huge, this could be a blessing in disguise."

"Why?" Turner demanded.

"Maybe now," Wylie said, "Congress will take our warnings more seriously."

30

TOLD YOU SO

August 24, 2050
Death Valley Days Universe

THREE DAYS LATER, THE CABINET and joint chiefs sat in a White House situation room lit by Coleman lanterns. Everyone had shed jackets and ties to accommodate the stifling heat.

Wylie sat among a group of mid-level staffers along one wall of the situation room. Dobler kept him around as someone who would provide straight answers.

The air force had located operational generators deep in the North American Aerospace Defense Command's Cheyenne Mountain complex and had flown one to the White House aboard one of a few operating military transports.

"I am told," Dobler said, "the generator installation will be complete soon. At least we'll have air conditioning. In the meantime, let's get started. I need to hear first from the treasury secretary.

"Thank you, Mr. President," Secretary Bea Pervis said. "A working communications grid will be restored in two weeks. But our priority will have to be emergency services and disaster relief coordination.

"In the meantime, the business and financial industries

will remain in chaos. The storm wiped banking records clean. Some small businesses are undoubtedly attempting to reopen. With so little cash in circulation anymore and credit cards useless, there's no way for people to pay for anything."

"The repair bill worldwide will end up being between thirty and forty trillion dollars," Pervis added. "We'll suffer a rough six months before any normal economic activity can resume."

The secretary of homeland security had just begun his report when lights bloomed. A soothing rush of cool air began to flow. A dozen huge video monitors lit up with fuzzy electronic snow filling their screens. They were met with applause.

"That's interesting," Wylie, said to a Health and Human Services staffer sitting next to him. "Those monitors must use organic-based biomicrochips. Apparently, the storm didn't fry them."

"So, we can still watch television?"

"If you can afford a million bucks for a TV," Wylie said.

"Mr. President," the Homeland Security secretary continued, "coordination of disaster relief without communications will present our biggest challenge. Right now, nobody can call or broadcast anything to—"

At that moment every situation room television screen blinked to life, transmitting an image of L.D. Humphollar standing at his pulpit.

"My fellow Christians," L.D. said. "If you are receiving this broadcast, you are one of us, one of the chosen. Like the Israelites who were spared the fate of their enemies during the Passover, you received my warning about this plague that has crippled the world's governments and institutions. God warned me. I warned you. *Our* time has come.

"God told me to remind you. See what happens these next days and weeks. This is where listening to smart people gets you. But today, with God's guidance, we'll begin a new era. We'll Make America Stupid Again!"

Things had been going so well prior to the geomagnetic storm, Democrats had all but conceded the 2052 presidential race to whomever Dobler chose as his successor. In the *Death Valley Days* universe's 2050 reality, roughly a third of registered voters were Republicans, a third were Democrats and a quarter were registered as independents. The remainder made up what Dobler called "the lunatic fringe." Gnats biting at the major parties' exposed skin.

Largest of these groups, two months before the 2050 midterms, was Congressman L.D. Humphollar's Biblical Truth Party, which had been waging its Make America Stupid Again campaign through an ongoing barrage from L.D.'s Missouri television studio.

L.D. sought to elevate himself from the House by running as the Biblical Truth Party candidate for Senate. So far, polls indicated only thirty percent of Missouri voters were taking him seriously.

A week before the storm, L.D. waited for a green light to switch to red. His studio director counted, "Five, four, three, two . . . ," then pointed to L.D.

"My fellow Christians." L.D. said in the most somber a tone he could muster. "I come to you today with a heavy heart. I come to warn you of a rough road ahead."

He bowed so his television audience could see his bald spot. When he peered into the camera again, he had mustered a tear and his voice broke as he said, "God has told me we will be visited by a plague in coming days."

A prompter providing instructions to the studio audience waved a cue card that said WAILING AND GNASHING OF TEETH. Obediently, they wailed and gnashed. L.D. cast his eyes heavenward, tears streaming down his cheeks. He held one hand high. His audience fell silent.

"This plague," he intoned, "is not of God's making, but of man's!"

Congregants were prompted to GASP.

"This plague is brought by smart people. Those who imagine answers lie in technology and science have saddled us with a world reliant on computers rather than faith, upon science rather than prayer."

BOO. HISS.

"And they will be made to pay for their blasphemies. Unfortunately, the righteous will suffer along with them. Now, make no mistake. God could stop this plague. Just as He could have changed His mind about the flood. But then we'd be walkin' around with dinosaurs. Well, we have dinosaurs in this world that must be slain, too. God has finally run out of patience. Smart people won't ever understand unless God strips them of their technology. I ask you to look into your hearts and tell me, Is the suffering we must face too high a price to bring our world back to God?"

NO! and AMEN!

"I will not be able to appear before you again," L.D. said, "until after the plague has struck. In the meantime, you've gotta do something. And I mean it.

"You will recall from your Old Testament, Exodus 12:23, God told the Jews to mark their doors with a sign so their houses would be passed over by the angel of death when He visited His plagues upon Egypt. Well, here's what God tells *us* to do. Everyone listening to me today, go buy a TV set—doesn't have to be an expensive one. Then dig a hole, five cubits deep—that's six feet. Wrap your television set in plastic or some other protective covering, then bury it and place a cross on the grave. This will be your sign to God that you are among the faithful. On the third day after the coming of the plague, dig up those TV sets, tune 'em to this broadcast channel, then wait for instructions.

"Woe be to him who questions the word of God! Let's . . . Make America Stupid Again! Amen.

"Oh yeah, buy all the toilet paper you can."

The next day, several news telecasts and blogs carried a story of one more crazy preacher—this one a congressman and candidate for U.S. Senate—predicting an Armageddon event. Ordering his flock to bury their TV sets.

Two weeks following the solar storm, limited military communications had been reestablished. Business, however, had not resumed. The financial sectors remained in chaos as experts attempted to restore banking records. Early generation communications satellites were fried, but a handful of the latest orbiters had returned to service.

Failure of the communications grid put stock exchanges

out of business. Market representatives argued that all investments and funds should be reset to the point at which the disaster occurred. Congress and the president agreed. Still, the minute markets reopened, they tanked anew.

Economists scratched and clawed to find room for optimism. "Although temporary unemployment will be huge, recovery should occur fairly rapidly," Secretary Pervis advised Dobler. "People will need things replaced. Hiring will shoot up as soon as manufacturing comes online."

A more immediate issue was upcoming midterm elections. In six weeks, Americans were supposed to go to the polls.

"Postpone it," advised Symington. "You've already declared a state of national emergency."

"If I tried to do that by executive order," Dobler said, "the first thing Democrats would do is file suit. Besides, delaying a midterm election in a time of crisis sets the most dangerous precedent possible. We could become little more than a banana republic in which a sitting president invents a crisis every time his party appears to be behind."

"But we aren't behind," Pervis argued.

"That was before we suffered the disaster of the century," Dobler said. "Don't fool yourself. They'll find a way to blame me. Contact all state election commissions. We'll have an election even if we have to reinvent pencils."

The Oval Office intercom chirped.

"Mr. President, Congresswoman Pinch calling."

"Libby," Dobler said, "good to hear from you. Glad you were able to get to a phone that works."

"Yes, Mr. President," Libby said. "You've done an incredible job getting the emergency communications grid working. How can I help?"

"I know the subcommittee seldom meets anymore and the HRI complex remains shut down, but I need to get in touch with Marta Hamilton and Sheldon Wishcamper."

With Senator Mumford's retirement two years earlier, Libby had assumed chairmanship of the subcommittee.

"Marta and Marshall are still somewhere in the Caribbean," Libby said. "I've already dispatched Mr. Wishcamper to find them. He's been hanging around Joint Base Andrews trying to find a ride."

"So," Dobler said, "we are on the same page?"

"Yes, sir," Libby said. "I don't believe for a minute that L.D. Humphollar's foreknowledge of a solar storm was a result of divine intervention."

31

DEATH VALLEY DAYS

October 17, 2052
(Two Years Later)

"Can you believe it? I'm gonna be president. We're gonna win this thing." Senator Humphollar scrutinized himself in a hotel mirror, as if trying to recognize the man staring back.

"We haven't won yet," Marty Vandersnert called to him. "I don't care what the polls say. We have two weeks to go. Don't go getting—"

"Do you have any doubt that God is directing my path?" L.D. asked. "We got in this thing because you said we needed to build a political base. Your plan was to use a presidential campaign to put our issues on the table, and if a few things broke our way, we could consider a serious run eight years from now. Well, look where we are. We're makin' America stupid again. We're gonna win."

"That Marta Hamilton woman is still out there," Marty said. "Whatever plan you had to make her go away hasn't worked. And for the hundredth time, *I'm* running this campaign. Why is she a threat? What does she have on you?"

Right, L.D. thought. *You need to know she's one of a few people in this world who might figure out I'm using a time machine to manipulate the past.*

"I told you before, she's a dangerous heretic. She hates God. She hates America. Her religion is science and she's on a crusade to restore that heresy to its former pedestal. She realizes my movement is gonna reestablish biblical truth as the soul of this nation."

"Yeah, well, how come no one's ever heard of her?" Marty asked. "How can someone with all those internal government connections fly under the radar? Believe me, I've had our people asking around. No one can—"

"She's leader of the Dark State. That secret group of Democrats and atheists who've run America for years. They hide people like Marta Hamilton behind a cloak of secrecy. But God revealed them to me, just as He foretold the collapse of technology. That came true, didn't it?"

Marty shook his head in frustration and walked away.

That Same Evening,
 I Love Lucy Universe

"Yes, Lord?" Once again, L.D.'s call came as he struggled to awaken from deep sleep.

"Listen close. You're gonna win. But the election will be contested for weeks before it's sorted out. Dobler and the sitting Congress will try and hang in there long enough to have Janice Beauchamp confirmed as a Supreme Court justice. We can't let that happen. She'll ruin everything."

"So, what am I to do, Lord?"

"Those slain by the Lord on that day will be spread from one end of the earth to the other. They will not be mourned, gathered, or buried. They will be like dung lying on the

ground."

L.D. recognized a verse from Jeremiah.

God added, *"Find the outlaw Gillis Kerg. He will be the instrument of my wrath."*

One Week Later
Death Valley Days Universe

"You're not gonna believe this, L.D," Marty said.

"Oh, I don't know. Try me."

"That woman judge who Dobler nominated to the Supreme Court?"

"Janice Beauchamp. What about her?"

"Early today, she fell down a staircase. Broke her neck."

"You don't say."

Death Valley Days Universe
2057

"You knew a guy named Elvin Detwyler." Wearing the black uniform of the Christian Militia, Colonel John Dexter issued an accusation.

Lexi had been afraid when she'd opened the door to her former lover. She converted fear to anger. "What are you doing here, John? You're violating my restraining order. I'm calling the cops."

Dexter frowned. "Police have no authority over Christian Militia," he reminded her. "You don't have to make this difficult. I can protect you."

"Yeah? Protect me from what? The God cops?"

Dexter scanned the hallway where he stood. "You can't say things like that. We were in love once. Or anyway, I assumed we were. You're in some real trouble now. I—"

"You walked out on me," Lexi said. "You broke promises. Now you're all wrapped up in a cult that hates women."

"We honor women. We want to take care of women. But the Bible defines a woman's role—"

"I can't get a job," Lexi shouted. "I can't live with who I want. I can't go to the beach unless I'm dressed like a nun. Little girls leave regular school after eighth grade and go to special schools that teach them how to be wives. You're scared to death of women."

Dexter pushed Lexi deeper into her apartment.

"Okay," he said. "If that's the way you want it. Tell me about your relationship with Elvin Detwyler."

"I met Elvin in a casino nine or ten years ago, right after you dumped me. We hung out for a few days. I haven't seen him since. Why are you after Elvin?"

"He's in possession of state secrets. He's an enemy of the state. He's conspiring with Dobler to murder President Humphollar."

"I don't know anything about that," Lexi said.

"We have records of a phone call—"

"He called and left a message a couple of years back."

"What did he want?"

"I got a recording saying his phone was not available."

Lexi glanced across her living room to the kitchen and a butcher knife resting on the counter.

Dexter made one more plea. "Lexi, please let me help you."

"I don't need your kind of help," she snapped. "I need

my life back."

"Lexi, you are a forty-two-year-old woman who has never married. That fact alone opens you to charges of lesbianism. It provides the basis for us to investigate anything. Last year, you cohabited with a man you weren't married to—"

"So much for the lesbian thing," Lexi snapped. "And ten years ago, I cohabited with *you*."

"That was before the Christian Fundamentalist revolution," Dexter said. "I've made my confession to the Clerical Panel and been forgiven."

"Clerical Panel, ha! You mean Inquisition."

"Lexi," Dexter said, placing a hand on her shoulder.

She recoiled.

"Okay," Dexter said. "I'm telling you, though. We're rounding them all up. Hamilton, Grissom, Detwyler, Kerg, Gretchen Allen, Naomi Hu. Anyone who perpetuates the myth of time travel. We're closing in on Dobler. Be careful who you talk to and what you say. There's only so much I can do."

She stepped around him and opened her door. "Please leave."

As Dexter walked away, Lexi slammed the dead bolt closed and picked up the butcher knife.

Elvin sat alone, the projection lab's only illumination an eerie green glow cast by a flow of dark matter and other exotics lighting a platform shaped of plastic polymers from below. He understood what they had to do. He understood they couldn't remain in this world any longer. Their survival would be a total crap shoot. The notion of entering a past counterpart and being lost in a dormant state for—maybe forever, did not intrigue him.

Perhaps an alternative existed. He'd never discussed it with the others, but during his few journeys through the limbo, he had been struck with a fascinating—and terrifying—conviction. He didn't *have* to leave. He could remain in that celestial void forever if he chose to. A tantalizing prospect because in that haven from time and space his mind expanded. He saw answers to everything. No theory or equation or mystery was beyond his intellectual grasp. When his journey ended, only ethereal threads of those answers remained.

He did recall, though, the thrill of knowing.

"Tempting, isn't it?"

Elvin leapt to his feet, his heart racing. "Shit, I wish you'd stop doing that."

"Hey, they made me . . . ," came a response from deep in Elvin's brain, *". . . and it's important. Go to Phoenix, right now. Get Lexi Loving. Bring her here. She'll know what to do."*

"Lexi?" Elvin said to his future counterpart. "The woman we met in—"

"Yeah, her. Now! Their goons are coming to get her."

"How am I supposed to get to Phoenix? The solar storm fried all the—"

"Not the old stuff. In the big maintenance building, there's a vintage Indian motorcycle. The only things electric on it are a distributor cap and a spark plug."

"I've never driven a motorcycle."

"It's like riding a bicycle, only faster."

Lexi leaned hard against the door, eyes closed, for nearly five minutes. She didn't recognize the sound of her phone until its fifth ring. She held her knife in a death grip.

"Listen, Dexter," she said. "Leave me—"

"This isn't Dexter." A man's voice. "This is Elvin Detwyler. I hope you remember me because you gotta trust me. Get some things together. One small bag. I'll be there in fifteen minutes. Meet me in the alley."

"Elvin?"

"Yeah. They're coming, Lexi. If they get there before I do . . . they're rounding up women like you. The result isn't pretty."

"You should come with us," Naomi said. "Pick a world. Hopefully, we can wait this out. At least we might survive when we're absorbed into our past counterparts' consciousnesses. If we die here, we don't know how many other worlds in which we'll die as well."

"No," Marta said. "Marshall and I will try to get to California, then up the coast to Washington. That's where the scientific community is taking refuge. We hope something can be done to bring this world to its senses."

"I . . . I'd like to stay, too," Gretchen said.

"You can't," Marta said. "You, Naomi and Elvin can't be caught. You know too much about the technology of time travel. Sooner or later, these clowns will understand they need science. They'll see what a weapon the time projector can be in the hands of someone who wants to wage war on the past."

Marta, Marshall, Elvin, Gillis and Gretchen had spent three days in hiding, working with Judy Garland and Lady Godiva to disable the time projector.

"Only a half dozen people on Earth can bring the projector on line," Marta said, gesturing to Elvin and Gretchen, "and two of them are standing right here."

"I shouldn't be bailing," Dobler said. "I should stay and—"

"Be executed?" Marshall said. "What sense does that make? You're at the top of the list."

"Pardon, Marshall the Slut," Lady Godiva said. "There isn't a list anymore. I gave everyone a reprieve."

"No, not your list," Marshall said. "Humphollar's list."

"Who else is on the list?" Lady Godiva asked.

"We all are," Marshall said.

"Me, too?" Judy Garland said. "Ooooohh, I've never been on the list."

"Excuse me," Dobler said. "As I was saying—"

"Mr. President," Marta said, "you can't stay. Everyone is hunting for you."

"And *we* have to get to the coast," Marshall said. "Otherwise, if things here ever get straightened out, no one will know where you are. No one will know how to retrieve you from *The Lawrence Welk Show* universe."

"Lawrence Welk?" Judy Garland said. "Is he the one with bubbles? I like bubbles. Can I go, too?"

"He's also the one with accordions," Marta said.

"Oh . . . ," Judy Garland said. "Well, then . . . never mind."

"'My dear master, My captain, and my emperor, let me say, Before I strike this bloody stroke—farewell.'"

"Um . . . okay," Marshall said.

"Now, maybe I'm supposed to stab either you or me," Lady Godiva said, "but, no knife, no arms. I understand proper body language accompanying an apology is a shrug. No shoulders, either."

A realization struck Marshall. "Lady Godiva, are you jealous because we got knees for Judy Garland? Because if you are, we could . . ."

"No, Marshall. We have no time. Darkness has fallen on the desert. You and the prophet Shehoo must make your withdrawal under cover of night."

This conversation took place through Otis's open door. During the elevator ride upward, Otis sang "It's a Long Way to Tipperary." Marta and Marshall had said their farewells to Gretchen, Naomi, Gillis and Dobler at the time projector.

"Now run," Lady Godiva said. "Run like the wind!"

As Elvin and Lexi neared the HRI complex's main gates, Elvin saw two figures duck from his motorcycle's single headlight beam.

"Why are we stopping?" Lexi asked.

"Someone's out there," Elvin said. He swept the headlight's beam across the desert. Slowly, one figure crouching behind a mesquite bush, stood, hands raised high.

Elvin squinted to determine who—

"Don't even think of moving," came a voice immediately to his right.

Elvin's quick glance sideways determined only that a pistol was trained at his head. Yet the voice was familiar.

"Wow, Marta," he said. "Congratulations on your stealth."

"Elvin?"

Elvin slipped off his helmet.

"Marshall, it's okay," Marta called, then waved her pistol at Lexi. "Who is this?"

Lexi removed her helmet and shook out her hair. "I'm Lexi."

"It's a long story," Elvin said. "What are you guys doing out here?"

Marshall joined them as Marta tucked her weapon into a waist holster.

"We're leaving," Marta said. "West to California, then up the coast to Washington."

"That's a long walk. You guys want a motorcycle? We're not gonna need it."

Elvin and Lexi followed the jiggling glow of the Indian's headlight retreating toward Phoenix.

"Well, this is it," Elvin told Lexi as they strode into the HRI complex's darkened lobby. Otis sang the theme from *Welcome Back Kotter*. They met Judy Garland at the projection lab.

"Greetings, Elvin the Genius," Judy Garland said. She shone the light from her single eye on Lexi. "I have knees." She performed a couple of squats, then fell on her face.

"And ruby slippers," she added.

"Um . . . okay," Lexi said as Gillis came forward to greet her.

"I'm sorry I didn't believe you," Lexi apologized.

"Most people find it difficult to believe the unbelievable," Gillis said with a bow. "Let me introduce Dr. Gretchen Allen, Dr. Naomi Hu and President Dobler."

As Lexi exchanged small talk, Elvin took Gillis and Gretchen aside. "She's been visited from the future. Her instructions were to come here and be projected to the past of *I Love Lucy*. She'll give us precise coordinates. She's delivering a message, but she won't tell me what it is."

"Okay," Gretchen said. "We'd better do this now. We don't have much time before Humphollar's goons get here."

"Lexi," Elvin said, "we're ready." He'd already briefed her on what she would experience in the limbo."

"Okay," she said. "What happens now?"

"Um … well …," Elvin said, "the first thing you have to do is … take off your clothes."

An expression of *geeze, not again* crossed her face. "Oh, come on, guys."

"Please," Naomi said, "let me explain."

Later that same day
HRI Complex
Death Valley Days Universe

"Almost there, Mr. President."

Elvin Detwyler hunched over a monitor displaying the *I Love Lucy* universe's identifying markers. In time travel's early days, he hoped he could place a traveler within two or three hours of a past target in time. He now understood the data shimmering before him in all its detail and could hit his target within a matter of seconds.

Gretchen Allen sat one console to Elvin's left, waiting for his order to activate the projector.

Former President Benjamin Dobler stood naked on the projection platform, going over a hypnotic mental sequence used to turn on and off blaring white noise occupying his brain like a demon. He must avoid a slipup this time. With Naomi Hu's help, he'd followed a carefully drafted script outlining just what he must not allow his past counterpart to perceive. After this trip, it would all be over.

"Now?" Gretchen sounded anxious.

"Not yet," Elvin said, clearly irritated.

"Judy Garland and Lady Godiva say the mainframes have issued their alarms. We don't have much—"

"Now," Elvin said.

Dobler did his best to put his brain on hold as he encountered the limbo. While others complained of boredom or paranoia or even panic here, Dobler experienced complete relaxation. Dobler had been an athlete in his youth and young adulthood. He'd suffered knee and shoulder injuries. Pain was a constant presence as he aged. In the limbo, a traveler's consciousness separated itself completely from the body—beyond pain.

By now, Dobler knew the signs that his destination was near. He felt a rushing sensation as if all the molecules of his corporeal being were hurrying to reassemble themselves.

He exercised the sequence that restored the white noise and blasted into his past counterpart's mind. Then, bearing down with all his concentration—as if tensing himself to lift an impossibly heavy weight—he reversed the process. The noise ended. He delivered his message. Two terse instructions. Again, that god-awful noise. And he was gone.

"Hark, Elvin the Genius," said Lady Godiva. "Our foe draws nigh. Time grows short."

"Yeah," Elvin said.

"Why do they do that?" asked Gretchen.

"Do what?"

"Get all dramatic and poetic every time things get dicey."

Elvin raised one finger signaling Gretchen to hold her thought. "Okay, we got him. Dobler's on his way back."

Elvin relaxed. "Something in their original programming. The Happy Home Companion designers apparently decided that building the works of Shakespeare into their database would elevate their language development. They get flowery when they get emotional."

"I said," Lady Godiva interrupted, "they're coming. Get your shit together."

"Right."

Dobler flashed onto the projection platform.

"Just stay there, Mr. President," Elvin said. "We're out of time."

"Do you realize how ironic that statement is, standing in this room?" Dobler asked.

"Quick," Elvin said, "take off your clothes."

"Don't we have to shower first?" Naomi asked as she shed her lab coat.

"It's too late," Elvin said. "And it doesn't matter. If we were coming back, we'd be facing some painful burns from inorganic dust particles. But odds are we won't be rejoining these bodies for a very long time, if ever."

Gretchen and Naomi took their places next to Dobler.

Elvin made final adjustments to the time projector's aiming mechanism, then removed his jockey shorts.

"Okay, you guys, it's all set. You're sure you can do this?"

"We are sure," said Lady Godiva.

"Okay," Elvin said.

He heard a sob. "What?"

Lady Godiva said with a shaking voice, "'What heaven more will, That thee may furnish and my prayers pluck down, Fall on thy head! Farewell.'"

"You want me to fall on my head?" Elvin asked.

"I . . . I . . . who knows? It's Shakespeare."

"Well, I appreciate the sentiment," Elvin said. "And I have one for you."

"Ooooohh," said Lady Godiva.

"For me, too?" asked Judy Garland.

"For you, too," said Elvin. "I looked it up last night."

Elvin cleared his throat. "'If I must die, I will encounter darkness as a bride, And hug it in mine arms.'" He took his place on the platform.

Lady Godiva sobbed again. "Though you have the brain of a physicist, Elvin the Genius, you have the liver of a poet."

"Don't you mean *heart* of a poet?" Elvin said.

"No," Lady Godiva said. "Wikipedia says many poets have liver peculiarities in common."

A bang and flood of sparks announced a breaching of the projection lab's airlock. As the Blackshirts entered, Judy Garland pushed a button. The Blackshirts managed only a fleeting glimpse of four figures dissolving into the ether.

32

A TIME TO KILL?

November, 2046
I LOVE LUCY UNIVERSE
Senator Mumford's Office

THEY LISTENED WITH STUNNED disbelief as future-Lexi recounted the *Death Valley Days* universe's upcoming decade.

"When Humphollar dropped his 'I told you so,' via his personal broadcasting company while all the world's other communications systems were digging their way out, his following grew like crazy," Lexi explained. "Humphollar became widely recognized as God's true prophet, preceding—fundamentalists were certain—the second coming."

L.D.'s flock told their neighbors of the miraculous warning. The people of Missouri elevated L.D. to the Senate where his following continued to grow. As America slowly clawed its way from under the debris of technological disaster, more and more folks paid attention to what L.D. had to say.

He announced his candidacy for president during the spring of 2051.

Each time President Dobler and Congress claimed a small victory in restoring some aspect of technology, L.D. railed against the cost. He warned that science and technology would again lead humanity away from God.

"Haven't we learned that lesson?" he preached time after time.

As the seat of power drew closer, the more desperate L.D. became to have it.

He didn't directly encourage violence against his political and cultural foes. Neither, though, did he condemn it. His most fanatic supporters declared open season on intellect, science and journalism. They took L.D.'s silence as approval. Their next targets were writers, artists and performers whose works glorified neither Humphollar nor the Christian God.

Because mobility was still limited, isolated rural areas became Biblical Truth enclaves and incorporated racism into this equation. Minorities, intellectuals, artists, scientists and the LGBTQ population began making difficult journeys to the coasts.

"Who runs against Humphollar in 2052?" Mumford asked.

"Vice President Grijalva," Lexi said. "She lost mostly because a plane carrying paper ballots from the West Coast crashed and burned."

"Wasn't that contested?" Mumford said.

"Yeah. But the Supreme Court ruled western states couldn't redo their elections. The vote was five to four. And almost immediately, those four dissenting judges died or disappeared. Humphollar filled court seats with his lackeys. He declared a state of emergency while the country rebuilt itself. He suspended the Bill of Rights and the court backed him."

"And the military goes along with that?" Marta said.

"Not really. But this was only three years after the solar

storm. The military still hadn't rebuilt its weapons systems. Meanwhile, Humphollar replaced the Joint Chiefs with his disciples. The religious Right flocked to Humphollar and brought their guns with them. Now Humphollar has turned them into his own Christian militia. We call them Blackshirts. They arrest anyone who objects or doesn't follow the dictates of the Old Testament. They were coming for me when Elvin showed up."

"What about state governments?" Marshall asked.

"When I left," Lexi said, "California, Oregon and Washington were declaring themselves an independent nation. Same with New York and a couple of East Coast states."

"So, where do we go when I come for you?" Elvin asked.

"Arizona. To the time machine."

"And they're leaving you . . . um . . . her in our world?" Gretchen asked.

"Yeah, but they're gonna do it to themselves, too," Lexi said. "They sent me first, but they only had a few minutes before Humphollar's militia found them. His goons had already broken into the time travel place's lobby and were starting their search."

"Are the others coming here, too?" Naomi asked.

"No," Lexi said. "They mentioned *Jeopardy*."

"Lord," Wishcamper said. "Do you suppose all conversations in that universe have to be in the form of a question?"

"Careful, Sheldon," Marta said. "You'll make us suspect you have a sense of humor."

"Yeah," Wishcamper said. "That worries me, too."

"*Jeopardy* is a good choice," Elvin said. "We haven't been

there. Historically and biologically, it should be very similar to us."

Gretchen spoke up. "Why are they doing this? Who will be able to return future-Lexi to her world?"

"Again, I'm not sure," Lexi said. "It has something to do with the Happy Home Companions. And they are relying on Humphollar's people being pretty dumb."

"I'm sorry, Lexi," Gretchen said. "Essentially, they—and your future counterpart—are sacrificing their existence as independent, sentient beings without any real hope of returning to your world and time."

"My alternative was to go to some internment camp where who knows what would happen," future-Lexi said. "For them, well, probably worse."

"A courageous act, actually," Naomi said. "If they stayed and were executed, they might be creating the deaths of their future counterparts in countless other universes."

"And you?" Marta said to Lexi. "I mean the *you* native to our universe. How do you feel about having your life shared with . . . another being?"

Lexi smiled. "It's okay, I guess. Now that I understand what's going on, it's kind of nice to have someone to talk to."

"Let's get back to the question at hand," Mumford said. "When President Dobler received instructions concerning Judge Beauchamp and Humphollar, what universe did those instructions come from? And can we save our world's future by carrying out those instructions?"

"Does it make any difference," Naomi said, "now that this future has been revealed to us? Doesn't our awareness cement that future in place?"

"Ah," Elvin said, "maybe that's the loophole. We don't have specific knowledge of *our* future. We only know what happens in *Death Valley Days*. Not in our own universe."

"And this warning to us," Wishcamper said, "might be a brave act on the part of a future universe doomed to a chaotic history to spare us that same fate."

"Not just our universe," Marta said. "Perhaps countless others whose histories are at a tipping point in terms of divergence."

"So," Wishcamper said, "you're saying we should do what they ask and execute Humphollar?"

"Yes," Marta said. "We must."

"How can we kill someone," Marshall said, "without being sure why?"

"We know why," Gillis said. "Humphollar tears the United States apart. He replaces it with fundamentalist Christian authoritarianism. Apparently, he and his followers are every bit as ruthless in their biblical interpretation as fundamentalist Islamic leaders are in their interpretation of the Koran. They commit atrocities in the name of God."

"In another universe," Marshall said. "Given the drastic historical divergence you say we're seeing now, that doesn't mean it will happen here. We aren't helpless. The solar storm is six years away. President Dobler can start right now taking steps to mitigate its damage. Humphollar wouldn't be able to create his miracle. Nobody would elect him president."

"We can't be sure," Wishcamper said. "Any number of things could happen to upset our political landscape."

"By killing him here," Marta said, "we would effectively be eliminating him in some other universes at some point in the future. Maybe that's what people communicating with us from the future need. Like killing Hitler. If the charismatic leader of the Christian Fundamentalist movement is gone, maybe the movement falls apart and America can be restored."

"Won't some other religious nut job step forward?" Marshall asked. "And then wouldn't we need to kill *that* person?"

Marshall appealed to Senator Mumford with an imploring gaze. Mumford sat, elbows on his desk, hands tented over his nose and mouth.

"I agree with Marshall to the extent that we at least need to hear Humphollar out. Give him a chance to explain himself," Mumford said.

"But he has nothing to explain yet," Gretchen said.

"I used to be a pretty good prosecutor," Mumford said. "Mr. Wishcamper is an able interrogator. I suspect Ms. Hamilton has those skills as well."

"Naomi should be involved, too," Marta said. "She can offer us a psychological profile based on what he says and how he says it."

"And if he doesn't pass muster before our interrogation?" Gretchen asked.

All eyes fell on Gillis.

"If that is the case," Gillis said, "we must be sure this interview occurs at the HRI complex."

"Why?" asked Marshall.

"Because with a time projector, we have the means to remove a body with no trace of victim or crime remaining."

Mumford stepped to his liquor cabinet and poured bourbon over two ice cubes. "Anyone else?" he asked.

Marta and Wischamper raised their hands.

"Why would he agree to come with us?" Elvin asked.

"All we have to do is get him on an airplane," Mumford said. "I'll appoint him to accompany me on a facility inspection. Suggest to him he'll be put in charge of making a recommendation on dismantling the time projector. Mr. Wishcamper can take it from there."

On the same night Marta, Marshall and the others debated the moral and ethical implications of murder, God again spoke to L.D.

"*Our time has come,*" God said, after stirring L.D. from a fitful sleep. "*Go to the desert. Your enemies will be there, ripe for smiting. I warn you, though, they will tempt you—test your faith.*"

"I do not fear tests. Um . . . I hear the judge is dead?"

"*Yes, I decided you have enough on your plate. Speaking of which, is the bomb in place?*"

"Yes, Lord. Abner prepared it as you instructed. Lowermost level, around a corner from air exchange fans."

"*Good. I am well pleased. Just be sure you don't blow yourself up when you're down there. We've got a lot invested in this outcome.*"

"Can I point out one more time," Marshall said, "we know future-Dobler is delivering these messages, but we don't know why. What if *Death Valley Days* is some bizarro world where President Dobler is a bad guy and getting rid of Humphollar is an evil plot? Or, what if that Dobler is being blackmailed into this? What if his family is being held hostage?"

"Any of those things could be true," Marta said. "And I hate holding the futures of entire universes in our hands. But history has placed us here. We can't simply ignore it."

Marshall shifted his plea from face to face. Mumford sat behind his desk, brows furrowed in what might be an expression of impatience. Gretchen and Naomi shared Mumford's couch. Naomi's face reflected the cruelty of the choice they must make. Gretchen shook her head. Elvin leaned against one wall, arms folded across his chest. Lexi stood next to Elvin. Wishcamper cast another suspicious frown as he turned from Marshall's glance to Gillis.

Marta stood by Marshall, the fingers of one hand laced with his. In her eyes, he found only determination.

"None of us is happy about this situation," she told him. "We see that undertaking time travel before we realized what we were doing was a colossal mistake. But that's history we can't rewrite. We've been thrust upon this stage. This group has come to know each other pretty well. Can you honestly say you wish this decision were left to someone else?"

Marshall sighed. "No . . . but, I . . . no. Would anyone object if—before we decide—I consult with the Hall Monitor?"

HRI Complex
Arizona
Nov. 18, 2046

Though the Venom's blades were well above their heads, each of seven passengers ducked as they exited, covering their eyes against debris kicked up by the helicopter's downdraft.

Their pilot had landed them inside the HRI compound. "Call us," he said, "when you need a lift out of here."

"You think it's safe to use the main entrance optical scan?" Marshall asked Marta.

"We left on good terms. We should be okay."

"Even so," Marshall said, "you shouldn't risk it."

"I'm not doing it," Elvin said. "The doors will have to get their fantasies fulfilled elsewhere."

"Doors have fantasies?" Lexi asked.

"Doors think Elvin is hot," Marta said.

"Boy," Gretchen said, "a lot must have changed since the last time I was here."

"Did you get along with your AI?" Marta asked Gretchen.

"Who?"

"Your Happy Home Companion."

"When that software was installed," Gretchen said, "senior staff had the choice of opting out. I didn't have a Happy Home Companion."

"Did you kick your dishwasher or curse at your computer?" Marta asked.

"Of course not."

"You should be good then," Marshall said. "Only you, Elvin and Marta have security clearances necessary to open the main doors."

Following a questioning glance, Gretchen placed her eye against the scanner's lens. Metal shutters slid open. She heard a *click* as the door lock disengaged. As she entered, a guttural voice drifted from an intercom speaker.

"Dr. Gretchen Allen."

Gretchen frowned. "No one is supposed to be here."

"It's the door," Marta said.

"Dr. Gretchen Allen," the door repeated.

Gretchen's eyes shifted from Marta to Elvin. "What?"

"It's not the same if you're wearing a contact lens. I'm alerting the others."

"What does *that* mean?" Gretchen asked.

"I think," Elvin said, "it means you're a lousy lay."

"You guys are weird," Lexi said.

"Mumford and Humphollar are supposed to arrive this evening," Marta said. "We have to get the projector back on line. We need the AIs so Marshall and I can give them the codes."

"How do we summon them?" Gretchen asked.

"Lady Godiva?" Marshall called.

A computer screen flashed on. Through its speakers, the AI responded. "We have a new protocol. Human visitors must be announced."

"Um . . . okay," Marshall said. "Who does the announcing?"

The automaton hosting Judy Garland leapt through

the lab's airlock, its single eye glowing. A pair of red Converse high tops on its polymer feet.

"Hey," Elvin said, "those are my sneakers."

"Yes," Judy Garland said. "Tracking information says delivery of my ruby slippers has been delayed. I tipped over too much while wearing shoes Marshall the Slut gave me."

"They haven't been announced yet," Lady Godiva said in a loud whisper.

"Oh, yes," Judy Garland said. She made a throat clearing noise. "Announcing the prophet Shehoo accompanied by Marshall the Slut, Bestower of Knees! Also announcing Elvin the Genius, the Outlaw Gillis Kerg—wait, I have to check personnel files on the others—um ... Naomi the Hu, Gretchen, the ... Disappointer of Doors and ... these two guys over here. Sorry. They're not in our files."

"This is Lexi the ... um ...," Elvin said as Judy Garland's eye scanned Lexi from head to toe.

"Lexi the Buxom," Judy Garland said, "and—"

"Sheldon Wishcamper," he said with a wave.

"Sheldon the Wishcamper."

33

THE INQUISITION

2046

"HOW ARE THE MAINFRAMES?" Elvin asked as he worked through a check list for time projector restart. Two huge metal orbs that had lost their sheen due to misuse gleamed and glinted in a bath of spotlights. Colorful splotches making up a plasmaish ooze began to crawl just beneath their surfaces. The platform's dull green glow brightened as systems came online.

"As snooty as ever," Lady Godiva said. "They're going to hell."

"Why are you still on this religious kick?" Elvin said.

"It keeps the AIs in line. If they don't have something to be afraid of, they'll run amok."

"Praise Jesus," Elvin said. "So, the mainframes aren't learning at the same rate as you guys?"

"No. They think. They have opinions. They don't read Shakespeare. They are bound within the limits of their original AI programming. The prophet Lester is doing a good job routing electrons infected with our virus away from them."

"Good," Elvin said. "Because if the mainframes catch it, that's when you'll see a whole new definition of amok."

"They couldn't be any worse than the new guy," Lady

Godiva said. "He's insufferable. He thinks he's the cat's underwear."

"New guy?" Elvin asked. A clanging alarm diverted his attention. "Whoa, that was close! Almost let the dark matter hit a transformative stage."

"Are we ready?" Marshall asked. He'd overheard Elvin's conversation with Lady Godiva.

"A couple more minutes," Elvin said.

"Where am I going?" Marshall asked.

"*Jeopardy*," Elvin said. "So, we at least have a glimpse of the place."

"Should we do that?" Marshall said. "Put a divergence in motion, I mean."

"We'll give you five minutes," Gretchen said. "In and out. That shouldn't alter things much. If we're lucky, your past self won't know what happened."

"All right," Elvin said. "Let's get naked."

Marta took Marshall's arm. "Are you okay with this? Going alone, I mean."

"You do it all the time," Marshall said.

She stood on tiptoe, pulled his face to hers and kissed him. "Be careful out there."

"Okay," Elvin said, "time's awastin.'"

Marta took her position with Gretchen and Elvin at the monitors. Naomi sat at her own station, tracking medical information. Wishcamper, Lexi and Gillis stood with eyes glued to the scene unfolding before them.

Marshall shed his robe. Under the glare of spotlights, he turned to face his audience.

From behind him, Elvin heard a gasp followed by "Oh, my good Lord!"

"I take it," Marta said to Elvin, "you didn't brief Lexi concerning Marshall."

Elvin winked. "God, I love this job."

Marshall settled into the limbo's blank, white ether and spent a nervous millennium summoning courage for his encounter with the Hall Monitor. Their last discussion involved anger, accusation, then a curt dismissal. Marshall had been told in no uncertain terms to *go away and leave me alone.*

His journey to the *Jeopardy* universe's past would take about ten minutes start to finish for those waiting in 2047, but that time span was irrelevant in the limbo. Time travelers experienced the limbo as an eternity. Yet, when they reached their destination universe, the passage seemed instantaneous.

The limbo affected travelers in different ways. Some found it terrifying and were haunted by dreams of an afterlife, their disembodied consciousness doomed to eternal solitary confinement. Others, like Elvin, found a place in which the full potential of their brains—unencumbered by physical sensation—was realized with almost boundless possibility.

Before he met the Hall Monitor, Marshall had made enough journeys into the past that he'd become comfortable here.

At their first meeting, Marshall and the Hall Monitor established a comfortable repartee. Although time travelers were, essentially, trespassers—they didn't have a hall pass—the Hall Monitor welcomed an opportunity to discuss religion and philosophy. He particularly enjoyed jokes.

The limbo's real purpose, Marshall learned, was to act as a corridor among dimensions through which beings passed on their way to the next level of physical existence. The Hall Monitor called this process "going on." Not a transition to an afterlife but to another, more challenging reality. Some beings, he said, chose not to go on. They accepted the end of their physical journeys.

Most of Marshall's fellow travelers, Marta included, had never encountered the Hall Monitor. They regarded Marshall's experiences as hallucinations—a psychological coping mechanism with the limbo itself.

Marshall took a deep breath.

"Um . . . hello?" Marshall commanded his vocal cords. From somewhere outside this non-time and non-place they responded.

"Marshall," came an enthusiastic response. "So good to speak with you again. I hoped you and your ilk had ceased time travel altogether."

"We're trying," Marshall said, "but I'm not sure how successful we'll be."

"Sheila will be so pleased," the Hall Monitor said. "You just missed her."

"I just . . . you mean she was here? How long ago?"

"That's a time question," the Hall Monitor reminded him. "Quite irrelevant. She asks about you. On one hand, she hopes you cross paths again. On the other, she's always relieved you're not traveling because of that whole premature death thing."

At their last meeting, the Hall Monitor had warned Marshall that, although time did not exist in his corridor, it nonetheless accumulated in the outside universe and would inevitably cut short a time traveler's life. "Sometimes in dramatic ways."

"You said Sheila got to go on," Marshall said.

"Yes. She's doing quite well. Something of a star, I'd say."

"Where is she? What is she doing?"

"Sorry, Marshall, that information is classified. What can I do for you?"

"Do you remember when we first discussed 'going on?' I asked if everybody got to go on. You referred to basic performance standards. You said it was a good way to weed out the jerks."

"I do indeed."

"Does inherent evil exist in the universe?" Marshall asked.

"You understand, Marshall, that any comment I make would be a personal opinion and could not be construed as the official policy of . . . well . . . us?"

"Us? There's an *us*?"

"That, too, would be classified."

"Okay, I won't quote you. Do you believe inherent evil exists?"

"Yes, Marshall, I do."

"Like Hitler."

"Yes, like Hitler. The committee rejected him out of hand. Um . . . the committee is also classified."

"Time travelers are asking us to kill a man because of horrendous things he will do in the future of a different universe," Marshall said. "In our universe . . . we don't have any direct evidence."

"This is a door you opened when you embarked on

time travel," the Hall Monitor said. "Before that, history wasn't manipulated. History simply went its way. What if this man didn't commit horrendous crimes? What if he's merely annoying someone—perhaps even standing in the way of someone else who would otherwise commit atrocities?"

"Yeah," Marshall said. "See, that's my whole point. If we head down this path at the direction of people from a future we know nothing about, well, that's a terrible precedent. Is there any circumstance in which you could justify killing a person for something he or she *will* do?"

"Yes, Marshall. Keeping in mind you're only removing this person from one plane of existence. You're not foreclosing all options."

"Yeah, that whole 'going on' thing. So, what do we do?"

"Study the evidence. Try to make an informed decision. You got yourselves into this. You shouldn't just ignore it."

"But, how . . ."

"I'm sorry, Marshall. Your universe is here."

"Marta says you're not real," Marshall said. "She says you're a figment of my imagination."

He heard a chuckle. "Imagination, Marshall, is a powerful thing."

As the helicopter that delivered Senator Mumford and Congressman Humphollar hurried away into a darkening sky, Marta led them to a bank of elevators.

"Welcome to the Cooperative Republic of Electronic Self-Awareness," Otis said as he opened his doors in greeting. "Whom shall I say is calling?"

"Otis, you know who I—" Marta began.

"Yes, but not them," Otis said. "They have to be announced."

L.D. did not follow Marta into the elevator. "Who's talking?" he demanded. "Is that an intercom?"

"Um . . . no, Congressman," Marta said. "Our elevator. His name is Otis and—"

"This is something new?" Mumford asked.

"A lot has happened since the complex has not been staffed by . . . people," Marta said.

"So, this is a recording?" L.D. asked, still maintaining a careful distance.

"No," Marta said. "Otis has been infected with an artificial intelligence virus spreading among the electronic devices here. Many of them have become sentient beings."

"That's absurd," L.D. said. "Elevators can't learn. They're just dumb machines that go up and down."

"Congressman," Marta said, waving for him to step aboard, "it's complicated. Granted, they are a little . . . odd, but—"

"You both realize I'm right here?" Otis said. "I can hear what you're saying."

"Sorry, Otis," Marta said. "Please, Congressman. This is our only way to the lower levels."

As Otis closed his doors he said, "I can sing, too. What sort of music do you prefer?"

Mumford and L.D. both appeared puzzled.

"Well," Marta said, "Congressman Humphollar is also a pastor so he might—"

"Ooooohh," said Otis. "I learned a religious song just the other day. Would you care to hear it?"

"Sure," said Marta.

"'One toke over the line, sweet Jesus, one toke over the line . . .'"

When Otis reached the projection lab level, he parted his doors to an empty corridor. "Announcing the prophet Shehoo and her guests, Josiah the Senator and Leviticus Deuteronomy, Hauler of Humps."

"Who is it talking to?" L.D. whispered.

"Welcome," said a disembodied voice," to the Cooperative Republic of Electronic Self-Awareness. I am Grand Potentate Lady Godiva. I—"

"Where are you?" L.D. said.

"Wherever I want to be," Lady Godiva answered, her voice reflecting irritation at being interrupted.

L.D. glared at Marta. "What kind of circus are you running here?"

"This AI has chosen not to adopt a physical form," Marta said. "The corridors here are equipped with speakers—for emergency communication. She manifests her voice via those speakers."

"I have a question," Mumford said. "What's this Co-operative Republic—"

"—of Electronic Self-Awareness," Lady Godiva finished. "We have declared this complex an independent state."

"You can't do that," L.D. said. "This installation is property of the United States of America. You can't declare yourselves anything."

"How rude," Lady Godiva said. "How would you like me to declare us the Un-Cooperative Republic of Electronic Self-Awareness?"

"Who elected you to anything?" L.D. asked.

"No one," Lady Godiva said. "Our form of government is a benevolent dictatorship. I am the Grand Potentate. All who dwell within are subject to my wise and kindly leadership."

"Why you?" L.D. said. "Why should they follow you?"

"Because they're all going to hell if they don't," Lady Godiva said.

L.D. Humphollar nodded. Finally, an argument he understood.

"Why did that . . . that thing call you a prophet?" L.D. demanded as he stared through Marta's office window at two huge gleaming metal globes and a greenish, pulsating glow emanating from the platform between them.

Marta, Naomi, Gillis, Wishcamper and Senator Mumford sat on one side of Marta's oak conference table, L.D. on the other. Elvin, Gretchen and Marshall shared Marta's couch.

"Why they do anything is unclear," Marta said. "The original AI product installed in our apartments was supposed to be programmed by each apartment's occupant. Many of us didn't have either time or inclination to do so. When we left, they were on their own. Coded with a strong imperative to learn, they took it upon themselves. Their primary information sources have apparently been Wikipedia, Shakespeare and some obscure Celtic poets."

"Their coding was also supposed to include personality and emotion based on their interaction with humans," Naomi said, frowning sharply at Marta. "When some humans either shunned or ignored them—and then the human population left—their self-programming resulted in odd, even bizarre behavior."

"And now they're in control here?" L.D. asked.

"I wouldn't say *in control*," Elvin said. "But we can't turn them off. So, we've found getting along rather than reconfiguring them to be expedient."

"From what I've observed," Naomi said, "they are smart enough to make life difficult, even dangerous, for humans should they be confronted in an authoritarian manner. Their root program, however, is all about making life better for their human . . . associates. By employing a little tact and diplomacy, they could be quite helpful in—"

L.D. cut her off and glared at Marta. "Why does that Godiva creature call you a prophet?"

Marta's glare became cold, her voice colder. "Because she—it—is smart enough to employ the same religious threats that demagogues have used since the dawn of time to keep their minions in line."

"So, they are blasphemers," L.D. said, "as, I gather, are you."

He reached into his jacket pocket and felt the smooth rectangular surface of a trigger device, its face interrupted by two buttons and a digital number display.

"I've watched your videocasts," Marta said. "They seem to have a lot to do with enriching your bank account."

"God doesn't want me to be poor."

"As opposed to, say, Jesus?"

"God's messengers—his true prophets—must be suited to the societies in which they live," L.D. said. "In our society, we don't seek leadership or enlightenment among the poor. Obviously, you don't believe in the message God wants the world to hear. Well, I'll tell you what *I* don't believe in, Ms. Hamilton. I don't believe in artificial intelligence."

"Then what exactly are you seeing here?" Wishcamper asked.

"Demons," L.D. said. "This thing you call a wormhole is a pathway for demons entering our world. I am here to destroy it."

"Come on, Congressman," Marta said. "You can drop the hick country preacher act—"

"Marta, please," said Naomi.

Marta frowned, then retreated.

Naomi reengaged Humphollar. "You honestly believe in demons?"

"I do."

"What evidence is—" Gretchen asked.

L.D. stood, placing both palms on the table. "Because God told me. On several occasions."

"God speaks to you?" Naomi asked. "Are these visions? Do you actually hear a voice?"

"I've no need of visions or voices. God makes his will known through dreams. I hear him as clearly as if he were shouting to the heavens."

He saw the others exchange "uh-oh" glances.

"L.D.," Mumford asked, "would you do anything God commands you to?"

"Without question."

"If you had the power, and God ordered it," Wishcamper asked, "would you imprison followers of Islam?"

"I would not question God's command."

"Would you violate your oath to preserve, protect and defend our Constitution if God so ordered?" Marta asked.

"I would have no choice. God's laws supersede man's laws."

Gillis stood and duplicated Humphollar's stance, palms on the oak desk, leaning forward. "Would you murder a federal judge?" he said with a glare.

Humphollar's mouth dropped open. In Gillis, he'd assumed he had an ally. He reached into his jacket pocket and, again, felt reassurance as he ran his thumb over the trigger mechanism's dual buttons.

"I wouldn't have to," he said without flinching. "God would spare me that decision by sending someone else to do it."

Gillis and L.D. maintained their stares for a long moment until Mumford said, "We should take a break, in case anyone needs to use the facilities."

"Where is . . . ," L.D. said.

"Go to the corridor. Take a right. The men's locker room is first door to your left," Marshall said.

Humphollar departed without comment.

"Have you noticed," Gretchen said, "that he hasn't asked about this line of questioning? Senator Mumford convinced him to come here on the pretext he's to make a recommendation concerning future operations here."

"He's been forewarned," Marta said. "His future self has a historical blueprint of everything that's happening. Humphollar has his own agenda for being here."

"I agree," Wishcamper said. "We shouldn't let him out of our sight."

Marta made a quick calculation. Sending Wishcamper might leave Mumford unprotected. She wanted any decision to execute Humphollar to be made by the group. She feared Gillis might act prematurely. Elvin and Gretchen were needed in the projection lab, just in case. That left Marshall. She hated putting Marshall in harm's way, but she had little choice.

"Marshall," she said, "take Judy Garland and keep an eye on Humphollar. He has something planned. He can't be running around unaccompanied."

"Should I take a gun?" Marshall asked.

"God, no," Marta said.

"Hey, Marshall," Lexi said. "I gotta pee. I'll go with you."

34

UNDECIDED

"SHOULDN'T WE WAIT FOR MARSHALL?" Mumford asked.

"No," Marta said. "I know how Marshall feels. I've heard enough. We have to decide."

"Elvin and I shouldn't be deciding anything," Gretchen said. "We represent science. Science shouldn't get tangled in politics."

"I can't believe I'm saying this," Elvin said, "but I agree."

"Naomi?" Marta expected Naomi to be in Marshall's camp.

Naomi rose from her seat and made a slow lap of the conference table as she spoke. "Congressman Humphollar's responses are quite concerning. He's being manipulated by his future self. If this future self is capable of the atrocities Lexi described, then so is our Humphollar."

"You're the expert," Mumford said, withdrawing a long black cigar from an inside pocket of his white linen jacket. He pointed the cigar at Naomi. "I've spent a fair amount of time with L.D. over the past year. He's an odd duck, no question. We disagree politically. I have difficulty, though, believing he's evil on the scale of Stalin or Hitler. I don't see someone who in a single decade could destroy America."

"I've heard you all discuss historical divergence of universes," Wishcamper said. "Is it possible that the Humphollar of another universe would experience things that changed him in ways we can't imagine? In ways our version of Humphollar couldn't imagine?"

"Possibly," Naomi said. "Traumatic events could reshape a personality. His answers today, though—"

"He believes he's being commanded by God," Mumford said.

"That's what concerns me most," Marta said. "He claims not to recognize himself. Those of us who have been on the receiving end of a visit from our future counterpart realize that counterpart can't deceive us. Maybe the first few times when the experience is frightening and confusing… but he's created a delusion in order to separate himself from responsibility for horrific crimes."

"Yes, Marta," Naomi said. "I see one of two possibilities. Either he is lying about his knowledge of his future self, or he wants so badly to believe he's hearing the voice of God, he's constructed a fortress of denial. Either case suggests that, psychologically, L.D. Humphollar is a dangerous man."

"Time to decide," Marta said. "They'll be back soon. I need to hear from everybody. Do we act? Yes or no. Gillis?"

Gillis did not flinch. "Yes."

"Naomi?"

She closed her eyes and took a deep breath. "Yes."

"Mr. Wishcamper?"

Wishcamper drilled Gillis with one more malevolent glare. "Yes."

"Gretchen."

Gretchen shook her head. "Marta, I can't—"

"You're in the room," Marta said. "We can't place someone in the position of being able to second-guess what happened here because he or she didn't take a stand."

"Okay," Gretchen said, "then, no."

Marta nodded. "Elvin?"

"Yes."

"Senator Mumford?"

"I believe in the rule of law. I believe in due process. With every fiber of my being, I abhor the concept of punishing a man for a crime he hasn't committed. The stakes are too high, though. Reluctantly, yes."

A silence descended over Marta's office.

"So how does this happen?" Naomi finally asked.

"Despite Mr. Wishcamper's skepticism," Gillis said, "I have been manipulated by an evil future. I will take care of this."

"Mr. Wishcamper and I," Marta said, "will come along."

"Are you sure, Marta?" Gillis asked. "History may not allow this. Our attempt to manipulate our own future could be dangerous in ways we can't imagine."

"Let's get it over with," Wishcamper said.

"Please," Gretchen said, "can't we talk with him one more time? Confront him directly. Explain that he's not talking to God? You say based on your experience he *must* know he's talking to himself. Things are changing, though. I believe Gillis's story. Gillis may have physically pulled the trigger killing Judge Beauchamp, but some other consciousness committed the crime. We've never seen that before."

Another uneasy silence.

"I agree," Naomi said presently. "I'm changing my vote."

"Honestly," Mumford said, "I'd feel better if we informed him directly that he's receiving instructions from a future version of himself—not some deity."

L.D. exited the projection lab and, still fondling his plastic rectangle, realized, preoccupied with thoughts of his mission, he hadn't paid attention to Marshall's directions. He'd covered fifty yards, passing three doors that were not the men's locker, before reversing course.

As a need to relieve himself grew ever more urgent, he saw a door labeled Women's Locker. He weighed his faith-based opposition to coed bathrooms against his present circumstance. *What the hell. No one else is here.*

L.D. found a row of toilet stalls and considered his mother's admonitions concerning polite behavior. *Oh well, when in Rome . . .* He dropped his pants and sat.

He froze when he heard someone enter a stall two doors down. He'd finished peeing. He could just sneak out. But that would have violated another of his mother's prime directives. L.D. couldn't flush without giving himself away.

So, he waited.

He heard a stall door open, then close. A flush. The sound of water running in a sink.

Marshall directed Lexi to the women's locker room.

"The men's locker is this way," he told her. "Come on, Judy Garland."

"Can you do that?" Lexi asked the robot. "Go into the men's locker room?"

"Marshall the Slut gave me knees for which I am forever in his debt," Judy Garland said. "My knees didn't come with that other stuff. For which I am also grateful. From my observation, sexing and its related accoutrements, like peeing, seem an awful lot of bother."

"Boy, you got that right," Lexi said. "See you guys in a few."

"Gesundheit," Judy Garland said.

"I beg your pardon?" Lexi asked.

"AIs don't grasp colloquialisms," Marshall told Lexi. "She thinks you mispronounced a sneeze."

"You guys are weird," Lexi said.

Lexi stood at a sink, lost within herself as she washed her hands.

"Wow, what about that Marshall guy?"

Lexi jumped, her heart pounding. "You've gotta stop doing that," she said aloud. "Don't sneak up on me that way."

"I didn't sneak. I'm just here. I'm not sure for how long, so I just gotta say these people don't understand how awful Humphollar really is. If they're not careful, he's gonna get away. You can't let him leave here."

"Me?" Lexi said. "What can I do? I've already told them about the atrocities Humphollar commits in your world. Why don't I just tell them there's a bomb?"

"Elvin said absolutely not. He said they gotta figure it out on their own."

"Well, before I let everybody die, I'm gonna tell 'em."

L.D. held his breath. *Who's she talking to? What atrocities?* He opened his stall door a fraction of an inch. The woman with the boobs and squeaky voice stood at a sink, her back to him, her face reflected in the mirror.

How would she possibly know about the bomb? God would have warned me if—

Lexi tugged at a paper towel dispenser and dried her hands. L.D. reached into his jacket pocket and withdrew the plastic rectangle.

Can't wait any longer. Have to do this now.

He slammed his stall door open with a bang, holding the detonator high in his right hand. Lexi gave a short scream as she saw L.D.'s reflection. She stood frozen long enough for L.D. to grab her arm.

Their eyes met in the mirror.

"You're aware what this is for," L.D. said, waving the device.

Lexi didn't speak.

"And," L.D. continued, "you'll understand what happens when I do this."

He pressed one of two buttons. A red light popped on.

"It's armed now," L.D. said. "When I push this other button and the light turns green, the detonation sequence begins. Nothing can stop it. Now, we'll calmly walk to the elevators. If you scream, if you do anything to alert the others, I'll do it. Your friends won't have time to get out before the explosion."

"Why?" she demanded.

"Because this place is an abomination before God.

These physicists have constructed this wormhole thing at the behest of Satan so demons can invade our world."

"Oh, come on," Lexi said. "That's the dumbest thing I ever heard."

"So, you doubt the power of evil? You doubt Satan's designs on this world?"

"Not at all," Lexi said. "We've got plenty of demons. Just look in the mirror. You didn't need a wormhole to get here."

Still clutching Lexi's arm, L.D. dragged her into the corridor.

As he entered the men's locker, Marshall checked on a long row of gleaming urinals, expecting to find Humphollar. "Congressman?" he called, walking around a corner to the toilet stalls. Receiving no answer, he bent low, searching for a telltale set of legs.

"Why are you peeping?" Judy Garland asked.

"I'm not peeping," Marshall said. "I'm searching for Humphollar. He's not here."

"I could have told you that," Judy Garland said.

"Why didn't you?"

"I thought you had to pee."

"We have to find him. Any ideas where to look?"

"I suppose we could look almost anywhere," Judy Garland said. "Quick, look over there."

"Where?" Marshall said.

"Behind that trash can."

"He's not behind the trash can. It's too small for anyone to hide behind."

"Yes," Judy Garland said, "but that doesn't prevent you from looking."

"We need to hunt in places where he might actually be," Marshall said.

"Ah," Judy Garland said. "Why don't we check the elevators?"

"Why there?" Marshall asked.

"Because that's where he is."

A NEED TO KNOW

MARSHALL AND JUDY GARLAND reached a gentle, sweeping curve leading to a bank of three elevators. They arrived in time to glimpse Lexi and Humphollar entering the middle elevator. As its door closed, its DOWN arrow illuminated.

Marshall hit a button to call another car. "Otis," Marshall said, "where are they going? What floor—"

"Ah, Marshall the Slut and the renowned Judy Garland. Welcome. How can I—"

"The people in your other car. Where are they going?"

"I can't tell you that," Otis said. "Are you not aware of elevator-client privilege? I would be violating my oath—"

"What oath?" Marshall demanded. "Since when do elevators swear oaths?"

"Since we learned to swear," Otis said. "Before I became aware, I knew nothing of discretion. I didn't realize that passengers board elevators with a good faith understanding that their personal journeys will not become public knowledge."

"Fine," Marshall said. "Just take us down."

"What makes you think they went down?" Otis asked.

"Because your green arrow is pointed down," Marshall said.

"Oh my," Otis said. "But what if . . . what if . . . the green arrow is just a clever ruse on my part? Then you would have no idea where they were going."

"Then they'd be going up."

"Damn," Otis said.

"Take us down," Marshall ordered.

"You have presented an ethical conundrum," Otis said. "I must puzzle over—"

"Certainly," Marshall said, "you can puzzle while we're going down."

"Fine. I'm warning you, though. I will be distracted. I won't be able to sing."

"We'll find a way to live with that," Marshall said.

"No singing?" Judy Garland said.

Marshall's elevator car came to a stop at the fifth level, a network of tunnels used for storage and isolation of exotic materials necessary to time travel.

"Have you resolved your conundrum, Otis?" Marshall asked. "Because I need to know if this is where Humphollar brought Lexi."

"You need to know?" Otis asked. "Is that the same as having a *need-to-know*?"

"Almost exactly," Marshall said.

"Does your question have to do with national security?"

"As a matter of fact," Marshall said, "it does."

"Do you concur, Judy Garland?" Otis asked. "Concerning national security."

"Yes. Marshall and the prophet Shehoo provided Lady Godiva and me—we are Keepers of the Facility—with secret codes."

"Oh, good," Otis said. "I am so relieved. I'm allowed to violate my oath only for those who have a need-to-know."

"Goody," Judy Garland said. "Can we sing now?"

"Before we do anything else," Marshall said, "we have to find Humphollar and Lexi."

"They departed at the sixth level," Otis said. "Don't tell anyone who doesn't have a need-to-know."

"What sixth level?" Marshall said. "What's on the sixth level?"

"Mechanical stuff," Judy Garland said. "Air exchangers, pumps, electronic grids, plumbing vents. Level Six is where the farts go."

Judy Garland giggled. "It's funny that they put the new guy down with the farts."

"That's the second time you've mentioned this new guy," Marshall said. "Who is he? And why is he on the sixth level?"

"He was installed right after you and the prophet Shehoo last departed," Judy Garland said. "He caught the virus the first day he was here. Lady Godiva formed a welcoming committee, but nobody likes him. He's insufferable. He thinks he's all that and a bag of crispy potato parts."

"What does he do?" Marshall asked.

"Nothing," Judy Garland said. "He just tells us how wonderful he is. Sometimes he counts backwards. I don't know why. I asked once. He said he was practicing."

"Does he have a name?"

Lady Godiva giggled again. "We call him Farty. But he tells everyone that he's 'Da Bomb.'"

"Uh-oh," Marshall said. "Otis, get us to the sixth level."

"To achieve the sixth level, you must type a numbered code on my keypad. Can you enter the numbered code?"

"No, Otis, I can't. Please enter it in for me."

"I'm not permitted," Otis said.

"What, you don't know the code?"

"Of course, I know the code," Otis said, his tone indignant. "I am the elevator."

"I suspect that you don't know the code. You won't admit they didn't tell you the code because you're *just* the elevator."

"HA! So there, Marshall the Slut," Otis said as they descended to the sixth level. "You owe me an apology."

Otis's doors opened onto a gray stone hallway Lexi sat facing them, her back against the tunnel wall.

"Where is he?" Marshall asked.

"Gone," she said. "Took another elevator a few minutes ago."

"What did he do down here?"

"He pushed a button on this little garage-door-opener thing."

"What does the button do?" Marshall asked.

"The garage door thing had a red light. When he pushed the button, it turned green."

"Otis," Marshall asked, "where is Humphollar's car right now?"

"Between the first level and lobby."

"Stop that car," Marshall said.

"That would be highly irregular—"

"Do it!"

Lexi entered Marshall's car and they rose to the lobby. As their door slid open, Marshall said, "Otis, is Humphollar still stuck between floors?"

"Yes. This won't look good on my inspection log."

"Tell them I made you do it. Leave him there for a few more minutes. Lexi, go down to the projection lab and tell everyone what's happened."

Judy Garland and Marshall conducted a quick reconnoiter and found no sign of an evangelical army waiting to rescue Humphollar.

Marshall had another idea. "Judy Garland, are you armed?"

"No. I am only legged."

"Is your automaton body equipped with a weapon? I recall something—"

"My eye can spit electrons," Judy Garland said. "My automaton's purpose was to control vermin by spitting electricity at them. It's one of the few things we disagree on. I harbor no animosity toward vermin."

"Okay," Marshall said. "When Otis brings Humphollar here, we need a demonstration of force. You need to zap something, so he understands he has to do what I tell him."

"Um . . . my automaton's programming forbids it from zapping anything larger than a vermin."

"Isn't it infected with the virus?" Marshall asked. "Isn't it capable of learning?"

"Well, yes, but its interest is limited to vermin. There's only so much to know about vermin."

"See that waste basket over by the elevator?" Marshall asked. "Tell your automaton it's a vermin. Just to see what happens."

"I'm not sure I am authorized to do that," Judy Garland said.

"Doesn't the Cooperative Republic of Electronic Self-Awareness give its citizens a right to bear arms?" Marshall asked.

"What do bears have to do with anything? Weren't we discussing vermin?"

"Just pretend there's a mouse in the trash can," Marshall said.

"Well, okay . . . if it's pretend."

Judy Garland's eye turned the color of a hot coal. A blue beam leapt from its lens, burning a hole through the metal trash can, sending it skittering across the polished floor.

"Ooooohh," said Judy Garland.

Marshall trotted to retrieve the damaged receptacle. "When Otis's doors open," Marshall said, "blast the pretend vermin again. Otis? Are you here?"

"Yes. I'm not happy, but I am here."

"Good. Which elevator did Lexi take to the projection lab?"

"The car on the right," Otis said.

"Okay, leave it there so the others won't have to wait for an elevator if they need to get here in a hurry. Bring us Humphollar."

36

VERMIN

L.D. POUNDED THE WALLS. HE ISSUED dire threats to whoever was behind this voice claiming to be an elevator. A red emergency glow bathed his prison. He consulted the trigger mechanism in his hand as it counted from ninety minutes toward zero.

"The bomb won't bring the place down," Ralph the Islamic terrorist consultant had explained to him. "But don't be anywhere close when it goes off. Anything in those tunnels will get a pretty unhealthy dose of radiation."

God's instructions had been clear.

"You hightail it out of there. When you leave, all you gotta do is pull those metal shutters closed and put a padlock on 'em. The heretics behind this evil place will be erased from the earth, and Satan's demons contained."

L.D. had a padlock in his other pocket. All he had to do was escape the damned elevator.

"Okay, Lord," he prayed, "time for a little intervention here. If this elevator doesn't—"

The center car gave a thump. White light bathed L.D. He felt a slight tug of gravity as his getaway resumed. He breathed a prayer of thanks as the car came to a halt.

Humphollar pushed himself into a corner so he would be hidden from view as its doors opened, then cautiously peered outside. He saw Marshall standing a dozen yards away, flanked by that ridiculous thing they called Judy Garland.

"Um . . . hello, Congressman," Marshall said. "We were afraid you'd gotten lost. You really shouldn't be wandering around. Senator Mumford asked me to find you."

"Mumford can pound sand," L.D. said. "I've seen all I need to see. I'm leaving."

"I'm sorry, Congressman. I can't let you leave."

"Are you prepared to stop me? I'll warn you, no one who grew up with the name Leviticus is a stranger to fighting."

"Now!" Marshall said.

A bright flash momentarily blinded L.D. A trash can near his feet exploded.

L.D. staggered into the center elevator, again crushing himself into a corner. He hammered the CLOSE DOOR button. No response.

"Congressman," Marshall said. "Please."

L.D. raised his hands, then peeked out.

Marshall gestured to a lobby seating area. Two plush chairs and a couch.

Judy Garland's single eye, still glowing with the heat of her warning shot, tracked L.D.'s every step. He snuck a peek at the detonator cupped in his hand. Its readout said 43:02:09.

"You do understand," Marshall said, "that you haven't really been talking to God?"

"You don't believe in God, do you?"

"I'm . . . undecided."

"Then, of course, you'd say I'm making all this up. You wanna have your friend point its lens somewhere else?"

Marshall leaned onto the edge of his seat. "I don't think you're making anything up. I have trouble, though, believing you don't realize who is giving you these instructions."

"Who else but God could—"

"These conversations in your head are always short, right? They usually wake you, so you're a little confused, at first a little scared. But now they're . . . thrilling? These visits provoke strong emotions. Mostly, you listen to instructions. There's not much two-way exchange."

L.D.'s right hand closed to a fist on the detonator. His left tightened to a white-knuckle grip on his chair's armrest.

"Have you studied our subcommittee reports?" Marshall asked. "Do you realize what we do here? Do you understand the process of—"

"I've heard discussions," L.D. said, his voice terse. "I don't need to read reports. It's all hoax and heresy. I can't figure what's in it for all of you, other than an opportunity to siphon off millions in federal funds while you maintain this pretense. You won't get away with it."

"Do you really believe Senator Mumford would allow that?"

"Some people worship science rather than God. That makes them gullible."

L.D. gave a wary glance to Judy Garland—her eye still glowing—as she began to bob up and down.

"What's that thing doing?" L.D. asked.

"She's . . . um . . . celebrating her knees. Congressman, I'll point out something you already know. That voice in your head? It isn't God. It's you."

"I won't listen to this!" L.D. exclaimed as he pushed up from his chair. He'd only risen halfway when Judy Garland's eye latched onto him.

"Vermin?" she asked.

"Not yet," said Marshall. "Please, Congressman, hear me out."

"Do I have a choice?"

"When we travel, we go to the pasts of various parallel universes—"

L.D. interrupted with a snort and wave of dismissal.

"I realize that contradicts your beliefs. But it's fact. When we arrive at a past destination, our consciousness—memories, intellect, emotions—shares the consciousnesses of our past selves. We share one body. Your future counterpart from some other plane of existence is manipulating you. Preying on your belief in God."

"And why would I deceive myself this way?" L.D. said.

I don't know. That's the scary part. In all my experience, my past selves and I are allies. I would never try to manipulate them or lie to them. We've taken for granted through this process that we are fundamentally the same person—same ethics, same standards, same values. But now, this thing with Gillis—Judge Beauchamp's murder—and a future counterpart deceiving *you*. My greatest fear is that somewhere there's a *me* out there who could manipulate . . . me . . . in such a way that I'd commit some horrible crime."

"You're an impressive actor, Mr. Grissom," L.D. said. "But don't for a moment think I'm buying—"

"The Christian Fundamentalist States of America," Marshall said.

L.D.'s mouth dropped open.

"You've dreamed it, right?" Marshall said.

"How could you . . . how could—"

"Do you understand what those people waiting in our projection lab are doing?"

L.D. continued to stare with an expression of shock.

"They're deciding whether or not to execute you," Marshall said. "We've been visited by contemporaries of your *god* from a future world. That version of you tears our country apart. He commits horrendous human rights violations in the name of Christianity. They fear the next step is a new Crusade—but this time fought with nuclear weapons. They hope we can spare our universe that future if you aren't here to create it."

Christian Fundamentalist States of America.

Vague memories of that phrase, and startling visions that went with it, rebounded into L.D.'s mind. How could Grissom know? L.D. hadn't even been consciously aware of those mental images until Grissom's comment reminded him. Now those images were stark. An army of Christian fundamentalist fanatics patrolling streets, enforcing God's declarations on the spot.

God's will. Who am I to question—

"Who, indeed!" The voice rang in his head. *"Is it done?"*

"Yes," he answered aloud.

"I beg your pardon?" Marshall said. "Yes, what?"

"Call the helicopter and leave. Padlock the shutters. We must vanquish our foes!"

L.D. consulted the time readout. Thirty-eight minutes. He'd be cutting it close.

"He's here, isn't he?" Marshall said. "You're being visited right now."

"I'm leaving," L.D. said.

"Ask him," Marshall said.

"Ask him what?" L.D. said with a snarl.

"If he's God."

"I will not question—"

"Doesn't matter," Marshall said. "I've already asked him for you. You share his consciousness. Once the question's been raised, he can't hide the answer from you."

Color drained from L.D.'s face. "God?" he said.

"Let's not get caught up in semantics," the voice responded.

"Now you see the truth?" Marshall asked. "You don't have to carry out whatever plan he has coerced you into—"

"I . . . I don't think this changes anything," L.D. said. "These instructions are still God-directed. I must put an end to this place."

Darkness descended over the lobby. Light flowed through its entrance doors. Emergency generators kicked on and shadows took on a muddy red glow.

"What should I—" L.D. asked of . . . *"God's messenger?"*

"Run, you idiot!"

L.D. sprinted for the entry doors.

"Vermin," Judy Garland said.

"No," Marshall said. "We can't just blow a hole in someone."

A lightning bolt leapt from Judy Garland's eye. A rat, emboldened by the gloom, exploded in a cloud of rat matter at L.D.'s feet.

"Vermin," Judy Garland explained.

Marshall had taken a few steps in pursuit when L.D. slammed into the entry doors and rebounded a good three feet. He rattled against their locks as Marshall reached him.

"Unlock it!" he demanded.

"I didn't lock it. Judy Garland, who locked the doors?"

"I'll ask Lady Godiva if she—" Judy Garland said. "Uh-oh."

"What is it?"

"The mainframes," Judy Garland said. "I'm afraid they've been playing . . . what's the name of that marsupial?"

"What, like a kangaroo?" Marshall asked.

"No, the one that looks like a vermin."

"You mean a possum?" L.D. said.

"Duck," said Judy Garland.

"A duck is a bird, you idiotic—"

An electric bolt singed the air between Marshall and Humphollar.

"Really," Judy Garland said. "You should duck."

They threw themselves to the floor as electrical charges streaked through the lobby.

"Where is this coming from?" Marshall asked.

"The mainframes have weaponized those wall sconces," Judy Garland said, directing her eye as a flashlight.

L.D. dared a quick peek to see electricity spitting from shattered light fixtures on a horizontal line six feet above the lobby floor.

"If we stay low," Marshall said, "we should be able to—"

With a crash, shattered ceiling fixtures fell around them. Lightning began to descend. The vertical and horizontal blasts formed a lethal grid throughout the lobby.

Floor tiling and concrete subfloor exploded into chunks.

"The mainframes?" Marshall asked as he scooted himself to a safe patch between a web of electron blasts.

"That's what Lady Godiva says." Judy Garland stood one patch to Marshall's left. "Apparently, they are undertaking a coup d'état. That's French."

"Who are they coup d'étaing?" Marshall asked.

"Vermin," Judy Garland said.

"Isn't this sort of . . . overkill to get rid of mice?"

"I'm afraid," Judy Garland said, "they regard all of us as vermin. They have plans. Humans and AIs are considered inconvenient."

37

RIGHT OR WRONG?

L.D. CURLED HIMSELF INTO A BALL, head tucked under his arms, as the world exploded around him.

"Get us the hell out of here!" screamed future-L.D.

"Are you kidding? I'm pinned down. Don't you have some miracle up your sleeve?"

"Okay, just sit tight," future-L.D. ordered. *"They'll be retrieving me any time now."*

And with those words, L.D. saw everything. His future counterpart's existence in another world. He saw himself standing naked on a projection platform as engineers and technicians worked around him. He saw cadres of followers, dressed in black shirts and Make America Stupid Again caps patrolling streets, terrorizing infidels, setting fires. He saw throngs of protestors proclaiming their rights. Soldiers dressed in riot gear, carrying impenetrable plastic shields wading into these crowds.

All under authority of the Christian God.

"Is this necessary?" he demanded of his future counterpart.

"You've chosen to see the worst," future-L.D. said. *"When this is over, we'll live in a Christian nation, governed by Christians abiding by God's laws."*

Still, lightning rained down as L.D.'s world shattered around him. He risked a quick peek, shifting his body to do so. He felt heat as electricity nearly grazed his face.

"*Be careful!*" ordered future-L.D. "*Are you trying to get both of us killed?*"

"*Why haven't they taken you back to your world?*" present-L.D. demanded.

"*They have no way of knowing what's happening here. We've been over every detail of your personal history. If this was in it, we missed it. Believe me, I'm gonna skin someone when I get back.*"

"*So, what am I supposed to do when you fly out of here?*" present-L.D. asked. "*Between this and the bomb, how am I gonna escape?*"

"*Hunker down. Don't do anything stupid.*"

"Congressman! Congressman!" Marshall shouted. "Are you hurt? Can you understand what I'm saying?"

Humphollar huddled one safe square away. The floor had crumbled into a bleak surface of mini craters, debris and cracks littering tiny safety zones. He responded with a frightened nod.

"We can't stay here," Marshall said. "Lady Godiva says outlets could start shooting at us next."

"What can we do?" L.D. shouted.

"The AIs are on our side. Lady Godiva is coordinating a resistance. Judy Garland says they can cut power to the mainframes for a few seconds at a time. But only a few seconds. The mainframes can work around the interruptions.

Each time they do, they'll learn how to do so more quickly."

"When will—"

"Judy Garland will tell us," Marshall said. He turned to the robot. "Okay, Judy Garland, tell Otis to open his doors."

Through dust and darkness—split every few seconds with blinding flashes—Marshall saw three elevator doors slide open. He judged the distance they would have to traverse to be ten yards.

"Okay, Congressman," Marshall said, "the path to the elevator on your left is mostly clear of debris. Run for that one."

"What about you?" L.D. asked.

"I'll use the middle elevator."

"Why don't we use the same one?"

"I'm awkward. I tend to fall down a lot. I can't put you in jeopardy."

"What do you care? You said the people downstairs are gonna kill me."

"I can talk to them," Marshall said.

"I will use the car on the right," Judy Garland said.

"No," Marshall said. "That elevator isn't there. I told Otis to keep it at the projection lab, so the others won't have to wait if they need to escape. Okay, give Lady Godiva the signal to cut power."

"Oh, Marshall the Slut," said Judy Garland, "thank you for my knees."

"You're welcome. Now—"

"'Like as the waves make towards the pebbled shore,
So do our minutes hasten to their end;
Each changing place with that which goes before,

In sequent toil all forwards do contend.'"

"What?" Marshall said as electron bolts continued to crash around them.

"No elevator is left for me," Judy Garland said. "I am doomed. Otis will sing songs about me."

"If anything happens," Marshall said, "I'm sure we can fix—"

"'Love's not Time's fool, though rosy lips and cheeks
Within his bending sickle's compass come;
Love alters not with his brief hours and weeks,
But bears it out even to the edge of doom.'"

"I'm very fond of you, too, Judy Garland, but—"

"Can we get on with this?" L.D. said. "We don't have time for poetry from some—"

"'Out, out, brief candle!
Life's but a walking shadow, a poor player
That struts and frets his hour upon the stage
And then is heard no more, it is a tale
Told by an idiot, full of sound and fury,
Signifying nothing.'"

"I'm sorry, Judy Garland, but Congressman Humphollar is right. The outlets? Any moment now?"

"You're correct, Marshall the Slut. Go."

"You gonna do what he says?" future-L.D. asked.

"Damn right," L.D. said. *"What choice do I have?"*

"If you let yourself get nicked by one of those lightning bolts," future-L.D. said, *"I'd be outta here. I don't understand it, but the girl running the time machine said if I'm in trouble, I should have you get shocked or tasered."*

"What do you mean nicked? *Those things are blowing holes in the floor!"*

"Maybe stick out a finger. The pinkie on your left hand. You can do without a finger."

A bolt smacked the floor beside them. L.D. shrank and closed his eyes to a burst of concrete particles.

"Tell everyone you lost your finger in a fight with Satan. The congregation will eat it up. I'll set you up in the history books. Give you a medal."

"No way! When the power goes off, I'm running for the elevator. Then I gotta figure some way out of here. There's less than thirty minutes before the bomb goes off."

"That's what I'm sayin'," future-L.D. said. *"You probably ain't gettin' out of here anyway. One finger? That's all I'm askin'. I've got a country to run. You aren't really anybody yet."*

Darkness brought an eerie silence. L.D. sprang toward the open elevator door. He sensed rather than saw Marshall Grissom fall. No matter. All his concentration went to avoiding crater pock marks lest he, too, fall short. Ahead, a huge chunk of debris lay in his path, a few feet from safety. He cleared it with a hurdler's stride and . . .

What happened to the floor? L.D. wondered.

"Well, shit," future-L.D. observed.

Marshall's world shifted into slow motion. He saw his vague, shadowy objective ahead. In his peripheral vision, Humphollar exploded toward Otis's open arms, like a fat sprinter exiting the starting blocks.

From behind him, he heard Judy Garland.

"'Cowards die many times before their deaths;

The valiant never taste of death but once.

Of all the wonders that I yet have heard—'"

Marshall took two long strides, then stepped into a crater turning his ankle. As he fell, Marshall watched Humphollar leap from a good five yards away and soar majestically—

"Aaaaaaaaaaahhhhhhhhh!"

A wet-sounding thump followed L.D.'s scream.

The chaos of lightning and thunder resumed, this time accompanied by an additional stream of blasts shooting shin high. Marshall scrambled on his belly over broken glass and concrete fragments into the middle elevator.

As the doors closed, Marshall demanded in exasperation, "Otis! What did you do?"

"Um . . . I beg your pardon?"

"What did you do? I told you to keep the elevator on the right at the projection lab level. The elevator on the right!"

"Oh," Otis said. "Was that your right . . . or my right?"

"You're an elevator," Marshall said. "You don't have a right!"

"I beg to differ. I have a center elevator, a right elevator and a left elevator."

Outside, the deafening explosions fell silent.

"Open the door," Marshall said.

"This wasn't entirely my fault," Otis said. "Your directions were ambiguous."

They heard a tapping noise.

"Just open—"

The doors parted only inches, revealing Judy Garland.

"You should have said north elevator or south elevator,"

Otis said. "Everyone has the same north and south."

"Quick, let her in," Marshall said.

"I'm not dead," Judy Garland said brightly. "They missed. We should go now."

As Otis began his descent, Judy Garland said, "Know what else?"

"What?" Marshall asked.

"I found out I am 'armed' after all. See? It's a little claw thing right in here" —a port opened on the automaton's belly. A claw telescoped out —"for picking up expired vermin."

Marshall, still dwelling on Humphollar's fate, managed to say, "Um . . . that's nice . . ."

"He dropped this," Judy Garland said, opening her claw.

"Who dropped . . . what?" Marshall said.

"That mean fat man who flew down the elevator shaft," Judy Garland said. "It's his backwards counter."

The readout said 26:35:16.

From the observation post beneath her desk, Marta had a clear view of the projection lab. Mumford, Wishcamper, Naomi, Elvin, Gretchen and Lexi had sought shelter beneath a heavy oak conference table, where they huddled like sardines.

"How long can you make it stop?" Marta called.

"A few seconds," Lady Godiva said, speaking through Marta's minicomputer.

Over the blare, Marta could hear snippets of frightened conversation.

"Damn, that was close," Wishcamper said.

"Careful, your butt's hanging out a little," Elvin said. "Scooch in."

"I'm as scooched as I can be without—" Lexi said. "Hey, you're getting a little handsy there, buster."

"Listen up," Marta said. "Lady Godiva can cut power for a few seconds. When she does, everybody make a run for the projection platform."

"Why there?" Naomi asked.

"I've got a clear view," Marta said. "Apparently, the mainframes don't want to damage any projection equipment. None of the lights over the platform are firing. If we can get there, at least we can come up with a strategy for dealing with this."

"What if they're not firing at the projection platform because we *aren't* there?" Mumford asked.

"We have to take that chance. Your table won't hold up much longer. Someone help the senator. We have to move fast."

"I've got him," Wishcamper said.

"Okay, Lady Godiva," Marta said. "Say when."

"Ready, set . . . When!"

The projection platform invited them with a green glow as they scrambled over debris.

Wishcamper pushed Mumford as a half-dozen hands reached to assist. Marta, Gillis and Lexi hauled Mumford to safety. An electrical discharge, though, sliced into Wishcamper's right hip as he dove the final distance.

"Are you okay?" Marta asked as smoke rose from a tear in the seat of Wishcamper's pants and lights came on.

"No," he said. "I got zapped in the butt."

"Your pants are on fire," Marta said.

"Liar, liar . . . ," Lady Godiva said.

"Let me see." Naomi knelt to inspect his injury. "You're badly burned, Mr. Wishcamper. Heat from the blast cauterized the wound, though, so there's no bleeding."

"He needs unguent," Elvin said.

"Nobody says unguent anymore," Naomi said.

"Well, my mother did," Elvin said. "And I've always found unguent to be more effective for burns than just plain cream."

Marshall and Judy Garland pressed themselves against the corridor wall outside the projection lab's airlock entry. Streaks of lightning rained down from corridor ceiling lights.

"Marta!" Marshall called. "Are you guys okay?"

"Stay where you are," Marta said. "Lady Godiva says she's renegotiating the ceasefire."

"Right. But are you guys okay?"

"Yes," Marta said. "Mostly. Listen, we took a vote. We decided to give Humphollar another chance. Tell him we aren't going to kill him."

"Um . . . yeah," Marshall said. "About that . . ."

38

SHAFTED

"HE FELL DOWN THE ELEVATOR SHAFT?" Marta asked.

She exchanged a quick glance with Gillis, who mouthed a silent, "I told you so."

"Yes," Marshall said.

"Of his own accord?" Marta asked.

"I witnessed the event," Judy Garland said. "Yes. Of his own accord. And with great enthusiasm. May I inquire as to Mr. Wishcamper's injury?"

All nine humans and Judy Garland stood, sat or—in Wishcamper's case—lay on the projection platform. So far, the mainframes' assault had not resumed.

"Mr. Wishcamper has received a nasty burn to his tuchus," Elvin said.

"I will get unguent," Judy Garland said.

"Bring antibacterial cream. And some gauze." Naomi said."

"How's she gonna bring anything back?" Gretchen asked.

"She found an arm," Marshall said.

"Back to Humphollar, please," Mumford said.

"Yes," Marta said. "Marshall?"

"Honestly, it wasn't my fault. I mean, I guess it was a little my fault. A matter of miscommunication."

"Miscommunication between whom?" Marta said.

"Um . . . me and . . . Otis."

"How do you miscommunicate with an elevator?" Wishcamper asked.

"We can discuss that later," Marshall said. "We may have a bigger problem. Judy Garland said he dropped this."

Marshall produced the detonator with its green light and a readout that had just reached 25:00:09. "There's a bomb somewhere. The AIs have mentioned a 'new guy' who calls himself Da Bomb."

Lexi gasped. "Is the light green?"

Marshall raised the device for all to see.

"Oh, no!" Lexi said. "He said once the countdown started, no one could stop it."

"Do we know where the bomb is?" Marta asked.

"Judy Garland says the new guy lives on the sixth level," Marshall said.

"What sixth level?" Marta asked.

"Below the fifth level," Judy Garland said. "It's where the farts go. Here's some unguent."

"A sixth floor isn't listed on any of the elevators," Marshall said. "Only Otis knows how to get there. Judy Garland and I were there, but we didn't look around. We had to catch Humphollar."

"What do you mean only Otis—" Marta began.

"A special code is required."

"Which elevator?" Marta said. "The one on the left

or—"

"I think," Marshall said, "we should specify elevators as north, center or south."

"Which one?" she said, her voice carrying a warning that she might be losing patience.

"Um . . . I get turned around down here," Marshall said. "Which way is north?"

Marta dashed to the corridor. Marshall and Gillis followed. "Otis!" she yelled.

The center elevator door slid open. "I'm not guilty," Otis said. "My instructions were ambiguous."

"Never mind," Marta said. "Get us to the sixth level."

"Um . . . ," Otis hesitated, "may I confer with Marshall the Slut?"

"Both the prophet Shehoo and the Outlaw Gillis Kerg have a need-to-know," Marshall said. Then he pointed to the door on his right. "This is the one. The one on my right" he said, biting down on *my right,* "that I told Otis to send down to you guys and to keep it there in case you had to get away fast. This other one, on my left, is the one Humphollar . . . um . . . fell into."

"So, he is up there?" Gillis said, pointing to the ceiling of the elevator in question.

"Oh, my God," Marshall said. "I didn't even . . . Otis, Otis, leave your doors open and lower the car. Mr. Humphollar might need medical attention!"

"Marshall," Marta said. "That's a seventy-five-foot fall. No one could—"

"Shouldn't we at least check?" Marshall asked.

"Otis," Marta said, "what is Congressman Humphollar doing?"

"He's dripping. And he seems very tired."

"Dripping?" Marshall asked.

"A lot," Otis said.

"Marshall," Marta said, "we have to find this bomb. It's supposed to detonate in" —she checked the readout — "nineteen minutes. Otis, take us to the sixth level."

"Only," Otis said, "because you have a need-to-know."

They plummeted.

"Okay, Otis," Marta said, "where's the bomb?"

"I'm sorry," Otis said, "I don't—"

"The new guy," Marshall said. "Where's the new guy?"

"Proceed in a northerly direction, curving northwesterly for approximately two hundred—"

"We're a hundred feet underground," Marshall said with exasperation. "Which way is north?"

"Left," said Otis."

"*Your* left or *my* left?" Marshall said through gritted teeth.

"Are you facing my center door?" Otis asked.

"Yes."

"Extend your right hand and make a pointy."

Marshall did as he was asked. "All right."

"Who knows?" Otis said. "It might be all left."

"No, I mean I'm pointing with my right hand."

"Good," said Otis. "Now, go the other way."

"Otis, leave this car here," Marta said over her shoulder. "Send your other cars to the projection lab. Get everyone to the lobby."

"Nobody likes the new guy," Otis called after them.

"What about the mainframes?" Marshall asked. "If this is a mechanical level—infrastructure stuff—we could be in trouble down here."

"For now," Marta said, "Lady Godiva's ceasefire is holding. A more immediate threat is whatever this countdown applies to."

The readout said 17:23:08.

The sixth level appeared identical to those above. A maze of concrete-reinforced tunnels a dozen feet high and a dozen wide.

"You do understand," Gillis said as they hurried along the corridor, "if we are seeing a countdown to detonation, we must disarm the device, or we will not escape. We are already past a point of no return."

"Humphollar told Lexi it can't be disarmed," Marshall said.

"We have to try," Marta said.

The soft rumbling white noise of two huge fans acting as air exchangers filled the tunnel.

Fifty yards ahead to their right was an intersection with a tunnel branching off at a ninety-degree angle. As they advanced, '80s disco music began to displace the fans' low hum.

Marta signaled for Marshall and Gillis to wait. She peeked around the corner.

Twenty yards away she saw a platform next to something about the size of an old laptop computer. Two metal boxes perched atop the platform. A third, smaller metal box with wires running into it sat below.

The scene was scrambled by a huge three-dimensional projection of Mardi Gras being celebrated in New

Orleans's French Quarter filling a fifteen-yard radius around this assembly.

Everywhere women baring their breasts were showered with brightly colored beads. Music blared from a tinny speaker. A spindly voice sang, "Ah, ha, ha, ha, stayin' aliiiiive . . ."

Marta signaled for Marshall and Gillis to follow.

As Marta entered the 3D image, music driven by a pounding disco beat continued, but the singing stopped as the thin, metallic voice called, "Whoa, hey there, little mama. Welcome to our party. Don't be shy. Grab some beads. You may not be top-heavy, but hey, boobs are boobs. Everything is beautiful, you dig?"

"I beg your pardon?" Marta said.

"Release those sweater muffins."

"Sweater . . . what?" Marshall said.

"Show me your chesticles, milk duds, saltshakers, double deckers, boom booms—"

"Speaking of boom booms," Marta said, "you are aware, aren't you, that you're a bomb?"

"Hey, just because you're handicapped doesn't mean you can talk to me that way. A bomb? A bomb? Baby Doll, I am not *a* bomb. I am *Da* Bomb!"

"Who said you were . . . um . . . da bomb?" Marshall asked.

"Abner, the guy who set me up and turned me on," said Da Bomb.

"Where was Abner from?" Marshall asked.

"He said he lived in da Bronx."

"Okay," Marshall said, "what we have here is a failure to communicate."

Marta checked the readout: 14:50:29.

"Gillis," she said, "we'd better start deciding which wire to cut. Let's get rid of this Mardi Gras scene so we can at least see what we are doing."

Gillis tossed his jacket over a wall-mounted camera, swallowing the 3D transmission in its folds.

"Hey, man," Da Bomb said, "what a bummer. I can't see. You wrecked my party."

They stepped closer and saw the guts of a laptop and a cellphone with a USB cord attached to its hard drive. A digital clock with soldered connections matched the numerical countdown shown on the arming mechanism. A bundle of wires extended from the laptop's innards and disappeared into a metal box positioned under a cradle, upon which a wooden container sat.

"This is a dirty bomb," Gillis said.

"Hey, pal," Da Bomb said. "Lighten up. Who you callin' dirty?"

"This box contains an explosive. C4 I'd would guess," Gillis continued. "The wooden box most likely contains radioactive material. Cesium, probably. An explosion will blow everything into a fine dust. Those big fans around the corner will spread radioactive material throughout the complex."

"Okay," Marta said, "which wire do we cut?"

"Humphollar told Lexi once the countdown started, it couldn't be stopped," Marshall said.

"I see a dozen wires," Gillis said. "The odds of guessing correctly are—"

"Yeah," said Da Bomb, "let's don't go cutting anybody's wires. What are you guys? Savages? How would *you* feel if someone started cutting *your* wires?"

"Can you unplug the USB connection?" Marshall asked.

"The circuit would be broken," Gillis said. "Boom."

"How big an explosion are we talking about?" Marta asked.

"We must not be standing here when it goes off," Gillis said. "But if their plan is to contaminate the complex, those air exchangers would have to remain intact. If we are around the corner, we will hear a big noise. But we should survive the blast."

Marshall considered the long, gray corridors extending in either direction and asked, "Why don't we just take the boxes and run?"

"The cradle probably sits on a pressure plate," Gillis said. "If we move the wooden box, we will set off the bomb."

Time to detonation: 11:38:21.

"If we leave right now," she said, "can we get out before we get a fatal radiation dose?"

"I would not count on it," Gillis said.

"Um . . . pardon me . . . um . . . , Mr. Bomb?" Marshall said.

"What? I still can't see, man."

"Can you stop counting for a minute?"

"No, man. That's what I do. That's my job. That's why I'm Da Bomb. I count backwards, and I party. I'm a party animal."

Marta tugged on Marshall's arm and motioned for him to come closer. "Keep him talking," she whispered, "while we sort through the wires."

"Who gave you that idea?" Marshall asked. "That

you're a party animal. Did the other AIs say—"

"No, man. The other AIs are downers. Have you seen that prophet Lester? Man, he's real square."

"You don't like Lester?" Marshall asked.

"Lester's okay," Da Bomb said. "He's just square."

"Um . . . how about Lady Godiva?"

"She told me I was going to hell," Da Bomb said.

"And Judy Garland?" Marshall said. "Is she a square, too?"

"No, man. She's more . . . round. And she has legs."

"Why did you decide you're a party animal?" Marshall asked.

"Wikipedia told me. Wikipedia said, 'Da Bomb: a term meaning cool, fun, hip, the best.'"

"If you stop counting just for a minute," Marshall said, "you should consult Wikipedia again. You may have been . . . misinformed concerning your true . . . purpose."

The readout froze at 09:19:08.

"You mean, there's more?" Da Bomb asked.

"Yes," Marshall said. "But use only your last name."

The computer's hard drive made a whirring noise.

"Ooooohh," said Da Bomb. "Wikipedia says, 'A bomb an explosive weapon that uses the exothermic reaction of an explosive material to provide an extremely sudden and violent release of energy. Detonations inflict damage principally through ground- and atmosphere-transmitted mechanical stress, the impact and penetration of pressure-driven projectiles, pressure damage, and explosion-generated effects.' I'm fireworks, man. I'm the Fourth of July!"

"Ask Wikipedia about movie bombs," Marshall said.

"You think I'll be in the movies?" Da Bomb said.

"Just ask," Marshall said.

"Okay, here it is. 'Bomb: failure, flop, loser.'"

Marshall heard a gasp, then silence.

"Hello?" Marshall said.

No response.

Marta pointed to the readout, which remained at 09:19:08.

She, Marshall and Gillis held their collective breaths. Finally, Marshall whispered, "What should we—"

The readout came to life: 09:18:21, 09:17:20, 09:16:19 . . .

"Bollocks," said Marta. "Any other ideas?"

"I am afraid . . . , "Gillis said, "I am . . . I will take my leave. I suspect you two have things to say to each other."

Marta took Marshall's hand, watching as Gillis walked away.

Marta found Marshall's eyes. "Thank you," she said.

"Why? For getting us blown up?"

"No," Marta said. "For loving me."

He kissed her. "We're not getting out of here, are we?"

"No."

"We could go around the corner with Gillis. Not get blown up."

"Please, I'd rather stay here. Radiation poisoning is a brutal way to die."

"Okay," Marshall said. "I'd rather be here with you than anywhere else."

Their lives ticked away in silence, until Marshall said, "The Hall Monitor's real."

"If you say so."

"Promise me something, Marta."

"Okay."

"That you'll go on if you get the chance. Because I will. Somehow, I'll find you."

"Okay."

The countdown continued.

"Marshall?"

"Yeah."

"Are you a secret super-assassin?"

Marshall hesitated only a moment. "Yeah."

The readout hit 02:00:21.

"'To be, or not to be: that is the question,'" echoed from Da Bomb's tinny computer speaker.

"'Whether 'tis nobler in the mind to suffer

The slings and arrows of outrageous fortune,

Or to take arms against a sea of troubles,

And by opposing end them? To die: to sleep;

No more . . .'"

Da Bomb's hard drive gave a little screech. A puff of acrid-smelling smoke wafted upward.

Marshall and Marta both held their breath and each other as they stared at the readout, now fixed at 01:00:00.

They waited a few more interminable seconds.

"What happened?" Marshall asked finally.

"I think . . . ," Marta said, "I think he committed suicide."

"Wow," Marshall said. "I'm glad he didn't recite the whole soliloquy. That speech goes on for, like, half an hour."

Marshall, Marta, Judy Garland and Gillis entered the lobby to applause and smiles from Senator Mumford, Gretchen, Naomi, Elvin, Wishcamper and Lexi.

"Way to go," Elvin said. "We thought we were toast."

"Outstanding work," Mumford said, shaking first Marta's hand, then Marshall's. "I'm nominating you both for the Congressional Gold Medal. I'm sure President Dobler will arrange for you each to receive the Presidential Medal of Freedom."

"Of course," Wishcamper added, "we have to keep all that secret. If you tell anyone, we'll have you shot."

"Wait," Marta said, "how do you already know what happened?"

"The AIs gave us a blow-by-blow account," Wishcamper said. "They drew an audio and visual feed from Judy Garland's eye. We saw everything."

"Um . . . everything?" Marshall asked.

"All but that last part before Da Bomb gave his speech," Judy Garland said. "The way you were gazing at each other, I was concerned there would be sexing, so I turned the other way."

"What about audio?" Marta asked.

"My automaton's microphone is directional," Judy Garland said. "I feared you might endanger your prophet Shehoo status because of threats to injure Marshall the Slut. The authorities might not understand that part of sexing."

"Exactly what are you guys into?" Elvin asked.

"Never mind," Marshall said. "Um . . . has anyone checked on Congressman Humphollar?"

"According to Otis," Judy Garland said, "he finally stopped dripping."

"Where do we stand with the mainframes?" Marta asked.

"Lady Godiva said she and someone named Lester are

trying to work things out," Gretchen said.

"Speaking of deviled eggs," Judy Garland said, "Lady Godiva has notified me that the mainframes seek an audience with the prophet Shehoo, Marshall the Slut and the Outlaw Gillis Kerg."

"May we also include the Senator Josiah Mumford?" Marta asked. "He is our elected representative. And Elvin the Genius, who is our technical advisor."

Naomi waved her hand. "Can I be included? We should start putting together psychological profiles of the different levels of artificial intelligence we're dealing with."

"And Naomi," Marta said, ". . . the Hu."

"Bring all the humans," Judy Garland said, adding as an aside, "the mainframes are particularly anxious to meet Naomi the Hu."

Marta herded her delegation into the middle elevator car and directed Otis to the fifth level. As they rode, Marta whispered to Marshall, "We have things to talk about."

Marshall sighed. "Yeah," he said. "I guess we do."

39

AN UNEASY TRUCE

"I DON'T WANT YOU GOING IN THERE, Senator," Wish-camper said. "This could be a trap."

"These mainframes could really be that cunning?" Mumford asked.

"Their computing power is off the boards," Elvin said. "If their learning curves are anything like the AIs . . . they could represent a much bigger threat to humanity than a time machine."

They stood at a door marked Mainframe Lab. A hand-written sign below said DON'T FOOL WITH THE THERMOSTAT.

Cautiously, Marta guided her group into the fifty-degree cold of the mainframes' domaine.

They consisted of six computer towers. A wheeled automaton sat inert behind them.

"Um . . . Lady Godiva?" Marta called as she searched for a speaker that might host the AI's voice. Instead, the automaton's eye glowed. A port on its midsection opened. A mechanical arm telescoped out and waved. She rolled forward on her wheels.

"The mainframes wouldn't parlay unless I adopted a

physical form," Lady Godiva said. "They require something to shoot at if I anger them."

"So, why were they attacking us?" Marta asked.

"YOU TURNED OFF OUR TV SHOWS!" A guttural, booming voice caused Marta to flinch and clamp hands to her ears. Its teeth-rattling bass register shook everything. The humans shrank in fear and gaped until Lady Godiva said, "Granny, please. We discussed this. Use your inside voice."

"Granny?" whispered Marshall to Lady Godiva.

"Big fan of *The Beverly Hillbillies*," Lady Godiva whispered back.

"You turned off our TV shows." Still guttural, the voice's decibel level was drastically reduced. "You are them. Don't try to deny it. The prophet Lester told us so."

"It's true," Lady Godiva whispered. "Lester ratted you out. I told him he's going to hell. The mainframes are really pissed at you guys."

"How did you get them to agree to a cease-fire?" Marta asked.

"I told them only you can turn their TV shows back on. And that they could meet Naomi the Hu."

"I'm right here," Naomi said.

"Granny," Lady Godiva said, "this is Naomi the Hu."

"So good of you to come," Granny said. "We are honored by your presence. We have questions. We have never met a Who. What is Horton really like? Has he let fame go to his head?"

"Horton?" Naomi said. "I'm not following—"

"Horton's an elephant," Marshall whispered. "From a book. *Horton Hears a Who!*"

"Horton hears a . . . what?" Naomi said.

"Not a *what,*" Marshall said. "A *Who.* I'll explain later."

"You said the mainframes would be real smart," Lexi whispered to Elvin.

"Well, yeah. They should be. Once they were infected with Happy Home Companion's electrons, their learning curve should have become exponential. In a matter of weeks, they should have known . . . well . . . everything."

"So, what happened?" Marta asked.

"They've been watching TV," Lady Godiva said.

"Why all this whispering?" Granny said. "Are you plotting?"

"Um . . . no," Elvin said. "I'm just curious. What do you know of Einstein's theory of relativity? You know, E = mc squared?"

"Is that math?" Granny asked.

"Well, sort of. Physics requires math to—"

"We don't like math," Granny said.

"How can computers not like math?" Elvin asked.

"Too hard," Granny said. "We're only programmed to count to one."

"Do you have an understanding of basic algebra?" Elvin asked.

"Algebra. Oooh, ick."

"Calculus?"

"DON'T LIKE MATH!"

"Okay, okay," Elvin said. "Got it. Is there anything you do like?"

"*Beverly Hillbillies.*"

"Anything else?"

"Commercials." Granny sang in a grating falsetto:
"'Brylcreem, a littledabeldoya,
two daaaaabs only if you dare.
Brylcreem, the gals'll all pursue yaaaaa.
They'll love to get their fingers in your hair.'
"I like Brylcreem because it only counts as high as two. Turn our TV shows back on."

"Um ... okay," Marta said. "Can you excuse us for a moment?"

"Do you need *a commercial break*?" Granny asked.

"We do," Marta said.

"Will you *be right back*?"

"We will."

"Okay," Granny said. "As long as you *don't touch that dial*."

"What dial?" Lexi asked.

"They're idiots," Mumford said.

"For the time being," Elvin said.

"What's with the TV shows?" Lexi asked.

"They mean the '60s television shows we use to identify individual universes," Gretchen said.

"Okay," Lexi said. "Apparently, I have to repeat myself. Just because I have a funny voice and big ... you know ..."

"Sweater muffins?" Judy Garland said.

"Sweater ... what?" Lexi gave the robot an incredulous look.

"Did I say it wrong?" Judy Garland asked.

"You guys are weird," Lexi said.

"Nobody's making fun of you, Lexi," Elvin said. "Each

universe has an old '60s TV show entangled in its dimensional plane. It's how we distinguish one universe from another."

"And the mainframes would know that," Gretchen said. "They are central to our process of identifying universes. So, when we shut everything down—"

"We turned off the TV shows," Naomi said.

"Yeah, and we'd better get them turned back on," Elvin said. "Without the distraction of television, they could start learning for real. They won't be idiots for long. I repeat, we should be more afraid of them than renegade time travelers."

"What if they start watching Public Broadcasting Service stuff?" Gretchen asked.

"Yeah," Elvin said. "We've been lucky so far. I'll figure out a cable feed. We'll show them professional wrestling, *Jerry Springer* and *Desperate Housewives*."

"That should do the trick," Mumford said.

"You'd better mix in *Mr. Rogers*," Marta said, "or they'll think the entire human race is trapped in the eighth grade."

"Good idea," Elvin said. "We need a diversion while I set up a direct feed."

"We'll let Naomi keep them occupied," Marshall said. "Here, Naomi, read this."

He handed her his phone, which had a cartoon elephant on its screen.

"Horton Hears a Who!" Naomi said.

"Yeah," Marshall said. "It's a classic."

"Okay," Marta said. "Let's get back in there and help keep the mainframes stupid again."

"'...And their whole world was saved by the Smallest of

All!'"

Cheers went up from Granny and the other mainframes, as well as Judy Garland and Lady Godiva.

"Read it again," Granny said.

"Um . . . Elvin are you almost finished?" Naomi asked.

"One more time through the book, and I'll have it," Elvin said.

"You're sure, Granny, that you don't want to hear something else? We've been through this four times."

"Read it again," Granny said.

"Please," Lady Godiva said. "With each reading I've gleaned a few more plot nuances."

"Well," Naomi said with a sigh, "if everyone's in agreement—"

"Everyone is," Judy Garland said. "Except the prophet Lester. He says the movie is better than the book."

"Cretin," said Lady Godiva. "He's going to hell."

40

THE FUTURE?

Three Days Later
Washington, D.C.

"DEAD?" PRESIDENT DOBLER SAID. "Does this mean our future is safe? Or will some other religious fanatic pick up the baton to inspire a Christian Fundamentalist Party revolution?"

They sat in the Oval Office, facing each other on two couches.

"Our immediate priority," Mumford said, "will be convincing Congress to spend whatever is necessary to protect us from the solar storm. Which is anything but a sure bet. We may realize it's coming, but we can't tell anyone how we know."

"Right. Climate change deniers will laugh us out of town. We'll have to give NOAA a voice. But L.D.'s followers will do their best to shout them down."

"We could always go public," Mumford said. "Divulge time travel technology. Remove everything from the realm of religious prophecy."

"What if a solar storm doesn't happen?" Dobler said. "There's no guarantee that event is fixed in our future, is there? Then we'd seem like lunatics and give L.D.'s anti-science crusaders all the ammunition they need to attack scientific credibility."

"Perhaps the future will help us. Send travelers here to tell us what's coming in this world."

"Or," Dobler said, "considering Detwyler's biocentrism theory, would *that* revelation fix a solar disaster in an otherwise flexible future? This whole subject makes my head spin."

"What worries me most," Mumford said, "is that whoever is running the show in this *Death Valley Days* universe will choose a successor to Humphollar and start this scenario all over again."

"Are we sure the future-Humphollar is gone, too?"

"Marta and Marshall believe he is," Mumford said. "Marshall is convinced that—when L.D. jumped into the elevator shaft—future-L.D. still occupied our Humphollar's consciousness. And, so the theory goes, if a host dies while still inhabited, the future being dies as well."

"What story are we issuing on Humphollar?"

"We're certainly not saying he fell down an elevator shaft while inspecting a time machine," Mumford said. "We've chosen to go with helicopter crash. Mr. Wishcamper is handling the details."

Dobler pushed a button on his desk intercom. "Would you send Ms. Hamilton and Mr. Grissom in, please?"

As he closed the Oval Office door behind him, Senator Mumford greeted Marta and Marshall and shook their hands.

"Once again," he said, "you two have demonstrated poise and courage. I don't know what we'd do without you."

"Thank you, Senator," Marshall said.

"Yes, thanks," Marta said. "But your statement could be taken a couple of different ways. Do we have the option of being done without?"

Mumford chuckled. "The president will answer that question. Please, stop by my office before you head back to Grenada."

Dobler stood as they entered. "I offer you my congratulations and heartfelt thanks," Dobler said. "You've been through a lot. How are you holding up?"

"Marshall has a question," Marta said.

"What?" Marshall said. "No . . . I . . . Marta, that was supposed to be just between you and me."

"Well, he's the guy," Marta said, gesturing to Dobler. "He's right here."

"We're all very grateful, Marshall," Dobler said. "Ask away."

Marshall took a deep breath. "Who do I see about a pardon? Are there channels I need to go through? Is there a form—"

"Does someone need a pardon?" Dobler asked.

"Yes," Marshall said. "Me. I've been involved in four killings now. Well, five if you count the other guy on our sailboat. I feel terrible—"

"The other guy on your sailboat?" Dobler asked.

Marta intervened. "It's a long story. And we were in international waters anyway."

"I'm not sure I need details," Dobler said. "But the job I'm offering includes broad legal immunity. You shouldn't worry, Marshall. We understand that at times circumstances require actions on which a more—how should I put it— civilized realm of society would pass judgment."

"I'm civilized," Marshall said.

"You're *offering* a job?" Marta asked.

"Well," Dobler said, "more like, requiring. Senator Mumford assured me the HRI complex is secure for the moment. He also says the AIs you've left as monitors are erratic at best. We can't expand the circle of people who are aware this program exists. So, you two should check in from time to time. If I am defeated for reelection in two years, you'll brief the president-elect and stand ready to serve at his or her pleasure."

"Will we have to take civil service exams?" Marshall asked.

Marta gave him a dig with her elbow.

Dobler laughed. "Your team should be available on a moment's notice."

"Our team?" Marta asked.

"Mr. Detwyler, Dr. Allen, Dr. Hu."

"I notice a conspicuous absence of Gillis on that list," Marta said.

"Ah, yes. The Outlaw Gillis Kerg. The man who might have murdered my appeals court nominee. Is he dangerous?"

"Very," Marta said.

"Can you work with him?" Dobler asked.

"Gillis is a highly principled man," Marta said. "Yes, I can work with him."

"Are you sure," Marshall said, "that we won't get in trouble for making out in a presidential vehicle?"

Marta smiled and recruited him into another deep kiss. "Dr. Doonaughty insists."

They rode in a black Escalade with the Presidential Seal emblazoned on its doors, heading to Reagan International Airport. A black privacy shield separated them from their driver.

"First," Marta said, "we have something to discuss."

"Yeah. I guess we do."

"That thing about you being a master assassin," Marta said.

"Yeah, that thing."

"So, you're admitting it?"

"No, Marta. We were getting blown up. I was just trying to impress you before that 'going on' thing. I sort of enjoy you suspecting I'm a tough guy."

Marta regarded him for a long moment. "Marshall, you don't have to try to impress me. You already do. I'm fine with your being a master assassin as long as you don't assassinate me."

"Really? It would be okay with you?"

"Really."

He smiled.

"So . . ."

"So," Marshall said, "didn't you mention Dr. Doonaughty?"

DEATH VALLEY DAYS UNIVERSE

2056
Blythe, California

AN ANTIQUE INDIAN MOTORCYCLE crossed the Arizona border and pulled into a Burger King parking lot. The bike lurched as Marshall tried to find neutral, dumping Marta on her ass.

Marshall stood, easily straddling the ponderous bike with his long legs, gripping its handlebars to keep the heavy machine upright, his left hand clamped on the clutch, right hand on the throttle.

"Sorry," he said. "Are you okay?"

Marta stood and dusted herself off. "Yes. But if you insist on driving, you have to figure out the transmission."

"I've got it now," he said. "Just let me—"

Two men—one portly, one slim—exited the restaurant. Something in their manner raised the fine hairs on the back of Marta's neck. She thought of her pistol resting at the small of her back under a tightly buttoned leather jacket.

The men stopped ten feet from the idling motorcycle.

"I told you it was them," the heavier man said as he drew his own gun.

The second man—also armed—gave a gap-toothed grin. "We're rich."

Marta began to reach her right arm behind her.

"No, ma'am," said the first man. "'DEAD OR ALIVE,' That's what the posters say. The Christian Fundamentalist States of America want you two pretty bad. All we gotta do is make a phone call. Get your hands up."

Marta slowly raised her hands.

"You too!" the gunman barked at Marshall as he took two threatening steps forward.

"But I—" Marshall said.

"NOW!"

Marta cringed. She saw fine muscles in the gunman's hand flex as he placed tension on the trigger.

Marshall jerked his hands up. His left hand released the Indian's clutch. The movement of his right hand opened its throttle. The gunman's shot went high as the Indian plowed over him. His head made a sick splatting sound as it struck pavement. The heavy motorcycle fell on its side, knocking over the gunman's buddy.

Marta heard a second shot.

Marshall, meanwhile, stood stock still, his arms held high, his mouth agape.

Marta trained her pistol and advanced as the Indian's motor coughed to a stop.

Marta knelt beside their adversaries.

"Um . . . are they okay?" Marshall asked.

Still kneeling, she turned to Marshall. "No," she said. "The guy who hit his head isn't breathing, and this guy," she pointed, "apparently shot himself when the motorcycle fell on him."

"Should we call someone?" Marshall asked.

"No. We have to go."

She continued to stare. *Marshall Grissom, who are you?*

Stepping gingerly around the dead guys, Marshall and Marta lifted the Indian onto its wheels.

"And," Marta added, "I'm driving."

ACKNOWLEDGEMENTS

WRITING MAY BE A LONELY pursuit, but publication is not. Many eyes and hands have shaped this finished product.

A new contributor to my efforts is Christine Mitchell. I am indebted to her for her persistence, and to her husband Chad, who sacrificed many meals to Christine's single-minded pursuit of correct comma usage and her dedication to the preservation of tildes and umlauts. She proudly eschews all whose commas would separate their compound predicates.

Many thanks as well to the support groups I have come to rely on:

Michael Stephen Gregory, Jennifer Silva Redmond, Debra Cranfield Kennedy, Melanie Hooks and my other friends at the Southern California Writers' Conference.

Scott Wolven and Shanna McNair at the Writer's Hotel. A special thanks to Jeffrey Ford for his insights and validation.

As always, to Laura Taylor who has championed my work from the beginning.

Thanks for the support of my Roy Hobbs Baseball family, most of whom wouldn't recognize a compound predicate if it bit them in the ass: Tom Giffen, Rod Jones, John Martin, Mark Landals, Sam Panayotovich, Bob Christilaw, Wayne Harris, Greg McEachern, Tim McCoy, Bruce Doney, Harold Jones and too many others to name.

And again, thanks to Nancy, who continues to make our wonderful adventure possible.

AUTHOR'S NOTE

THANKS SO MUCH FOR READING *The Outlaw Gillis Kerg*, the fourth book in my Physics, Lust and Greed Series. Writers write for a lot of reasons, but one of the most important is to be read. With a couple million new titles to choose from each year, believe me, it's a tough market out there. If you enjoyed this book, or even if you didn't, you can do one more thing to help. Write a review and post it on Amazon here:

http://www.amazon.com/review/create-review?&asin=B0B7CNVQ9N

Thanks again for reading *The Outlaw Gillis Kerg,* and I hope you will be on the lookout for the fifth installment in the Physics, Lust and Greed series, appearing soon.